ALMOST INFAMUS

ALMOST INFAMOUS

A SUPERVILLAIN NOVEL

MATT CARTER

TALOS

Talos Press

Talos Press books may be purchased in bulk at special discounts for sales promotion, corporate gifts, fund-raising, or educational purposes. Special editions can also be created to specifications. For details, contact the Special Sales Department, Talos Press, 307 West 36th Street, 11th Floor, New York, NY 10018 or info@skyhorsepublishing.com.

Talos Press is an imprint of Skyhorse Publishing, Inc.®, a Delaware corporation.

Visit our website at www.talospress.com.

10 9 8 7 6 5 4 3 2

Library of Congress Cataloging-in-Publication Data is available on file.

Cover illustration by Adam Wallenta
Cover design by Jason Snair

Print ISBN: 978–1–940456–50–8
Ebook ISBN 978–1–940456–51-5

Printed in the United States of America

To Scott Carter,

The greatest hero I've ever known.

1944–2015

A BRIEF HISTORY OF SUPERHEROES

The Stone Age of Superheroes

1854: At the Battle of Balaclava, shields created by Corporal Langston Hicks protect charging British cavalry and result in an overwhelming victory for the British over Russian forces. The "Charge of the Light Brigade" is henceforth known as the first public confirmation of superhuman existence.

1854–1900 (approx.): Amid intense fascination and fear of superhumans due to the British Empire augmenting their military and political strength with superhuman aid, a general wave of fear and disgust by humanity keeps many supers in hiding.

1867: Infamous Wild West outlaw, Jill "Blackjack" Winchester, outs herself as a superhuman, widely regarded as both the first professional supervillain and superhuman to use a codename.

1871: Sailors of the HMS *White Walrus* become the first humans to survive first contact with the xenophobic, reptilian natives of Lemuria. Shortly after, representatives of Atlantis reach out to the British Crown with an offer of peace in an effort to outdo their Lemurian rivals.

1870–1900 (approx.): With superhuman aid, scientists like Tesla, Moreau, and Edison make scientific discoveries decades past what conventional technological wisdom believes possible, helping reshape the public image of supers more in their favor. Many smaller, less ethical "mad" scientists push the boundaries of science and accidentally create many proto-supervillains.

The Iron Age of Superheroes

1898: The 1st United States Volunteer Cavalry, under commander Theodore Roosevelt, is one of the first military units primarily filled with superhumans. Their battlefield prowess and raw power brings a swift end to the Spanish-American War. Cuba is soon after made the forty-sixth state to enter the Union.

1914–1916: World War I is triggered by the assassination of Archduke Franz Ferdinand. This global conflict (exacerbated by the navy of Atlantis informally aiding the Central Powers) sees widespread use of superhumans in battle, improving their public image and bringing a swift end to the conflict while bringing a singular brutality to warfare that had yet to be seen. Conditions under the Treaty of Verdun financially punishing Germany and illegalizing humanity's use of Lemurian and Atlantean technology keep tensions around the world lingering.

1917: The islands of Hawaii are seized and claimed by cultists and redubbed New R'lyeh. Weakened by the war and not seeking the wrath of such powerful magic, world leaders acknowledge the new nation.

1917: Bolstered by superhuman forces, the Bolsheviks seize power in the Russian Revolution. Through efficient programs managing the superhuman population and putting them to work for the greater good, the Soviet Union rapidly becomes one of the most prosperous and powerful empires of the twentieth century.

1922: An Egyptian tomb unearthed by Howard Carter releases the trapped energies of the Egyptian pantheon upon the world. Their public revelation and general declaration of peace (some outliers aside), as well as the acknowledgment of other deities including Maui, Ishtar, Raven, Tezcatlipoca, and Sun Wukong, confirm to the world that gods walk among us.

The Golden Age of Superheroes

1930: Miguel Díaz dons a handmade luchador outfit and emigrates from Mexico to the United States as El Capitán. Declaring neutrality from any government influence, he decides to use his powers for the betterment of mankind and soon becomes the world's greatest superhero. His example of costumed vigilantism is soon followed by many with increasingly flamboyant identities and costumes.

1938: The Empire of Japan's invasion of China combined with border tensions with the USSR trigger World War II, an even more destructive and globe-spanning conflict than its predecessor. Superhumans around the world are pressed into service, while costumed superheroes use their celebrity influence to drum up support.

1940: After Japanese naval attacks on America's west coast, President Roosevelt orders the internment of Japanese-American citizens. Sixteen-year-old Kazuo Nagano escapes internment and, despite lacking superpowers, uses his genius intellect to transform himself into vigilante the Gamemaster, fighting against government oppression and corruption.

1941: Seeking an end to the war, El Capitán, the Gamemaster, and French superhero Stone Spirit meet in Amber City. From this meeting they create the idea for the Protectors, a civilian team of superheroes not answering to any particular government and aligned with the goal of saving humanity from this destructive conflict. Nearly a dozen other heroes soon join this team with the goal of world peace.

1942: One year and a day after the founding of the Protectors, El Capitán raises an American flag in Berlin, declaring an end to the war.

1943–1950 (approx.): Despite postwar prosperity, tensions begin to rise between the allied empires of the United States, the USSR, the British Empire, and Atlantis in a nonviolent but vaguely hostile "Cold War."

1947: At the height of a competitive "Space Race" between the United States, USSR, and Britain, a spacecraft from the mysterious Gray race crash-lands in Roswell, New Mexico, confirming the existence of alien life. Technology salvaged from this craft makes the US the dominant spacefaring nation for decades to come.

1949: United States president Thomas E. Dewey is the first sitting world leader to walk on the moon, and is famously photographed shaking hands with El Capitán in the Sea of Tranquility.

The Silver Age of Superheroes

1950: Triggered by humanity's deeper exploration of space, the First Gray Invasion of Earth occurs. Millions of lives are lost and large portions of East Asia and Africa, still recovering from World War II, are laid to waste. With most militaries disabled by Gray technology, humanity is saved by an expanded roster of Protectors, who repel the invasion and kill the Gray Emperor.

1951–1964 (approx.): Earth is invaded periodically by alien races including the Grays, the Traknet, and the Roball Empire. An increased emphasis on Earth defense technology and a higher superhero population help defend Earth from serious damage. The required global unity in defending against these attacks prevents the Cold War from escalating.

1950–1969 (approx.): Postwar prosperity creates an explosion of supervillains looking to acquire this wealth for themselves. Looking to stand out from others, villains often strive to become more over-the-top and flamboyant than their peers. In response, superheroes become more flamboyant and colorful. Campy one-liners, themed schemes and henchmen, and ostentatious displays of wealth become common for both superheroes and villains.

The Bronze Age of Superheroes

1969: In response to the foundation of the Villains Union, the world's first major team of supervillains, El Capitán and the Gamemaster, with the help of a reformed Blackjack, recreate the Protectors as a world-spanning team of superheroes in many subteams. The villains escalate their numbers and plots in kind, kicking off a conflict they dub the "War on Villainy."

1970: The Protectors open the Tower, the world's greatest prison designed for housing supervillains.

1969–1993: The War on Villainy is waged around the world, with civilian- and government-sponsored superheroes slowly imprisoning and exterminating the entire world supervillain population. Superheroes get an increasingly militarized look, with increasingly violent tactics approved, and edgier attitudes beloved, by the public.

1993: With the defeat of Otis Shylock in Chile, and every last known supervillain eliminated, the War on Villainy is declared over.

The Digital Age of Superheroes

1993–Present: Even without supervillains and few wars to fight, superheroes are still a part of daily life. They star in movies, dominate tabloids, and wield tremendous political power for the betterment of mankind. Occasional attempts at villainy are made, but the heroes quickly defeat them before any damage can truly be done. Losing their edge from the War on Villainy, they take on colorful costumes and kinder images.

Under their benevolent protection, all is well.

1

THE REQUISITE
ORIGIN STORY

Like anyone who ever attended a public high school, I first considered becoming a supervillain during a mandatory assembly on the dangers of peer pressure.

They'd promised us a superhero guest speaker this time, and not just some guy off the street in a cape and spandex suit who hangs around playgrounds (like last year), but a real one with powers and corporate sponsors who would offer us a truly "life-enriching experience." Whether or not this was worth getting excited about was yet to be seen, but considering the fact that the last "life-enriching experience" we had came in the form of a guy in a bright green bunny suit rapping about saving the rainforest, we had reason for skepticism.

Still, when the lights dimmed and the stage curtains were raised to reveal a large, cardboard cutout of the Protectors' logo and a banner that read DO YOU HAVE WHAT IT TAKES TO BE A HERO?, most of the students in attendance sounded impressed.

Well, except for some junior in back who shouted, "YOU SUCK!"

The air fell still and, with a dramatic flourish, one of the windows at the side of the auditorium burst open. There were shouts of surprise and screams from the freshman girls, and almost as many cell phone cameras held in the air as there were people in attendance as a glowing, crackling ball of electricity floated in through the window and hovered above the stage. With a dramatic explosion and a roaring clap of thunder, the ball transformed into a muscular man clad in bright-green spandex, a flowing blue cape, and brighter blue, spiked hair. His eyes were hidden by a bright-yellow domino mask, but his smile was so broad and toothy and white that you could see it shining from the back of the auditorium.

"Hello, boys and girls and inter-gendered Lemurian residents of Hacklin's Hall High School. I . . . AM . . . THUNDER-HEAD!" he said with a dramatic flourish of his cape, surrounding himself with a shower of sparks. For emphasis, a curtain behind him was ripped aside, revealing a cardboard cutout of him and his Twitter handle (@YourHeroThunderhead).

He laughed heartily at the audience's cheers, unaware that he had set his cardboard cutout and one of the stage curtains on fire. A couple of his personal assistants were quick to run from backstage and extinguish the ignited curtain before the sprinklers went off.

"I know that life today is tough for children like you. I know . . . I was a child once myself," he said, giving us a knowing, sympathetic nod. "You are faced with daily challenges that are almost as great as the ones superheroes, like myself, fought against during the War on Villainy! Every day you are faced with gang violence, sexual assault, drug abuse, deforestation . . ."

Saying all that, I severely doubted he'd ever visited Hacklin's Hall, Indiana. Our town was as innocuous as any American suburb in the country. You might find all of these issues in locations like on the eastside of Amber City or New R'lyeh or the Detroit Exclusion Zone, but not in Hacklin's Hall.

Problems like those would make this town too interesting.
"... political dissidence, and genocide. But those are easy problems to fix—ones we superheroes strive to eliminate every day. There is one problem, however, that you face that takes everyday heroes, heroes like *you*, to fix: PEER PRESSURE!"

He paused for dramatic impact, letting the words sink in.

Again the junior in the back shouted, "YOU SUCK!"

Then a childish voice from off stage chimed in. "Golly, Thunderhead, what's peer pressure?"

Thunderhead looked to the side of the stage with an exaggerated searching look. His smile broadened.

"Why if it isn't my newly appointed sidekick: Iguana Boy!"

A spotlight shone on the curtain to his left, illuminating a small lizard that clung to it. With a dramatic leap, the lizard flew onto the stage, transforming into a teenage boy (he had to have been at most thirteen), dressed in a garish, green-scaled bodysuit complete with claws and a tail. The small microphone taped to his chest led me to believe his appearance was not as impromptu as Thunderhead had wanted us to believe.

He waved to us enthusiastically and barely flinched when the ball of paper chucked from the audience hit him in the shoulder.

"That is an *excellent* question!" Thunderhead said, slapping Iguana Boy on the back hard enough to knock him forward a step. "According to the fine people at Merriam-Webster, peer pressure is . . ."

"We know what peer pressure is," Vic grumbled beside me. He had enough sense to be quiet about it, especially after the paper-thrower was escorted from the auditorium by several of Thunderhead's entourage, with a few faculty following close behind.

"Yeah, but there's gotta be like, what, five or six people here who missed all the lectures? This assembly is for them," I said, twirling a pen between my fingers, bored.

"This sucks balls, Aids."

That's Vic Benedict for ya, always the poet.

3

Vic had been my best friend by default, since we grew up on the same street. He said he called me Aids because it was easier to say than Aidan, but I think he just liked calling me Aids. I enjoyed hanging out with him because he was funny, sometimes, and occasionally got his hands on explosives. He claimed to like hanging out with me because he thought I was cool, but that was a bold-faced lie and we both knew it. The thing was, I didn't really care because being best friends with Vic—even if he talked to my video games more than me—was better than being best friends with no one.

While we didn't have much in common, the key to our friendship—at least for me—was that he didn't care that my life was going nowhere. It was obvious to everyone (including myself) that my future likely entailed graduating high school the middle of Hacklin Hall High School's Class of 2016, moving on to community college, then real college, as I would probably have no idea what the hell I wanted to do with my life. (Grad school was even an option if I so chose, as both my folks had met at one and always said how it changed their lives.) Then I would end up Aidan Salt, middle-manager of some low-level company that moved paper from one warehouse to another, had a wife that resented me, two-and-a-half kids who didn't want anything to do with me, and a heavy drinking problem. He also didn't care that I'd probably die at the age of fifty-seven from something like pancreatic cancer or a car accident or maybe just eating a bullet like my old Uncle Rex.

No, Vic didn't care about much but what was right in front of him, and with graduation right around the corner, it was kinda nice to have one person who didn't care about my future.

"They should've gotten El Capitán," he said.

"They'd never get us El Capitán," I replied.

"How do you know?"

"Well, first, El Capitán's appearance fee has to be through the roof, and I don't think our PTA is that generous. Second, El

Capitán is 'America's Greatest Protector,'" I said, trying to add the emphasis they always put in El Capitán's commercials.

"He did one for those kids in Somalia!" Vic said, defensively. "They were refugees. He saved them."

"Lucky bastards," Vic pouted.

"And we're nowhere near *that* lucky," I said, tapping my pen on the chair in front of me for emphasis. "We're lucky they even sprang for a Protectors reserve member. I was thinking they'd get someone from one of the satellite teams, or maybe one of those corporate heroes."

"Captain Cola would've been cool. He's a pretty kickass dancer."

"Captain Cola versus Lemon-Lime Lad would have been better," I said with a snicker.

"Yeah, but they'd still find some way of turning this all into an ad," he complained.

"Like this one won't?" I asked, trying to remember any of Thunderhead's sponsors.

Vic raised an eyebrow. "Wanna bet on that, Aids?" He always liked making bets with me, mostly because he usually didn't have money and I sucked at gambling.

"No."

"Aw, come on, five bucks!" he pleaded.

"No."

"A five-dollar bill! Minuteman's face on a rectangle of green paper! Almost enough to buy a cup of coffee!" he continued.

"I don't drink coffee"

"Almost enough to buy *her* a cup of coffee."

Damn. He got me.

I fished through my wallet and found a five-dollar bill hiding between a couple of twenties and handed it to him. Minuteman's face stared up at me solemnly from the bill, the tip of his tri-corner hat shading the eye he'd lost fighting during World War I. Vaguely, part of me wondered if he knew back when he first strapped on that star-spangled cape and chestplate that someday his sacrifices would immortalize him on the dollar bill that might finally get me into Kelly Shingle's good graces (and, hopefully, her pants).

I'd like to think that would make him proud.

I checked the stage. Thunderhead was flying around, lazily punching cardboard cutouts of supervillains and making some long-winded point about how if unchecked, peer pressure would transform us into date rapists. Iguana Boy stood by raptly, asking enough dumb questions to keep Thunderhead talking.

"So I take it you bitched out and didn't ask her out?"

I glowered. "I didn't bitch out . . . but I didn't ask her out either."

"You bitched out," Vic said, nodding.

"I didn't! I froze up! Talking to girls isn't easy!" I said, my voice getting higher with every word.

He rolled his eyes. "Yes it is. All you have to do is say, 'Hey, beautiful. Here are some flowers. Wanna go out sometime and give each other hand jobs?'"

"I don't think it's called a hand job when you do it to girls."

"Semantics," Vic said, waving off my comment. "Or you can show her your new trick! That'll get any girls' loins aquiver!"

"Do you even know what any of those words mean?"

"Mostly," he said with a shrug.

"I'm not showing her my trick," I said. "It's . . . not ready."

"See, that's your problem! You just need confidence, and then you'll be on easy street!"

Confidence. Easy street. Right.

Vic could say that because he had confidence to spare and was moderately good-looking. Sure, he may have been dim and poor, but he stood out from the crowd just enough that he had no trouble getting first dates.

I, on the other hand, was the utter definition of nondescript. Brown hair, average appearance, below-average height, average clothes . . . the list went on and on.

I'd never get Kelly Shingle. She was the hottest, sweetest, smartest girl in our senior class. We were never friends, but she talked to me if we passed each other in the halls or when we shared classes. She was always nicer to me than she had to be. I knew that if I could just find some way to stand out that she might go out with me. Maybe I'd impress her with my trick, and then maybe she'd take off her top and let me touch her boobs.

Several actors in cartoonish, black-and-white striped shirts and masks had joined Thunderhead and Iguana Boy onstage. They had attempted to peer pressure Iguana Boy into jumping off of a bridge because it would be "groovy," and when he said no they had tied him up and were preparing to throw him off while Thunderhead ran around the stage, inconsolable.

"I cannot take on the forces of peer pressure alone! Tell me, are there any heroes in the audience who can help me save my sidekick?"

Almost every hand shot up. Very few of them could have qualified as superheroes. Sure, there was Jim Abernathy from my trig class, who could move metal objects with his mind, that sophomore girl who could enhance the smells of whatever she was looking at, or those three scaleface juniors (*Lemurians*, the politically correct part of my mind reminded me) whose names I couldn't pronounce. They might have been able to put up a fight against the forces of villainy and, who knows, maybe even peer pressure, but they couldn't make it as superheroes.

Vic raised his hand, and then looked to me. "Why aren't you raising your hand?"

"Not interested."

He smirked. "Worried they might find out your—"

I punched him in the side, hard, hissing, "Shut up!"

He laughed. "Fine, fine, whatever."

Naturally, Thunderhead picked three of the cutest girls he could find from the audience, and one freshman boy with a leg brace to prove he was equal opportunity. He taught them, and us, several silly catchphrases we could use to fight peer pressure in our everyday lives. Most of the audience shouted them back obligingly, and he had his volunteers scream them loud enough to knock the cartoon thugs away from Iguana Boy, who sprung to his feet, hugging each of the girls who had "saved" him, copping a feel on at least two of them.

Smart kid.

I must have dazed off, because when I stopped twirling my pen and looked around, I realized that everyone's attention was on the stage. It was still public, and I knew this was stupid, but also couldn't help myself.

The trick was like a new toy, and I couldn't help playing with it.

I looked at the pen.

Focus.

Jerkily, it hopped out of my hand and hovered a few inches above my palm. It took some effort, but it began to spin.

I then tried to focus it back into my hand.

The cheap pen crushed into a tiny ball in midair, splattering ink all over my face and shirt. I dropped my focus—and what was left of my pen—as I looked frantically to make sure nobody had seen me.

They hadn't.

Phew.

This power was unexpected. Most superpowers are supposed to develop right around puberty, but mine decided to hit me just slightly after my eighteenth birthday.

Dad always said I was a late bloomer.

I'd have to report this soon, too, because there are nothing but horror stories out there about people trying to hide their powers from the Department of Superhuman Affairs (DSA), but for now I liked having it as my little secret. (I shouldn't have told Vic, but I was excited that first night when I accidentally blew up our mailbox and had to tell someone.)

And then I saw something that pushed all thoughts of responsibility aside.

Thunderhead took a wrong step in his fight choreography and tripped over one of the cartoon thug's legs, falling flat on his face.

He looked dazed, surprised.

Everyone else onstage didn't know what to do.

Finally, achingly, he got up, pretending it was all part of the show . . . but I knew what it was: A non-powered actor had taken out a professional superhero.

Suddenly, it all made sense. My mediocrity. My new trick. Wanting to stand out so I could see Kelly naked. Thunderhead on his face on the stage. They were all individual pieces to the greater puzzle of my life, and I could finally see how they all fit together.

I could finally see where my life was supposed to lead.

"I think I can take him," I said.

"What?" asked Vic, glaring at me out of the corner of his eye.

"Thunderhead. I think I can take him."

#Supervillainy101: Lester & Lyle

You've probably heard a million stories like the one of Lester Luck and Lyle Laughlin. Lester and Lyle were identical twins, separated at birth, yet both led remarkably similar lives. They both got poor grades in school, both married women named Mildred after knocking them up at the age of sixteen, both fought in the army during World War II, both drove Buicks . . . and the list goes on from there. The important similarity is that, in 1948, both of them manifested the ability to control fire, and both decided to become supervillains.

This is where the similarities end.

Wearing a fedora and trench coat whilst throwing fireballs, Lester first made headlines when he robbed a bank in his hometown of Vancouver, American Columbia. He got away with just shy of six grand, but was arrested later that night after being identified by more than a dozen eyewitnesses. Since this was before the Tower existed, he was sent to a local prison, where he probably would have gotten out in fifteen to twenty if he hadn't been stabbed to death with a pair of scissors in the fall of '49.

Lyle, on the other hand, draped himself in a garish black and orange costume with a flowing cape and a shocking, face-covering mask while going by the name of Mr. Smoke. He robbed a bank in Richmond, Virginia, and made off with five grand, but because he could disappear by simply taking off his mask, he was never caught. Mr. Smoke enjoyed a long career as a supervillain, working with the earliest iterations of the Villain's Union and the Offenders supervillain teams while amassing a fortune of close to fifty million dollars during his career. He enjoyed one of America's longest and most successful careers as a supervillain, that is, until he was shot in the head by the Gamemaster during the War on Villainy.

#LessonLearned: For an enduring career in supervillainy, invest in a good costume and secret identity.

10

I AM . . . APEX
STRIKE!

I hope you weren't too set on the idea of me hooking up with Kelly or seeing Vic again, because neither of those is going to happen. Considering how busy my next year would be, they never really made an appearance. That's not to say I stopped thinking about them. In fact, during some of my drugged-out self-pitying stages, I'd stalk them online to see what they were up to.

Kelly became prom queen (naturally), dated the star quarterback (naturally), and attended a nice college out of state, far away from the crushing boredom of Hacklin's Hall (naturally).

Vic got arrested after blowing two-and-three-quarters of the fingers off his right hand playing around with some illegal Lemurian explosives he bought off of one of the scalefaces at school (naturally). He probably would have gotten away with it if he hadn't posted it to YouTube (naturally), but at last report it had close to 11.5 million hits and was pretty damn funny, which made him a local celebrity (naturally). Sometimes, during my really dark days, I would watch that clip and pause on his laughing, stupid face as he held up his mutilated hand and think: *That should have been me, dammit.*

Everything changed after that assembly. I was consumed with the image of Thunderhead faceplanting on that stage and wondering just how I was going to take advantage of it.

Villainy, however, wasn't my first idea.

At first, like every kid, I wanted to be a superhero. They got all the money and endorsements, and had their faces smeared across numerous posters (yeah, I had posters of El Capitán and the Gamemaster on my walls, so what?), and pussy . . . lots of it. If I was ever going to stand a chance at fame, fortune, and pussy, becoming a superhero was my best bet.

The only reason I didn't pursue this path was because becoming a superhero was difficult . . . very difficult. Unless you're one of the lucky few to win *America's Next Protector* (a pretty crappy show, but it has its moments), you have to wait for the annual hero Spring Training, where you try out with something like twenty thousand wannabe heroes from around the world for a spot with the Protectors or one of their satellite teams. At these training events, potential heroes are put through mental and physical tests, psychological and moral evaluations, boatloads of paperwork, and the hassle of dealing with the DSA . . .

Like I said, heroism was hard.

If I really wanted to take a risk, I could always go vigilante, like the Gamemaster back before he helped found the Protectors. But unlicensed heroism held little to no reward. Everything you did had to be out of your own pocket and you spent about as much time running from heroes as you did fighting crime.

Yeah, no thanks.

So, with those unappealing options aside, supervillainy just sounded like the perfect fit for me. It had its risks, of course, but you'd get to keep 100 percent of the profits and gained automatic bad boy sex appeal with a lot of the groupies out there.

I'd be a fool *not* to try supervillainy.

There hadn't been a real supervillain since the heroes won the War on Villainy back in 1993, when the Protectors captured, exiled, or killed all the villains who opposed them. Sure, every so often you'd hear of some idiot with a superpower pulling on a cape and a mask and declaring himself the next great villain, but the Protectors would usually take them out within a few hours.

Idiots.

These wannabe heels were being taken down by heroes with more experience filming commercials than fighting crime. The old heroes had gotten soft, and the young ones didn't know what *real* villains were like.

Even so, these villains-in-training didn't properly prepare, didn't think, and when push came to shove, rarely even fought back.

I was going to be different.

Better.

No, *the best.*

I knew that I could succeed where all of them had failed.

While all of them rushed out to buy spandex and bust open the nearest bank, I studied. I absorbed all the information I could on historical supervillainy. When I should have been doing homework and worrying about graduation, I was reading Villainpedia articles and books while streaming every true crime special on supervillains I could find.

During this time, I worked out with my powers some, enough to learn some pretty good tricks. I could levitate things pretty well, and was even better at breaking things. I could've spent more time trying to hone these, maybe do some real cool stuff like flying, but that would take years, and I couldn't wait that long. Besides, I was confident that I was strong enough to deal with any problems, heroes or otherwise, that might come up.

Only then, after I was confident in my strength, did I let myself work on my costume and codename.

The costume part was easy. The thrift store two towns over had everything I was looking for: black leather jacket, black leather pants, and black leather boots. None of them were the right sizes, as the pants were too tight and the jacket was too big, but I figured I could make it work. Especially seeing as I had no sewing skills nor access to those tailors and polymers the heroes could afford.

It took a separate trip to the bike shop (while sneaking some money out of my dad's emergency stash) to get a motorcycle helmet, and another to the craft store to get the bright-blue puffy and spray paints I'd need. They wouldn't sell me the spray paint, something about them not trusting teenagers, so I had to pay a not-too-terrible-smelling bum off the street to buy it for me.

After getting some advice from my mother on how to use puffy paint (for an unrelated school project, of course), I set about decking out the jacket and pants with bold blue lightning bolts, while spray-painting the same pattern on the helmet. They didn't come out straight, but I felt they got the point across. Then some duct tape and strategic cuts to an old electric-blue tablecloth I "borrowed" from grandma's house gave me the cape to complete the costume.

I looked good. In the right light, I could almost pass for a real hero or villain. I spent a lot of time in front of the bathroom mirror posing, taking a few selfies for posterity.

So I had my costume. That just left the codename.

After gathering all my online resources, I'd made a list of nearly five thousand supervillains that used codenames. Almost two-thirds of them were from English-speaking countries (stupid British Empire), and no way was I going to use one that had already been taken. I mean, the last thing a newbie villain wants to do is worry about some ex-villain breaking out of the Tower and seeking vengeance for stealing his gig. I mean, yeah, the Tower's supposed to be inescapable (with its miles and miles of smiles), but I didn't want to take my chances; most of those old villains are really scary people.

I spent a lot of time with my thesaurus app looking for something that sounded tough and menacing. The first word that called to me was Apex, because it means being the top of something. Research told me that there had been six superheroes who'd gone by the name of Apex, so unless I wanted to call myself Apex (the Supervillain), I knew I'd had to expand on it.

Don't ask me how, but that led to Apex Strike.

I could just see it on the news: "Apex Strike Strikes Again!"

Wait, no, that was awful.

"The Wrath of Apex Strike!"

Better, but still pretty cheesy.

"All Shall Kneel Before Apex Strike!"

. . .

All right, I'd have to trust the news guys to come up with the headlines. That was their job anyway.

So I had a codename, and I had a costume. Now to break them in.

It took nearly a month of planning, but I was finally ready to introduce the world to Apex Strike.

There were some pretty big butterflies in my stomach on that "Administrative Leave Day" from school as I biked two towns over to my first target, my backpack bulging full of costume, my helmet barely balanced on the handlebars.

I parked in an alley two blocks away from the target, allowing myself some privacy to change. Actually walking around in the full outfit proved more difficult than posing in front of a mirror; the pants rode up my crotch more than I liked and were very squeaky, while the jacket sleeves almost completely covered my gloved hands.

At least the cape covered up the fact that the puffy paint on my jacket was starting to flake from being crammed in my backpack for so long.

I reminded myself that I didn't have to be functional; I just had to look cool.

Everything else would come out of that.

I stood outside the door, my heart pounding as I prepared to pull it open.

*All right Aidan—**Apex Strike**, time to be a legend. Time to be a badass.*

Seeing the sign above the handle that said PUSH, I swung the door open and stepped inside the Sunnyside Liquor Store.

The store was empty, save for the clerk, who was an aging hippie chick with thick, tied-back gray hair that seemed to stretch to the floor, and a fat guy mopping near one of the beer displays. Neither of them paid me much mind, even when the bell jingled above the door.

Showtime.

"I AM . . . APEX STRIKE!" I announced, proudly.

The fat guy kept on mopping, his attention held by the music in his earbuds. The clerk behind the register looked up at me, idly, a slow smile crossing her face as if she recognized me.

"Don't tell me the Malkinsons are having another cape party. Which one are you supposed to be, Electronaut?" she asked.

This wasn't quite what I planned.

Again, I announced, "I AM . . . APEX STRIKE!"

The clerk shook her head. "Speak up, darlin', can't hear nothin' through that helmet."

Fine, time to try something else.

With slight focus, I waved a hand at the beer cases, exploding them outward in a shower of glass. The mop guy yelped, diving into a rack of Twinkies and sending them all over the floor.

Raising the visor from my helmet with my free hand, I yelled again, "I AM . . . APEX STRIKE!"

For emphasis, I whipped my cape over my shoulder, dropping the visor back down to cover my face.

The clerk was startled, but looked more angry than scared.

"You asshole," she said, defiantly.

16

Fine. If that was how she was going to play this, I'd take the lead. I pointed and focused on the cash register. I meant to make the drawer pop open dramatically, but instead dented it so hard and deep that it looked like it'd been hit by a sledgehammer. The drawer did pop open with a ding, so I got that much right.

I made it nearly three steps to the counter before I was jerked off my feet and slammed to the floor on my back.

> **Pro-tip, kids:** If you're going to dramatically toss your cape over your shoulder, make sure you're not tossing it onto the metal spokes of a magazine rack that's bolted to the floor.

I got back to my feet and was about to free my cape from the magazine rack when the first liquor bottle shattered against my helmet.

I couldn't see where it came from, not with the damn helmet cutting off my peripheral vision, and probably looked like an idiot darting my head from left to right.

I expected it was the mop guy, probably trying to play superhero.

Instead I saw the clerk behind the counter. She had undone her massive ponytail, which now writhed around like a mass of gnarled pythons, grabbing liquor bottles and hurling them at me.

She's super, too. Shit!

Bottle after bottle smashed around me before one shattered against my helmet, then another in the chest.

"Get the hell out of here!" she shrieked. "Jimmy, get my gun!"

I didn't see Jimmy run for the gun, and I didn't want to. I ripped a large portion of my cape away, finally freeing myself from the magazine rack. I waved a hand at the rack of liquor bottles behind her, shattering them all and taking away her ammo.

Instead of throwing bottles, now she started throwing the larger shards of glass my way. One of them bit into the left arm of my jacket and I screamed in pain as I felt it slice at my elbow.

No, this wasn't working out at all.

I couldn't get to the register without this crazy bitch slicing me to ribbons. Now if I could only get it to come to me . . .

I hadn't made any attempts at grabbing objects when testing my powers, but there was a first time for everything.

I reached out, again focusing on the register. It rattled, and even crushed inward some, but didn't move from the counter. The plastic jar that sat next to it, however, flew right toward me. It was full of odd bits of change and crunched up dollar bills, with a sticker on it saying that all donations would go to the Lemurian Civil War Orphans Fund. There had to be at least seventeen dollars inside.

Jar in hand, I ran for the door, trying to push my way out, but it wouldn't budge.

I placed my hand against it, focusing on the glass and metal frame, and exploding it outward into the street.

With one last thought, I turned back to the clerk and raised my helmet's visor. "Remember to tell people that Apex Strike did this!"

She shrieked, "You crazy motherf—!"

I ran away, smiling and scared out of my mind with the hope that I could get out of there before Jimmy found that gun.

As I headed for my bike, I turned to the sound of a car horn blaring. Not taking traffic into consideration, I stopped in my tracks as the truck bore down on me, slamming on its brakes.

Before I could think, I put my hand out in a desperate attempt to stop the truck that was now inches away.

I didn't stop it.

I did, however, rip it in half down the middle. Each half rolled around me, falling on its sides in twin twisted heaps.

Everything went silent. People on the street mostly stopped and stared, though some had the presence of mind to pull out their phones to take pictures or call for help.

I should have tried to make my escape, but I couldn't help myself. With adrenaline pumping through my veins, I raised the visor and yelled, "Remember, today you saw the birth of Apex Strike! A-P-E-X, STRIKE! When posting about me, remember to hashtag it, or I will destroy you!"

I smiled, dropping my visor back down and feeling pretty damn proud of myself.

Then I saw the money.

Dollar bills of all denominations rained down around me and coins jangled as they rolled down the street at my feet. For the first time, I got a good look at the truck I'd torn in two.

It wasn't a truck, it was an armored van.

"Sweet!" I exclaimed, cramming handfuls of cash into the orphan jar. I must have grabbed a couple thousand dollars, which was more than enough to make up for how much of a mess this day had turned into.

I was still cramming cash when I heard the crackle of electricity explode behind me, filling the air with green light.

My heart lurched. I knew this was a possibility, I just never thought it would actually happen . . . not on my first time.

Tossing one more handful of cash into the jar, I began sprinting down the street, knocking people down and smashing storefronts to cause confusion and wishing I had better fitting pants that didn't squeeze so uncomfortably with every leaping step I took. I made it nearly a block before I finally looked over my shoulder.

The glowing, crackling green triangle of energy floated several feet off the ground near the wreckage of the truck.

A Tri-Hole. The preferred method of transportation for any respectable Protector.

When the Tri-Hole first exploded behind me, it must have been no bigger than a postcard. Now it was at least eight feet across, big enough to let one of them through.

And, sure enough, the shadowy outline of a superhero began to appear. It waved a hand out, creating a ramp of solid ice and sliding down, revealing a young masked man with spiked blue hair in a light blue and silver bodysuit. Then a second figure flew through the Tri-Hole. He was muscular, blond and shiny, bedecked in a bodysuit of gold and white with a shimmering cape that flapped in the breeze behind him.

A small part of my mind was thinking: *Wow, Icicle Man and Helios.*

They weren't big heroes, but they were *almost* big heroes, so that was enough to be impressed with.

The rest of me was thinking, *Ohshitohshitohshitohshit- ohshitohshitohshitohshitohshit!*

The last thing I wanted—especially on my first caper—was to get captured and sent to the Tower. I didn't want to die. I just wanted to go home and enjoy my money and power and, if I had to quit villainy to do so, I would . . . *oh God I just don't want to get in trouble.*

I ran, tired and sweating and cursing this damn suit. I was certain that if I could just dodge down one of the side streets and find a quiet place where no one could see me, I could ditch the costume and look like any innocent kid holding a jar full of money that was totally not stolen, no sir, Mr. Superhero.

Icicle Man and Helios went off in different directions, people pointing them every which way as the chaos I'd attempted to spread seemed to kick in.

Almost there, almost there, just a little bit farther—

The ground beneath me turned to ice. I slipped and fell, sliding down the street and smashing into a snow drift. Massive spikes of ice burst from the ground, surrounding me like the bars of a cage.

Aching from the fall, I turned onto my back. Looking around, I saw people cheering and clapping and holding up their phones as Icicle Man smiled and waved, crouching a few feet off the ground on a ramp of ice he'd made. Once he was done with the crowd, he turned in my direction.

I raised the visor on my helmet and screamed, "Please! Please don't hurt me! I surrender! I'll do anything! I surrender!"

To show him I was serious, I raised my hands and tossed the plastic jar of money at his feet.

He laughed, jauntily, shooting a couple of icicles from his hands and spearing the arms of my jacket to the ground.

"Sorry, villain, but that's not good enough!" he said, getting another uproarious burst of applause and cheers.

The cage of icicles began to close in around me, sharp tips pressing into my flesh. He wouldn't kill me; he couldn't. No villain since the War on Villainy ended had been killed, not like the old days; they'd just been sent to the Tower for the rest of their lives. It wouldn't be fun, but it had to be better than being publicly impaled by a dozen icy spikes.

Even though he couldn't, that didn't mean he wouldn't. He was a superhero. I was a supervillain. Nobody here would think worse of him for it.

There was only one way out of this that I could see.

Focus.

The icicles immediately shattered, freeing me from my frozen cage. The wave I created shattered pavement and knocked nearly everyone within a fifty-foot radius to the ground. I stumbled to my feet as Icicle Man tried to regain his footing on a new ice ramp. Attempting smooth, he slid towards me.

I raised my hand to him.

Focus.

In my defense, I was just trying to push him away.

And I did . . . sort of.

He did lurch backward in midair before going completely rigid. He levitated off the ramp at least a foot, shuddering and jerking as his hovering body contorted violently. Blood burst everywhere as a terrible ripping, slurping sound filled the air, with bones and organs and various bits of meat swirling around in on themselves before exploding outward like a piñata full of roadkill and cherry bombs. What used to be inside Icicle Man was everywhere, spread across the street, the screaming audience, me.

I had turned him inside out.

In retrospect, this would have been a great time for a witty catchphrase, cementing my legacy as the next great supervillain.

Instead, I just screamed, "FUCK!"

#Supervillainy101: Ned Kelly

In the late 1870s, the Stone Age of Superheroes, there was no more feared an outlaw in Victoria, Australia, than Ned Kelly. A petty criminal throughout his youth, he gained notoriety when he and his gang murdered three police officers sent to bring them in for questioning. This set off a crime spree of violence and bank robbery that, well, probably would have gone relatively unnoticed in this otherwise lawless section of pre-hero Australia.

Toward the end, aware that police would soon be closing in, Ned Kelly procured the help of one of the many mad scientists hiding out in Australia to build him a weapon that would allow for one great last stand against the police. In the town of Glenrowan, Kelly brought out this fearsome weapon: a steam-powered suit of mechanized armor. Using this semi-robotic suit of armor to deadly effect, witnesses reported Kelly killing at least a dozen police officers before taking a rifle shot to the boiler in his back.

Reports of what exactly happened after this are sketchy at best, but it is known that the subsequent boiler explosion killed Kelly, his gang, and all of the police who had tracked them down and set a good stretch of the town on fire.

To this day, you can still see occasional news stories of people finding chunks of his armor, and if they're really lucky, bone.

#LessonLearned: Always have a well-planned exit strategy.

I AM NOT
APEX STRIKE!

I got away.

Everyone was so focused on the puddle of meat that used to be one of their beloved superheroes that they didn't see the lowly, gore-covered supervillain escape. I was running on auto-pilot, fleeing in fear, hearing only the dull thud of my heart in my ears as I ran blindly. After a block I started climbing people's fences, going from backyard to backyard, convinced that at any moment a Tri-Hole would open and spew out more heroes who would arrest me and take me to the Tower, telling my parents what awful things I'd done. I was in so much trouble . . .

No, *Apex Strike* was the one in trouble! Aidan Salt had never even left town. Aidan Salt had never even seen a real superhero in person (except Thunderhead), let alone killed one.

If they asked me I'd say, "Apex Strike? Who's that?"

Finding a shovel in some random backyard made destroying the evidence easy. I dug up one of their flower beds (it was ugly anyway) and buried the costume as deep as I could.

Retracing my steps back to my bike, I was afraid that people would look at me and laugh, since I was just in my tank top and boxers. Fortunately they seemed more interested in the growing crowd back where Icicle Man was killed.

I made it home with time to spare, parking my bike, showering about four or five times, and parking myself on the living room couch with a bible. If anyone asked, I'd been home all day, reading. I hadn't been online, hadn't seen the news, and had no reason to know that anything of interest had happened today.

Mom and Andy came in about an hour later, both looking grave.

I snapped the book shut. "I'vebeenhomealldayreading!"

I'd like to thank the Academy . . .

They were too lost in their own world to even notice me. Given her glassed-over look, I think Mom might have even popped a Valium. Andy was on the verge of tears.

"Is something the matter?" I managed to say, pretty sure I didn't sound *that* suspicious.

Andy immediately ran upstairs, bawling, while Mom steadied herself on the doorframe.

She looked at me, questioning, "You mean, you haven't—"

"No, I haven't heard what happened."

She ran to me, throwing her arms around me. "Oh, it was terrible! Someone . . . a terrible, inhuman, un-American, *supervillain*, killed . . . Icicle Man!"

I got off the couch to console her. As she sobbed into my shoulder, I gently rubbed her back, trying to calm her down.

"It's all right, Mom, everything's going to be fine," I said in my best soothing voice, trying not to sound too scared.

Of course, it wasn't fine.

For the next week, our fight was the number one trending topic in the media and nearly every channel was focused on the death of Icicle Man and the disappearance of the mysterious and evil Apex Strike. There were memorials. There were retrospectives of his brief career in heroism, which was tragically cut short. Lots of time was spent focusing on his extensive charity work. His album of jazz standards shot to the top of the charts in less than twelve hours.

It was easy to get lost in the headlines:

"A Nation Mourns"
"Death of a Hero"
Helios: "If Only I'd Gotten There Sooner"
El Capitán : "I Will Pray for His Loved Ones"
Protectors Spokesman: "This Death in Our Family Will Be Avenged"

One week after the autopsy proved that he had, indeed, been turned inside out, every channel showed the live broadcast of his funeral. Though a native Korean, his career with the Protectors granted him an honored burial at Arlington National Cemetery. Tens of thousands of people lined the streets of Washington, DC, to watch his funeral procession. There were speeches from both the President of the United States and El Capitán. They spoke of the tragic loss of life and how this reminds us of the need for constant vigilance in the face of villainy.

The most famous image of this aftermath was of a small boy, dressed in an Icicle Man costume, standing on the sidewalk along the funeral procession with a single tear rolling down his cheek as he held a sign, saying "I'LL MISS YOU!"

The picture later went on to win a Pulitzer.

I'd hoped that, given all of this mourning, people would be more focused on the hero than the villain, but for every two headlines about the sad death of Icicle Man, there was one that went like this:

"Apex Strike: The New Mask of Evil"
"Is This the Return of the Supervillains?"
"Who is Apex Strike?"

Several online communities sprung up trying to crowdsource Apex Strike's identity from every picture and video clip that had been taken from the fight. One user determined that Apex Strike couldn't be human based on the funny way he walked, leading to a brief period of violence against local Atlanteans, scalefaces, and gene-jobs.

Multiple conspiracy theories came out that Icicle Man's death must have been an inside job from the heroes to legitimize their liberal, anti-freedom-based agenda.

Fangirls started crawling out of the woodwork, making social media pages dedicated to how cute Apex Strike must be beneath that mask and how they wanted to have his babies. Not just sleep with him, but actually give birth to his children. I didn't mind the first part, but the second . . .

For reasons good, bad, and otherwise, everyone just wanted to know who Apex Strike was.

That was the question everyone at school spent all their waking hours speculating on. Who could it be? Why would they do such a terrible thing? Where would they strike next?

In reverse order, my answers to those questions were: I don't know, I don't know, and I don't know, but it sure as hell isn't me. I might have said that last part one too many times, but the way people laughed afterwards gave me the feeling that they just thought it was my sick sense of humor. After all, there was no way *I* could be Apex Strike. According to the news he was a dangerous criminal mastermind who would have gotten away with an expertly planned armored car robbery if it hadn't been interrupted by the Protectors. His ability to stay concealed even with all the surveillance technology the heroes and government had to offer had to be a sign of skill and practice of years at being on the run.

Apex Strike was clearly a master villain.

I was just Aidan Salt.

Of course, I wasn't half-assing my innocence either. I put my nose to the grindstone and studied hard at school, earning more

A's than I had since freshman year. I joined my family at a few of our church's candlelight vigils in Icicle Man's honor. I even started spending time on weekends working with local charities. Mom, Dad, and even Andy all thought I'd lost my mind. All I had to say was that Icicle Man's sacrifice had inspired me to improve my life.

I was a *good* boy, after all. There was no way I had anything to do with the death of Icicle Man. And there was no way that I could be Apex Strike.

None whatsoever.

After a while, I thought I just might get away with it as life slowly went back to normal.

I started sleeping again, no longer jumping or screaming at the slightest sound. After a few weeks I'd dropped out of the Top 10 trending topics and the news started spending less time talking about Icicle Man's death and more time on its favorite topics: war and superhero gossip.

In retrospect, my devastating failure at the Sunnyside Liquor Store didn't seem *that* bad. After all, I'd gotten away with some cash, and even proved myself against a superhero. He really didn't stand a chance. And I was famous—just a step or two away from being rich and feared. Maybe if I could retrace my steps, find that yard where I'd buried the costume, I could possibly even resurrect Apex Strike (*maybe even hit up a few of those fangirls . . .*).

After all, if I'd gotten away with it once . . .

I was thinking something much like this while walking home one day in late March when a man in a black trench coat and sunglasses dropped out of the sky in front of me.

"Aidan Salt," he said, reaching into his coat.

"Ididn'tdoit!" I shrieked back, turning on my heels and running. I looked back long enough to see him tapping his earpiece and speaking rapidly.

Two more men in identical suits appeared in front of me, one dropping out of the sky like the first, the second materializing out of the ground.

The last thing I remember before everything went black was holding my hands up and screaming, "Wait!"

I didn't wake up dead. That was a good start.

I did, however, wake up tied to a chair in a dark room with a bright light shining in my face. I seemed to only be wearing my underwear and a thin metal collar wrapped around my forehead.

I quickly realized waking up dead might have been a better option.

I tried to focus, but couldn't. My power had been disabled.

From somewhere beyond the light, someone threw a bucket of icy cold water in my face.

"I was already awake!" I shrieked.

"We know," a firm, amused voice said from somewhere else in the room. "That was for Icicle Man. And don't bother trying to use your power. The halo you're wearing lets us control your powers whenever we want."

I nearly screamed. Everyone knew the horror stories about what had happened to supervillains who'd been forced to wear halos for too long.

I babbled freely, "I didn't do anything, I swear! I don't know what you're talking about! Don't hurt me! I'm sorry!"

Tears were streaming down my face, when I heard someone in the dark chuckle.

"We're not here to hurt you . . . yet," the voice said.

"YET? Then . . . why . . . ?"

They continued, "We have a question for you, *Apex Strike.*"

"I'm sorry . . ." I muttered.

"Apex Strike . . . do you love America?" the voice asked.

There were a thousand questions I'd expected to be asked before this one, but at least it was one I could fake a quick answer to easily. "Yes! Yes, of course I do! My parents put a flag out every President's Day, and one day I want to visit all fifty-eight states!"

"Excellent . . ." the voice said. "And what of her allies?"

"They're awesome!" I said, even though I had no strong feelings toward the Brits or the Soviets or any of the others.

"And Earth?"

"Love it," I said. I was willing to agree with whatever they asked me if it kept me alive.

"Very good. You see, Apex Strike, America, her allies, and Earth itself have enemies. To maintain the *freedom* we enjoy, we need superheroes. They maintain the peace and order that allows us to sleep at night. You do like a good night's sleep, don't you?"

"Yes!" I exclaimed.

"Good, I'm glad we agree, because not everybody does. They believe that, because there are no more supervillains, because the non-human empires of Earth and beyond are not currently hostile, that we do not need as many superheroes. Already many corporations and governments are considering cutting back on superhero funding. Do you understand how bad that would be?"

"Yes!" I exclaimed, completely answering on autopilot.

"It would be anarchy! People would run lawless through the streets, committing crimes at will! Governments would fall! We would suffer attacks from Lemuria, Atlantis, the less-civilized Sasquatch tribes, maybe even the Grays! The world needs its superheroes!"

The voice fell silent for a moment, and then sighed. "But to have superheroes, we need supervillains. Supervillains keep heroes relevant and funded. That's where you come in."

I was still on autopilot. "Yes! I'll do it! I'll do whatever you want!"

"You know, we were hoping you would say something like that. I think he's ready for us to shed some light on this situation, don't you?"

The spotlight that had been blinding me was shut off, and replaced by dull, harsh fluorescents that lit this otherwise stark, concrete interrogation room.

Standing before me were at least a dozen heroes. Some I knew, while others I didn't: Everywhere Man, Helios, Crystal Skull, husband and wife team Morningstar and Silver Shrike, Armada, Captain Cola, and even Extreme Man, who I thought had retired in the 90s.

A muscular man, the left half of his body human, the right half a Gray alien, walked toward me, smiling.

It was Fifty-Fifty, who I went as for Halloween when I was a child.

"Welcome to 'Project Kayfabe,' kid," Fifty-Fifty said. "So guys, think he's ready for Death Island?"

He raised a control device towards me, his finger hovering over a button in the center.

Fearfully, I asked, "What isl—"

#Supervillainy101: Blackjack

If you choose to believe her story, even knowing her history of lies and cons, Jill "Blackjack" Winchester was cursed by a voodoo witch doctor on her plantation in Georgia in the 1760s so that she could never touch anyone without them feeling her pain. From that day forward, the last person she touched would feel all the pain, suffer every injury, and even age every day that she was meant to age, effectively making her into an immortal voodoo doll.

Realizing this power's potential (and always having an attitude problem), she started posing as a man, "Jack," and purveyed this curse into a career as an outlaw and mercenary, traveling the world, fighting in wars, and running gangs from the Wild West to Prohibition-era Chicago. Her Old West bravado and style made her a notable and colorful figure in the rising superhuman underworld of the early twentieth century. She was fearless, dangerous, and widely regarded as the first true supervillain of the Golden Age of Superheroes.

When the War on Villainy was announced and the superheroes organized, Blackjack knew that her time was short if she decided to stay a villain. A survivor till the end, she broke into the first ever meeting of the Protectors and offered them all of her criminal contacts in exchange for freedom and a spot on the team.

Naturally, they took her up on this offer, and she enjoys to this day an enduring career as one of America's favorite antiheroes.

#LessonLearned: Superheroes can be surprisingly reasonable if you learn to play ball.

PROJECT KAYFABE

I was getting tired of having my brain turned off and on by the time they finally put me on the boat, but it happened half a dozen times between my interrogation and then.

Three times it was to ask me some follow-up questions about myself; about how my power manifested and how strong I was.

Twice I was woken up by technicians who were working to calibrate my halo. Given their terrified cursing, I think there were accidents.

The last time before the boat I was woken by Armada, decked out in all of his body armor and weapons and reeking of vodka.

"Look scared," he ordered in his Russian accent.

This wasn't hard.

"Thanks," he said, posing himself next to me to take a selfie. Picture taken, he ruffled his fingers through my hair.

"Tell anyone I did that, little boy, and I'll shove a fucking flamethrower up your ass and pull the trigger," he said before shutting down my brain.

The next time I came to, I was on my back, staring at a gray, blank ceiling. My head was pounding as the world was slowly rocking back and forth. The sound of water lapping at one of the walls told me that I was on a boat, which had to be better than being in the Tower . . . or dead.

I sat up, the world righting itself more than my empty and angry stomach wanted to. I could see that I was in a small room with a thick metal door, a toilet, a sink, and my cot. A single flickering bulb in the ceiling bathed the room in a faint yellow light.

I had been in public school classrooms that were more comfortable than this.

The rocking. The pounding in my head. That sour ball forming in my empty stomach.

Something was about to give.

I ran for the toilet, sank to my hands and knees, and vomited, painfully.

I quickly realized three things after doing this:

1. The heroes had found my Apex Strike costume and helmet.
2. I was now wearing my Apex Strike costume and helmet.
3. The visor for my Apex Strike helmet was closed.

"Fuck."

I ripped the helmet off and dropped it into the toilet, retching at the stench that filled the air and covered much of my face. I turned both sink handles on full blast. There was a hiss of air and the heavy thudding of something vibrating in the wall before thick, brown water burst from the pipe with an explosive bang. I yelped, falling back onto my cot and banging my head against the wall and suddenly wishing I hadn't taken off my puke-filled helmet, as the wall had no give against my skull.

"This sucks," I muttered, wiping my face on the back of my jacket's sleeve.

There was a thudding sound from the head of my cot, followed by a puff of black smoke and the smell of brimstone.

A small man was standing on the end of my bed. Only he wasn't a man . . . not quite. Barely three feet tall, he had the upper body of a man and even wore a small white collared shirt with an even smaller black tie that made him look like an engineer for NASA back during the Silver Age. Assuming of course that Silver Age NASA engineers had triangular heads with seven beady black eyes around the rim, quill-like hair, a toothy mouth surrounded by tentacles, and four wafer-thin ears that fluttered next to his face like moth's wings. And, of course, assuming that they had a bulbous black lower body beneath their shirt the size of a basketball with seven spider-like legs sticking out from the sides.

He cocked his head, looking at me curiously, before raising a clawed, four-fingered hand and waving it at me.

"Hello! Odigjod likes how you smell!" it said cheerfully.

I screamed, trying to climb up the wall in some attempt to get away from this . . . thing.

I then felt someone pound from the other side of the wall. "FUCKING SHUT UP, TESTA DI CAZZO!"

The little monster on my bed waved his hands at me. "Apologies! Apologies! No need for fearing! Just a fan of the villain Apex Strike wanting to hello before competition beginning!"

I backed into a corner and asked, shakily, "What the hell are you?"

"Ah, my topside manners are needing working. Apologies, apologies," he said, taking a dramatic bow. "I am Odigjod, son of Bamtalegrissnkareayganitikanikan and Bob the Dietician. Odigjod is imp, up topside from Third Circle of Hell on work exchange program to try to be supervillain like you! Odigjod's big fan of your work! Can Odigjod have autograph?"

Still shaken, and the fact that I'd never signed an autograph before, I shakily agreed. "Umm, sure."

He snapped three of his fingers and made an autograph book and pen appear in midair. I took both and signed my name, and hoping I didn't misspell his (I did, writing it like he'd pronounced it: "Odd-dig-jodd.").

"Thank you, Mr. Strike, I look forward to competition with you," he said politely.

There was that word again.

"What competition?"

Before he could answer, two of his ears perked up vertically, cocked toward the door.

"Coming for us now. Everything beginning! Have to go back to room! Thanks!" Odigjod said, disappearing with another puff of brimstone and smoke.

The door swung open with a heavy metallic squeal. A large man in a black, SWAT-like outfit with body armor and a gas mask waved an automatic rifle at me.

"Out now! Costume on!" he commanded.

I looked at my helmet, sitting in a couple inches of rusty toilet water and vomit.

"Do I have to?" I asked.

He flipped a switch on the side of the rifle. The red pinpoint of a laser sight appeared on my chest.

"Got it," I said, running to the toilet and pulling my helmet out, shaking it free as best I could and slamming it down on my head.

I didn't think it was possible for the helmet to smell worse.

I was wrong.

The guard led me down a long hallway past many similar rooms with locked and guarded doors. I don't imagine I looked terribly intimidating in my mud-caked outfit, tattered cape, and stinking helmet, but they didn't let their guard down around me. It was up a long, creaking flight of stairs before I was out in the sunlight and on the deck of a large freighter in the middle of the ocean. There were more guards along the railing, some armed, some not (supers). About a hundred yards away from the boat was a foreboding island teeming with dense, thick jungle (including many twisted trees that didn't look like they belonged in nature) and a mountain that I could have sworn had half a face carved in it.

The guard dragged me to the middle of the deck and quickly disappeared into the darkness below.

Moments later, another larger cargo door opened on the opposite side of the deck, and out stomped a vaguely human-shaped robot with a hunched back and glowing green eyes (*or was it a mech suit like ATHENA?*). It looked cobbled together, as very few of its heavy metal parts had matching paint jobs, with some of them dented and rusted. It came to a stop next to me, close enough for me to see that one of its right thighs had a few names painted on it and crossed out, the most recent one reading FIREWALL.

Never having seen a robot (or mech suit) before, I couldn't help but touch it.

"Touch me again and I will fucking destroy you," a distorted female voice with a vaguely British accent said from within.

"Sorry," I muttered, stepping away.

Another door opened, and out stepped a young dark-skinned man in a faded green army jacket and ski mask.

"Bloody hell, I gotta share?" he said with an Irish accent, shaking his head.

More supervillains, great.

They came out from the hold one at a time. Some of them had costumes, both homemade and professional looking. Others wore street clothes or prison issue jumpsuits. Not all of them were human; aside from Odigjod, who came up on deck bouncing and gushing over villains that he must have recognized, I noticed three scalefaces, a Sasquatch, a Cyclops, and one guy who appeared to be made of lava. There was another who was made of large, jagged crystals, and an Atlantean showing off their trademark pride. There were some gene-jobs, too, asymmetrical and misshapen from going to one of those illegal clinics to change their DNA to become super, or having it forced on them by some mad scientist. One of the bigger ones looked like he'd taken a hyena-shark-lizard cocktail and appeared so vicious that he had to be escorted by two guards with noose poles around his neck. He snapped and yipped for effect, but didn't try to seriously attack them.

Most of these "villains" appeared to be young, in their late teens or early twenties. While the guys ran the gamut from ugly as sin to movie-star good looks, the girls were universally gorgeous. Beautiful faces, firm, toned bodies with tight asses and high, firm, big breasts . . . *well, whatever was happening here couldn't be that bad*, I realized.

Many of the other villains looked at me, but didn't try to initiate a conversation. Some smiled and nodded (not as many girls as I'd have liked), while others looked disgusted by my presence.

Everyone had heard of me, yet I hadn't heard of any of them. It was a pretty cool feeling, one I definitely was not used to.

After the last villain had been led onto the deck (a girl in a tight white bodysuit and black hooded cloak, her face covered with a porcelain doll mask), there had to be at least ninety of us there, standing around confused, watching the guards, wondering if we were all brought here to die or if we'd have to fight our way out. Since the fight option seemed more likely, I scanned the deck, trying to find anything to hide behi—

"Welcome to Death Island!"

The voice was proud and powerful and very Southern. We all looked to the raised section of the deck to our right.

She stood there looking like she'd just jumped out of one of her posters; long black coat stretching almost to the floor, faded cowboy hat obscuring the top half of her face, showing only a square, tanned chin that had seen a few too many fights, two faded auburn braids tied loosely at the back of her neck, and a half burnt-down cigar sticking out of the corner of her yellow smile. Seeing she had our attention, she jumped the twenty feet down to the main deck in front of us, brushing off her coat.

The fluttering breeze revealed a pair of pearl-handled revolvers holstered at her waist.

Blackjack.

She was shorter than I'd expected.

Seriously, she had to be like four-and-a-half feet tall, tops.

Though looking like a middle-aged soccer mom who'd spent a bit too much time in the sun, her frame was powerful and quick, like a coiled snake.

"This island used to be home to Professor Death, one of the greatest supervillains of his day, just like all y'all. And just like all y'all, we heroes took him down," Blackjack said, pacing the deck in front of us, her spurs jangling as she went.

"Now, I know some of you may take umbrage at the term 'supervillain.' You may not be like the rest of the sonsabitches on this boat who strapped on some spandex, gave 'emselves a new name, and decided to mo-lest po-lite society. You may not have come out of a superprison. You may just be some hard-luck kid who just happened to break the law while coincidentally having a superpower. Well, despite your o-ppression complex, I got a harsh reality for you: to the rest of the world, you *are* supervillains. You deserve to be removed from po-lite society with extreme prejudice so people can go about their everyday lives."

She smiled, broadly, tipping up her hat slightly to reveal the palest eyes I'd ever seen. "But I got news for you. Like the recruitin' speech each of you got said, Earth's in need of some villains to keep po-lite society po-lite. That's why some of us in the Protectors have decided to put Project Kayfabe together. Its goal is puttin' together a team of supervillains."

Well there's one puzzle piece in place, but why so many?

"We want the best, the brightest, and the *worst* out and about, giving us superheroes a hard time. You will commit crimes. You will fight us. Sometimes you'll win, sometimes you'll lose. Mostly you'll lose, because you losin' makes people know that the heroes are out there to protect them. Do this for us, and you will live the kind of life you've always dreamed of.

38

Fame, fortune, freedom, women, men . . . *respect*, they'll all be yours."

As afraid and uncomfortable as I was, what she promised sounded awesome, more than I would have expected when I first went to hold up Sunnyside Liquor Store.

"But this ain't gonna be a walk in the park. The team we're puttin' together's only got space for seven of y'all, and as you can see, there's a damn sight more'n seven of you."

I flashed back to being the last one picked for kickball, and for being the first one hurt on purpose so I could get kicked out of the game. Seeing that happen here, where I'd be just as likely to be set on fire or turned inside out . . .

"So, we're gonna test you. We're gonna tear you apart and put you back together. If you pass muster, you move on to the next round of suffering. If you don't . . . well, this ain't some self-esteem course where everybody gets a trophy and moves on because you're all so darn special. As of today, none of you legally exist. All of your records? Gone. The memories of those who knew, loved, or even vaguely recognized you? Erased. From now on, you are your codename and no more. If you don't have one, one will be provided for you. You belong to us, and if we don't want to play with you anymore, we'll send you on a one-way trip to the Tower with its *miles and miles of smiles* . . ."

I shuddered. Everyone shuddered. Everyone in their right mind who'd heard about the Tower and its smiles should shudder.

I don't know if it was this, or the erasure of our lives that hit people the hardest. Erasure mostly, I'm sure. It didn't hit me as hard as I thought it might. My parents liked Andy better anyway, and I knew Vic would find someone new to play video games with.

Being erased gave me a clean slate.

Cool.

"The only real rule you're gonna live under is this: play nice. This ain't some 'Most Dangerous Game' competition where we just want you killing each other off until only seven of you are left. We want an honest assessment. You kill someone here and you will be punished. You fight us too much, or you try to escape, and . . ."

She flicked her wrist, and a small controller popped out of her sleeve and into her hand. She pointed it at the lava man and pressed a button. He screamed in pain, grabbing his chest and trying to tear it open. He soon stopped screaming, pitching forward and falling to the ground, his flesh melting away on the floor and leaving a crispy skeleton in its place. There were some shocked gasps, even a few screams (mine among them, though the helmet thankfully muted much of it), though most barely reacted.

"And we activate your Creeper." She looked down at the steaming mess. "Creepers let us keep track of you and make sure you're playin' nice. I know there's some pretty big brains in the crowd here who might think you can cut it outta your chest and beat the system. Go ahead and try. These things are set to go off if you even *think* about tampering with them. I also know there are some tough guys and gals among you who think this is bullshit. You think you're hot shit and can fight your way out of here, and to that I say . . . be my guest. We won't touch your Creepers, make it a fair fight. Those of you who want fame, fortune, and glory, those who want to live . . ."

She waved her hand dramatically to the island. "The island awaits. Now there's barracks for y'all 'bout a mile or two inland. We didn't clear out the island much, so you're gonna want to watch for—"

I was off and running before she could finish the sentence. I jumped over the railing, catching my foot on the lip and sending myself cartwheeling through the air. It would have been bad enough if this was a five-foot fall. But the twenty feet it actually was *really* sucked.

I hit the water hard, thrashing and coughing when it filled my helmet. I ditched one boot and started pulling off my jacket.

There were more splashes around me as others jumped in. My lungs burned as I took a panicked breath and sucked in water. I coughed. I thrashed some more. Things started going dim. *Dammit, not again. Maybe if I just focus—*

A large, hard hand wrapped around my chest and lifted me above water, setting me down on what felt like a small, jagged island. As my eyes cleared, I could see that I was on the back of the large boy made of crystals. He had grown into a giant since the boat, the top half of his body sticking out of the water while he calmly walked along the bottom. Large crystal points jutted out in every direction. He turned what I guess had to be his head to me.

"Do you need help getting to shore?" he asked, his voice thick and rocky.

"Yes!" I coughed.

"Hold on," he said, picking up three more people along the way (including the Sasquatch, who smelled like a wet dog) and setting us all down on the sand. Collapsing to the ground, I had hopes that I was at least one of the first to make it here, but that didn't last long. There were a number of fliers who had probably gotten to the beach in a couple seconds, several speedsters who could run on water even faster, and the Atlantean swimming in quick circles, showing off his "skills." Firewall hovered a few feet off the ground with her crude jetpack, while Odigjod teleported excitedly from tree to tree as if he had never seen anything so strange or wonderful.

The boy made of crystals ran back out into the water, grabbing more people who were having trouble swimming. I pulled off my helmet, shaking the water out and feeling bad for him.

Didn't he get that this was a competition? Didn't he understand that helping them only hurt his chances?

While I was shaking out the final drops from my helmet, an explosion went off from the boat. When I looked over I saw that most of the upper decks were engulfed in flames. Blackjack and the guards were giving the ten or so villains who decided to stay back and fight a real time of it. Several from each side were draped over the rails, either dead or dying, while a couple of charred bodies floated in the water. One of the villains started a tornado that tipped the freighter onto its side.

There goes our ride.

More people made it to shore, some like me, standing around confused, others headed into the jungle, remembering what Blackjack said. I thought about following some of them, even made to do so, when my foot caught on something buried in the sand.

As I pushed the sand away with my foot, I uncovered a half-buried mask made to look like a porcelain doll. I bent over and began to dig it out, turning it over in my hands.

"Excuse me?" I heard from behind my kneeled-over self. The voice was sexy and soft, an accent vaguely British with something a little more exotic mixed in. I turned to face this mystery woman, hoping the face was as beautiful as the voice.

It wasn't. At least not the part she wasn't able to hide with the hood of her black cloak. It looked like someone had tried melting her face, and then tried to put it back together while blindfolded. It took everything I had not to recoil.

Instinctively I cast my eyes down. This view was a lot nicer. The white cotton bodysuit she wore was soaking wet, clinging to a body that belonged on a swimsuit calendar. Long, toned legs, wide hips, big boobs, with the faint hint of nipples sticking through in all that wet cotton.

All right, maybe she's salvageable.

"Here," I said, handing her the mask. Without saying a word, she pulled the hood of her cloak back and put the face-concealing mask back on.

Running a hand through her pixie-cut, dirty blonde hair and pulling her hood back up, she said, "Thank you for not screaming. I know you wanted to."

"Uh huh," I said, unable to take my eyes off her chest.

"The heroes want you to call me Ghost Girl, but my name's actually Emma," she said.

"Uh huh," I said. If all the girls here looked like her (at least from the neck down), I would have a hard time focusing.

She shied away, trying to hide herself in the cloak before turning and darting into the jungle. *Did I say something wrong?*

The next voice that came from behind me was laughing, high and yipping, sending chills down my spine.

I turned to face the large gene-job that had been fighting with the guards. One of the noose-poles still hung around his neck, broken in half and hanging against his chest like a tie.

"You're Apex Strike," he said, revealing a mouth with way too many sharp teeth for my liking.

"Yes," I said.

"I'm Carnivore. They say you're the strongest villain here."

"Well . . ." I shrugged, trying not to sound terrified. He leapt toward me, clearing twelve feet in the blink of an eye. Long strings of drool trailed down from his teeth and onto my jacket as he stood over me, casting a large shadow and putting me in the shade.

"And if you're the strongest, and I eat you, that'd make me the strongest, wouldn't it?" he asked, his drool dripping onto the sand.

"No it wouldn't!" I exclaimed, turning and running to the forest. He was on me fast, flinging me to the ground as I tried to crawl away.

"You can't do this!" I pleaded. "This is against the rules!"

He laughed again, high and yipping, raising a hand over his head to tear me open. "Rules? We're *supervillains!*"

He had me there.

Right before Carnivore could dissect me, a large villain barreled into him, knocking him off me and onto the sand. This newcomer was a pale, burly man clad in a suit of armor made of rusty scrap metal, its cowl shaped like a bear's head. He was barely older than me, but twice as large (more in that suit of armor) and was more than a match for Carnivore.

"Don't you know who that is, monster? That's Apex Strike! Show some respect!" he shouted, his accent thick and Eastern European.

"He's mine, you commie fuck," Carnivore hissed back, dropping to all fours and baring his teeth, the hair on his back standing tall. The newcomer flexed his wrists. Several pieces of his armor uncurled from his body, hovered in midair and straightened into spears pointed at Carnivore.

"You were saying, my Yankee friend?" my new personal hero said cockily. Carnivore hissed, then turned and bounded off into the jungle. The new guy simply flexed his wrists again, causing the shards of metal to rejoin his armor.

"You saved . . . oh God . . . I mean—thank you, thank you so much!" I stammered, bounding over to him.

He laughed loudly, slamming one of his metal-encased hands into my back. "It is my pleasure!"

"Ow," I said, trying to hold my smile. Thankfully he didn't notice my grimace over all his laughter.

"I am Iron Bear. It is not my real name, but everybody calls me that. It is so great to finally meet a real, successful villain like you! You must have so many stories! I think we should be moving soon, I believe night will fall sooner than we'd like, and I do not know about you, but I would rather not sleep in the jungle. Like the *hero* said, 'monsters are in these trees.'"

"She said that?" I gulped.

Iron Bear laughed, pounding me on the back again. "Come, we will walk together! I will tell you what she said if you tell me some of your villain stories, maybe give some tips so we might be a better team together, yes?"

Let's see. He idolized me, was big enough to fight off Carnivore (and whatever else this island had to offer), and had information vital for survival?

I was pretty sure I'd just found my new best friend.

#Supervillainy101: Bad Bug & Dart Lad

Like most people, Samuel Grunnings dreamed of being super.

And like most people, he wasn't.

Unlike most people, Samuel Grunnings had escaped from an institute for the criminally insane. Even though it was the early 80s, the height of the War on Villainy, he was able to find the lair of Dr. Tongue, the premiere mad scientist and gene-splicer of the day. He told Dr. Tongue that he loved bugs and wanted to be one of them. The mad doctor didn't hesitate to mix Grunnings's DNA in a blender (or whatever it is mad geneticists use) with that of an ant, wasp, scorpion, praying mantis, and something like twenty other bugs to create the world's greatest gene-job supervillain: Bad Bug.

Yeah, I know, it's a pretty awful name, but what else can you expect from an escaped mental patient whose brain's been fried even further by illegal gene-splicing?

Bad Bug set up shop in the Gamemaster's hometown of Los Angeles, California, reasoning that a non-powered hero's town would be easy pickings. As most villains found out, this was a mistake, as the Gamemaster was more than a match mentally and always managed to foil Bad Bug's devious plans.

Dart Lad (the Gamemaster's sidekick at the time) was known for being cocky and wasn't particularly beloved by anyone, let alone the Gamemaster. During Bad Bug's reign of terror, Dart Lad famously gave a press conference where he called Bad Bug a "brainless [expletive deleted by news station]," and dared Bad Bug to take them on in one final battle. Knowing how proud Bad Bug was, Dart Lad meant to use this chance to ambush Bad Bug with the rest of the Fresh Protectors (a Protectors sub-team made of all the sidekicks) in an attempt to step out of the Gamemaster's shadow.

Bad Bug didn't quite follow the plan.

If he'd been human, maybe he would have just taken the insult and moved on, or maybe he would have fallen for it. But the splicing fried his brain so much that he couldn't help but overreact.

He didn't spring the trap.

He did, however, track down Dart Lad's family and kill his mother, father, five sisters, two brothers, eight cousins, three grandparents, an aunt, an uncle, the paperboy who happened to witness the death of said aunt and uncle, his favorite elementary school teacher (though she was set on fire and partially fed to flesh-eating ants, she actually survived), and fifteen separate pets between all of them.

The videos and Polaroids that Bad Bug sent Dart Lad were rumored to have been so horrible that veteran homicide detectives resigned after seeing them.

Dart Lad suffered a nervous breakdown, dropped out from superhero life, developed a crippling heroin addiction, and briefly worked the underground pornography circuit to make ends meet. Eventually he pulled out his old costume and rebranded himself as a villain. He was captured by the Gamemaster just two months before Bad Bug was taken in.

When being hauled off to the Tower, Bad Bug was famously quoted as he shouted to the media, "Make sure I have a cell next to Dart Lad!"

#LessonLearned: Don't fuck with gene-jobs.

5

SWEETHEARTS

We had expected dinosaurs, as they were a really hot status symbol with supervillains back during the Silver Age, when Professor Death was active. Lucky for us.

They were easy enough to deal with.

I'd focus on the ground in front of them, or Iron Bear would fling a piece of jagged metal, or Odigjod would brew up a little hellfire and blast them to smithereens.

It was when we saw that car-sized gene-job, some mix of snapping turtle and scorpion, crouched over the half-eaten remains of some villain who'd tried going at it alone (sadly, it wasn't Carnivore), that I was most glad to be surrounded by people more eager to fight and more likely to die than me.

"STAND BACK!" the scaleface loudly proclaimed. He unsheathed a curved sword from his back and a crystalline, blue dagger from his belt. "THIS ONE IS MINE!"

"Go nuts," I said.

Weapons drawn and leather tassels trailing behind his red and gold plated armor, the scaleface charged the beast. "FOR KOSAL!"

"Think he stands a chance?" Showstopper asked.

"He comes from Lemuria, the land of dinosaurs. He has probably seen much worse," Iron Bear said.

"Green-skins are loud, violent scum with no appreciation for beauty and logic, but never doubt one in a fight," Artok, (*Prince* Artok, of Atlantis, he'd quickly correct, currently exiled, if you believed him, which I didn't) said in his high, shrieky voice.

"Should we help him?" Showstopper asked. The scaleface laughed, chopping off one of the beast's front legs with his sword.

"I think he's got this covered," I said.

You don't become a supervillain by sticking your neck out and volunteering to get killed. We all knew that (well, maybe the scaleface didn't, but their heads work differently, so they don't really count), and I think that's why we just stood back and watched.

Of course, you also don't get to be a supervillain by dying, which was why we'd all decided to band together in the first place, and probably why everyone except Artok and me were actually considering helping him.

There were six of us now, including the scaleface. Odigjod joined us first; he'd teleported to the barracks just to check them out, but decided to come back to join us because we "seemed fun." I think he just wanted to moon over me. He was like what you'd get if you combined a hyperactive little brother and an overeager puppy and given them godlike powers.

Still, he was friendly, so I didn't mind him.

The others came gradually.

Showstopper, a fat Aussie kid a little older than me with a patchy beard, blond hair tied back in a ponytail, and a gaudy, sequined, and far-too-tight-for-his-body spandex suit, came out of the forest casually whistling with hands in his pockets and asking if we'd like some company.

Artok joined us more dramatically. While he was at home in the water, on land he was fearful and jumpy and really had no idea of what dangers were around. He came running towards us, his scream more high-pitched than I thought possible, as he was being chased by a velociraptor. Iron Bear and I tried to take it out first, but both missed. I then hid behind the closest tree, and Showstopper was smart enough to join me. Odigjod just looked at the raptor, smiled (I think, it's hard to tell with his face), and made the dinosaur disappear with a clap of his hands.

"Mother would like an new dog with me gone," he explained, fluttering his ears.

I have no idea how the scaleface joined us. One minute we were walking, and the next he was walking with us.

He fought the gene-job with gusto, laughing and loudly proclaiming, "I AM VETANK'ILIJ, EXILED WARRIOR OF THE GRAND LEMURIAN HOUSE OF KOSAL! BY MY OATH TO THE GODS OF HARVEST AND FIRE, I WILL DESTROY YOU AND ALL WHO OPPOSE ME AND MY HOUSE UNTIL THEIR HONOR IS RESTORED!"

"Chatty, isn't he?" I said.

"Nobody talks things up like a Lemurian," Showstopper added. "I've worked with a few of 'em on one of my uncle's cattle ranches, and they treat everything like a battle. One of 'em goes to take a dump, he'll come out speechifying about how he slew and conquered the slimy beasts that once dwelled within his bowels."

Artok hissed. Lemuria and Atlantis had hated each other for centuries.

"Disgusting," Artok said.

Showstopper shrugged. "Maybe, but they tell their stories well."

"They are boastful and proud," Artok said, haughty.

"And you aren't?" Iron Bear laughed. "I've worked with both your kinds when I was an enforcer on the black markets. Lemurians, they speak big but tell the truth. Atlanteans, they talk flowery, but almost all of it is a lie."

Artok looked scandalized. "We speak the pure truth, only embellishing for greatest dramatic impact because we have true respect for the art that is speech! And if you wish to split fins, our women are *far* more beautiful than theirs, and you can trust that they were always women."

He did have us there. For better or worse, Atlanteans were near-universally gorgeous.

I had nothing to add to this conversation. These people had been around, had seen and done things that I could only dream of. They'd make far more interesting additions to the team than me.

I had to work on that if I wanted to make it.

With two more chops severing the gene-job's tail and one of its hind legs, the scaleface darted in for the kill, stabbing it with his dagger in the middle of its back. Stroking a jewel at the base of the weapon, the dagger glowed a bright blue. The monster let loose one last, plaintive scream of pain before wisps of steam shot from its wounds and mouth. The scaleface knelt down beside it, whispering a quick, wordy prayer in his native tongue.

"Cooked 'er up real nice from the inside out. Not bad," Showstopper said, impressed.

"Indeed. She'll make a fine meal," the scaleface replied, looking to all of us except Artok. Looking at the charred monstrosity, my stomach did a somersault.

"You don't expect us to actually eat that, do you?" I asked. I didn't want to vomit a second time today.

The scaleface sneered, "Let not your human squeamishness guide you, psychic warrior."

Psychic Warrior. That had a nice ring to it.

"The rules as you know them do not exist out here. We know not if we will sleep on fine feather beds or on the dirt beneath our feet—"

"Cots," Odigjod interjected, waggling a hand back and forth in a noncommittal gesture. "Not fine, not floor."

"—we do not know if they will feed us, or if we must find our own food—"

"They've an mess hall. Mostly cold stuff, but they said they'd have an Subway truck by the end of week," Odigjod said again.

"Subway? Nice," I said. Odigjod nodded.

"They're putting in a metro?" Iron Bear asked.

"No, Subway, they make sandwiches," I explained.

"We do not have these in Lithuania."

"Your *Iron Curtain* has its disadvantages, no?" Artok smiled.

I said, "Oh man, you don't know what you're missing, you can—"

The scaleface roared primally, stabbing his sword into the ground.

"Do none of you realize that we are trapped here, and that without each other we will not survive? This island is harsh, and our captors are harsher. You may think you are strong, but I have watched you all. None of you knows how to fight. I am a warrior of the House of Kosal. I survived the War of the Thirteen Houses! I have defeated the Sons of R'lyeh cultists on the Plains of M'tsalka! I have been to war against foes greater and more dangerous than any of you have ever seen. This land is harsh, but it is nothing compared to my home; I can teach you how to thrive off it. Stand by my side and together we can survive and become the team that is needed to bring order to this world!"

Showstopper was right. The scaleface was good at making speeches. He may have looked like a giant lizard stuffed into red and gold medieval knight's armor, but he knew what he was talking about. I didn't want him to be *my* leader or anything, but I started thinking that maybe, just maybe, he'd be good to keep around.

I stopped thinking that about two seconds later when the tree behind him bent over, opened its jagged, toothy mouth and gobbled the scaleface up. He tried to fight the tree as it reared back up, screaming and hollering and kicking his legs. The screaming stopped when the tree bit down on his armor with a loud, meaty crunch. The kicking stopped then, too, but that probably had more to do with the fact that his bloody, severed legs dropped free from the tree's mouth not long after it bit down.

Artok, Showstopper, and I screamed in horror.

Odigjod simply looked up at the tree and said, "Wow."

The tree belched, loudly.

"Can we go find the barracks now?" I asked Iron Bear.

We were the first walkers to arrive at the barracks, though there were nearly twenty others already there when we entered. Fliers, mostly, with a couple speedsters and teleporters to even things out. We'd been set up in the remains of a small company town Professor Death had made for his minions, and while most of the buildings were burned out and full of bullet holes from when the Protectors invaded in the early 70s, there were a couple sets of barracks, a mess hall, and group showers still intact. There was some electricity, and running water that was clear more often than it was brown. We even had a great view of the force field that bisected the island, keeping us prisoner on this side under the ever watchful gaze of Death Mountain.

Word had it that the Protectors invaded before Professor Death could finish carving his face into the island.

I hated it already. It was hot and humid and full of bugs, the food was mediocre, and the barracks slept like fifty people and had no privacy.

How was this supposed to lead to fame and fortune?

How would this lead to anything that Blackjack promised?

Well, everything except the pussy at least. That was pretty prime here.

She also had the freedom part right. If you ignored the Creepers buried under our skin, we were pretty much left to our own devices. We could eat what we wanted, when we wanted.

We could go to bed whenever we wanted, hang out with whoever we wanted. By nightfall, when the last of the stragglers had made it to the barracks (by then there were seventy-three of us left), we had a few bonfires going. It felt like summer camp, or at least what I always imagined summer camp to be like since my parents never shelled out the dough to send me.

There was a surprising amount of singing and dancing considering that there wasn't any alcohol going around. Artok had an audience of nearly a dozen girls swooning by his fire as he played an Atlantean lyre, singing songs of home and telling stories of his heroics on the hike over, saving us poor humans from monsters and scalefaces.

There were stories and gossip aplenty.

Everybody was talking about the competition.

Everybody was certain they'd make the team.

There were small cliques and alliances forming already, just like on TV. Carnivore (yeah, he'd made it this far, unfortunately) had made some fast friends with a guy dressed like a pirate, the ten-foot-tall Cyclops, and a short, fast-moving kid who literally looked like a brightly colored, angular, anime clown.

Seriously, if you caught him at just the right angle, he had only two dimensions. It was creepy.

People were laughing.

People were making out.

People were having fun.

None of them were me.

I sat by our bonfire, occasionally hovering a log into the flames and watching it burn. Odigjod kept Showstopper and Iron Bear laughing, jumping into the fire and making it transform into various funny faces. Firewall joined us, not so much out of desire as finding the least populated fire to work on her suit by. She'd destroyed a robot in the jungle and was adapting its tech to her suit. It was weird, seeing her outside of it; an average-looking (compared to the rest of the girls around here) girl with light brown skin and short, mussed-up black hair, her legs missing just below the knees and hands that moved with machine-like precision. Occasionally she'd say something like "Impressive, for its time," but she mostly left us boys alone.

"It's not fair," I finally said.

"What? Us being trapped here?" Showstopper asked.

"No. I'm the most famous villain here. I killed Icicle Man! Why doesn't everyone want to hang around me?" I complained.

Odigjod teleported out of the fire, putting a comforting claw on my shoulder. "We want to hanging around you!"

"Yeah, that helps," I said, sarcastically. Odigjod let out a low coo before stepping back and again teleporting into the flames.

"It is not as bad as you think, I think," Iron Bear said. "You are correct when saying that you are the most famous here. I doubt that anyone else here has made headlines like you, and I think they are jealous."

Jealous? That perked me up.

"Keep going," I said.

"Well, look at it from their view. They enter into a competition that means either freedom or prison, and they think they all have a chance, but then they see you. They see *Celebrity Supervillain Apex Strike*. They see someone they think is going to be on the team for sure, and they are jealous that they do not have that," he explained.

I looked to Showstopper. "You think that's true?"

He shrugged. "Maybe. Who cares about those assholes anyway? Once we get to competing and you show off what you can really do, they'll be begging for your friendship just so they can get a few pointers from someone who's actually been there. Not like some posers who want to make everyone think they have."

He didn't have to point to Artok or Carnivore, but I got the idea.

"Thanks guys, that really means a lot."

Odigjod teleported in front of me. "Even Odigjod?"

I smiled, ruffling a hand through his fluttery ears. "Yeah, you too, Odigjod."

There was a sharp, sarcastic laugh from across the flames. "You really believe all that bullshit?"

"It's not bullshit," Iron Bear said.

"Yeah, it is. You guys have just piled it so fucking high you can't see what it is anymore," Firewall said, using a severed, robotic arm to pull herself across the ground toward us.

"What's bullshit?" I asked.

"The way they jack you off just because you got in a lucky shot at a superhero that had probably never fought a supervillain before," she said.

"That wasn't luck—"

"Yeah, it was. You were running, he caught you, he almost killed you, you killed him first, and you couldn't run away fast enough."

"You don't know what it was like. You weren't there."

"No, I wasn't. But I watched that video a few dozen times, and I know you're not the hot shit you think you are. None of us are, really. Some of us are petty criminals, sure, and even a few real bad guys, but mostly if you look at our files we're just a bunch of stupid kids the heroes know they can push around."

"You've seen our files?" I asked, a bit taken aback.

She rolled her eyes as if I'd just asked the stupidest question in the world. "I can talk to machines. They do what I want them to. The computers on the boat had really shitty encryption."

She looked down and started talking at her chest. "And yes, I know you guys are listening in on this, and if this was a big surprise you would have killed me by now. I know you want me here on the team because I'm that good, so don't even give me a suspense shock, all right? That'd annoy me and slow down the upgrades on my suit and will mess up your whole 'show and tell' day tomorrow because I can put on a really, really good show if you don't annoy me."

It took me a moment to realize that she'd started talking to her Creeper.

"Hey, we're bad guys," Iron Bear said, defensively.

"No, you're sweethearts," Firewall stated.

"Wanna bet?" he asked, flexing his suit as if it were a second set of muscles.

She raised an eyebrow. "You've broken some legs for a black market mob boss, but you've smuggled goods to dissidents and refugees—for free—under your boss's nose if you thought you could get away with it."

She turned to Showstopper. "You've used your hive mind powers to create flash mob musical numbers in an effort to pick up women and jumpstart your career as a performance artist, and the heroes branded you a villain just to shut you up."

"That works?" I asked.

He chuckled. "The girls and getting arrested part, yeah. The art . . . not so much, no."

She turned to Odigjod. "And you . . . actually, they don't have a file on you."

Odigjod nodded. "Hell magic. We cannot show up in an formal file, it just does not working."

"File or no, though, it doesn't take a genius to see you're a sweetheart," she said.

He bowed. "Guilty."

"See?" she said, moving her hand as though showing off a host of prizes. "Sweethearts."

"So what you're saying is, you don't think we can cut it as supervillains?" I asked.

"Supervillains like Bad Bug and Otis Shylock? Fuck no. But the supervillains they're going to want on this team to push around? Yeah, I'd say you guys are perfect."

Both Iron Bear and I stood up to object.

But before an altercation could arise, a crashing at the edge of the forest stopped everyone in their tracks.

"It sounds huge!" I exclaimed, running to the other side of the fire with Firewall.

"I've heard bigger!" Iron Bear laughed, unwrapping several shards of metal from his armor and hovering them like spears at the ready.

No monster came out of the trees, at least not any that were native to the island. It was only the giant boy made of crystals. He cradled another villain in his arms, setting them down by the fire. Though they ran off, the crystal boy stood looking at us for a moment while breathing heavily. Finally, he smiled crookedly.

"*Hola!*" he said, conversationally, collapsing on the ground. The crystals began to retreat into his body, shrinking him down to a slender, handsome boy maybe slightly taller than me in a tattered soccer jersey and shorts with about a week's worth of black stubble.

"Are you all right, friend?" Iron Bear asked.

"Fine, I'm fine," the boy said. "Just exhausted. Spent all day searching the waters for those in need of help. I found some, but not a lot wanted help. Can you believe some actually took shots at me?"

I don't know why he sounded so sad. He shouldn't have been surprised.

"Have you eaten? Had water?" Iron Bear asked.

The downed boy shook his head. He looked on the verge of death.

"Apex Strike and I will get you some food and water."

"We will?" I asked, surprised that he recommended me for this expedition.

"Yes. And you two will watch him. Make sure he does not lose consciousness," motioning to Odigjod and Showstopper.

"With pleasure," Showstopper said, pulling Odigjod over to sit by the boy. "Now, have you heard the one about the bloke who tried smuggling cane toads up his bum?"

Though I would have been more comfortable sitting by our bonfire, I walked with Iron Bear, ignoring Firewall's echoing call of, "Sweethearts!"

"Why did he do it? Why are we doing this?"

"Doing what?"

"Helping *them*, helping *him*? Isn't this a competition? Doesn't it help us to go every man for himself?"

"In something like this, no. We will be a team, remember? We are to depend on one another someday. I think you can only benefit from playing nice," he proposed.

On paper, what he said made sense. In reality, it sounded hard as hell. People never liked me. They'd never really disliked me, either, and usually just walked around me. Playing nice would take the effort of pretending to be interested in them.

I shook my head. "This sucks."

Iron Bear laughed, playfully punching my shoulder. "Nobody ever called being a supervillain easy. Come on, you get the water, I'll get the food."

We went our separate ways, both of which were long and winding. I hoped that as the competition went on that they'd figure out how to speed this along. I mean, we'd starve out here if we had to wait like this *every* day, wouldn't we?

It had only been a few hours and I already heard people fighting in the food line. There was some shoving, some accusations about getting seconds when some people hadn't had firsts. Someone defensively saying they were getting food for a friend.

This was a problem that was going to get worse before it got any better if nobody took control of the situation.

With all the commotion, the forest went silent with the sound of screams, followed by a loud gurgling and someone laughing loudly. Everyone ran out of the water line to see what was going on. I cut to the front, grabbing a couple canteens before seeing what had happened.

Everyone stood in a circle around Carnivore, as blood ran down his cheeks and neck. Another boy lay dead in front of him, with a large pool of blood spreading on the ground. His dead eyes stared out blankly into the night.

Iron Bear.

Carnivore had ripped out his throat.

Suddenly, Carnivore's body went rigid. He let out a high, yipping scream, grabbing at his chest and falling to the ground in a violent seizure.

Blackjack's voice echoed across loudspeakers on the island, "We told you kids, no killin'. This time, y'all got a warning. Next time, we set the Creepers to kill. Now somebody bury that poor SOB before he stinks up the place and get on with your party. You'll want this free time while you still got it."

Carnivore stopped seizing and crawled away, grumbling.

Nobody wanted to touch Iron Bear, but because I'd spent the most time with him, everybody expected me to do something. Sighing, I focused, dragging his body across the ground while still keeping my distance so I wouldn't have to smell him, or look at all the blood.

Or the guy I thought might've been a friend.

Odigjod simply hissed a low, "Oh no." when I brought the body back by our fire.

The crystal boy took the water from me gratefully, but sadly. "If he hadn't been getting me food . . . it's my fault."

"Yeah, it is," I said. Firewall chucked a small piece of metal at the back of my head, shooting me a harsh glare.

Weakly, the boy stood up, transforming one of his arms into a crystalline monstrosity. "I will bury him."

"Odigjod will help," Odigjod said.

"We all will," Showstopper said, standing to join us. Even Firewall set down her work long enough to suit up and join them. *Great, now I'll look like a dick if I don't help.*

Between the five of us and our powers, it didn't take long to bury him. Showstopper even made a simple cross out of a couple sticks and stuck it in the ground.

"Think he'd have liked that?" he asked.

"I think he'd have liked being alive more," I said.

"But . . . never mind," Showstopper said, turning to Odigjod. "Did he go to hell?"

Odigjod shrugged. "Not my department. Odigjod will looking him up when visiting home next. Maybe put in an good word, if I can, if he's there."

"What do we put on the marker? Iron Bear or . . . what was his real name?" Showstopper asked. Nobody knew. Firewall probably did, but she wasn't saying.

"Seriously?" Showstopper asked. "None of you even took a second to ask his name?"

"Did you?" I asked.

He grumbled. "That's not the poin—"

"Supposed to use our codenames," Odigjod said.

"You don't," Showstopper said.

"Don't have one, yet," Odigjod said.

"His name was Sacha," a voice said from behind us.

It was Ghost Girl.

Her eyes glowed vaguely gold behind her mask. "Sacha Sakalauskas. He wasn't evil, he just worked the black market so he could provide for his sister. She's been ill for a long time. He hoped he'd make the team so he could provide a better life for her, maybe smuggle her into France. Even though she wouldn't remember him, he would have done this. He was a good man. He's sad to have died, he's sad that he will never see his family again, and to have died without anyone knowing his name."

Suddenly her name made a lot more sense.

"You see ghosts," I said.

"I see lots of things," she said.

It was quiet by our fire as we took in what she said.

Then the crystal boy spoke, "Felix Platero."

"Nick Nesbit," Showstopper said.

"Helen Campbell," Firewall said.

"Emma Hendriks," Ghost Girl said.

At last, they all looked to me. Sighing, I said, "Aidan Salt. Just don't go spreading that around too much, 'kay?"

I barely slept that first night, as I was afraid of what was ahead. What if I screwed up? What if I freaked out? What if I failed? That'd all be a one way trip to the Tower.

I couldn't handle that.

Those thoughts were rough. Almost as rough was realizing just how much I missed.

I missed having a bed that wasn't rock hard and swarming with mosquitoes and other weird bugs that kept trying to burrow beneath my skin.

I missed technology.

I missed all the familiar sounds of home.

I think I might have even missed my family some, though there's every chance that was just some side effect of missing home.

I missed having dreams that didn't include people dying. Since I didn't sleep much, there weren't many of them, but the few minutes I caught here and there were full of them. Icicle Man. The people on the boat. Iron Bear. Even the scaleface.

But most of all I missed sleeping in a roomy bedroom, and not having to share it with forty other guys. They were always moving, tossing and turning. Some snored. Some wept softly. Every so often we'd hear something horrible in the jungle and everyone would wake up, cursing.

And the sex . . .

They started meeting up around one in the morning, when they thought everyone else was asleep. Usually it just meant a girl sneaking in, meeting up with a guy, and them heading out to do their business. Some were less discrete, getting busy on a cot.

Most of them kept it down.

Some didn't.

So mixed in with all the tossing and turning and snoring and crying you'd occasionally hear the low and not-so-low moans and grunts of people fucking.

I tried to block it out by wrapping my head in my pillow. But it's easier said than done when there's a couple screwing right next to you.

"Yeah, tell me how amazing I am!" Artok whispered, his voice still somehow shrill. *So, I guess one of the girls bought his shtick.*

"You're all right," the girl said.

"Just all right?" he asked.

"That remains to be seen," she said, her accent foreign and sultry.

I could focus, tilt his bed over, and mess things up for him. Atlanteans were supposed to be good fighters, but he seemed weak and there was no way he could take my power.

It'd be easy. Fun. Maybe even help me sleep.

I rolled over, ready to take him down a peg.

Then I saw her.

She was completely naked, straddling the Atlantean's hips and riding him slowly. Her skin was pale white, practically glowing in the moonlight, offset by a large number of ornate tattoos that covered her back and arms. Long, perfectly straight jet-black hair rolled down her back, with a few odd locks spilling over onto her amazing breasts.

This was the first time I'd seen a naked girl in person.

It looked better than it did on the Internet.

She turned to me. Her face was serene, unlike Artok, who kept grunting and shrilly muttering about how awesome he was. Her lips, painted black, matching her goth goddess look, curled into a confident smile.

Then she winked at me.

She winked at me!

Arching her back and rocking her hips, she gave a hell of a show. Then, before anything could get real good, she stroked a tattoo on her arm. Briefly, it appeared as though all of her tattoos had come to life, dancing about her body before a swirling flock of black birds burst from her arm, surrounding their bed and blocking it from view.

"Show's over," some guy with an Irish accent said from across the room. "Time to get some sleep."

There were scattered mutters of agreement. Not from me, though. She winked at me! Maybe that meant she knew who I was! Maybe that meant I stood a chance! I mean, she was putting out on the first night, so I guess that meant anyone—and by anyone I mean I—had to stand a chance at nailing her too, right?

#Supervillainy101: Locust Lad & Illusor

All the best superheroes had their rogues' gallery of villains. I'm sure a lot of them would want you to think that they had some major vendettas against these particular heroes, but more often than not it came down to them being unable to afford working any city other than the one their particular hero operated in.

Of all the heroes that operated in the last days of the Silver Age, before the War on Villainy, perhaps the most colorful rogues' gallery belonged to Locust Lad. Though Denver was not as illustrious a center for superheroism as Los Angeles, New York, or Amber City, it attracted a surprising number of mad scientists specializing in experiments gone awry, giving it one of the highest populations of supervillains per capita in the United States. Though only possessing the powers bestowed upon him by a radioactive grasshopper (or was it a mystical grasshopper totem? He's never been clear on his origin), Locust Lad fought them all for years, even when his voice started to break and he redubbed himself Locust Man.

The least respected of all his villains was Illusor. An ex-magician, he was utterly pitiful in a fight, instead relying on parlor tricks and flashy illusions to escape. He rarely engaged Locust Lad in direct fights, preferring to distract him to the opposite side of the city from where he plotted his evil schemes, and when he did have to engage the hero, it was with a shotgun.

No weapon themed to his outfit, no witty quips, just a shotgun.

Purist villain fans hate him for having some of the most boring hero-villain fights of the War on Villainy.

I think his record speaks for itself.

Of the forty-two villains usually counted among Locust Lad's rogue's gallery, Illusor was the last one captured. He used his tricks and illusions to stay hidden until long after the War on Villainy ended and the Digital Age of Superheroes began, surrendering himself in 2009. Apparently, after a cancer scare, he found God and decided it was the "right thing to do."

All right, the "Illusor Sucks" crowd does have some points.

#LessonLearned: Sometimes being flashy is better than being dangerous.

#LessonLearned: Also, don't find God.

SHOW AND TELL DAY

Nevermore.

Her name was Nevermore. She was from Paris, France, a Virgo, could make her tattoos become real world objects, was a huge fan of Edgar Allen Poe, and was "a shining blossom of femininity whose petals only needed the slightest of coaxing to bloom." These were all details I got from Artok on the breakfast line. He said he'd gotten what he needed from her and that I was welcome to her if I wanted.

I did.

Knowing that I did was the easy part.

Knowing what to do next wasn't.

I'd never been on a date and had never been able to muster the courage to even ask Kelly Shingle out, and she was only the prettiest girl at school.

Out here, surrounded by some of the hottest bad girls in the world, I needed some serious help.

Lacking Vic for advice on such matters, I went to the few people I knew well enough to ask for advice.

Odigjod didn't know much of human courtship, and I'm still doing my best to forget the nightmarish details he provided on the imp reproductive process.

Felix was gay, so I didn't think he'd be much help.

I was sure Firewall had experience asking girls out, but for some reason she was offended by my question and threatened to blow me to pieces if I ever asked it again.

Showstopper went into a long-winded speech about how a good sense of humor, listening to girls, and occasionally sacrificing my dignity would help.

So, they weren't any help. I'd have to improvise.

I'd have to watch, and wait, and plan, and find my moment.

That moment came about an hour later.

It arrived not long after the morning announcement. Blackjack said that our first test would be that afternoon, and they would deliver some more comfortable clothing than our "pitiful attempts at costumes." We each got a foot locker at the base of our beds stocked with t-shirts, athletic shorts, clean socks and underwear, running shoes, and toiletries (never had I thought I'd be so glad to see a bar of soap). Everything gray and navy blue, hardly stylish, but heaven compared to saltwater-soaked leather.

With some time to kill, I decided to take in the sights of our little shanty town.

There weren't many.

A lot of people scoured the town ruins, bored, occasionally finding the odd bits of treasure or one of the many skeletons of Professor Death's minions. Carnivore and his friends found an old death ray in the ruins of a daycare center and spent some time trying to get it working, but were only successful in blowing up a tree and fighting and exchanging various ethnic/sexual slurs with each other. They ended up tossing the ray aside and wandering off.

Since I couldn't get it to work either, I found Firewall and gave the gun to her. It didn't completely smooth over my question from that morning, but it did get a rare smile and a "Thanks" from her.

After wandering around the town, I finally found Showstopper, Ghost Girl, and a couple other villains at the edge of the forest, chucking rocks and pieces of rubble at a tree.

"Another one of those killer trees getting close?" I asked.

"Nah, just mangoes this time," Ghost Girl said, chucking another stone and missing a mango.

"Little help?" Showstopper asked.

Normally, this would have been when I'd have made some excuse and not helped out, mostly because I didn't want to fail and have them laugh at me. That would have been the case if I didn't see *her* sidling on over to our group, curiously looking up at the tree.

Suddenly, my newly gained confidence (thank you, Icicle Man) returned. *I'm Apex Strike, the greatest supervillain in the world. I can do anything if I put my mind to it.* With a grin, I raised both of my hands, focusing on the hanging fruit. I watched as a heavy limb, covered with ripe, juicy mangoes began to shudder. I had it. I looked back to the others. I looked to Nevermore. I pulled.

I remember a loud snapping sound and some screams.

I remember the world violently tilting on its end before going black.

I vaguely remember hearing the words "Holy shit!," "Impaled," and "Should we call Spasm?"

Most of all, I just remember wondering if Nevermore would like to fill her hair with scrambled eggs before or after I gave her a mango.

Serious head injuries can make you wonder things like that.

"Tell me if this hurts." I recognized his voice. It was the Irish guy who told us all to shut up last night.

"Huh?" I muttered, slowly regaining consciousness.

The searing pain of a lit cigarette being pressed to the inside of my wrist sped that process up considerably.

"FUCK!" I screamed, eyes bolting open to see a grimy, stubbly, dark-skinned young man with wire-rimmed glasses and a faded green army jacket sitting in a chair by my cot. I waved a hand at him, flinging him across the room and into the wall.

He laughed, putting the cigarette back between his lips. "I'll take it from your response that your answer would be yes?"

"Why did you do that?"

He got up, shrugging and sitting back in his chair. "Why not?"

"Because . . . fuck! You burned me with a cigarette!"

"That I did. I can also fix that," he said, pointing at me. I felt a sudden wave of euphoria, and all at once didn't even notice or care what he'd done.

"This island's living up to its name quite well. I've seen about as many injuries here since last night as I would a good week in Belfast: broken bones, gashes, burns, bug bites like crazy. But you and your infinite stupidity truly took the cake, for today at least. I imagine worse to come, especially if they keep you on."

"It wasn't stupid," I said.

"Nearly killing yourself to impress some girls, even lovely girls, is stupid. You probably woulda died if your associates hadn't brought you to me. The name's Long, by the way. Liam Long, though I guess you're supposed to call me Spasm, and body control's my specialty. I put your healing response, immune system, and blood production into overdrive and made you good as new. There, pretty as a picture," he said, waving a hand and sending the euphoria away.

I was suddenly aware of my bloodstained t-shirt full of holes, but that was probably better than having Ghost Girl tell everyone what my last thoughts were while they buried me next to Iron Bear. I doubt I would've sounded very good.

"This is . . . impressive," I said, looking myself over.

"A 'thank you' would have sufficed, but I'll take the compliment as well. Just remember to put in a good word for your old pal Spasm if the heroes start asking who you are and aren't fond of," he said, shaking a cigarette out from his pack and offering one to me. I declined.

I wanted to ask him a thousand questions. How long had I been out? Where was everybody else? Were they laughing at me?

"So . . . were they impressed?" I asked.

Spasm stared at me as if he suddenly saw worms crawling out of my mouth. Then he walked away, laughing.

"Don't be late. Our test's starting soon."

I found some clean clothes in my foot locker, changed, and ran outside. I was in such a hurry I barely even heard her calling for me.

"That was very foolish what you did, Apex Strike!"

She stood just outside the door to the men's barracks, tossing a mango back and forth between her hands. Nevermore. She'd tied her gray t-shirt into a knot just below her rack, showing off some of the unsettling tattoos on her stomach. She would have been kind of scary if she didn't have a mischievous smile.

And, I gotta admit, the French accent did it for me too.

She tossed over the mango. "I had to save this for you, before the rest of the vultures swooped in. What you did may have been foolish, but still deserves its rewards."

Is this the only reward I get?

"Thanks," I said. I had no idea what to do with it. She looked at me expectantly. I lifted it to my mouth and took a big, juicy bite out of it. The skin was waxy and bitter, and the juice and bits of fruit poured down my face.

"It's good," I said, trying not to choke on a piece of skin as I swallowed.

"And you are very sweet, as well as foolish," she said, kissing me on the cheek. "Would you like to walk with me to our test?"

She could have asked me to set myself on fire at that moment and I probably would have. "Sure."

Who am I kidding. Probably?!

We talked about inconsequential things, our trip across the island, costumes, our favorite superheroes, what the upcoming tests might be like. I caught some of what she said, but the rest was a blur. There was probably some important information in there that I missed, but I mostly remember images (her smile, the tightness of her shirt across her chest, her laughing when I might have said something funny), and thinking *don'tfuckupdon't fuckupdon'tfuckup.*

We were among the last to arrive. There were rows of folding chairs—enough to fit everyone on the boat—by the ruins of a building that had since been made to look like a cartoon bank. Blackjack stood by a table with three chairs lined up behind it, checking her watch and doing a head count; a man about two heads taller than her, dressed up as a rent-a-cop, stood behind her, looking bored. Nevermore ran off to join some friends. I found Odigjod, Showstopper, Ghost Girl, Felix, and Firewall in a row of seats toward the front. Firewall had come in her newly modified suit, with a couple robot arms and the ray gun I'd found added to her arsenal.

Satisfied that we were all here, Blackjack pulled a microphone from her pocket.

"Glad y'all showed up . . . what's left of you, anyway. Welcome to your first assessment. Make it past this, and you've earned yourself a few more days on the island. Don't, and, well, you've earned yourself a bed, a room, and three square meals a day in the Tower with its miles and miles of smiles!"

Yeah, reminding us of the stakes was going to get an honest assessment. Those who weren't completely arrogant and full of themselves were trying to keep from shaking, shitting themselves, or vomiting.

Maybe even all three, like me.

"Today's what we like to call Show and Tell Day. Each of you's gonna have three minutes to impress us. Trick us into believin' that you're *real* supervillains. Now of course, since this is a competition, we're gonna need some judges." With that said, Blackjack pulled a small controller from her pocket and pressed a button.

From behind her appeared a Tri-Hole, which opened as three heroes stepped out. First came Black Blur, a dark-skinned, middle-aged superhero from London who smiled broadly and waved. The second was a bubbly, twenty-something blonde in a bright red, white, and blue costume with a lot of bare midriff and a domino mask. Shooting Star. She'd won a spot on the Protectors two seasons ago on *America's Next Protector*. Though she hadn't done any major heroism, she did have a rather lucrative career as a Christian pop singer, which made seeing her here unlikely. *Everybody needs a hobby, I guess.*

The last to step out was a large, muscular man. Completely bald and in his early seventies, he had a dour, scarred face from decades of superheroism. The Voice of the People, one of the Soviet Union's finest.

He didn't look very nice.

They all took seats at the table facing what I assumed was the stage as Blackjack explained the test. She went on about how all good heroes and villains had catchphrases, and how even though some were good and others were bad, when said with conviction they were vital to a super's branding. So, in addition to showing our stuff, we would be given a card with three increasingly silly things to say to see how well we would commit ourselves to doing as we were told.

"First up . . . Apex Strike!"

At first, I didn't hear my name; I was so focused on wondering how embarrassing these catchphrases would be. Then I felt hands, some encouraging, some glad it wasn't them, pushing me along the aisles, others offering encouragement, whispering that they wanted to see me crash and burn. Blackjack guided me to the judge's table, where Shooting Star handed me a card.

"Knock 'em dead, cutie," she said, shooting me a quick wink. My confidence swelled.

"Impress us or else," the Voice of the People said. And just as it had risen, my confidence immediately shrunk.

Quickly, I looked at the card. They had to be kidding.

"I'm really supposed to say this?" I asked.

"It's easier than it looks, trust me," Black Blur said. "Once the adrenaline's flowing, you can do anything."

I walked up to the mock bank set, keeping most of my shakes in check. The fake rent-a-cop pulled a baton from his belt, beating it against his free hand and smiling. Something about him looked familiar . . .

Blackjack smiled back at me, shaking her head slightly before turning to the rest, "Now, one of you versus an ordinary Joe may be fun to watch, but it's hardly what we're lookin' for here. So, to make this more interestin', I'd like to introduce you all to our special guest judge today, Everywhere Man."

So that's where I recognized him from! *Fuck!*

Everywhere Man clapped his hands together, causing about a dozen duplicates of himself to pop up around me in a circle, each beating their baton in their free hand in unison.

"Now, these duplicates got no souls and can't feel a thing, so feel free to fuck 'em up all you want.

"All right, the clock starts . . . now!"

"What?" I shrieked as his duplicates pounced on me. One cracked me across the back of the legs, taking me down in agony. Soon after I fell, the others pounced on me, clubbing my entire body. They were pulling their punches, not trying to kill me, but that didn't stop the pain, blinding and sharp. It felt like they were breaking every bone in my body. I could hear some cheering in the distance, others laughing. I held my hands out for mercy, begging them to stop, thinking that the Tower couldn't possibly be worse than this pain.

Then . . . something strange happened. The pain brought a strange clarity.

I remembered where I was.

I remembered who I was.

I remembered what had happened the last time I fought a superhero.

I can take him.

Focus!

The energy bubble I created was enough to knock them all back, enough to help me roll painfully onto my hands and knees and regain my footing. Triumphantly, with fists balled, I faced the audience and roared.

"I'M APEX STRIKE, MOTHERFUCKERS!"

This wasn't one of my lines, and it probably wouldn't make a very good catchphrase, but it got the audience cheering.

For the moment, at least, Aidan Salt was gone, and I was all Apex Strike.

I found the card I'd dropped, mashed into the ground and covered in mud. I wiped off some of the muck before the first of the Everywhere Men got back to their feet.

The first catchphrase was easy enough to shout.

"WOULD YOU LIKE TO SEE A PICTURE OF MY ITTY BITTY KITTY MITTENS?" I cried out, launching three of the Everywhere Men into the fake bank's wall so hard they disintegrated with three resounding pops.

Some of the others had regained their feet and started chasing me. Having had some experience running from superheroes already, this didn't scare me as much as I thought it might. I shot some focus back at them, crushing one into a small ball and sending the others sailing into the audience, each disappearing once they'd been hit hard enough. The next catchphrase was smudged too heavily, so I'd have to improvise.

"I LIKE WEARING WOMEN'S UNDERWEAR!" I practically screamed as I dodged another clumsy attack from one of the Everywhere Men. I think that's what the card said, at least.

"One minute left!" Blackjack called out.

Gotta finish this one with a bang.

There were five left.

They surrounded me.

I had an idea.

I wasn't sure I could pull it off (precision had never really been my thing), but even if I couldn't, I was pretty sure it'd look cool.

After all, I was Apex Strike.

Focus.

One by one, I grabbed each of the five and lifted them off the ground. I must have squeezed two of them too tightly, because they popped like grapes and disappeared. I was able to hold on to the other three just fine as they kicked and thrashed in midair. I flicked my hand up, and each of them shot into the sky like bullets. I have no idea how far they would have gone if they hadn't exploded against the curve of the force field, but I like to think I'd have been able to get them out of the atmosphere.

Finally, turning back to the audience, I put my hands on my hips and tried to deliver the last phrase from the card as confidently as I could.

"Now THAT is how you make a perfect batch of macaroons!"

The crowd broke out in applause; even some of those who had wished me dead earlier clapping (except Carnivore, but I thought I had scared him enough to make him back off).

At Blackjack's direction, I hobbled over to stand in front of the judge's table for their assessment.

"A little sloppy in the beginning and the end, but I think you nailed it once you found your confidence! You really made it your own!" Black Blur said.

"That was awesome!" Shooting Star added. "I mean, my word, I could see you had some trouble for a little while, but you really brought what's unique and special about you to put on a great show. Plus, you're a cutie, and you seem to have real fun doing what you're doing. My word, I could see you fighting the Protectors *tomorrow*."

Again, I swelled with pride . . . or maybe that was just fluid collecting from the beating.

The Voice of the People, as usual, looked like he was sitting on something very sharp.

"I believe you are a danger. To yourself. To others. You lack the focus necessary to be an effective member of a team as important as this, and you are a coward who could get people killed unnecessarily. Further, you did not take the time to remember your second line when following the script is key to our glorious plan, and you did not do even that. . . . You failed in my book."

I'd expected worse from him, so that was a relief.

I hobbled back to my seat, and thankfully Spasm wasn't far behind, fixing me up as we watched Artok step up next. I enjoyed watching him fumble. Out of the water he was useless, and though he put up a solid fight, he got scathing reviews from all three judges.

My pleasure didn't last too long, sadly. Everyone put on a much better show than I did. They clearly had better control over their powers, and nobody took a beating like I did.

Firewall didn't scream when surrounded, but rather just unleashed the death ray I'd given her, wiping out the Everywhere Men so quickly that they had to send in more.

When Felix was knocked down, he didn't whimper and beg, but instead transformed into a crystal giant and destroyed his attackers.

When the Gnome Caller had her arms pinned behind her by one of the Everywhere Men, she didn't even break a sweat. She just let out a piercing Nordic cry that summoned a few hundred sentient lawn gnomes from a pocket dimension that tore the Everywhere Men apart with their sharp little teeth.

While many excelled, some stumbled worse than me. Carnivore was so focused on ripping his victims to shreds that he forgot to say two of his catchphrases and Nevermore, though she put on one of the best shows with her tattoos, said hers out of order. Some (especially the fliers) were more boring than me, but not by much.

Seeing Showstopper force the Everywhere Men into a dance number out of *West Side Story*, the cartoon clown boy, Circus, bending reality like a video game with all the cheat codes on, and Ghost Girl's acrobatics that made it look like she could predict their moves, I got nervous.

Not *too* nervous, but nervous enough.

Finally, after the Zone Runner had finished doing whatever it is that Zone Runners do (it was hard to pay attention after nearly five hours of these, including a dinner break), Blackjack talked with the judges. They compared notes, even bringing in Everywhere Man for his opinion on how we'd all done. The tension in the air was thick. Odigjod grasped my hand tightly in one of his claws. Despite having one of the best showings of all of us, he was shaking like a leaf.

Finally, Blackjack took the stage. She opened up another Tri-Hole behind her.

She didn't have to tell us that this one led to the Tower.

"All right. Just wanna thank y'all for your patience. We had some tough choices to make, but we've come to an agreement. There's seventy-three of you here, and only seven spots on the team. Fifty-two of you are moving on to the next round. Twenty of you aren't. Black Blur?"

The middle-aged judge stood, arching his back. Then, true to his name, he disappeared in a blur. He was allegedly the fourth-fastest person on the planet, capable of breaking the time barrier if he tried hard enough. I wouldn't have believed it until today. Occasionally you'd hear a surprised yelp as he plucked someone up and hurled them through the Tri-Hole, but usually he was too fast for them to even notice something had happened.

Afraid again, I closed my eyes tightly. *I'mfineI'mfineI'mfine I'mfineI'mfine . . .*

"All right, thank y'all for your patience!" Blackjack said over the loudspeakers. "Get yourselves some rest, because classes start tomorrow!"

I opened my eyes, seeing Blackjack and Everywhere Man leave through the Tri-Hole before it disappeared. Relief flooded through every part of my body as I collapsed back into my chair. I wasn't the only one. The suddenness had past, and one by one everyone started looking around, seeing who was left and who wasn't. Most of the fliers and some of the others with more boring powers were gone, as well as the Cyclops from Carnivore's gang.

So was Artok. *Yes!*

Everyone I liked was still here. Cheers and cries of relief started circling those of us still left as everyone shared hugs and high fives. Though I've never been much for closeness, it felt good to hug Showstopper, Felix, and even Odigjod and Firewall, though through her suit it felt like she was trying to break my back.

I saw Nevermore in a small group hugging her two remaining friends, and we exchanged smiles and nods.

Now that wasn't so bad, was it?

#Supervillainy101: The Third Cataclysm

Every thirty to forty years since the rise of the supers, Earth has gone through what scientists have called "Cataclysms." Apparently, our universe has something close to an infinite number of alternate universes sharing the same space (roughly) full of the same planets and people, just slightly off. (Makes me wonder what all the alternate versions of *me* are like.) Sometimes these universes get slightly out of sync and collide, and in order to make things right again, a battle needs to take place.

Don't ask me to explain the whys here. I don't know why they only started happening once the supers rose, nor do I understand why a battle's supposed to take place to fix it. All I know is that all the superheroes of all the participating dimensions have to take part, and occasionally a universe is destroyed or merged with another, and sometimes we get new heroes out of it.

The Third Cataclysm occurred in 1969, when some brainwashed clone of El Capitán from an alternate universe grabbed the fabric of reality and ripped it in half, nearly destroying all existence. Most of our heroes were involved in repelling a Gray invasion on the moon and couldn't come back to Earth in time to save it.

Seeing this, several of the most influential villains of the day decided to step in to save the world. Led by Otis Shylock, Professor Death, Blackjack, and Dr. Tongue, an army of nearly one hundred supervillains and a few stray heroes and sidekicks worked around the clock to right the fabric of existence, ending this Cataclysm faster than either of the previous two had under the heroes.

Realizing what they could do together, Otis Shylock and Professor Death did something that had never been dreamt of in the past: they created a team of supervillains. With nearly thirty members, the Villain's Union created a criminal empire the likes of which the world had never seen, elevating this odd group of petty thugs to celebrity status almost overnight.

Of course, the sight of a group of villains working together was too dangerous to let stand, and in response the heroes reformed a new version of the Protectors (a group temporarily created to fight in World War II and disbanded shortly thereafter) to confront the threat that this group clearly posed.

The War on Villainy had begun.

#**LessonLearned:** Sometimes adversity has a way of bonding people.

THE CHIN

It was three weeks before we felt strong enough to make it to "The Chin."

Three weeks of struggle.

Three weeks of nonstop classes in performance and diction, in stage fighting and real fighting, in using our powers and gaining the confidence to look like we'd been using them forever.

Three weeks of lousy sleep and lousier food.

Three weeks of watching pretty much everyone but me get laid.

Three weeks of constant judgment by heroes and the ever-present threat of elimination.

With all this going on, the six of us never should have had the time to make it to the Chin, but we did.

I blame Felix.

Not for making it to the Chin. He'd have done that anyway, probably just for fun. No, I blame him for convincing us, somehow, that jogging and hiking would be fun.

Without using our powers. *Pre*-dawn.

The man was a sadist.

"Come on guys, it'll be fun!" he said.

"Come on guys, it'll be good for you!" he said.

"Come on guys, what else do we have to do for fun here?" he said.

While I could answer "No it won't" quite handily to his first two statements, he had me on the third. If the heroes had given us some video games and tablets, this would be like home and we'd never have to leave the town ruins . . . or Firewall would have stolen all of them from us and made them into a machine that would help her escape the island or end the world.

One or the other, it was kind of hard to tell with her.

Without those things to keep my mind busy, I'd gained a crippling case of stir fever whenever we had any downtime. It made me susceptible to such crazy suggestions as voluntary, pre-dawn exercise in the jungle of death and mystery.

So we started hiking, just a little bit at a time, clearing out bits of forest of the monsters and traps as we went, building ourselves up until we could make it to the Chin.

"Come on, we're almost there!" Felix cried out enthusiastically, jogging ahead of us on the darkened trail, the bouncing beam of his flashlight the only sign he was still alive.

"We heard you the last time!" I shouted back to him.

"And the time before that!" Showstopper shouted more hoarsely, coughing and spitting into the bushes. In Felix's defense, Showstopper wasn't breathing as heavily as he used to on these hikes, so the exercise was actually doing some good.

"It's called positive reinforcement!" he called out, laughing.

Positive reinforcement? Who the hell was he kidding? He was a maniac. Besides, I didn't see what he had to be so positive about. Back home in Uruguay he'd been a rising soccer star, and might have actually made something of himself if his father hadn't found out he was gay and forced him onto the streets, committing petty, superhuman crimes to survive. His life had sucked up to that, but now here he was, bright and chipper.

If I didn't like hanging out with him so much, I might have hated him.

"I can guarantee you that once we make the Chin, we'll have a view of sunrise like nowhere else on the island!" Felix proclaimed.

"And how's that an incentive?" I asked between breaths.

"Where's your appreciation of the beauty of nature?" he asked, steering clear of a humming hornet's nest the size of a watermelon that bulged dangerously from a nearby tree.

"At home. On the Internet. Safely away from the beauty of nature," I said.

He looked to the others for support. "Can someone back me up here? Gentlemen? Ladies? Imps?" Not even Odigjod chimed in. Just shy of a month topside had him about as sick of nature as the rest of us. Neither Firewall, balanced on the pair of robot legs she'd modified for her personal use, nor Ghost Girl looked ready to support him either.

Firewall laughed viciously. "No ladies here, I'm afraid. We are *supervillainesses*! Right, Ghost Girl?"

Ghost Girl adjusted her mask as if trying to hide. "Leave me out of this?"

Firewall scoffed, "We are not mere ladies bound by society's rules of propriety and dignity! We have no time for nature! We are 'self-empowered' and 'actualized by our beauty and femininity and independent, inner-strength to be powerful, easily underestimated foes.' At least if you believe any of that bullshit the heroes are heaping on us."

"They actually said that?" Showstopper asked.

"With less sarcasm and anger, but yes, those words were there," Ghost Girl replied.

"We didn't get that speech," I chimed in.

"No, you got cocks," Firewall said. "What kind of line are they giving you in your confidence classes?"

"Mostly how we're tough badasses who are so powerful that we don't have to take shit from anyone," Showstopper said.

Firewall snorted. "Fucking figures . . ."

I was lost, but no way in hell was I going to say that out loud. That was just opening the door for one of Firewall's indignant speeches that I'm sure she was absolutely correct on but I just didn't want to listen to, at least not at this hour.

Odigjod, on the other hand, hadn't figured out my strategy just yet. "What is figuring?"

"Objectification. That's the name of the game for us, isn't it?" Firewall said. "They try and give us the big *fucking* speeches about how our powers are everything and our other differences are meaningless, but they're just full of shit. All you guys have to focus on is being tough. We have to focus on being tough, seductive, desirable, mysterious, confident, and about a thousand other things. Every one of us has to be the girl that every boy wants to take to bed but doesn't want mom to meet. All our bodies have to be shaped exactly right, which is *not* the same as actually being in good, strong shape, and then we have to do everything you do in high heels and just enough light, easily torn fabric to leave something to the imagination while still showing as much vulnerable skin as possible. You . . . *you* can be fat . . ."

"Hey!" Showstopper said, feigning anger.

". . . or fuck ugly . . ." she said, pointing at Odigjod, quickly adding, "No offense."

"Back home, Odigjod's quite handsome, but I'm understanding your topside point."

". . . or, well, whatever word sums up best whatever you are," she said, pointing at me.

"I'm complicated," I said smoothly, recalling every lesson they'd taught us in acting class.

"No, you're not."

"Yes I am!"

Firewall looked to Ghost Girl for backup, who chimed in, "He's more complicated than you think, not as complicated as he thinks."

"Thanks?" I said, glad for the support, if not entirely sure what she meant. Nobody could read people like Ghost Girl, and I hadn't seen her wrong yet.

Firewall sighed. "I'm just . . . so tired of all the bullshit that's going on around here. They've got our lives in their hands. The least they could do is show us some honesty."

"Honesty? Like what?" Showstopper asked.

"Like telling me that if I didn't have this mech suit, and they weren't trending right now, that I wouldn't rank pretty enough for freedom no matter how powerful or skilled I am. It's not *fucking* fair!"

Well that was a helluva conversation killer. Firewall tried to look away from all our lights. I don't know if she was shaking because she was on the verge of tears of anger or sadness. Odigjod sidled up to her cautiously, placing a claw on one of her mechanical legs.

"Odigjod thinks you're pretty," he said carefully. She turned to us, smiling slightly, rubbing a hand through the mess of slimy quills that Odigjod called hair.

Looking more energetic than he normally did at this hour, Showstopper clapped his hands together. "We can't be that far off from the Chin now, what would you all say if I proposed a race?"

"I'd say you're insane," Firewall quickly responded.

"Insane, or brilliant? You're all emotionally compromised; I might just stand a chance this time!" Showstopper proclaimed.

"No, she was right about you being insane! We haven't cleared everything out of this part of the island yet!" Felix protested.

"You say it's not safe, I say I'll meet you at the Chin!" Showstopper shouted, crashing off into the darkness. I'm sure he planned this out as soon as the conversation started turning south. He always had this kind of rodeo clown spirit to him, keeping morale up and trying to deflect any darkness no matter the cost. I'd always thought it was an attitude that was going to get him killed, but since it had served him well so far, maybe he had the right idea.

Felix and Firewall chased after him. Odigjod looked up to me.

"Odigjod shall protecting them," he said with a bow. Before I could say that I would have also liked his protection, Odigjod teleported out of sight.

"At least we can protect each other," Ghost Girl said, amused.

Ghost Girl. Of course I had to get stuck with her.

Of our group, she was the one I had figured out the least. The rest of us, we all had our roles: Felix was the good-looking athlete, Showstopper was the joker, Odigjod was the eager-to-please little brother, Firewall was the smart spitfire.

I was the leader, obviously.

All roles you could easily see on a team of supervillains. Ghost Girl, though, she was different. She was nice enough—and could even be funny sometimes—though she tried not to show it. She wasn't bad-looking from the neck down, though God help you if you tried telling her that. Her powers were vague yet impressive, making her probably the third most powerful member of our group, I think, but that way she always looked at you like she could look right through you, combined with her reserved demeanor, made her hard to get to know.

"Reading my mind again, Ghost Girl?" I asked.

"For the last time, *Aidan*, I read auras, not minds . . . and it's Emma. They've dehumanized us enough, can't we at least keep our real names?"

"But we're supposed to use the codenames."

Even behind her mask, I could see her roll her eyes. "Did you get here by doing what you were supposed to?"

"Yes," I said. I followed all the rules the heroes had given us, and aside from occasional run-ins with Carnivore and his gang and the fact that Nevermore still wouldn't do more than flirt mercilessly with me, I thought I'd been doing pretty well. Blackjack and my other teachers were as hard on me as anyone else, and when it came to the judges I was pretty sure I had both Black Blur and Shooting Star on my side. Even the Voice of the People had managed an odd compliment or two.

She shook her head. "Have it your way then, *Apex Strike*."

She said the name almost disgustedly. A flash from one of my classes hit me. *Your codename is who you are. Don't ever let anyone diminish it.*

"Hey, I like being Apex Strike a helluva lot more than I ever liked being Aidan Salt," I defended. "Apex Strike is strong. Apex Strike has potential. Hell, Apex Strike's got some people who might even actually *like* him."

"You mean *friends*?" she interjected.

"I don't know if I'd go that far, but the basic principle's there! Apex Strike could be somebody! Aidan Salt was as good as he was ever going to get."

"You don't know that," she said.

"So you're saying your life would have been better if you never put on that mask?"

"My life? Maybe, but goddammit I made a whole lot of other people's lives better because of it! And even when I put on the mask, I never forget who I am. My name is Emma Hendriks. Ghost Girl . . . she's a media creation."

"But if you never take off the mask, don't you kinda become it?"

Defiantly, she pulled off her mask. I recoiled.

Seeing my reaction, she put it right back on. "That's why I never take off my mask in public. I hate that look of fear, or worse, that look people have of *should-I-or-shouldn't-I-pity-her*. It's exhausting."

"I'm sorry. I get it, I mean, I imagine it would be tiring, with a face like that."

She looked at me for a long moment before shaking her head. "God, I must be high."

"What?"

"It's nothing, but . . . you know, you're an expert at saying the worst thing at the worst time."

I couldn't see it, but her voice told me that she was smiling behind that mask.

"Thanks?"

"Not really. No," she said, continuing to the Chin.

"So you made people's lives better?" I asked, trying to restart the conversation.

"I dabbled in vigilantism. I did the things the redcapes were afraid to do."

I nodded, impressed. "You beat up bad guys?"

"And 'good' guys, when they deserved it."

"Is that why they sent you here?"

"It was either here or the Tower. I hate evil. I love freedom more."

"Did you ever kill anyone?"

"Maybe," she said, her words cautious, trying to change the subject. "Or maybe I'm considering it for the first time now."

I laughed. She didn't laugh back. "You're joking, right?"

Ghost Girl was able to pick up their trail pretty easily with her power. Since auras existed in the past, present, and near-future, her power allowed her to see the remnants of anything that would leave a strong psychic impact (like someone dying) or what a person's actions would be within a few seconds.

Our flashlights wouldn't be necessary much longer, as the sky was beginning to turn orange. If we didn't want Felix to be telling us "I told you so," we'd have to pick up the pace.

"Not all of us are handling the stress of this place the same way," she said.

"What do you mean?"

"Helen is crusading. Felix is working out. Nick is trying to focus on raising everyone else's spirits. You distract yourself with idle pursuits like looking cool and sabotaging your efforts at bedding girls so you can give yourself something to focus on other than the nightmares."

Whoa, that wasn't cool. "Hey, I don't sabotage my own efforts!"

"Yes, you do."

"Really?"

"My answer hasn't changed from two seconds ago."

"Shit."

"That's an apt response to that."

"How do I stop doing that?"

She shrugged. "Stop obsessing over making it onto the team and just accept the inevitability that whatever happens, happens."

"Even if it means miles and miles of smiles?" I asked. She didn't have an answer for that. I didn't expect her to.

I couldn't stop obsessing. None of us could. It was off to the Tower if we lost that focus. But no way in hell was I going to stop hoping for the chance to hook up with Nevermore. She was too hot.

"I thought so," Ghost Girl said, nodding knowingly.

"You're sure you can't read minds?"

"Very," she said, pushing a carnivorous vine out of the way.

The trees were beginning to clear out. I hoped we would get there soon.

"You won't tell anyone about the dreams, will you?" I asked.

"Wouldn't dream of it."

As I looked ahead, a puff of dark smoke appeared in the distance, shading the almost orange sky. Odigjod.

"Almost there! Almost there! Beautiful view! Felix was right!" Odigjod exclaimed, clapping and pointing ahead. At this hour his enthusiasm was hardly contagious, but it was impossible to hate him. He scuttled ahead, and we quickened to follow. Soon the trees ended, and there was nothing but Death Mountain above us. We followed the trail through the foothills to an old maintenance path dotted with burned-out and bullet-riddled vehicles.

And then we made it to the Chin. It was one of the only parts of Professor Death that had been carved in full into the side of the mountain. The Chin had to be bigger than my high school, and time and elements hadn't been entirely kind to it, but we'd finally made it.

Felix unshouldered his duffel bag and pulled out its contents: six cans of energy drink from the mess hall and a Polaroid camera, with timer, that Firewall had snuck in with her armor.

The drinks were passed around, and at Felix's suggestion we raised them all in a toast.

"To the future!" he said.

At Firewall's suggestion, we climbed on top of the Chin and set up the camera to take a half-dozen pictures of us as the sun rose. They were cool souvenirs. Whether we'd be allowed to keep them was up for grabs, but for now it felt good to have a memory of my . . . come to think of it, the word friends didn't sound all that far off after all.

And, much as I hated to say it, Felix was right: we did have a helluva view of the new day from here.

#Supervillainy101: The Radiation Queens

Heroes and villains have always had something of a gentleman's agreement in terms of not repeating codenames. To put it plainly, it hurts brand recognition and makes it harder for people to tell you apart. The only acceptable time you can take someone else's codename is when they die. Who gets that name, on the other hand, has led to its share of problems.

In 1975, Radiation Queen was killed after a prolonged battle with the Protectors. Her daughter, Emily Ender, had been born with the same power of radiation manipulation and readily stepped into the identity as the new Radiation Queen, intending to take over her mother's criminal empire and avenge her death.

The problem was, she wasn't the only one to pounce on the Radiation Queen mantle. A street-tough chick from Detroit named Myra Mont who was born with similar powers (she could only manipulate the microwave spectrum) decided to start calling herself Radiation Queen around the same time.

Thinking this was a miscommunication, Emily kindly asked Myra to stop using the name.

She declined.

Emily then sent in her lawyers.

Myra sent them to the burn ward.

Emily then sent in some thugs to beat up Myra's family.

Since they succeeded, Myra sent them to the morgue.

Finally, Emily went in herself to confront this rapidly escalating annoyance.

Nobody really knows what went down after that, but around six in the morning of March 24, 1975, one of the largest nuclear blasts in recorded history erased most of Detroit from the map. The Protectors responding to the explosion found Emily and Myra still clawing at each other and throwing balls of glowing energy, even as they were being haloed.

Detroit remains to this day one of the most dangerous and polluted places in America.

Rumor has it Emily and Myra share adjacent cells in the Tower.

#LessonLearned: Avoid pointless rivalries whenever possible.

APEX STRIKE VS. CARNIVORE

If it weren't so insultingly blasphemous to him, I'd say God bless Odigjod, because without him, life on Death Island would have been really boring. Sure, there were our hikes, and there were the classes and tests, but they all took something out of you. Sometimes you just needed to relax and unwind.

And I couldn't think of a better way to unwind than watching Odigjod make one of the walls of the girls' shower transparent . . . while the girls used it, of course.

The show included a full view of Nevermore, the Gnome Caller, and Apsara, a beautiful telekinetic girl from India who was kicking my ass in all our Power Perfection classes. (I would have held it against her had she not looked so good wearing a thin sheen of water and soap.) Contrary to what the Internet had taught me, girls' group showers were not a nonstop lesbian orgy, but were still pretty nice. We made sure to be stealthy, and Odigjod said he could make it so that we could see them but they couldn't see us. But, to be completely honest, the way they pranced and spent so much time lathering themselves up, part of me was pretty sure they knew and were putting on a show.

"You think they're using a new shampoo?" Showstopper asked.

"Same as always I think," Spasm said, munching from a bag of popcorn.

"Seems to be taking a lot longer than usual to wash out," Showstopper said, stealing some of his popcorn.

"This one's on me," Circus said, smiling and bouncing back and forth spastically in his lawn chair. "Touch a bottle, change its molecular composition just so slightly that it still looks, feels, and smells the same but takes ten percent longer to wash out. Don't all thank me at once."

For someone who usually hung out with Carnivore, Circus wasn't so bad. On the rare occasions when he dropped the cartoon look and slowed down, he was almost decent to hang around, at least as pudgy, fifteen-year-old Japanese nerds go. However, given his ability to hold complete control over reality within six inches of himself and the fact that puberty was hitting him like a ton of bricks, he could also be unpredictable and annoying as shit.

"Thank you," I said before he might have decided to do something more attention-grabbing . . . at least more attention-grabbing than what he was already doing.

Some of the other guys were able to ignore him. Sitting right next to him, Spasm wasn't.

"Could you restrain yourself, or perhaps just go to the bushes?"

Circus scoffed, "I see a hot girl, I'm gonna ogle. I see a hot naked girl, I'm gonna file that in the spank bank. I see *three* hot naked girls showering, I'm gonna jack it. It's biology. Can't be helped. Besides, I put up the censor bar! What's the problem?"

I had to give him that. He did put up a floating black bar in front of his hand and crotch, but you could still see *what* he was doing, even though you couldn't actually see it.

"Your bar's too big," Showstopper suggested.

"Yeah, but it's still there! I'm totally fucking PG-13, cut me some slack!"

Spasm had less patience for Circus. He pointed at him.

The younger boy looked like he'd been kicked in the gut, jerking and falling out of his chair with a face that looked equal parts pleasure and pain.

"You're done," Spasm said.

"The fuck, dude!" Circus exclaimed. "Did you just—"

"Now wash your hands and let us watch in peace," Spasm said, never once taking his eyes off the shower. Staggering to his feet and looking confused, Circus took on his cartoon clown form and bounced away towards the men's showers.

"Thanks for taking one for the team," Showstopper said, joining the rest of us in patting Spasm on the back.

Spasm shrugged, lighting up another cigarette. "I've done worse for better reasons."

Too soon for our liking, the girls finished. Though this got some groans, it wasn't the end of the world; the girls traveled in packs when it came to the showers, so we knew that more would come soon.

Unfortunately for us, that more happened to be Ghost Girl and Firewall.

"Okay, guys, show's over. Shut it down, Odigjod," I said, to the groans of the rest of the group. Though Firewall and Ghost Girl were probably the two least attractive girls on the island, they weren't that bad looking, and these guys would take anything.

I couldn't look in on *their* private time, though, something about it just felt . . . weird. So we went off in search of breakfast and Felix. Breakfast was in the mess hall, as usual (though boasting a waffle bar today), but Felix wasn't. Since he hadn't announced a hike, though, we had an idea of where we could hunt him down.

Sure enough, he was in a dark corner of the ruins, making out with Swashbuckler (Carnivore's pirate friend).

Showstopper decided to announce our presence by touching a finger to his temple and making Felix and Swashbuckler engage in an elaborate tap dance routine.

"You're getting better at these," I said.

"That's the thing about art, you always have to outdo yourself," Showstopper replied. "Wanna join them? Make it a threesome?"

I shuddered. "Don't even try getting in my head."

"Fine, fine, ruin all my fun," he said, letting them go. Swashbuckler bounced off a couple walls parkour-style and leapt over us, yelling a long string of British profanity (which, to my ears at least, wasn't dirty in the slightest). Felix was only slightly less offended.

"Seriously guys, what the fuck? When's the last time I ever cockblocked you?" he said, crystallizing the palms of his hands before smacking Showstopper and me in the backs of our heads.

"We'd need dates first, so, never I guess," Showstopper replied, rubbing the back of his head.

Even with the pain, I started laughing like hell. "So we gonna plan a wedding for you guys or what?"

Showstopper poked me in the ribs. "That joke was funny until you started laughing."

Felix took up most of our walk to the mess hall explaining how he and Swashbuckler weren't serious, that they were just making the most of being the only two gay guys here and had what fun they could. He didn't need to defend himself, not to me at least. Though Swashbuckler was a douche who wore more makeup than most of the girls here, I was glad at least someone in our group was getting some.

Of course, dealing with Swashbuckler's friends was another matter entirely.

Swashbuckler, Circus, and, of course, Carnivore intercepted us before we could make the mess hall. As usual, Carnivore was angry, and as usual he directed that anger towards me.

"You shouldn't have cut the shower show off. Some of us weren't finished," he growled.

Three-plus weeks on this island, and I still hadn't figured out how not to feel like a deer in headlights around Carnivore.

"He was," Showstopper said, pointing at Circus.

"But I wasn't," Carnivore said.

"Well, you could have always used your imagination, or did they remove that when they gang-raped your genes?" Showstopper goaded.

Carnivore hissed, flicking a snake-like tongue at Showstopper and baring his fangs. That got Showstopper to shut up. Taking a step forward, Carnivore put a clawed hand on my chest. Threatening, but not enough to set off his Creeper.

"Next time, I don't care if it's your girlfriends or your mommy showering, we'll tell you when we're done."

"They're not my girlfriends," I said, trying to sound tough while hiding my shattered nerves.

Carnivore cocked his head, sniffing something on the wind, and turned toward the mess hall with his gang.

"We'll finish this after classes," he said as they walked away.

After classes? What was this, high school?

The hero-led classes were a mixed bag.

Most of them were like being in school again, at least, what I'd imagine being in an acting school would be like. We had classes on diction and inflection, on line memorization and stage presence, on boosting our confidence and being able to radiate an air of being a professional supervillain. These were all right, and I did pretty well thanks in most part to the superhero teachers, who seemed to like me. Frankly, these subjects weren't the sort of thing I'd have thought the superheroes would be good at teaching, but since most of them did more film and TV shows than actual heroing these days, it made sense. Periodically we would get pulled out of these classes for a sit-down with a personal image consultant who would run us through ideas for costumes and ways of improving our supervillain persona. I was good here as well, so they didn't have much to change, but Felix, Firewall, and Odigjod were run through the ringer with suggestions.

The physical fitness and fighting classes that Blackjack led ran us ragged, but after the first couple weeks (combined with Felix's hikes) I was beginning to feel pretty damn good about myself. I was getting the hang of Cape Fu (the showy and deadly mixed-martial-arts all respectable supers prefer), and was starting to figure out how to merge it with the stage fighting courses so that I could look cool without killing whoever I was fighting. Some of us even got special training in weapons; Ghost Girl had become fairly lethal with a retractable quarterstaff that her consultant thought would make her look cooler.

. The class that I always looked forward to and dreaded the most was my Power Perfection class, where all of us with similar powers were put into small classes to be taught by a specialist hero who could help us "maximize our superhuman potential."

I looked forward to it because I got to sit next to Nevermore. Though she wasn't telekinetic, her powers of projection were deemed close enough, so I got at least a good hour every day to ogle and flirt with her. And by flirting, of course I mean her looking good and occasionally giggling at me and me trying not to say the worst thing possible (as Ghost Girl would say).

She was good at flirting. I was pretty sure I was improving.

I dreaded the class because of pretty much everything else . . . like the fact that I was at the bottom of the class. Apsara, the two other guys whose codenames I could never remember, and Nevermore all had precision, enough to a point where they could safely use their powers to fly. I was easily the strongest one there, but no way was I going to risk trying to pick myself up off the ground. I could break things too easily, lift some things with a bit more difficulty, and according to my teacher I was a long way away from having control over my power. Hell, I'd almost killed myself with a mango!

My teacher was the other problem.

I didn't doubt Helios's credentials as a superhero. In his mid-twenties, he had the devastatingly handsome look of a movie star and knew how to pull off his white and gold suit. His mastery of telekinesis was impressive, as were his energy blasts and superstrength, and I'd seen enough of his commercials and movies to know he was a pretty good actor.

I also didn't doubt that he had it out for me for what I did to Icicle Man.

While he put the others through basic exercises, he put me through the most difficult tests where I'd always make a fool out of myself. There were times during exercises where I'd be covered in mud and bruises, and the only sound I could hear was everyone else's laughter. I was sure I was gone after each class, but I kept passing on to the next stage.

I was pretty sure he just kept me around to torture me, and nothing he said or did contradicted this theory.

Yet even after my run-in with Carnivore that morning, I was feeling pretty good heading to Power Perfection class. Not even Helios dropping the bomb that we'd have our fifth elimination test later in the day could ruin my mood. Our lesson of the day was to see how many clay pigeons we could shoot out of the air when ten were launched. Apsara, normally the overachiever, managed to get eight. The other two guys managed five each. Nevermore projected multiple tattoos at once, sending out a swarm of birds, a swinging bladed pendulum, and a stylized (and surprisingly limber) orangutan to destroy nine targets before they hit the ground.

I was sure I could take all ten; this wasn't a test of precision, as I could send one wave and destroy them all. This would be easy, just *focus* and done. Maybe I'd even impress Nevermore enough to finally get her naked.

I got up to the line and prepared to strike.

The pigeons were in the air. I began to *focus*.

There was a roar behind me, and I half-turned to face it. Before I could, I was face down on the ground after being hit from behind.

Then the *focus* kicked in, blasting me—and my attacker—off the ground. I was confused when I first saw the ground flying away from me. I only started to get scared when I saw the trees start to fly away from me.

What do they say?: It's not the fall that kills you, just the sudden stop?

I must've started screaming around the time gravity kicked back. I don't know how long I kept screaming, but it was a while. Even after Helios flew up and brought me down to Earth I was still shaking and gibbering with a rapidly expanding piss stain forming in the front of my shorts.

"What the fuck were you thinking? You almost got us all killed!" Helios roared at my attacker.

"I was just doing an assignment for class! You can ask Mr. Creature! He wanted us to stalk and take down someone without them seeing!" Carnivore said, his voice dripping innocence.

The two argued back and forth for a while as the rest of our class looked on in confusion and amusement and maybe some fear for me, as I finally started to calm down. Carnivore was good at faking innocence, but when Helios turned away to call for Creature, he snuck me a wink.

He'd humiliated me in front of a superhero *and* Nevermore. I had to destroy him.

There were only thirty-one of us left by the time the fifth elimination test rolled around. In the past three weeks we'd buried five people next to Iron Bear; one because of a dinosaur attack, two from suicide (a hanging and a guy who fed himself to some vampire vines), and another two who had their Creepers activated in front of us after attempting escape.

The rest had been cut from the competition by the judges and sent straight to the Tower.

On their own, the tests weren't so bad; they were mostly to see how we'd do under pressure in simulations of various challenges supervillains would face in the field. Wardrobe problems, delivering a powerful monologue to the press, containing a group of hostages. Simple stuff.

They weren't that difficult so long as you did exactly what the heroes told you, and though I was rarely the top of any of them, I always did well enough to move on.

This test wasn't any different. Blackjack told us that, while most of our encounters with superheroes would be coordinated and choreographed, there might be times when we would need to escape from prying eyes and blend in to our surroundings. As such, we were given a thirty-second head start into the forest before having a half-dozen robotic drones sent to hunt us down. Without attacking the drones, we had to evade them for as long as possible.

Easy enough. I'd spent enough of my life blending in that this wasn't a difficult task, and I made it five minutes in the jungle before they got me, which was actually pretty long compared to the others. Black Blur and Shooting Star gave me top marks, and even the Voice of the People had to give me slight praise for using my powers for tearing down a part of a tree for cover. Based on my performance and the hero's praise, I was confident that I'd make it through to the next round.

Now it was time to make sure that Carnivore wouldn't.

I was so focused on his turn coming up that the rest of the world around me might as well have not existed. I didn't even hear what my friends were joking about. All my attention was on Carnivore.

Then Showstopper said the one thing that could have stolen my attention from revenge.

"You know, I think she likes you, mate," he said, punching me in the shoulder.

"Nevermore?"

"No, Shooting Star," he said, pointing to the judge's table. She was looking at me, even flashing that million-dollar smile of hers she always showed off in her toothpaste commercials before turning back to the other judges.

"She wants you," Showstopper joked.

"No, she doesn't."

"Yes, she does."

"No, she doesn't."

"Actually, she does," Ghost Girl said.

"Really?" Showstopper and I said simultaneously.

"Oh yeah."

"Why?" Firewall asked. That would have been my question, too, but I would've sounded less disgusted.

"She keeps a prim and proper public image, but she dreams of fucking bad boys. Or girls even, if she gets drunk enough," said Ghost Girl.

"Why'd you look at me when you said that?" Firewall asked.

"I was looking at Aidan, you just happen to be in between."

"Because I like guys."

"So you've made abundantly clear," Showstopper chimed in.

Firewall shot back, "Look, just because I don't spread my legs like all the girls here doesn't mean I'm—"

"Shooting Star?" I said to Ghost Girl, trying to get things back on track.

"She's always wanted to fuck a supervillain, and with the pickings of straight male villains pretty low, she looks at you as the most fuckable by default," Ghost Girl said.

It was times like this I really loved her aura-reading power.

"I can work with default," I said. Trying to hook up with Shooting Star had never even entered my mind. I mean, sure, like any red-blooded American I'd spent my time jacking it to her back home, but she was a celebrity, impossible for someone like me to have dreamed about getting with before.

*But you **are** a celebrity now. You're Apex Strike. You can get her.*

Then it hit me.

"Wait, you can see who wants to have sex with who?" I asked.

Ghost Girl nodded. "I see lots of things."

"What about Nevermore? Do I stand a chance with her?"

"Of course you do. Just ask to have sex with her and you're in."

"Really? It's that easy?"

"Of course. She's desperately unhappy from a hard and depressing life and thusly has incredibly low self-esteem. She's been used by people so often she's confused sex with happiness and has so tied her identity to her sexuality she's lost who she is. So if you just want sex, then yes, it is that easy. If you would truly like to touch her soul and forge an enduring romantic bond, then I would recommend talking to her. Getting to know her. No one has given her that courtesy in a long time."

Most of what she'd said was awful, but the rest swelled my hope (among other parts).

"So . . . she would fuck me?"

Ghost Girl shook her head, cursing in Afrikaans.

"Felix, smack him please?" Firewall asked.

"With pleasure," Felix said, transforming most of his hand into crystal and slapping me in the back of the head.

"Ow."

There was applause around us as the judges finished critiquing someone. Tapping her microphone, Blackjack called Carnivore to the starting line.

This was it. No more distractions, no more thoughts of what Shooting Star might want to do to me. It was time to pay attention.

For the harassment. For the threats. For keeping Iron Bear in my nightmares.

For *revenge*.

They gave him a countdown.

Five . . .

Four . . .

Three . . .

Two . . .

O(*focus*)ne . . .

I only meant to trip him, maybe distract him long enough so the drones would catch up to him quickly, and then knock him out of the competition once and for all. Then I wouldn't have to put up with his shit anymore.

Snapping his shin bone the moment he took a step forward was just a happy accident. He howled, falling down on his face. He called back to the judges, asking if he could see Spasm before the competition continued, but they refused. His head start continued to count down. I thought he would give up, hopefully even start crying.

Somehow, he got back up. He grabbed a downed tree branch and started using it as a walking stick. Then, somehow, he ran limping into the jungle.

The drones followed after him five seconds later.

I thought we'd hear the bell of his defeat in seconds, but we didn't.

One minute passed. Nothing.

Two minutes. Still no bell. There was some roaring, some thrashing in the distance, but still he eluded them.

Three minutes. Three and a half minutes.

The bell rang at just shy of four minutes.

Carnivore hobbled out of the forest, sweating and panting, looking near-death. He stood before the judges and took his criticism well. According to them, he was brave and strong for making it through despite his handicap. They called him an inspiration. *Shit.*

He collapsed back in his seat, looking at me smugly as Spasm came over and mended his broken bone. I doubt he knew what I did, I think he just wanted to gloat.

I fumed for the rest of the test. Odigjod and Nevermore did well, using teleportation and dark projections respectively to hide well at ten minutes each. With powers that didn't really line up with the test, Felix, Showstopper, and Firewall didn't do as well. Firewall could at least fly above the trees, but was hardly subtle, while all Showstopper and Felix could do was run through the jungle and hope for the best. They all got caught pretty quick . . . but most people did.

This test was definitely a tough one. While I could normally tell who was going on to the next round, this one was up for grabs. By rights, most of my friends would be eliminated, but most of them had done well on the previous tests and I was confident that had to be enough to keep them moving on.

Finally, with everyone finished, Blackjack and the judges tabulated their results. We knew our time was up when they opened the Tri-Hole.

"All right. Just wanna thank y'all again for your patience," Blackjack said, as usual. "Tonight's cuts are the toughest ones yet. A lot of y'all did great, some of you not so much. Some of y'all who didn't do so hot will make it based on the results from your previous tests and classes—but barely. There's thirty-one of you here, and only seven spots on the team. Twenty-three of you are moving on tonight. Eight aren't. Black Blur?"

As I did every time an elimination came around, I closed my eyes and kept repeating *I'mfineI'mfineI'mfineI'mfineI'mfine* . . .

This time, however, Ghost Girl sat next to me and (against her better judgment, I'm sure) grabbed my hand tightly.

Black Blur whirred through the chairs, grabbing people and dragging them to the Tri-Hole. He ran uncomfortably close to us, and for one fearful moment I thought I'd felt his hands clamp onto me. Instead, I just heard a nearby grunt, and the whirring was gone.

Then, so was Black Blur.

I'd made it another round. Relief flooded my body. Ghost Girl finally let go.

"All right, thanks again for your patience everyone! You guys are doing great!" Blackjack said over the loudspeakers. "Now you get tomorrow off, pure rest and relaxation. You're gonna need it, because day after's gonna be your final elimination test before the final choosing. Congrats on makin' it this far!"

I opened my eyes in time to see the heroes disappear through the Tri-Hole. *We got a free day tomorrow? Sweet! We hadn't had free time in ages! I'd get a day with friends, we could hike, we could explore, make some trouble, or we could relax, and maybe, just maybe I'd even finally get the courage to hook up with Nevermore.*

It was going to be a good day. I knew it.

It was only when I heard Odigjod crying, only when I turned to see Firewall setting a comforting metal hand on one of his tiny shoulders, that I realized Showstopper was gone.

The sadness hit me harder than I'd expected. Somehow, I'd thought the six of us were invincible. I was sure we'd all make it onto the team, that one day we'd run the world together. Seeing him gone made me feel so unbelievably . . . vulnerable. So alone.

This was suddenly so . . . *real.*

#Supervillainy101: The Family Maxx

While most villains have done well keeping their family and careers separate, some have attempted to make supervillainy into a family affair. The Maxx family consisted of some of the greatest supervillains of the 90s (you can tell they worked in the 90s because of the extra x in their name). The father, Jonathan, controlled fire, while his wife, Ginny, controlled ice. Their twin teenage sons, Lucien and Sammy, were speedsters, while twelve-year-old Hannah was considered one of the greatest florakinetics the world had ever seen. They were a powerful, intimidating team that had defeated every group of heroes that the Protectors had thrown at them.

It was when Lucien started dating Maria Modesto, the daughter of superhero Crystal Skull, that everything went to hell.

Neither family approved of their love, so the young couple tried to elope. Crystal Skull and a team of Protectors caught up to them, capturing the young lovers and using Lucien as bait for the rest of the family.

While Jonathan and Sammy fought Crystal Skull, Ginny and Hannah tried to free Lucien. They failed; Hannah was captured, while Ginny was accidentally killed while trying to imprison the Golem in a block of solid ice.

Insane with grief, Jonathan and Sammy were able to convince a few of the lesser members of the Offenders to join their cause and led an attack on the floating island headquarters of the Protectors, *The Pearl*, just off the coast of Seattle.

To no one's surprise but their own, I'm sure, they were killed to the last man.

#LessonLearned: Sentimentality and supervillainy don't mix.

9

SPONGEMAN RISES

It wasn't the free day I was hoping for. It should have been fun. Instead, it felt unbelievably oppressing.

Showstopper was *gone*.

Any of us could be next. *I* could be next. It was a lot to absorb, and I wasn't in any mood to absorb.

I wasn't in a particular mood to do anything, really. I didn't want to talk to anyone, and thankfully they didn't seem to want to talk much either.

Odigjod tried to follow in Showstopper's footsteps to keep our spirits up. Watching him teleport a dozen velociraptors he'd managed to fit into tutus to the main street of the town ruins was kind of funny. Even seeing him line them up and try to get them to dance was amusing as well, but that only lasted a few seconds as well. Overall nothing—not even raptors in tutus—would have cheered us up.

I should have planned for the test, but I didn't. How could I? They didn't give us any clue as to what it would be. It was probably going to be the toughest of them all, but I wasn't going to kill myself preparing for it (especially when I didn't know what to prepare for). If I was going to freak out over it, I was going to freak out over it after a good night's sleep.

When the next day rolled around, I wasn't a rested man. None of us were. You don't go into a final well-rested, no matter how much you want to. Pure force of will can get you so far, fear can get you even further. The rest requires a few energy drinks.

Thankfully, they delivered a new crate of those with breakfast.

Four energy drinks, three tabs of aspirin, two pieces of toast with butter and jam, and one hot shower later, I almost felt human. I felt more like a twitchy ball of fear, but closer to human than when I'd woken up.

They delivered the clothes and costumes we originally wore to the island after breakfast, laundered so they wouldn't smell of seawater and puke, and told us to put them on for the test. After doing my tests in gym clothes for so long, my old costume felt claustrophobic.

Most of the town ruins had been rebuilt overnight with facades to look like the main street of a small town. At least a hundred people walked the streets, though on closer inspection I could see that they were all costumed Everywhere Men.

We all walked to meet Blackjack and the judges at the edge as she explained our final test.

"Congratulations for makin' it to your final elimination test. Fourteen of you will move on to the final choosing, where seven of you will be picked for the team. Until then . . ."

She waved a hand dramatically to the fake town behind her. "Welcome, one and all, to Anytown, USA. It's a nice place to live, the kind of place where people can walk after dark with no fear of being mo-lested by unkind so-ciety. Until today. You're soon gonna give them a supervillain problem. In randomly selected teams, each of you holdin' a specific job, you will break into this town's bank. You will then make your escape to an extraction point at the other end of town. At some point—we won't tell you when—a Tri-Hole will open and you will face some genu-ine superheroes. These won't be our shining stars. They will be . . . mediocre. You will engage them, and you will lose. But this ain't no school play. You have to make it look convincing, because if you don't, if some poor fuck on the street sees that you're fakin' this, Project Kayfabe's done with you."

"How badly *should* we lose, then?" Firewall asked.

"Think a Silver Age Escape," Blackjack said.

That didn't sound so bad. A Silver Age Escape basically meant escaping, maybe a little bloodied, and with some but not all of the loot while shaking our fists and yelling to the heroes that next time they wouldn't be so lucky, even though we all knew that they would.

She looked at us gravely as she gave a final warning: "And whatever you do, do *not* kill any civilians; you can't scare people if they're dead. We're puttin' everything you've learned to the test. Impress us. Convince us, and you just might make it to the next round. Now, your teams are as follows . . ."

We were broken up into five teams of four or five people. I was lucky enough to be in one of the teams with five, and also not the first to go up; Ghost Girl was stuck in that unlucky spot along with Circus, Apsara, and a hulking monster of a boy with stone skin and acid blood called Biocide. Right around the time that I was think-ing that would be a fun show, Blackjack dropped the bomb that for this test, we wouldn't be able to see the other teams perform.

Great. No learning from their mistakes.

I shot Ghost Girl a thumbs-up before I was guided with the rest to a large tent that would be our staging area. Hard to read as ever behind that mask of hers, she just nodded her head.

The energy drinks were starting to kick in pretty fierce when we got to the tent. I was rocking back and forth, hands shaking, mind going a mile a minute, and needing to take a leak, but they didn't have any bathrooms nearby and weren't letting us out of the tent and I really didn't want to have to hold it in but was beginning to realize that that would be the case and . . .

And I still had to plan with my team.

I got lucky with my team. I got Firewall, Nevermore, Spasm, and Swashbuckler. I knew I could trust Firewall and Spasm to carry things if it got bad. Nevermore was powerful and good at following instructions. Swashbuckler was a wild card, but he was given the same menial job as Spasm (Crowd Control), so I didn't think he could cause too much trouble. With Firewall and Nevermore tasked with the Breaking & Entering and Entry & Removal jobs, I was given the role of Shock & Awe.

That sounded easy enough.

We could hear explosions and screams coming from the Anytown set, but couldn't tell what was going on. We tried strategizing some, like the other teams were doing, but after a few minutes of half-assing we just shut up and tried to remember our lessons. This may have been a team exercise, but it was still everyone for themselves, and I was trying not to piss myself.

Lessons. Enunciate. Remember your puns. Project. Ignore Shooting Star's cleavage. Show nothing but pride. She sells seashells by the seash—

"Team Two, you're up!" Blackjack said, lifting the flap of the tent. *How long had I been doing those stupid rhymes?*

At least the helmet could cover up my sudden terror.

We marched to the edge of town in silence as the judges eyed us, their faces solemn. The Everywhere Men wandered up and down the street, living out ordinary lives. Mailmen. Families walking around (*far too many Everywhere Men in dresses*). Riding bicycles. A milkman tipping his cap to a passing family (*there are still milkmen?*). Cars driving up and down the street. A perfect slice of Americana, circa sometime in the Silver Age. Still no bathrooms in sight, though there were a couple alleys that looked tempting.

Chewing on a short stub of a cigar, Blackjack smiled at us grimly. "Ladies. Gentlemen. Villains. Kick some ass."

That was all the cue we were given. No bells. No cheers. This was our time to shine.

Not like anyone knew what to do. We stood in a line looking at each other stupidly, hoping someone would get the ball rolling. Not even Firewall and Swashbuckler, who were two exceptional showboats, looked like they knew what to do.

I was as surprised as anyone when I took that first step forward, put my hands on my hips, and shouted, "Shock and awe!"

I focused, sending two cars flying end over end into buildings on opposite sides of the street. More focus sent a deep, long crack down the middle of the barely paved street, fracturing the sidewalk and sending people sprawling.

Taking charge wasn't my first idea; up until the last moment I was still hoping someone else would do it. I only stepped forward when I realized that the sooner we got this over with, the sooner I'd get to a bathroom.

My opening got everyone moving. Firewall took off, hovering a few feet off the street as she fired lasers and small rockets at buildings, blowing them apart and setting them ablaze. Nevermore wasn't far behind, sending a black cat—larger and fiercer than a tiger—from her chest, chasing people away from the bank. A few scattered police officers and guards ran from the bank, half of whom doubled over vomiting violently as Spasm pointed at them, the rest taken down when Swashbuckler darted through the crowd and cut a tree down with one quick slash of his sword.

I ran after them. I must've looked unvillainous as hell, shaking violently and with my thighs pressed together, but I made it to the bank just as Firewall ripped the front wall away with her four arms.

"Do you have this situation under control?" I asked no one in particular.

"We got it, friend," Spasm said, pointing at a few pedestrians who'd started to take pictures with their phones and sending them running away, bent over with gushing nosebleeds.

"Good," I said, darting for a nearby alley.

This couldn't wait. Not anymore. Maybe I wouldn't look cool, maybe it would deduct points, but I'd started this off strongly enough that I didn't think it would be too terrible a problem if I stepped away.

I ran down the alley and started to struggle with the too-tight leather pants I never should have bought.

I'd just gotten the zipper loose when he spoke up.

"Surrender, villain!" His voice was shrill and cocky.

You couldn't have waited thirty seconds?

Zipping back up, I faced a superhero I'd never seen before. "Who the fuck are you?"

"I am Spongeman!" he proclaimed proudly, putting his hands on his hips. "Absorber of evil and scrubber of crime great and small! Your days are numbered, villain!"

Well, that would explain why he looked like a giant man-shaped sponge wearing a cape. That *didn't* explain the Speedo, or the domino mask that did little to hide the fact that he was still a giant man-shaped sponge, but one thing at a time, I guess.

Hold it in. It's showtime.

Trying to look threatening while holding my legs together, I faced him, hands raised. Remembering my lessons, I focused, picking up some odds and ends of garbage and pieces of brick from the ground, and hurled them at Spongeman. *Grab a lot of small pieces and throw them one at a time. Very showy, but it does little permanent damage*, Helios had said during training.

True to his word, each of them bounced off of Spongeman as if they were nothing.

Once your first powered attack fails, always make a clumsy run at the hero. Try to hit them a few times, let them dodge, then let them get in a hit.

I dove for Spongeman with an awkward haymaker punch to his chest. He didn't dodge. In fact, he let it sink in a few inches, enveloping my hand in soggy sponge. *Gross.*

He tossed his head back in another booming laugh. "Foolish villain, whatever you throw at me, I absorb, and the more I absorb, the stronger I get!"

Well, that ruled out pissing on him.

To illustrate his point, he swung his body around, lifting me off the ground by my arm and throwing me back out into the street.

All right, this guy was starting to irritate me.

Hands still on hips, he laughed again. "Do you have anything more for me to absorb, fiend?"

A plan formed quickly. A witty comeback, not so much. "Absorb this, cocksucker!"

I focused on the ground at his feet, ripping a large section of it up and hurling it—and Spongeman—through the air.

His scream was as glorious as I'd hoped.

Wonder where he'll land . . .

A deafening roar brought me back to Earth, at least long enough to see the others engaged in battle with some of the biggest names in D-List heroes I'd ever seen in one place outside a celebrity rehab show.

Nevermore fought the Darklighter, a man in a black trench coat, fedora, and goggles who shot balls of brilliant white light that destroyed her projections. Foghorn Girl let out another blaring roar, taking Firewall to her knees. Former standup comic and rehab reality show mainstay Furious Frank punched Swashbuckler in the shoulder, taking him down so overdramatically that it wouldn't have passed muster in a daytime soap.

Spasm had it worst. Sea Cowboy (*huh, he's still alive?*), the half-cowboy, half-seahorse superhero, had Spasm tied up in a lasso and was spinning him over his head while shouting out the heartiest "YEE-HAW!" I could imagine. Spasm's face said he wasn't acting.

Focus.

The rope snapped, sending Spasm flying onto the hood of a parked car. I ran to him, helping him up and out of the rope. No way was I going to deal with these guys alone.

"I don't think these guys were told to stage-fight!" Spasm said, tearing the remains of the lasso off.

"I don't think these guys were told to be sane!" I replied, looking back over my shoulder to see Spongeman running at us and screaming like a maniac.

"We gotta lose!" he said.

"Running away still counts as losing!" I said, looking to see that our finish line was not that far away. All that stood in our way was four (soon to be five) almost-heroes and a few dozen copies of Everywhere Man watching us from the sidewalk, pretending to be pedestrians.

"Got any ideas?" I asked. Spasm always had plans, probably all his IRA training, which was pretty nice when you had him on a team.

"A few, you?"

"Just one."

I told him mine and he told me his. We put them together in a way that I was pretty sure would get us out with a loss and a victory. All that was left was hoping these heroes were as noble as they thought they were.

Sticking his hands out and separating them in a wave, Spasm made nearly all of the pedestrians double over sick and vomiting, distracting the heroes. He made sure to leave the two Everywhere Man copies closest to us alone, and we ran for them, each wrapping an arm around one of their necks.

"Heroes, surrender, or we will kill this woman and . . . child?" I proclaimed. The hostages were my idea. I was almost giddy when I saw it work.

Huffing and wheezing from his run, Spongeman shouted back, "We'll never surrender to your likes!"

"Well—wait, you did hear that we'd kill them, right?" I asked.

The other heroes looked at Spongeman like he was an idiot. My Everywhere Man copy even broke character, saying, "See, this is why you never made the big leagues, Stan."

"Shut up, Waldo," Spongeman shot back.

"Is everyone all right?" I asked the others. Firewall and Nevermore flashed me a thumbs-up.

Swashbuckler simply called back, "Furious Frank said I was knocked unconscious in the fray!"

Keeping in character, we marched our hostages, and the rest of our team (with Firewall dragging Swashbuckler by one of his legs) to the finish line. Some of the loot had been lost in the battle, but we'd gotten enough of it that this would easily qualify as a good loss. A textbook Silver Age Escape.

Feeling a moment of inspiration, I turned to the heroes, raised my fist and shook it, screaming, "WE'LL GET YOU NEXT TIME, HEROES!"

The judges didn't stop to give us comments, but rather sent us to another tent set up near the end of town. This one had picnic tables covered with food and drinks, and thank merciful God in heaven several porta-potties. I think the relief I felt visiting one of those was about as close as I'll ever get to heaven.

Firewall and Ghost Girl had a table to themselves. They both looked about as happy as I'd ever seen them. Firewall beckoned me over with a wave and a smile, but I was intercepted before I could make it to them.

"You were very impressive out there."

"Thanks," I said, turning to Nevermore. "I don't like to brag or anything, but . . ." I shrugged, hoping to look roguish and have the opportunity to brag.

"I think you will make it to the final choosing."

I looked over to Firewall and Ghost Girl, who now turned away from me. Ghost Girl was shaking her head softly.

"I'm hoping I will, but that's really up to the judges," I said, trying to sound humble, but agreeing with her completely. I *owned* that test.

"I am worried I won't," she said, looking away, slightly sad.

"I think you will!"

"Do you?"

"Of course!"

We danced this dance for a while, her showing a new doubt about her performance, me reassuring her, her face brightening up before darkening again, rinse and repeat. I was pretty sure that she was using me for compliments, but if it made the approach to getting her in bed easier, I would let her use me however she wanted.

After about ten minutes of this, the third group, containing Odigjod and Carnivore, came in. Most of the team looked hurt, bleeding and limping. The way Carnivore roared and kicked over a table before stalking off to the edge of the tent made me think their run didn't go so well. Odigjod running to the table with Firewall and Ghost Girl and burying his head in his hands confirmed it.

Nevermore was still talking, but I lost track of what she was saying, making my way to their table.

"—couldn't have been that bad," Firewall was saying, patting him on the back.

"It *was*," he sobbed, pounding one of his tiny fists on the table and burning a hole clear through it.

"What happened?" I asked.

"Their attempt didn't go so well," Ghost Girl said, then motioning her head to Carnivore. "There was a breakdown in leadership, maybe a misplaced teleportation or two, Carnivore lost his shit because of his perception of Odigjod as the team's weak link and wound up killing some civilians . . . you know the story."

"Carnivore?" I said, taking a seat at the table next to Odigjod. "He's just an asshole, don't listen to him."

"But Odigjod *did* screw up!" Odigjod said. "Odigjod failed for his team, and now he won't making the team and is going to be sent away!"

"You're not going to the Tower," I said, patting him on the back.

"No, Odigjod's work exchange program prevents that. Going to an worse place if losing. *Home.*"

Going home sure didn't sound worse than the Tower. I mean, I know home for him was hell, but he was used to it, so it couldn't be that bad.

He continued, "Home's where Odigjod's expected to keep the family business, to torment the gluttonous damned. For generations the family has done it and never dreamed of more. But Odigjod dreams! Odigjod wants to be more than just a imp like the rest! Odigjod wants to be special! Odigjod could be an real demon if he tried, but can't try back home! Out here . . . there's ambition. Chances. Opportunities. If not in the villain's team . . . no second chance topside."

It still didn't sound as bad as the Tower, but I still felt for him. Odigjod may have been ugly as sin, a minion of Hell, a bit naïve, and in need of some English classes, but he meant well. I didn't want to see him crying like this.

This would require some drastic measures.

"Did you have to fight Spongeman?" I asked.

He shook his head. "That was for the Zone Runner."

"Well, I'm sure he did fine, anyone could against Spongeman. But did you see him?"

"Yes."

"Did you know I made him scream?"

He shook his head.

"It was great. Back me up, Firewall."

I doubt she saw it, but she could pick up where I was going. "It *was* probably the funniest thing I've seen you do on purpose."

"It was?" Odigjod asked.

"Oh yeah," I said, describing the battle with just enough embellishment to make Odigjod laugh. Firewall liked Odigjod enough that she let me get away with more than usual, which was nice, especially when I focused on the table Carnivore had kicked over, crudely shaped it like Spongeman and launched it through the ceiling with my best imitation of his scream. I don't think it made him forget his fear or anything, but it was a distraction and made him laugh just long enough that the fear wasn't all he was focused on.

Firewall and Ghost Girl did the same, sharing our war stories, most of them at the expense of Spongeman. Even Felix joined in when his team finished. After a while we got a few funny stories out of Odigjod when he'd calmed down enough. It didn't sound as bad as he'd first said, especially once he got laughing, but it did sound like one big mess that might get him cut if the judges weren't feeling merciful.

I worried that he might be another Showstopper; I didn't know how any of us would last without Odigjod.

Finally, the fifth team came in. If it was possible, they looked even worse than Odigjod's team, which only boosted the imp's confidence.

Once we were all in the tent, Blackjack summoned us back to Anytown. For the first time after a test, I was eager to hear the results. I was pretty confident that I'd make it to the final choosing, which meant a fifty-fifty chance to make the team, and those were great odds by my estimation.

"I'm going to hazard a guess that that was the nicest thing you've ever done," Ghost Girl said, strolling beside me.

"Maybe."

She rolled her eyes behind her mask. "I love that you still think you can hide things from me."

As usual, I couldn't fool her. Making sure nobody was looking closely at us, I was able to drop the Apex Strike bravura. "Can't blame me for trying, can you?"

"I can, but I won't."

"And why's that?"

"Because when you're not trying to impress anyone, you're actually a pretty decent guy, and maybe, almost, kinda cute."

"Maybe? Almost? *Kinda*?"

"If I were to be generous," she said, offhand. "Don't make me reconsider."

"Hey, I'm cute all the time!" I protested, too loudly, even though I knew it was a lie, but it was the only defense I could think of to what she said.

"No, you're not!" Firewall called from the head of the group.

Ghost Girl and I looked at each other for a moment before we burst out laughing.

Come to think of it, I was pretty sure that was the first time I'd ever heard her laugh. I'd have commented on it, but by the time I realized it, we were at the judges table.

The Tri-Hole was already open behind them. They meant to do this quick. As usual, Blackjack gave us her speech about how many of us were eliminated and how many were moving on. As usual, I closed my eyes.

I'mfineI'mfineI'mfineI'mfineI'mfine . . .

Black Blur whirred past us. People were plucked off their feet.

I wasn't one of them.

I opened my eyes. Odigjod, Firewall, Felix, and Ghost Girl had all made it through. So had Carnivore, Circus, Nevermore, Spasm, and a few others I didn't know very well.

We were the final fourteen. Half of us would make the team, half of us wouldn't.

The judges disappeared one at a time into the Tri-Hole. Blackjack was last. She took the bare stub of the cigar from her lips and crushed it out underfoot.

"This one's off the record, but I just want to say I'm damn proud of you kids. You've all earned your spots here. We got a surprise for you tomorrow before the final choosing. Not gonna spoil it now, but consider it your informal, final test."

My stomach sank at the thought. I thought we were done with tests. We all had.

"But don't fret, I'm sure y'all are gonna do great. To take the edge off, I've had a little something I think you're gonna like delivered to camp. Just take it easy, relax, and have fun."

Fun. Right. How the hell were we gonna have fun after *that* bombshell?

Alcohol.

The answer to that question was alcohol.

While we were away at the test, a bar had been installed just outside the mess hall stocked with a wide selection of beers and liquors. There were also games, balls, and even a few musical instruments dropped off for our enjoyment, though most of these went unused. Felix was pretty good with a guitar though, and after a few shots he started to cut loose on 80s South American pop songs. After we got the bonfire started and Carnivore passed out from the three bottles of whiskey he'd polished off, it felt pretty close to the party we had on the first night.

Just without anyone dying.

I didn't drink. I wanted to, and there was a lot of liquor I'd have liked to try, but I didn't want to be hungover for tomorrow. I couldn't fuck up, not after making it this far, not after all I'd done. I considered finally propositioning Nevermore, but not an hour into the party she was sloppy drunk and stumbling about. It might have made things easier for me, but the odds were that she'd pass out the moment she was horizontal, and while I might have been a supervillain, I wasn't *that* evil.

Out of the corner of my eye, I saw Ghost Girl walking slowly toward the town ruins, her black cloak almost completely masking her in the night. Was she crazy? Leaving the barracks area at night wasn't safe. I mean, she knew how to take care of herself better than most people here, but this . . .

Sighing, I followed her.

"Wait up!"

She slowed her stroll just enough to let me catch up. We walked among the leftover facades from the day's test, most of them torn down or damaged, but a few intact, making the place look all the more like a ghost town under the light of a full moon.

"What are you doing here?"

Her eyes glowed gold in the dark. "This place is ridiculously haunted, but it has its charms."

That didn't answer my question. Seeing this, she added, "I haven't had a home, or a family, for a while, and even though this place is hell on my power, I've started to get attached to it, and to all of you. After tomorrow, that all goes away."

"It doesn't have to," I said. "You could still make the team. We all could!"

"As ever, your optimism is refreshing," she said, looking at me long and hard. Her eyes had stopped glowing, her face completely disappearing behind that porcelain doll mask.

Finally, she said, "So, do you want to fuck?"

If I had a drink in my mouth, I would have spit it out. "What?"

"I asked if you wanted to fuck."

"Yes! Why? Here?" I don't know which word I blurted out louder, but they all sounded deafening.

She sighed. "It was never this difficult back home . . ."

"But—"

"To answer your first question: There's a good chance one of us, or even both of us, will be in the Tower tomorrow. I haven't had sex in three years, and you're a virgin. I want to get laid at least once before a lifetime of imprisonment, and you don't want to go a virgin, do you?"

"I find absolutely no problems with that logic."

"And, for the second question . . ."

She took me by the hand, pulling me through the doorway of one of the facades that was still mostly standing. There were cheap plywood walls around us, and most of a roof, though it had enough holes to let the moonlight in. My heart was beating so heavily it made my ears ring. Was this really happening?

She pulled her cloak off and spread it out on the ground, running a hand through her pixie-cut hair. "You know, Aidan, this would be easier if you started to undress."

Yeah, this was happening.

She made getting undressed look good, turning away from me to unzip her formfitting bodysuit, slowly stripping it off to reveal her body, removing her sports bra, and sliding her panties to the ground.

I had to give myself points for not falling over once in my melee to tear off my clothes. With the pants not giving way, I wound up focusing on the crotch of them and sending them rocketing off my legs in an explosion of leather strips and torn boxers.

In retrospect, I was really lucky not to have blown my balls off.

I turned back to see her. She still faced away from me.

"Are you ready?" she said, her voice wavering only slightly.

"YES! I mean . . . yeah, I'm ready."

Slowly, she turned to face me. Save her mask, she was completely naked. Her breasts sagged more and had a slightly different shape from all the girls I'd seen online, and she wasn't as diligent at trimming the hair above her pussy either, but she was naked and willing to have sex with me. At this point I could look past a lot of things. I was just hoping she wouldn't laugh at the size of my dick; I knew I didn't stack up to the guys online, but I hoped it wasn't enough to send her running.

She didn't. She just approached me slowly. If it weren't for the mask, and her face, I guess we'd have kissed. Knowing this wasn't possible, I just pointed at her boobs. I'd wanted to do this since I first noticed boobs.

"Can I?"

"Sure," she said, cooing briefly when I first grabbed them. "That's good. No, not that, no, not that hard . . . no, they're attached, okay, better, yeah, like that . . . wait, no, not like—yeah, your mouth is nice on—no, too much teeth, I can feel that and—that's better, that's good, keep doing that . . ."

That got a moan. Unless she was faking on me, I must have been doing something right. Enough right that she took me in her hand and started stroking.

"Lie down," she said.

I did as she said, and for a moment that felt like a mouth, I started to wonder just what this meant.

Were we still friends? Was this supposed to be something more? Was *she* thinking this was something more? Was *I* supposed to? What the hell was going on?

The questions stopped when she straddled my hips, grabbed me and lined me up with her.

"You can still back out if you want to," she said.

I wanted to say I didn't, but only wound up shaking my head.

She rocked her hips.

I was inside her.

"Congratulations," she said.

"Thanks," I whimpered, still trying to get that ringing out of my ears so I could fully absorb just what was happening.

She started rocking her hips. I didn't know if I was supposed to move or stay still. I was feeling good, mostly, but I wasn't used to my dick being stuck at this angle and it kind of hurt. Feeling more and more awkward as I just lay there, I grabbed onto her hips and tried arching into her fast and hard like I'd seen online.

This didn't do either of us any good.

She pinned me down, slowing my thrusting. "You've got a lot to learn. Just take it easy. This is supposed to be fun."

"I'm having fun!" I said, falling back into her cloak as, too soon, I erupted inside of her.

My world went black as it felt like I was completely drained.

So that was sex. Cool.

I thought I was finished, but I wasn't. She rolled off of me, telling me to help her out so she could finish. Her fingers occupied her pussy pretty effectively, but I played with her boobs some more, stroking, pinching, and sucking until she came too.

Panting, she looked up at me. "Never leave a girl unsatisfied; you'll look like an asshole. Leave one with superpowers unsatisfied, you're liable to wind up dead."

"Good safety tip," was all I could think to say.

Rolling off the stained and dirty cloak, she started to gather up her clothes. "Come on. We should get dressed before people start to miss us."

"So, we're finished?" I asked. I thought there were supposed to be a lot more positions involved.

"*You* are," she said, pulling her panties back on.

"I guess . . ." I said, looking around. "Thanks."

"Don't get all mushy, at least emotionally, Aidan. It was just sex."

"So . . . we're still friends, right?"

"If you want to be," she shrugged. I couldn't tell, but I think this time she was the one hiding something in her voice.

"I do," I said. "Think we can try that again sometime?"

"Maybe," she said, laughing softly. "Let's see how tomorrow goes."

"Sure," I said. "Say, have you seen my pants?"

She laughed more loudly. "You blew them off in a fit of passion. Which I guess I should take as a compliment."

She might have taken it as a compliment. I took it as a guy with a shrinking, sticky penis having to walk pantsless—and underwearless—across a dark stretch of Death Island into a camp of supervillains. Only one word seemed adequate to sum up that problem.

"Fuck."

#Supervillainy101: El Capitán & Edward Edge

They say that if you're a norm, you dream of being a super, and if you're a super, you dream of being a Titan, and if you're a Titan, you dream of being El Capitán.

The world's seventeenth confirmed Titan, El Capitán is considered America's, and often the world's, greatest hero. While many of the Titans have used their near-limitless strength, invulnerability, and myriad other powers to create an elite and aloof clique of supers, El Capitán has always fought for the little guy. Growing up poor in Baja California (before it was added as our fifty-eighth state, mostly at his request), he knew hardship that most heroes never would and vowed to fight injustice however he could. Upon discovering his status as a Titan, he donned his trademark red, green, and gold luchador outfit and immigrated north, joining the United States in World War II and almost single-handedly repelling a joint Canadian-Lemurian invasion from the north. His constant charity work and efforts during the War on Villainy are seen as a beacon of American virtue.

And he probably wouldn't have made it that far if he didn't have his archnemesis.

Millionaire industrialist and inventor Edward Edge, founder of Edge Industries and all its subsidiaries (there's at least a 70 percent chance they made the e-reader you're reading this on), was one of the greatest voices in the anti-super movement of the late 30s and early 40s. Seeing them as a menace to American life, he led a public campaign to discredit them, and a private campaign to have them killed, mostly to keep his vast and secretive criminal empire profitable. El Capitán was his number one target, and though the two fought many times over the decades, neither could truly win. Nothing Edge tried could kill El Capitán (though he came close on a few occasions), and he was so good at covering his tracks that El Capitán could never get enough evidence to imprison him. On his deathbed, Edge summoned the media and El Capitán to make a full confession, stating that he wouldn't have been as great a villain if it weren't for the hero.

The last thing he heard before dying was El Capitán admitting the same.

Of course, being one of the world's greatest supervillains, Edge wouldn't let El Capitán get the last word. Moments after he died, a pacemaker installed in Edge's heart sent a signal to a bomb planted in the newspaper office where El Capitán's girlfriend worked, killing everyone inside.

The epitaph on Edward Edge's memorial simply read, "I won."

#LessonLearned: Nothing brings greatness like a good archnemesis.

10

ARCHNEMESIS DAY

The world looks a whole lot different after you've gotten laid. It's like there's a switch that goes off that just gives you hope that things just aren't as bad as they previously seemed . . . or maybe that all comes from knowing you're not going to die a virgin.

I didn't know where Ghost Girl's head was, since we didn't have a lot of time to talk before we had to sleep. I did know that I was still riding pretty high when Blackjack's voice came over the loudspeakers at four in the morning, telling us all to wake up and get dressed.

Get dressed at four? Sure, why the hell not?

I wasn't a virgin anymore. I was a *man*. I could do anything.

Whatever we were doing, it wasn't too formal; they'd delivered street clothes on top of our foot lockers. I recognized the t-shirt, jeans, shoes, and socks as my own.

We got dressed in silence, the others nervous and excited and fearful, and maybe I had some of that too, but it wasn't what

I was focusing on. For the first time since I'd gotten here, I had complete confidence.

That lasted until I heard the announcement.

"Apex Strike, report to the mess hall ASAP!" Blackjack barked over the loudspeaker.

I walked through the men's barrack, getting some best wishes, some glares, and a very hungover growl from Carnivore as I walked to my final test. My shakes returned more the closer I got to the mess hall.

Are they going to send you to the Tower? Is that why they gave you street clothes? No, that doesn't make any sense. Maybe they're letting you go? Wait, why the hell would they do that? Now you're really thinking crazy.

I finally stopped my hands from shaking when I opened the mess hall door.

Blackjack sat on one of the hall's long tables, an open Tri-Hole floating a foot off the ground next to her. Instead of her usual cigar, this morning she was chewing on a Hot Pocket.

"Mornin', Apex Strike," she said conversationally, wiping melted cheese from her chin with the back of her hand, then wiping it on the table.

"Good morning, ma'am," I said, walking to meet her only when she waved a hand.

"Don't gimme any of that ma'am shit today, boy. There's a fifty-fifty chance we're gonna be coworkers at the end of the day. Why not just try calling me Blackjack?"

"Okay . . . Blackjack," I said, trying not to sound too terribly awkward about it.

"You know what? You kinda remind me of me before I got cursed," she said, smiling wryly.

"Thanks?"

"No. Not really. Before I was as immortal as a Titan, I was a pretty girl who was more concerned with what my daddy thought and impressing some high-society gents and stayin' pretty and clean and rich and safe. For a while after my curse, I thought things could stay the same, but they couldn't. Nothing ever stays the same when this life chooses you, no matter how much you try," she said, her voice sounding tired. She pulled a flask from her jacket and took a hit, then tipped it to me.

"It's not even, like, five in the morning," I said.

"Trust me, today, you're gonna need it."

Fair enough. I took a quick hit of her flask. It tasted of burning and Hot Pockets. I coughed, spitting half of it out, which got her to crack a smile.

"That'll put hair on your balls," she said, taking another long swig and pocketing it. "On the other side of that Tri-Hole is your final test. This one's not like any other you've done before. Just gonna be one-on-one, you and a hero, trying to see if you've got what it takes to be archnemeses. You'll spend the day together and if they think you hit it off enough, you're on the team. Think of it like a first date, except if you fail here you don't go home with blue balls and a black eye, but rather a one-way ticket to the Tower for eternity."

Miles and miles of smiles . . .

That wasn't really comforting, though, come to think of it, I was pretty sure she didn't mean it to be.

"I've never been on a first date before," I said.

"It shows," Blackjack said. "Just don't be a pussy. And don't fuck up."

"Thanks," I said. I gulped, flexing my hands and trying not to let the nervous energy take over.

"Look, kid. You did this to yourself, but life's still given you a raw deal. It's shitty, but try and make the most of it. If this is the start of a new life, remember what this last day of being you is like. If it's your last day of freedom, just enjoy it for all it's worth, you hear me?"

I did hear her. I didn't like it, but I heard it, and if I wasn't mistaken, that almost sounded like concern.

I was going to spend a day with a superhero, trying to impress them and get them to like me so I could convince them to let me on the team. If I'd had the confidence and ability to make a good first impression, I wouldn't have been here in the first place! I'd be back home, with more friends and maybe even a fighting chance of fucking Kelly Shingle (not that I had any complaints about what Ghost Girl and I did the night before).

Maybe that was why Blackjack finally had to push me through.

I'd teleported a couple times when Odigjod was trying to perfect teleporting an extra person with him, but that was instantaneous and kind of fun if you didn't mind smelling like brimstone for fifteen minutes after.

Teleporting through a Tri-Hole was like being flung through the air by my own powers: flying out of control through a bright green tunnel of glowing energy, loud, piercing sounds, like the screams of the damned that Odigjod sometimes summoned during tests, only mechanical and trying to get under my skin. I didn't like traveling through a Tri-Hole; I couldn't see how the heroes did this every day.

I was probably only in the tunnel for fifteen seconds or so, but it felt like twenty minutes had passed before I could see the light at the end. The piercing shrieks got louder, I was moving faster, and by the time I started screaming I couldn't even hear myself.

Then I slammed face-first into white sand.

I could hear the ocean, and some seagulls, and not too far off the faint sound of rock music and people laughing. I coughed, spitting out a mouthful of sand.

"First time Tri-Holing? Blackjack should have warned you about the landing, but she enjoys being a bitch sometimes. Want a donut?"

The man who stood beside me was maybe ten years older, tall, handsome, and blond, in a button-down white silk shirt with the sleeves rolled up, faded jeans, and designer sunglasses. True to his word, he carried a bag of fresh donuts that smelled damn good.

His brilliant white smile, wavy, perfectly slicked-back hair, and slight—but not too heavy—tan made him look like every Hollywood director's dream of California, which would explain how he kept getting cast in parts like that.

"Helios?"

He laughed, reaching out and helping me to my feet. "Please, it's my day off; I'm just Adam Archer. Call me Adam. And have a donut, they're fresh, and really good."

I'd never had a celebrity ask me to address them by their first name before . . . or offer me a donut.

I got the feeling that this would be a day of firsts.

I took the donut he offered me. He was right, it was good.

"We gotta watch our calories in this business, but if we can't treat ourselves occasionally, what's the point?"

"I don't know," I said.

"That's all right, you'll learn," he said, looking over his shoulder. "Look, we've got a busy day ahead of us, and even with all the Tri-Holing it won't take long for the paparazzi to find us, so if anyone asks, you're training as my new personal assistant, and if you're going to be doing that, you gotta look the part."

He reached into his pocket and tossed me a pair of sunglasses that matched his. I wouldn't have been surprised if they cost more than my mom's SUV.

"Where are we?"

"Southern California. I always like to spend at least a few minutes by the ocean when I've got free time, and of course . . . today we've got an extra bonus I wanted to show you," he said, pointing out to sea.

I finally looked out to the ocean and saw what he meant. A few miles offshore, hovering a couple hundred feet off the water, was an artificial island covered in high-tech, futuristic buildings.

"*The Pearl!*" I exclaimed.

"The one and only."

The Pearl was designed by the Gamemaster, Caveman, and ATHENA back in the earliest days of the War on Villainy as a mobile base of operations for the Protectors. Its armament and mobility made it a decisive factor in many battles, though it has since become more of a tourist destination, hovering up and down the West Coast. I'd always wanted to see it in person, but never thought I'd have the chance.

"I remember the first time I saw it in person. I was a few years younger than you, I think, before I'd gotten any of my powers, and I just had this thought. I knew that someday, I'd call that place home. And while I won't say I call it home now, it is a pretty awesome place to work. Walk with me."

This was too much to take in. Seeing *The Pearl?* Helios *wanting* to be my archnemesis? I was convinced that he hated me after I killed his friend, Icicle Man.

He guided me away from the beach and to the boardwalk. It was still early in the morning and most of the businesses were closed, but there were enough oddballs and street performers setting up shop for the day to justify everything weird I'd heard about California. A gene-job with quills covering half his face offered to melt into a puddle for five dollars. A few missionaries from New R'lyeh handed us pamphlets praising the glories of the Great Old Ones; we threw them out at the nearest trash can.

This was all too much. I had to ask, "Why me?"

"Because I see the potential for greatness in you, Aidan," he said without hesitation.

"Really?" I asked. Greatness and me were two concepts I don't think anyone had seriously put in the same sentence before.

"Of course! I wouldn't have asked you here if I didn't believe you could be one of the greatest supervillains ever. God knows I wouldn't want just anyone to be my archnemesis; I got an image to maintain," he said with a chuckle.

"Well, sure."

"And, while you may not be the bravest, or the most power-ful, you know how to work a crowd, and you *really* know how to follow orders. Every one of the other villains with you, they talk back, they question us, they plot against us, but you've never once argued, because you understand the importance of what we do, don't you?"

It wasn't so much that I understood the importance of the plan as I didn't want to be sent to the Tower, but I wasn't going to tell him that.

"Of course!"

"See, I knew the other heroes were wrong. You aren't stupid," he said, smiling.

"They think I'm stupid?"

He laughed. "I'm not gonna name names, don't want any more Icicle Man problems, do we?"

"No, we don't," I said, casting my eyes down. Now we got to the real point of the day. "I'm really sorry about that. It was an accident. I know you guys were friends, and—"

He brushed the thought off. "Icicle Man was dangerous and a pervert and you did the world a favor. You also did the Protectors a favor by killing him before any of that went public, so, really, *we* should be thanking *you*."

"No problem," I said, relief hitting me in a wave.

"You ever been fitted for a suit?"

"No."

He pulled a Tri-Hole controller from his pocket and opened one up before us.

"Then this will be new for you," he said, grinning.

The second trip through the Tri-Hole was a lot easier than the first, though this may have come from Helios being there to catch me upon exiting. We were in a nice suit shop in San Francisco (according to Helios), and it seemed like we were expected, even though it must have been way before business hours. Tailors flocked over to take my measurements like vultures.

"Before all this, did you know what you wanted to do with your life?" I looked at the tailors questioningly. Helios continued, "Don't worry about them. They're cool."

"No, I didn't. I guess I would have gone to college, but I didn't have any plans, really. I wasn't special then."

"Hey, don't let me hear that. *Everyone* is special, even the norms. I mean it's true that some of us are more special than others, but everyone has something to offer the world. It just takes some of us longer than others to figure out just what that is. You're lucky, really. I've got friends in their thirties who don't know what they want to do with their lives. Figuring out that you wanted to be a supervillain when you were *just eighteen*, that's damned impressive." I couldn't help but swell with pride at the thought. Helios had never been one of my favorite heroes, or even one of the most recognizable (he was B-List, on the cusp of breaking into the A-List), but I was beginning to regret not giving him more credit.

"Well, it seemed like the right thing for me to do . . ." I said, allowing myself a casual shrug.

"Strictly speaking, it wasn't. I'm supposed to tell you it's the worst choice you've ever made in your life because villains are, officially, an evil that needs to be eradicated for the peace and greater good of this planet. Unofficially . . . well, let's just say you decided to make the worst choice of your life at the right time. We've been putting Project Kayfabe together for about two years now, gradually removing candidates from society, and then you came along and killed Icicle Man and changed the whole game. You moved our plans up by something like six months, because we knew we had to get our hands on you right away."

"Thanks."

"No problem. I just wish you knew how really important you were. You study much history in school?"

"It was my favorite subject."

Amazingly enough, this wasn't a lie.

"You ever hear of the old limey concept called 'The White Man's Burden'?" he asked.

I shook my head.

"I don't blame you, it's a bullshit concept from a bullshit time that was made irrelevant by the public rise of the supers. It basically stated that the white, *civilized* world had an obligation to spread its values and protect the rest of the world from itself, which is complete nonsense. Skin color doesn't determine superiority; the very fact that anyone can be born super or made super through a hundred different external factors proves that. As for values, who's to say what's right and wrong in a society so long as nobody's getting hurt? But that's the problem: people can get hurt, and that's where the theory has some merit. Some of us do have an obligation to protect the world from itself. But you've already heard that speech, haven't you?"

I had, but hearing it from him somehow gave it a lot more weight. Now I could see that they were making, no, *asking* us to be both villains *and* heroes.

"Wow."

He smiled. "Yeah, wow sums it up, doesn't it? Nicolai, have that suit ready and waiting at the New York store by six o'clock local."

"Yes sir, Mr. Archer," the tailor said, making a beeline for their computer.

"What's this for?"

"It's a surprise. Kind of a way to cap off the day. Don't worry, I think you'll like it," he said. "So, what would you like to do until then?"

"What do you mean?"

"I've got a fully charged Tri-Hole generator, and we've got six hours until showtime. The world is our playground. Just name it, and we'll do it."

"Anything?"

"Anything."

Images of sweaty, naked women entwined around me flashed before my eyes, but not as readily as I'd have expected, not after last night. Other ideas, things I'd always wanted to try but couldn't do within the confines of Hacklin's Hall, Indiana, came to mind.

And so we spent much of the day hopping around the world through Tri-Holes. Within half an hour I got to sightsee what felt like half the world, from the Taj Mahal to the Grand Canyon to the ruins of Honolulu in New R'lyeh. We went to theme parks, sang karaoke in Tokyo, rode go-karts, played paintball, and had the most fun I'd ever had in a single day. Everywhere we went, we got the celebrity treatment, people cheering and loving Helios and asking for his autograph, and I got to be there soaking it all in.

Helios himself turned out to be a lot cooler than I would have expected. I mean, you see the ads, you see the movies, you watch all the gossip and paparazzi shows and you think you know who a person really is, but then you spend time with them and you learn all sorts of new things. Like how he studied philosophy and collected art in his free time. Like how before he was a celebrity with a mansion and a supermodel girlfriend he was awkward and bad at school and didn't become anyone until he'd manifested his powers. Or how he was one of the only people I'd ever met who actually asked me questions about who I was and what I liked, and even though I didn't have much to say, he still listened.

He got us to New York in time for whatever his surprise was. We dressed to the nines in the suits he'd ordered up (not too formal, very cool, very classy) and met a limo outside the shop. Inside were two of the most beautiful women I'd ever seen. One I recognized from all the gossip shows as Adriana Alton, one of the most famous supermodels in the world. The other, a slender and seductive Atlantean (even with her pale blue skin) was introduced to me as Venera, Adriana's protégé. Apparently we were going to the annual Carina's Corner lingerie show, and since Venera's date had backed out at the last minute, Helios had roped me in as backup. *Oh darn.*

So I walked the red carpet with Helios on one side and one of the most beautiful women in the world on my arm. We got front row seats along with a number of other celebrities to watch these women walk the runway in some of the hottest and skimpiest outfits I had ever seen. After the show we attended an after-party where Helios introduced me to all the models and a lot of the other celebrities who showed up (rappers, athletes, actors, politicians, superheroes, you name it). As none of them knew about Project Kayfabe, I had to keep up the personal assistant act. He kept me by his side the entire time as a friend and confidante.

He made me feel *special*.

I now had an answer for what I'd say if he'd asked what I wanted to do with my life: I wanted to be Helios.

Just, you know, the supervillain version.

We left the party early after Helios had gotten a call from one of the other Kayfabe superheroes. They talked for a long time out of earshot, and when he took me to the limo, I couldn't read his face.

I couldn't help asking, "So . . . how'd I do?"

"If it were up to me, I'd say you were in, but my vote only counts for so much," he said.

"I know. Thanks, at least."

He pulled the Tri-Hole generator from his pocket and opened one up before us.

"You know how this goes," he said. "I really hope to see you on the team, because I had an awesome time today."

"Me too," I said, reaching out to shake his hand.

"Ah, come here," he said, pulling me in for a bear hug. "Good luck. Hope to see you out in a cape soon."

"Me too," I said, looking at the glowing, crackling hole that floated a few feet before me. I was struck, briefly, with the crazy urge to make a run for it. He was tipsy, I could probably give him the slip, maybe even a good fight if I had to. *But then you wouldn't have a chance at this life. You'd be a runaway your entire life, an enemy of the state and the heroes, and where's the fun in that?*

Feeling the Creeper twitch beneath my sternum confirmed my decision.

I stepped through the Tri-Hole.

I landed hard in a dark room. The floor was cold and hard. Marble. I could sense people around me.

Then there was a drum roll. A dramatic musical swell. Dim lights fading up, showing us in a large round room. A proud, male voice on a loudspeaker.

"Ladies and gentlemen, let me introduce you to the world's newest supervillain team: the New Offenders!"

There was applause, artificial, for our benefit I'm sure, but I could barely hold back my excitement.

A bright light before me illuminated first the flag of Indiana, almost hovering in midair, before shining on a glass tube beneath it that held a mannequin in a stylized and very cool, professional version of my Apex Strike suit.

"From the United States, hailing from the great state of Indiana . . . APEX STRIKE!"

A spotlight hit me. I cheered and jumped as the fake applause grew louder.

Another light illuminating a swirling orange, round flag. A glass tube holding a wax figure of a terrifying, green-furred demon.

"From the Third Circle of Hell . . . HELLSPAWN!"

The light then hit a teenage boy with spiky brown hair who quickly transformed back into Odigjod. He collapsed onto the ground, laughing and clapping.

"From the British Empire's Realm of New Zealand . . . TROJAN FOX!"

The stylized silver and orange mech suit in the glass tube was as sleek and sexy as the name was awful. I was sure it'd give Firewall (Trojan Fox) a fit, but she just looked relieved. She had the beginning of a black eye, which when combined with her sparkly cocktail dress, bloodied knuckles, and new mechanical legs really had me wondering just what happened on her Archnemesis Day.

"From France . . . NEVERMORE!"

Nice.

"From Tokyo Prefecture, Japan . . . CIRCUS!"

I was indifferent toward Circus, but was sure he'd make for a fun teammate.

"From Uruguay . . . GEODE!"

Felix looked like he was ready to pass out.

That left one spot. I had a good feeling that it would be Ghost Girl. Everybody else I liked was here (well, minus Showstopper), so why wouldn't they put her on the team? She was smart, she was sexy, and even a little creepy, everything they should have wanted in a supervillain.

"And finally . . . from the United States, hailing from the great state of Ontario . . . CARNIVORE!"

He raised his arms in the air and let out a primal roar when the light hit him.

My heart sank slightly. I liked Ghost Girl; I was really hoping to improve my sex with her too. But there was something more to that, wasn't there? Something more than what happened that night. She was my friend. My best friend, probably. We may not always have agreed, but I always looked forward to my time with her.

I tried to put a good spin on it, I tried to think positively. I'd gotten what I'd wanted, and shouldn't that have been enough?

After all, I'd made it.

I was a supervillain.

#Supervillainy101: Lairs

If you want to be a supervillain, you're going to need a lair. Sure, some villains stayed mobile, but most of them were among the first captured during the War on Villainy. Lairs give you a place to take off your costume, relax, and enjoy your piles of money.

Of course, if you're going to have a lair, you need to put some thought into it.

Don't Operate Out of Your Home
The Skeleton Brothers and Crazy Cassie learned that, even with superpowers, urban apartment complexes and suburban condos (respectively) aren't secure when the Protectors start bursting through the doors, walls, ceiling, and even floors if Muck was on duty. No amount of powers, guns, or guard dogs are going to keep them out when all you've got between them and your loot is some cheap drywall.

Don't Be Too Clever
Sure, you might think camping out in an abandoned facility themed to your particular identity and power set may be fun, but whenever a clown-themed villain is on the loose, the first place the heroes will come looking is the abandoned playing card factory or amusement park.

Don't Use Security Systems You Can't Control
The Zombie King learned this one the hard way. His compound in central Nevada was well-fortified, and his army of ten thousand radioactive zombies was certainly dangerous (and radioactive). Of course, being zombies, they turned on him and his minions the moment they were unleashed (on live television, no less, when he was making a speech about how unbeatable he

was). Since this problem more or less fixed itself and was still highly radioactive, the Protectors just put a fence around his territory and said they'd take care of it when the War was over. Budget reasons kept this from ever happening, but the Great Fence of the Zombie King is an impressive tourist destination to this day.

#LessonLearned: Be sensible when choosing and setting up your lair.

#LessonLearned: If you can't or don't want to be sensible, invest in a good force field.

11

THE NEW OFFENDERS

It was only after the lights came up, revealing us to be in the lush foyer of a mansion, that someone posed the obvious question.

"Where the fuck are we?" Carnivore asked.

"Death Manor. Other side of the island," Odigjod said, touching the glass tube with his giant, wax counterpart inside, a look like awe on his tiny, terrible face. The image consultants were right to pick Hellspawn as a good villain name for him, but I'd never be able to think of him that way.

"How do you know that?" I asked.

"Odigjod did exploring on the other side of the force field in training. Curious what island was like. Saw the heroes fixing this place up."

As usual, the imp never ceased to amaze.

"We're still stuck here?" Carnivore said, running a hand through his coarse hair. "Son of a bitch."

"Would you rather see the Tower's miles of smiles?" Trojan Fox said, trying to readjust her torn dress.

143

"No," Carnivore replied.

"Then stop bitching and lighten up. We've made the team. You don't have to keep the macho bullshit up," she said, climbing one of the nearby curving staircases. "We gotta have rooms here somewhere. I'm gonna find some real clothes and see if Professor Death's lab is still intact! God knows that suit's gonna need some work!"

She was only slightly unsteady on the mechanical legs her archnemesis must have given her, but they looked close enough to the real thing that she clearly didn't mind.

Carnivore, Odigjod, and Circus soon went in search of the kitchen, leaving Nevermore, Felix, and myself.

Felix looked at his glass tube with less awe and more nervousness than Odigjod had, but his relief was plain.

"So, Geode, huh?" I said.

He shot me a faint smile. "Yes. The image consultants thought it would be best."

"It's cool. Strong. I could totally see that on a meme. Awesome name for a villain."

"It would have been better for a hero."

"But you're not a hero."

He sighed. "No, I guess I'm not. But I'm not in the Tower, either. That will have to do."

"Want to check out the mansion?"

"No," he shook his head. "I think I will find my room too and sleep. It has been a long month."

With that he climbed the curving staircase and was quickly out of sight.

"I would like to check out the mansion," Nevermore said. She was looking at a tablet, scrolling across what appeared to be a floor plan. "It looks quite luxurious."

"Where'd you get that?" I asked.

"This? I found it in a compartment beneath my costume, you should have one too." She was right. I pulled out my tablet and turned it on, getting a cheerful message welcoming me to

144

the rechristened "New Offenders Mansion," and giving a long list of rules for our stay here that all ended with threats of us being sent to the Tower or having our Creepers (which would stay in us as long as we were villains) set off. The tablet couldn't connect to the Internet (at least, not yet; Trojan Fox could probably fix that), but it did have detailed files on the mansion, our costumes, basically everything a supervillain could need.

There was no Tetris, but it was better than the tablet I had at home, so I wasn't going to complain.

Nevermore looked gorgeous, in her usual goth sort of way. Her long-sleeved shirt covered up all her tattoos, but it, and her leather skirt for that matter, were tight enough to make it not matter. Besides, I'd already seen her naked a lot, but somehow seeing her clothed seemed hotter.

I wonder if her boobs feel the same, or better, than Ghost Girl's.

That hurt to think about—more than I would have expected.

As usual, talking with Nevermore was a struggle. It wasn't as easy to find common ground like it was with Ghost Girl (*stop it*), and we both got through talking about what had happened on our Archnemesis Days quickly, though we both got a laugh when she brought up how, in the middle of their high-end shopping trip, Morningstar had proposed a threesome with her husband.

"What'd you say?"

"I said I'd think about it."

"Seriously?"

She shrugged, brushing some of that perfect black hair from her eye. "What? Morningstar is gorgeous, and have you seen Silver Shrike's calendars? Stretched out on the beach, oiled and glistening and tanned . . ."

"Well, that's not something I ever really put a lot of thought into."

"You should," she said. "I mean, not necessarily about Silver Shrike, because I know that's not what you are interested in. I just meant . . . we could die at any time. One moment we're swirling our capes around us, the next we are shot in the head by some security guard with superhero dreams. We have to live like we are dying tomorrow, and the opportunities provided to us now mean we could live a lot more excitingly than we could have before, no?"

Call it getting caught up in the moment, call it stupid, pent up frustration, or call it a switch that got flipped after having sex with Ghost Girl (*stop it!*), but I walked over to her and kissed her on the lips. She kissed me back, and though she tasted vaguely of liquor and tobacco, it was nice.

How many people have their first kiss after they've lost their virginity?

She smiled when we parted. "See, that's the spirit."

"What's your name? I mean, your real name."

She took a step back, her face not entirely pleasant, but reforming the smile quickly. "Nevermore."

"But your—"

"It's all that matters now, right?" she said. "Who we were, *what* we were, none of that matters anymore. Come on, let's explore."

And so, we ignored our problems together and explored our new lair. They must have refurbished the mansion to look a lot like it had in its heyday, because it was decked out with swinging 60s stylings, lots of bright colors, mirrors, fake potted plants, and even a couple go-go cages in the rec room (though the giant flatscreen and rack of game systems were nice additions as modernizations go).

It was when we got to the armory that we first got our hands on our new costumes, hanging in lockers.

"We should try them on," she said.

"Sure!" I agreed, though I was indifferent to wearing more clothes now.

Our lockers were on opposite sides of the row, so we could not look at each other as we changed.

"This is much better than what I used to wear," she said. "An old corset, tattered skirt, fishnet stockings and sleeves, cheap domino mask held on by string. It was what could be put together on a budget, but it made me look more like a cheap dominatrix. So glad I was not caught in it, or I'd have had to train in it."

"Sounds hot."

"It was, but was also quite uncomfortable."

"Sounds better than what I had," I said, trying to figure out just how the hell my costume was supposed to work.

"Have you ever committed a crime in high heels?"

"No," I admitted.

"Then mine was not better than yours."

Most of my new costume was a one-piece, formfitting black bodysuit with blue lightning bolt highlights made of some very flexible, very tough fabric I'd never seen up close before (Super-Spandex, most heroes call it), with a long zipper down the front and another smaller one at the crotch, which made me smile.

No more Spongeman problems!

After that, there were heavy, but comfortable boots, gloves, and odd bits of lightweight but near-indestructible plate armor for my shins, knees, wrists, shoulders, and chest. The chest plate (molded to make it look like I had awesome abs and pecs) had two crossed blue lightning bolts that stylishly formed the words *Apex Strike*. The cape, lighter and sturdier and more detachable than the one I'd made myself, clipped easily into the shoulder plates, leaving just the helmet.

I was hoping there'd be some way around it, but apparently that was a part of my image now.

The new helmet was simple, light and black, leaving my face open while sweeping back dramatically down my neck, like a samurai. Only once it was settled on my head and I started to think about how I was going to cover my face did I hear the mechanisms inside whir to life, covering my face in a dark, plastic-like visor that looked a lot like my motorcycle helmet once I got to see it in a mirror. Heads-up display information scrolled across the inside of the mask. When I thought it away, it disappeared. When I thought it back, it returned. When I thought to open and close the mask again, it did.

Cool.

I must have spent five minutes playing around with my helmet while Nevermore got dressed. It was only when I heard her tapping her shoe on the ground and clearing her throat that I remembered just where we were.

I really wished she'd chosen a better moment than me sticking my tongue out at the mirror to surprise me. Closing the visor on it hurt like hell.

Seeing her in her costume took most of the pain away (metaphorically, I mean, really my tongue still hurt like hell). They'd chosen crimson and black for her colors; black lipstick, a crimson domino mask, which each side of her cape bearing one of the colors. Her hair was bright red and long, probably a wig. Knee-high, high-heeled boots added an extra six inches to her height. The rest of her costume looked barely more concealing than anything the lingerie models I'd seen earlier in the day had worn, showing off all of Nevermore's tattoos.

She twirled around. "It covers more than you'd think. Where you see skin they have some mesh. Invisible, but very tough, probably like your suit."

I nodded.

"You like?"

I nodded again.

"How much?"

I nodded a third time.

"That was not a good answer."

I nodded a fourth time. She giggled.

"Have you ever fucked in costume before?"

I shook my head.

"Then you should try it; it's very nice!" she said, pressing her body against mine.

Though I didn't entirely believe her, once her hand found its way into my zipper, I was in no position to argue.

I was going to like life in Death Manor. I had my own, gigantic bedroom (customized to my suit's blue-and-black color scheme) with a comfortable bed, more clothes than I knew what to do with, and a TV the size of my bed back in Hacklin's Hall. We had to be on call for whenever the heroes needed us, but otherwise we could sleep as long as we wanted, do whatever we wanted, and even use Odigjod to travel wherever and whenever we wanted since they could keep an eye on us with the Creepers. The force field that had previously cut Death Island in half was gone, which now gave us access to the entire island, while the perimeter force field was strong enough that it would keep us safe and hidden from any of the non-Kayfabe superheroes. I had most of my friends, and I even finally hooked up with Nevermore, with every chance for a sequel.

In short, life was good.

We even had a half-decent cook, even if he was hardly a half-decent person. Or a half person, really.

"The secret to a good omelet is in the cheese," Carnivore said as he cooked us breakfast on our first morning in the mansion. "Too much, too many different kinds, you just create a muddy mess of cheese. Too little cheese or variety, and it loses personality."

"What if we don't want any cheese?" Trojan Fox asked, pouring herself a very, very large cup of coffee.

Carnivore snorted. "What are you, a commie?"

"The commies have cheese, too. That joke doesn't make any sense," Trojan Fox said.

He shook his head, letting out one of his yipping chuckles. "I wouldn't expect *you* to get it."

"And I wouldn't expect an omelet to have so much hair in it."

"Hey, I'm wearing a hairnet!"

"On your head; you've got fur everywhere you don't have scales!"

"Five bucks saying she kicks his behind royal," Odigjod whispered to me and Circus across the kitchen table.

"Are we talking fair fight or her in a suit, because that makes a difference," Circus said.

"Either or. She's wily," Odigjod said.

"You're on." I wasn't going to take that action, but mostly because I agreed with Odigjod.

"Do you think it's safe to have him cooking for us?" I whispered to them.

"What, think I'm gonna poison ya, *celebrity*?" Carnivore snapped, throwing back his head in another loud, yipping laugh. "First off, I got the ears of a fox so don't think I can't hear you. Second, poisoning is a bitch's way of killing, and I ain't no bitch. Thirdly, there's two things I pride myself on: killing those who got it coming, and cooking. I may not have no fancy college cooking education, but I got years behind the grill of pretty much every diner from Ottawa to Hamilton, and I know what I'm doing."

"Sounds like you and job security have only had a passing acquaintance," Trojan Fox said mockingly. He bared his teeth, but didn't take his attention away from the grill.

"Because every time some partially eaten whore turns up face down in a river, they blame the nearest gene-job. They blame the guy who was stolen out of his bed by Dr. Tongue when he was four, who was experimented on and genetically altered for a year until he was dropped back into the world as an angry killing machine. They blame the guy who's more animal than man and who the world would never give a fair shake," Carnivore said, hanging his head.

"But you did kill prostitutes. That's why you're here," Circus chimed in.

"Yeah, but only three of them! They blamed me for *eight*!"

"Three what?" Geode said, yawning as he entered the kitchen.

"Dead prostitutes that Carnivore made," I said. Geode didn't even try to hide his disgust.

"They had it coming! Everyone else was just persecuting me."

"Maybe if you didn't have a reputation for killing prostitutes that wouldn't be such an issue," Trojan Fox said.

"Look, do you want your damn omelet or not?"

"Yes, please!" Trojan Fox replied, as cheerful as I'd ever seen her.

Carnivore brought the platters of food to the table. I had to admit, even though he was an asshole, the food tasted good. I could almost feel bad for him, even; I mean, if he was telling the truth, he'd led a pretty fucked life. Any sympathy was temporary, at best, when I remembered what he did to Iron Bear and how readily he'd do the same to any of us if the notion struck him.

Plus the fact that he was still a major asshole.

All the same, our first breakfast in Death Manor was downright peaceful and courteous after we actually sat down to eat, especially when Nevermore joined us. Her smile for me was shy and almost embarrassed, but it didn't stop her from sitting next to me and joking with the group. I was a little worried after last night. She seemed a little teary and distant after we did it, but said she'd probably be up for it again sometime soon.

The peace wouldn't last (especially once Circus decided to cartoon himself again), but for that one moment, life almost felt normal.

"Attention New Offenders! Make your way to the War Room in thirty minutes for the briefing on your first assignments!" blared the loudspeakers, bringing us back to reality.

This was it. This was what we trained for.

Now don't fuck it up.

#Supervillainy101: The Whipfather

No one knows who the Whipfather was or why he did what he did, because the last thing he did before beginning his crime spree was eliminate every trace of his previous existence. All that's known about him was that he was a white male, maybe forty-two years old who wore bifocals, was dying of a brain tumor, and was obsessed with Christmas. His "Twelve Days of Christmas Rampage" made sure the holiday season around Amber City in 1983 ran red.

On the first day of Christmas, city councilman Steve Partridge was found impaled on a pear tree.

On the second day of Christmas, two trained doves pecked out the eyes of the mayor.

On the third day of Christmas, three hens strapped with grenades were released in a crowded shopping mall, killing three and wounding eighteen.

On the fourth day of Christmas, four parrots trained to shout obscenities were released in an elementary school.

On the fifth day of Christmas, the Olympic Rings from the under-construction Amber City Arena were stolen.

On the sixth day of Christmas, six geese from a local butcher's shop were found to be stuffed with severed hands.

On the seventh day of Christmas, seven swans were found drowned in Amber Park.

On the eighth day of Christmas, eight housemaids were found drowned in a milk truck.

On the ninth day of Christmas, the Whipfather kidnapped nine members of the Amber City ballet and broke their legs.

On the tenth day of Christmas, ten car bombs planted beneath cars owned by Lord Alley Locksmiths blew up, killing seventeen and wounding close to fifty.

On the eleventh day of Christmas, eleven plumbers were found impaled on pieces of PVC pipe.

On the twelfth and final day of Christmas, he captured twelve drummers from a local high school marching band, tied them up, and drove over them with a steam roller.

Reports had him laughing and shrieking "I did it!" even while he was being riddled with bullets by the Gamemaster.

#LessonLearned: There's nothing as satisfying as seeing your plan come together.

12

GREEN

When I heard the call for our first assignment, I had this image of us hurriedly pulling on our costumes and meeting in front of a giant, wall-sized monitor where our first mission would be outlined for us. We would then run out, battle the heroes, run back home, and *BOOM*! Instant celebrity.

Instead, we ambled on up to the War Room, in our pajamas, coffee in hand, and listened as Fifty-Fifty and Everywhere Man explained that our first big gig would involve robbing the First National Bank of Amber City . . . in three weeks. Until then, we had other work to do.

They did brief us via a giant, wall-sized monitor though, so I got that part right.

Before we could make our debut, we had to "establish a presence." Since the last of the supervillains went extinct in the mid-90s, back when every hero and villain was covered in guns, pouches, steroids, bad hair, and worse attitude, none of us had any idea what a modern villain was supposed to look like. The heroes had taken some opinion polls and surveys to give us an idea of what people would look for in a modern supervillain, and we had to mold ourselves to meet that ideal.

We had to be bad guys. *Check.*

We couldn't be *too* bad. According to polls, as much as villains terrified people, a large number of them wanted to be able to relate to and sympathize with us, so it's not like we could be villains *and* war criminals. We couldn't kill people or animals (especially dogs) unless we absolutely had no other choice. With the exception of Carnivore, I think we had this one as a *check*.

We had to look good as a team. Given our new professional costumes and the way our image consultants made sure each of us had a unique, bold color scheme, this was also a big *check*.

We had to be savvy in terms of social media and viral marketing. The heroes could manipulate the media enough to elevate us to rockstar status, but to keep us in the public consciousness we had to be able to promote ourselves. Since this would really define us as modern supervillains, this was where we needed the most work.

This meant that, even as we coordinated with our archnemeses on the Amber City gig, we had to practice getting comfortable talking in front of cameras and crowds. We also had to be prepared to take a lot of publicity photos for future circulation, dressed in full costume and striking poses to make us look powerful, or sexy, or scary, or whatever our designated role on the team was meant to be (I was powerful, though it took some Photoshop work to make it look like I could fly). For some of us it meant training on how to effectively use social media platforms. I had all the major sites down, while Odigjod and Carnivore needed a lesson on how to turn a computer on.

That was the easy stuff we could do from Death Island. The viral stuff . . . that meant getting out in the field.

The heroes said that people needed to fear us before they even saw us, since most of us weren't that well known outside our home countries, if at all, so we were given assignments to raise our individual awareness before we broke out as a team. I was exempted from this because everybody knew Apex Strike, so I saw the others off as Odigjod teleported them around the world, committing petty crimes, making sure they were *just barely* caught by security cameras, and leaving cryptic messages hinting at a new age of villainy. Circus was really good at these, especially the giant, glowing THE OFFENDERS LIVE! he scrawled across the south face of the Palace of the Soviets (even though I'm told his Cyrillic sucked).

Crazy as it sounded, it worked. None of us were seen clearly, but supervillainy started to trend like crazy. News from around the world was suddenly full of talking heads wondering if this was all some elaborate hoax, or if the villains had truly returned. There was so much fear and speculation, so little hard news, so many replays of my "battle" with Icicle Man.

It was awesome. Nobody saw us, yet we were changing the world.

On game day, they'd told us to suit up and gather in the mansion's "Green Room," so named for the grassy coating that covered every square inch of wall. It was dark and small, but had comfortable chairs to spare, a flat screen to kill some time, and the healing pods.

According to Adam (Helios, but I can call him Adam), they were some of Professor Death's finest genetic mutations. There were ten of them, growing out of the walls. Bulbous, pulsating seed pods the size of small cars, each covered in thick blue veins, each with a quivering, glistening slit down the middle that looked far too much like a pussy for comfort. He said that a few hours in one of them would heal pretty much any wound or sickness shy of being killed. While I hoped I'd never have to see the inside of one of them, I knew the odds were that I would.

And somehow, they paled in comparison to what that damn light did to me.

It was a simple bulb, jutting out of the wall right above the flat screen. At the moment it was red. But when it was show time, it would turn green.

Until then, we had to wait, which meant listening to Trojan Fox continue working on the unauthorized alterations to her suit (the war paint she'd put on her helmet's face to reflect her mother's Maori heritage was pretty awesome, though), Carnivore occasionally mauling Circus when he cheated at cards (which was often), or watching TV.

Odigjod and I chose TV, though his choice of reality shows left something to be desired.

"I do not understand this family. They are famous, why?" Odigjod griped.

"Because they're famous."

"But how did they getting famous?"

"Because they're rich, I think."

"But how did they—"

"The stepdad used to be a reservist for the Protectors, until he blew out his knee. He got enough sponsors in the meantime though to be pretty rich."

"But the daughters, the wifes?"

"Not super, no. Unless you count leaking sex tapes a power. Why do you watch if all you do is bag on it?"

Odigjod shrugged. "Trying to figure out which circle they go to when they die, tell some cousins they might getting an famous face or two."

"Well, you might too, right?"

"Not thinking so. Only sin they not showing is gluttony," Odigjod sighed.

"Eating disorders must be hell for your circle."

Odigjod waggled his hand back and forth. "Sometimes my parents fear for jobs, but your American companies and their corn syrup help."

"Well, glad to hear we're doing our part."

Geode stopped pacing under the TV.

"Can I say something?" he said.

This was as good an excuse as any to mute the TV.

"Look . . . I know we don't always get along. I know some of us maybe even hate each other—"

"Maybe?" Carnivore interrupted, a nonplussed Circus impaled on his claws. They'd have continued fighting if Trojan Fox hadn't trained her suit's weapons on them.

"Thanks," Geode said, smiling. "I just wanted to say, I know we got our differences, but we're in this together. We're all we've got, I think. The superheroes . . ."

He looked like he wanted to say more, but thought better of it. ". . . I just want to say, I think we're really the only people we can truly depend on, and that even if you don't like me very much, I will protect you all."

Carnivore sat up, the snarl on his face turning to a vague smile. "Awww, how sweet. We love you too, babykins . . ."

His smile curled into a yipping laugh, and for some insane reason we all found it hard not to join in, maybe, just maybe, because there was something about laughing all at once that made us feel like a team, even for just this moment.

So, of course, that's when the light went green.

"IT'S TIME! SUIT UP!" I yelped, too loud, trying to keep the nerves from coming back entirely. Odigjod and Geode transformed into the larger, hulking, monstrous forms our image consultants had devised for them. Carnivore roared, pounding on his chest. Trojan Fox closed the last few plates of her suit.

I didn't have anything cool to do like them, but I did close my visor and strike a pose so I wouldn't be left out.

Odigjod placed one of his massive, shaggy hands on my shoulder. Though he looked like a big, goofy Muppet, the way his neon green fur wriggled like worms still unsettled me.

"Now?" he asked.

I didn't want to go. I wanted to put this off as long as possible. I wanted to get over this stage fright that wouldn't leave. I didn't want to embarrass myself. I didn't want to go to the Tower. I wanted a lot of things, but going now wasn't one of them and it wouldn't be—

We disappeared in a puff of smoke. Seconds later, I fell six feet to the ground in the middle of a busy street. I would have landed on my knees, hard, but the miniature anti-grav generators they'd built into my shin pads (the same kind they put into all girls' tops and high heels to keep them looking hot and functional all at once) helped me land, and get back to my feet, looking cool and smooth.

Buildings towered all around me, some old, some modern, some so tall they blotted out the sun. Cars, buses, and taxis drove around me, honking, while hundreds of people on the sidewalks went about their daily lives, unaware that everything was about to change.

Welcome to Amber City.

I had to be the first. Everyone knew me, and I would look like the leader if I was first, especially if the team started appearing around me one at a time. I wanted to wait for them to show before doing anything, but I knew that wasn't part of the plan.

Focus.

With arms raised and cape billowing behind me, I brought down several streetlights and signals, smashing them into cars. The hundreds of people walking the streets now noticed me, and all screamed at once.

We weren't supposed to kill anyone, and we weren't supposed to hurt them all that badly, so I really had to hold back my focus, but I think I made a good show of it. I stomped on the ground, sending out a wave of focus that blew out tires for a block, and waved at a few nearby office buildings, shattering all their windows.

People ran, screaming my name in terror. More importantly, they pulled out their cell phones to get this on video. Some braver, or at least stupider, souls even tried for selfies with me in frame.

Odigjod soon brought in Geode, who made a fine entrance by doubling his crystalline size and ripping a bus in half, followed by Carnivore, who chased after people and used his powerful claws to rip into cars as if they were made of tissue paper. Trojan Fox, Nevermore, and Circus, who started jumping around on a cartoony, powerful, and very destructive pogo stick, came right after, leaving Odigjod (Hellspawn) the last to make an official entrance.

I climbed on top of a ruined bus half, sending enough focus behind me to make my cape look dramatic.

Time to remember my speech.

I turned up the volume from my helmet's speakers, turning it into a bullhorn that people would be able to hear from blocks away.

"CITIZENS OF THE WORLD, PAY ATTENTION! THE AGE OF THE SUPERHERO IS AT AN END! TOO LONG YOU HAVE LIVED IN COMPLACENCY WITH THEIR PROTECTION, AND NOW YOU WILL PAY FOR IT! WE ARE THE NEW OFFENDERS! WE ARE VILLAINY REBORN, AND NONE OF YOU ARE SAFE!"

A familiar voice came in my ear. "Nice job. Very dramatic."

"THANKS!"

"Cut the loudspeakers, Aidan."

"Sorry, Adam."

"It happens. Make your way to the bank. We'll be there in three."

"You got it."

"And Aidan?"

"Yeah?"

"It's Helios when we're in costume."

"Got it. Sorry." I'd gotten used to being on a first name basis with him, but had to remember we were on the job now, so I had to keep in character.

I rushed to join the rest of the team when I heard gunshots. Cops. They weren't part of the plan. Fear gripped me. *Our suits were bulletproof, right?* Nevermore projected a brick wall in front of the cops, deflecting their bullets while Trojan Fox cut their guns to pieces with her lasers. *All right, back on track.*

With one strike from his massive right arm, Geode ripped open the front of the bank. Beams of hellfire and lasers from Odigjod and Trojan Fox opened up the vault, leaving Circus and the giant cartoon sack (with a oversized dollar sign on the front) he'd created to clear out the cash. I stepped up on an abandoned mailbox to give another speech, while Geode, Carnivore, and Nevermore kept the crowd in check (which, per their assigned personas, meant Geode stayed silent and intimidating, Carnivore paced around snapping and yipping, and Nevermore kissed a guard before punching him out). It was going like clockwork.

"We're gonna be there in thirty. You loaded that playlist I gave you into your suit, right?" Helios asked.

"Yeah," I said again.

"Cue up 'Ballroom Blitz' by the Sweet and press play when you throw the mailbox. I know it's before your time, but it'll add a lot to the fight. I'm gonna do the same."

"Will do."

"And Apex?"

"Yeah?"

"Have fun."

I smiled as I cued up the song. "Yeah."

A Tri-Hole opened in the middle of the bank, sparkling and green. As we were taught, we struck dramatic poses, ready for battle. *That's right everyone, just keep taking pictures.*

Even though I was still afraid, I was smiling under my visor and ready to put on a show.

Helios came out first, glorious and golden in his full costume, along with the rest of the archnemeses. We traded our scripted banter back and forth, him calling for our surrender, me telling him to fuck off, but with PG-13 words so our battle could be shown on the evening news. He gave us one last chance to surrender. Per the script, I flung some debris at him, and I started the song.

He was right, it did add to the fight.

Actually, it was about the only fun I had. I spent so much time focusing on the choreography, so many times trying not to miss a punch or a demonstration of my powers, that I couldn't really get lost in the moment. Oh sure, I could improvise some, like when I needed to catch my breath and took a few human shields when our battle spilled out onto the street, but for the most part I had to stick to the script.

There were two main reasons for this:

1. Because the scripted battle would look cool as hell.
2. Following the script would keep us from getting really hurt.

Number two was the real important one. Our suits were designed to absorb a lot of abuse so we wouldn't have to, but they could only do so much. When you're flung to the ground by a telekinetic superhero, no amount of padding and rolling and telekinetic shielding is going to keep you from getting bruised. Or tasting blood. Or hearing the kind of pop in your knee that sends fire up your spine and makes you cry out like a little girl.

Looks like you'll have to spend some time in one of the healing pods after all.

I could protect myself with my powers, some, but not like Helios. He had to act more than I did whenever I hit him with my powers, or flung a piece of debris at his face. He was in better shape, so he didn't need to constantly find excuses to catch his breath, but I held to the script. I didn't break character.

I was a good villain.

And like any good villain, I knew when to call our retreat.

Some of the heroes had herded civilians beneath the marquee of an old theatre, keeping them out of harm's way. We knew this to be our cue to end the fight and get out of here.

I turned my outer speakers on full blast. "YOU WILL REGRET THIS, HELIOS!"

"As you will regret KILLING MY FRIEND!" he roared back, really selling the line as he shot energy beams from his hands to split the street in front of me. I rolled out of the way—as we'd planned—and focused on the marquee. It collapsed on the screaming people.

"NOW, HELIOS, YOU CAN LET US GO . . . OR LET THEM DIE!!!"

The look on his face was pained, with maybe the slightest bit of overacting so people further away could see. Still, he flew to help the trapped citizens. If I were watching this on TV, I'd wonder why; the marquee was cheap wood and plaster and most of the people could have freed themselves if they wanted to, but it was expected of him as a hero.

I turned the speakers off. "Odigjod, get us out of here."

"Understood." He appeared and disappeared in several puffs of smoke, taking Circus, Nevermore, Trojan Fox, and Geode with him. I was setting up for my grand finale, leveling a nearby, ancient tenement that the Protectors said I could destroy to my heart's content, when I heard Carnivore cry out in pain. I turned around to see that a silver arrow had pierced his chest. Another soon erupted from his stomach. Silver Shrike and Morningstar followed the arrows by violently beating him to the ground, soon joined by Fifty-Fifty and Extreme Man. They tied him up and haloed him and almost made me forget to destroy the tenement in my shock.

This wasn't part of the script.

I kept up my end. I focused on the building as people ran out, screaming. Odigjod appeared, grabbed my shoulder, and in a flash I was back in the Green Room.

The others were cheering and out of breath, ditching pieces of costume as they celebrated our first success. I removed my helmet and tried not to look too confused.

Nevermore grabbed me by the shoulders and planted a hot, wet kiss on my mouth. She tasted of lip balm and blood, but I suddenly didn't mind so much.

"When this is done, let's go to my room and fuck. God, villainy makes me so horny," she whispered, chewing on my ear until it actually started to hurt.

Odigjod had disappeared right after dropping me off, and he was gone for a good minute before returning and transforming back to his usual, small self.

"Carnivore?" I asked.

He shook his head. "Went to rescue him, but the heroes wouldn't let me get close enough and said to leave; that Carnivore was now their prisoner."

I was glad, but not as glad as I thought I'd be. It must have been shock, but I'd have to get over it. They must have had their reasons for not telling us they were going to capture Carnivore, and I was sure they would fill us in.

"Hey guys," Circus said, opening his massive sack of money, "who wants to get drunk, roll around naked in forty million dollars cash, and watch how much ass we kicked on YouTube?"

Doing that with Circus, no way. The same with Nevermore . . .

"Can I borrow some of it first?" I asked.

#Supervillainy101: The Face Thief

The Face Thief was one of the earliest members of the Gamemaster's Rogues' Gallery, and though his career was never as notable as Bad Bug's, his ability to transform himself into anyone he'd ever touched made him a successful art thief and a recurrent thorn in the Gamemaster's side. However, when remembered in the history books, the Face Thief's embarrassing end is often given more attention than his decades-long career in villainy.

Paranoid and antisocial in his later years after a few betrayals by underlings and the rise of the Protectors, he'd become reclusive and violent, rarely leaving his lair so he could keep a constant watch on his vast collection of art, which he carefully kept in crates in a high-tech, hermetically sealed vault, away from prying eyes and thieving hands. After a while he stopped leaving his house at all, and even the Gamemaster forgot about him with how busy the War on Villainy had kept him.

After his numerous battles with the Gamemaster, it wasn't the Protectors who uncovered his hidden lair, but the bank. After the water and electricity had been shut off, a repossession team entered the Face Thief's mansion. His mummified body was found locked in his vault, pinned under a crate that had fallen on him. All evidence pointed to him having bled to death after trying to eat his left hand.

#LessonLearned: What good is being a villain if you can't enjoy the spoils of villainy?

13

DRUMMERS & DRAGONS

After a few hours of sitting in a healing pod for my cuts, bruises, and knee, I wouldn't have thought I was in need of any more R&R time, but when Adam announced that I looked tense and offered a day at a spa, I wasn't going to turn him down.

Madame Kedist'olara's was not quite what you'd expected in a celebrity day spa. I mean, it was in Hollywood, it did have a lot of fruity iced drinks and a few hours there did cost more than a year at a half-decent community college, but its design as a traditional Lemurian bathhouse pretty much ended the similarities.

It had to be more than a hundred degrees inside, with near complete humidity. The carved stone in the walls made it look like we were walking through a cave, and the walls were dripping with water. The spa treatments involved a lot of heavy massages, being rubbed down in fragrant oils, and having layers of dead skin and body hair scraped away with glowing Lemurian daggers. According to Adam, these ancient techniques were designed by scalefaces to make shedding their skin a social event, and were considered quite trendy.

I just wanted to make it through the day with some of my skin still intact.

The scaleface women massaging us wore nothing but thin satin sashes tied around their waists, which would have been pretty hot if they had breasts, or hips, or any definable curves.

It was like being massaged by freakishly strong Olympic gymnasts covered in scales. *Fucking non-mammalian biology.*

I yelped in pain when mine started working on my lower back.

"I keep telling you to relax," Adam said from the massage table across from me.

"I thought I was relaxed."

"Not," my masseuse said.

"It shouldn't be this bad," Adam said.

"Well I'm hot and missing skin and sore and, and—"

No, I wouldn't go that far.

"And what?" he asked.

"It's nothing."

"No, really, what's on your mind?" Adam asked, turning over. His towel fell away, and I had to turn my head to avoid seeing his superhero cock.

I didn't want to tell him what was bothering me. We'd grown friendly in the weeks we'd been archnemeses. Adam was a better friend than I ever had back home, and was almost as good as some of the others I'd met on Death Island. Better even, in ways that only being famous could improve.

"Is it safe to talk, with them here?" I asked.

"Of course it is. They barely speak a lick of English and owe their citizenship and paychecks to Crystal Skull. You're not gonna say anything, are you, love?" Adam asked, trailing a hand up his masseuse's side.

"Not," she said, digging her hands into his chest and abs.

"Fine," I said, letting the words spill out. "Just what the hell happened with Carnivore? I mean, I hate the guy, but why did you capture him and not tell us? Was that always part of the plan or was that just something that came up? And, and . . . why are you laughing?"

"Because you babble when you're nervous, and if you're so nervous that you're gonna continue to babble, then we're gonna have to work harder to get you to relax," he said, then muttering something quickly in Lemurian. My masseuse then flipped me onto my back and pulled my towel away. She bent down, putting her head between my thighs.

"Not struggle," she said, getting me hard with a flick of her forked tongue.

"She's right, you don't want to fuck around with all those teeth. But those lips are a lot softer than they look."

That wasn't exactly comforting. She wasn't beautiful in any way, and those rows of many small, pointed reptilian teeth did look frightening, but when she took me in her mouth, all my concerns seemed to fade away.

He was right, her lips were a lot softer than they looked.

His masseuse then did the same. I had a crazy, fleeting thought I had to get out: "Does your, oh God, does Adriana know?"

Adam closed his eyes, but didn't falter. "She knows that a man has needs, and that I'm a man, so she's okay. But she's faithful to me, God love her. So, about Carnivore . . ."

"Can't we talk about that later?" I asked, running my hand through the short blue feathers that grew at the base of my masseuse's skull and trailed down her spine.

"There's never any time like the present," Adam said. "You ever been in a band? No, of course not, you'd have gotten laid earlier. Every band member plays a specific part. You got your front-man lead singer, you got the nerd on the keys, you got the hot girl singing backup and occasionally hitting a tambourine but mostly just standing there looking hot. Then you got your drummer. The drummer's the wild man, the one who lives hard and dies of a drug overdose after a year or two, then is immediately replaced by another drummer who'll repeat the process. If you were in a band, Carnivore would be your drummer."

Everything went blank for a moment as the scaleface finished me off, slurping with her forked tongue before cleaning the rest with a towel. Adam was nice enough to let me finish before continuing. He wasn't in as big a hurry to finish.

"You need drummers because they make you look like bad guys. We need you to have drummers because we wouldn't look good if we let you *all* get away. We stop you, we capture one of the real sick, scary villains people wouldn't want on the street, the crowd goes wild, and everybody goes home happy."

"But couldn't you have at least told us first? I mean, what if we'd been so surprised something bad had happened?"

"You guys still need to work on your acting, so we thought this time it would help to get an honest reaction. Next time we rotate a drummer in, you'll know what to expect."

"Thanks, I guess."

"Look, you did great out there. I'm sorry we didn't keep you in the loop the whole way, but from now on, we'll tell you everything."

"You really think I did great out there?"

"Are you kidding? The people feared you almost as much as they loved me for wailing on you. You're a media darling. If it weren't for keeping our secrets, these two lovely ladies would be singing songs to their people tonight about how they had the honor of pleasuring the greatest hero and the greatest villain in America, isn't that right?" he said. Though his was still busy, mine confirmed his point.

"So, feeling any more relaxed?"

"More, yeah. Getting better every minute actually," I said, meaning every word. Now that I knew that what happened to Carnivore was all part of the show, my worries started to fade away. They would take away all the real bad guys, while the rest of us would remain the core. It made perfect sense.

"Good, because tonight'll be a lot more fun if you're relaxed."

"Oh yeah?" I said, sipping from an ice-cold bottle of water my masseuse brought from a nearby refrigerator.

"Yeah. Because tonight, we're gonna party like superheroes!"

I had to take a quick trip back to Death Island to clean up (gingerly, since I was missing more skin than I'd started the day with) and get dressed. The others were mostly ready by the time I arrived. Circus and Trojan Fox had dummied up some fake IDs for us, in case they were needed, but I didn't think they would be. Trojan Fox and Geode were over twenty-one, Nevermore and I could pass with a little work, and Odigjod and Circus could change their appearance at will.

Besides, we had the heroes with us.

We waited for their call in the rec room, not having the appearance of a typical group that would normally go clubbing. Geode was dressed and groomed so well that I was sure he'd break a lot of girls' and guys' hearts tonight. Trojan Fox looked disgruntled, in a short dress I'm sure Nevermore insisted she wear. Nevermore looked amazing, though with all of her tattoos pulled back into an ornate (and very busy) tramp stamp, I barely recognized her with all the skin showing. She looked used to the club scene. Circus and Odigjod, both in human form, looked like kids about to knock over a candy store. Come to think of it, I probably did too.

We'd spent so much time working that it was finally time for us to enjoy the fruits of our labor.

The Tri-Hole the heroes sent put us in the back of an empty delivery truck. Once we were all through, the door at the back of the truck opened. A portly, middle-aged man whose head was replaced by a clear crystal skull with glowing red eyes stood there. I'm sure if he'd been able to, he would have been smiling.

"Ladies and gentlemen!" Crystal Skull said theatrically, his booming, Spanish-accented voice almost covering the heavy clicking sound his jaw made. "Welcome to my club!"

Excitement flowed through us all. I'm sure some of them had hoped—I know I did—that we'd be going here, but I had no serious expectations that we'd actually be going *here*.

Stepping out of the van, we all looked up and smiled. Nevermore squealed, wrapped her arms around Trojan Fox, and kissed her on the cheek. For her part, even Trojan Fox looked impressed.

The large neon sign before us read MODESTO'S KEEP. The actual club floated about thirty feet off the ground, probably using the same kind of anti-grav generator that kept *The Pearl* afloat. A series of spiral steel stairways connected it to the ground, while searchlights beneath it lit the club up as bright as day, even though the sky above us was black (well, as black as the sky above Los Angeles can get at night, which isn't all that black). A small mob of paparazzi stood by each stairway, some of them fighting with security when they saw a limo pull up. A line of people looking to get in stretched more than a block, many wearing capes and masks in fashion inspired by the heroes.

If they only knew what it was like to wear the real thing.

Crystal Skull led us to the VIP entrance, a Tri-Hole set in an elaborate iron frame on the ground and into the club proper.

It was everything I'd ever imagined. Booming music, darkness broken up by swirling colored lights. Beautiful, famous people grinding and dancing, passing drinks and drugs around. Since the club was owned by an ex-hero, there were plenty of supers employed to keep the theme going: scantily clad girls in cages changing their skin colors with the beat of the music, a telekinetic bartender putting on a show as he mixed six drinks at once in midair, balls of colored light forming and floating lazily from the chest of the DJ.

"It's like heaven," I said.

"More like the Gates of Home," Odigjod said wistfully.

"Come on, guys, we've earned this," I said, leading the way.

There was plenty of cash to go around after the Amber City job. We had a VIP room all to ourselves, so after purchasing a couple bottles of champagne and some shots, we hit the dance floor. I danced with Nevermore for a while, and even Trojan Fox (though her new legs were top notch, she wasn't a very good dancer).

A lot of the heroes there were part of Kayfabe, so I got to hang out and dance with most of them. True to what Ghost Girl (*dammit*) said, Shooting Star propositioned me after only one dance, nibbling on my ear and rubbing her hand against the front of my pants. I told her I'd think about it before making her jealous by moving on to dance with another hero. When Adam and Adriana showed up, they introduced me around to a number of their friends. Actors, athletes, even people just famous for being famous, like Erika Edge, professional heiress to the Edge Industries fortune. And to my surprise, she wasn't nearly as much a blonde bimbo as she appeared on TV (well, not so much a bimbo, but she was every bit as blonde).

It was hard to fully grasp the fact that I was really Apex Strike, the world's most famous supervillain. But I managed as best I could, every so often passing a sly wink to Adam.

After a few drinks my head began to swim, and the drugs that everyone was passing around started to look good. Pot, E, coke (Adam's favorite), a bunch of pills I couldn't identify, even this blue powder called "Montage" that people would sometimes pinch into their eyes. The others were already digging into these. Aside from taking a few hits off a joint, I didn't really experiment with that stuff. Though I was tempted, too many old PSAs swam through my head.

After I don't know how many hours of this, I had to take a break at the bar, looking at the parade of flesh and fame before me and considering how lucky I was.

This shouldn't have been my life. I should've been back home, trying to cram for one test or another, filling out college applications. Maybe Dad would have finally forced me to get a weekend job, or Mom would have given in and talked him into getting me a used car. There were a lot of maybes with that life, but one thing was for sure: if I hadn't put on the cape and accidentally killed Icicle Man, I would still be a nobody.

Now I had power. I had more money than I could ever spend. I was famous.

I had *everything*.

Well, *almost* everything, but that *almost* could still be remedied.

Everybody else had paired up nicely. Trojan Fox danced to a slow song with her archnemesis, Photon, looking every bit the reject from a 90s boy band; Geode was making out with some basketball player; Circus somehow seemed to have stolen the attention of one of the cocktail waitresses; and even Odigjod sat at a table chatting up Erika Edge.

Nevermore, however, was nowhere to be seen, but Circus told me he'd seen her go up to the VIP room. With all the excitement going on, I was craving her . . . I had to have her right now.

Sex with us wasn't a regular thing, but when we did it, it was a lot of fun. I was learning to go longer each time, and she'd stopped hurting me after the first couple times. The way she sometimes got teary and wound up asking me how good she was afterwards was confusing, but it was still sex (inventive too, damn she had an imagination), and she was so hot I wasn't going to complain.

I walked upstairs to our VIP room, found the door closed. It was too loud to knock, so I just opened it.

Nevermore was in there, all right, moaning and pinned to a wall by Silver Shrike, his pants around his ankles as he impaled her differently from how he'd impaled Carnivore.

"FUCK . . . ME . . . SUPER . . . HERO!" she cried out as he pounded her.

Morningstar, his wife and Nevermore's archnemesis, sat on one of the couches nearby, one hand moving vigorously under her skirt, the other holding up her phone to record the scene.

I slammed the door. I felt like I was going to be sick—or explode—it was hard to tell the difference. I realized I'd crushed the door handle without thinking, and stormed down the hall.

Maybe you should go back. If this were like porn, they'd let you join. God knows Morningstar looked in the mood, and that is how things work in the cape and mask world, right?

I stormed down the hall, anger mixing with betrayal as I tried to get the image of them out of my head. *Fine, if that's what she wants to do, two can play at that game . . .*

Shooting Star was still out on the dance floor. I found her and pulled her towards me, kissing her deeply. Following her lead from earlier, I reached under her almost non-existent skirt and found her not to be wearing panties. The way she cooed let me know I was doing something right.

"You have a VIP room?" I asked.

She nodded, not seeming to mind how clumsy my fingers were.

"Let's go," I said.

She nodded again, leading on. Her VIP room was smaller than ours, but just as plush. After we made out for a few minutes, she pulled a small vial of blue powder from her purse.

"Do this first," she said, taking a pinch of it and dropping it in her eyes.

"Montage?"

"It's good stuff, my word . . . it makes time speed up, slow down, only lets you see the good times, doesn't let anything feel bad . . ."

She didn't need another word to sell me on it. I took a pinch and dropped it directly into my eye. It dissolved quickly, burning like shampoo dripping into your eyes, and immediately transformed my entire whole world into a vague shade of blue. I almost didn't think it was working until I realized that the music had slowed to a crawl. Shooting Star sauntered over to me, faintly glowing, dropping her top to the floor as she pushed me to the couch.

Then time skipped. She was riding me, screaming out words no good Christian girl like her should know as I slid in and out of her. Every nerve in my body felt like it was being pleasured.

Another time skip. I was naked, she was dressed and running out of the room, telling me to stay put. I didn't know why, until she came back with her partner, Comet Girl.

I could get used to this.

#Supervillain101: Addict Man

Nobody knows the true origin of the supervillain Addict Man, since by his very nature he was unreliable, but most seem to accept his usual story that some experimental chemicals at a meth lab exploded all over him, granting him superpowers.

On his own, he was just an ordinary junkie, but under the influence of different drugs he could unlock special abilities. Steroids gave him superstrength, meth gave him super speed, crack could make him burst into flames without killing him, LSD allowed him to alter the world around him in a number of bizarre and disturbing ways . . . I could go on, but you get the idea. He was hardly the most dangerous supervillain of the War on Villainy, but his low profile and ability to blend into homeless communities helped him elude the Protectors for a lot longer than he should have.

In the end, his powers were his ultimate downfall. While the various drugs he ingested, shot up, and snorted gave him powers, he still felt all the side effects that came along with them, often bungling the easiest jobs because he was too wasted. It made him a particularly unambitious villain, knocking over liquor and grocery stores instead of banks, making out with a few hundred dollars at most on a good day. He was ultimately captured by Locust Man in Denver, not in some epic struggle of wills, but with a needle in his arm and enough heroin in his blood to land him in a permanent vegetative state.

#LessonLearned: Drugs and superpowers don't mix.

14

MONTAGE

I don't remember a lot of the next months, but I do remember getting into a pretty easy routine.

Get up, shower, eat, take some pills to open my eyes, see if we have work that day, do it if we do, don't if we don't. Travel some. Work out some. Try to get laid. Sometimes it works, sometimes it doesn't. It's night somewhere in the world. Teleport over. Get drunk, get wasted, try to get laid again, go home, sleep, rinse and repeat.

We'd all gotten pretty good at it, and thanks to a steady supply of Montage, I didn't even have to see anything that might make me feel bad.

Through the haze, there were jobs I do remember. Fights with the Protectors, "Vehicle" by the Ides of March blaring over my suit's sound system as if on a loop. There were Black Cape Jobs; the kinds of jobs where they didn't fight us, evil for the sake of evil because we had to sometimes win in order for people to fear us. Those were the easiest. Empty out a diamond mine in a developing nation here, break up a group of protestors there, hospitalize some pesky reporters and environmentalists . . . stuff like that. Sometimes we'd get hurt, and those days sucked, but pop some painkillers and uppers and spend some time in a healing pod and you begin to forget what being hurt meant.

We went through drummers pretty quick. Moon Warrior and Biocide only lasted a mission each, same with that girl who could turn into a panther. The Zone Runner lasted a bit longer, even though to this day I still can't quite tell you what zone running is. The longest-lasting drummer was a girl from Thailand called Backbreaker, but after two Black Cape Jobs and two hero fights, she was gone. Sometimes, when my head was clear and I was moderately sober, I hoped to see Showstopper, or Spasm, or Ghost Girl rotate in as a drummer, but then realizing what that meant, I would make myself wish to never see them again.

Thankfully those moments of clarity were few and far between. Partying all night and a whole lot of Montage let us keep the good times rolling. We clubbed in Hollywood and Amber City, Paris and Tokyo, London and Moscow. Wherever there were capes and parties to be found, we were there.

I hooked up with a lot of heroes during this time. Most of them were in Project Kayfabe, like Shooting Star, Comet Girl, Airburst, and Jenny Blade, but with some of their help I was even able to hook up with a couple who *weren't* in on it, like Dark Corner and Sidewinder. I got selfies of myself with most of them naked, and even some signed trading cards. It got to be a pretty cool collection, one I looked forward to expanding. There were times I felt like showing it off to Nevermore to show her I didn't need her anymore . . . and maybe I did, but it's kind of hard to remember the down times while you're on Montage, or if those memories I had of doing her again were really memories or just dreams or fantasies (*really hoping me tweeting that dick pic was just a dream*).

Montage does that to you.

The job I remember best, before everything started to clear again, was the last one. We were knocking over a museum somewhere, maybe in Berlin, maybe in Bombay, it's hard to remember. All I remember is that it started with a B.

Anyway, we were all pretty strung out on little sleep and liquor and uppers and teleportation-lag, and were definitely not at our best. Nevermore was home sick with the flu (read: hangover), so it was up to the five of us plus whatever drummer we had at the time. I couldn't tell you if they were a guy or a girl, but they threw lightning, I think, or maybe they could walk through walls, I forget.

Like clockwork, in came our archnemeses. It was harder to fight them than usual. My stomach kept roiling and my head would not stop pounding. Remembering the choreography was impossible. Our attacks were clumsy, Trojan Fox accidentally flew through a building, Geode bent over vomiting so much and so hard that he caved in the roof of a parked car. I barely remembered half my lines.

We weren't having fun.

Somewhere in my ear, I heard Helios and Fifty-Fifty simultaneously call out an early abort code. They sounded pissed, but I really didn't care. I was just glad to get out of there early. Odigjod started taking everyone out. Circus was toying around with some hostages, being a real prick, when he suddenly started foaming at the mouth, collapsing to the ground in a seizure that stripped him of his cartoon form. A couple of the heroes stood around him, looking back and forth to each other like they didn't know what to do.

Before they could force me to help, Odigjod took me home.

It was just me, Odigjod, Trojan Fox, and Geode in the Green Room after that, stripping off our costumes.

Somewhere, faintly I knew we were in trouble, but I was beyond caring by that point.

All I cared about was finding a place to puke. After that, I started to feel better.

#Supervillainy101: Nick Stone

Efforts at creating prisons for supervillains were attempted before the Tower, but most of them were abysmal failures. They were generally incapable of containing supers and were prone to constant breakouts. That was why, once the War on Villainy had been declared, the Gamemaster, ATHENA, Caveman, and a few of the Protectors' other best technical minds got together and constructed the Tower to be the greatest and most inescapable prison ever created. Nobody knows where it is, or what it's like on the inside, and unless you've got a really good lawyer, you're not even gonna get a trial (not that if you *do* get a trial will you get out, as nobody has ever before).

Unless, maybe, you're Nick Stone.

The man the media would dub Nick Stone (because his skin appeared to be made of stone and he had a prominent nick in his forehead) was discovered in 1986, wandering the Atacama Desert between Chile and Bolivia. He was naked, save for a few torn wires that led to probes buried deep in his stony flesh. Aside from being malnourished, dehydrated, and severely sun bleached, he bore multiple scars that indicated invasive medical experimentation and was covered in a faint trace of a powerful toxin authorities were unable to identify. When interviewed on his hospital bed, he claimed, in thick Danish, to have escaped from the Tower and its "miles and miles of smiles." It was all he said, babbling and raving, and it was all he would say until he was healthy enough to jump to his death from his hospital room window.

He was never identified, and the Protectors vehemently denied that he escaped from the Tower, so odds are we'll never know who he really was. Maybe he really was an escapee, or maybe the conspiracy theorists are right and he was planted by the heroes to give everyone a reason to fear the Tower.

Either way, would you want to chance it?

#LessonLearned: Fear the Tower.

MILES AND MILES OF
SMILES . . .

When I wasn't awake, or having the weird, scary dreams that Montage binges bring, I was in the black.

The black was where nothing could bother me. Sure, the dreams made their way in sometimes, but they were gone quick and forgotten even quicker. Only the outside world could break the black, and that was always awful for a moment, but there were things I could always take for that.

They'd left me in the black a lot longer than usual this time. No alarms. No training. No urgent missions. It was nice, hiding in the black. I knew the outside world was there. I could hear some voices and some things moving, sometimes far away (usually far away) but sometimes close, but nothing liable to take me out of it. Not until . . .

Aidan.

Not now.

No, now, wake up.

Fuck off. In the black.

Have it your way.

There was wet and cold over my body, but it wasn't enough. There was too much black. The wet and cold couldn't make me leave. I would fight it. I would—

BLAM!

The pitcher of water that'd been poured on me wasn't enough to wake me from the black, but firing a gun into my bedroom ceiling worked perfectly.

Everything was blurry, but I knew I was in bed. Naked, face down. Blearily, I pulled myself up. There was a puddle of vomit nearby, stinking and stinging even though it was dry. Another on the pillow beside me, a different color. *Whose is that?* Half a moldy ham sandwich was stuck to my chest. The other half was on my crotch. I threw them both to the floor.

"You're fuckin' pitiful, you know that?" I knew that voice. I didn't want to hear it. Not with my head like this.

"I'm not pitiful. I'm *Apex Strike*," I said. My mouth felt like death. My stomach roiled, and I suddenly realized that the bed smelled of piss. *How long was I out?*

"You can be both," she said.

I reached for the nightstand. Painkillers. Stronger stuff. Stuff to clear my head. Anything. I had a good collection sitting there normally, but not now.

"We cleared all your stashes out," she said. "Needed all your pretty little heads clear today."

A dull rage flared within me, followed by a need I'd never been conscious of before. *Today's gonna hurt, but you can get more when you're free.*

I turned to face her, wiping crusted mustard from my chest. I was in a foul mood and I wanted to share it. "Blackjack, you can be a real cunt sometimes."

She laughed. "I've been called worse by better *and* worse folk than you. Wanna know what I did to them?"

"Just lemme alone, all right? I'm hungover, I'm hungry, I'm—"

In the blink of the eye she was standing, a revolver in her hand and the boom of a gunshot filling my room. I could feel the wind of the shot passing right between my thighs, hear the slap as it hit the bed half an inch beneath my dick.

"JESUS, FUCK!"

She laughed.

I'd have pissed myself if I hadn't already done so while in the black, and still a thin jet of water shot out between my legs.

"You got a water bed?"

I didn't remember doing that. "I guess?"

"Look, unless you want the next shot to take off your twig 'n berries, I'd recommend hittin' the showers and gettin' dressed."

I liked my twig and berries just where they were. I tried to get up, but almost immediately fell to the ground, moaning in pain. My joints were stiff. My muscles screamed. I just wanted to roll into a ball on the floor, moaning until I passed back into the black again.

Anything was better than this.

Instead Blackjack lifted me up in her powerful arms and tossed me over her shoulder, taking me into the bathroom. She gave me the option of showering myself or having her do it for me.

I opted for the latter.

She poured half a bottle of shampoo in my hair, and a bottle of body wash over my pale, sticky skin before turning the showerhead up to scalding and blasting me. I moaned and protested feebly, choking and coughing.

"You can't do this!" I cried out.

"Really? I thought I was doin' a pretty good job, actually!" I reached out to her, my hand shaking and blasted a pretty weak wave of focus at her. It would have normally sent her across the room. Instead, I was flung into the shower, hitting my head hard enough to send the world spinning. *Right, she touched me.*

Finally, she turned the water off.

"You want me to dress you too?"

"No."

"Good. Finish cleaning up and meet down in the rec room in fifteen minutes. I gotta wake the rest of y'all," she said, leaving. Slowly, painfully, I got back to my feet. I gripped the wall, a towel rack, slowly remembering how to stand. I grabbed a towel and started drying myself off, letting the anger build.

She had no right. She wasn't one of the lead Kayfabe heroes, not like Helios or Fifty-Fifty. She was just supposed to be our trainer, a glorified drill sergeant. When I found my phone, I was going to call Helios and tell him, oh man, would she be in trouble . . .

But first things first . . .

She was right about clearing out my stashes. My medicine cabinet was empty, save for a couple tabs of aspirin she left on one of the shelves. I dry swallowed them, almost choking on them, sipping water straight from the tap to force them down, hoping they'd kick in soon.

I closed the medicine cabinet, almost screaming for the ghost I saw in the mirror.

Only it wasn't a ghost. It was me, somehow. My face had gotten long and slack. There were heavy bags beneath my eyes, and close to a month of patchy beard stubble on my chin, cheeks, and neck. My hair had never been this long. *Just what the hell is going on?*

I managed to stumble to my room and pull on a clean T-shirt, jeans, socks, and shoes without dying. My phone was gone. *Have to find one downst—*

A heavy blow hit me in the gut, knocking me to the floor. I cried out in pain and began to dry heave, but there was nothing to come up, nothing except two chunks of aspirin that stayed halfway between my mouth and stomach that felt like two dice wedged in my esophagus and a little water that just gurgled in place.

I knew that heavy blow. That was just as hard as Trojan Fox could punch out of her suit.

"FUCKING . . . BLACKJACK!" I cried out in pain.

I made my way downstairs, collapsing onto one of the rec room couches. Soon Geode was sitting next to me, asking some question in a faraway voice.

"Fine," was all I could say, pulling my eyes open with effort. Geode looked just as bad as I did, maybe even worse, which must have taken some work considering how much more handsome he was than me, normally.

"Are we dying?" I asked.

"No. But we are in trouble," he said, cradling his head in his hands.

Trojan Fox came down next, a thick pair of sunglasses obscuring her eyes and a bathrobe her body. *Wish I'd thought of that.*

Odigjod teleported in next, crying out when he came in merged halfway through the coffee table. With another puff of smoke, he teleported to a nearby couch, no worse for wear, though the hole in the coffee table remained. Odigjod seemed unable to decide whether he wanted to be human or imp, and was now some awful mix between the little imp we all knew and loved and his less impressive raver kid human form.

Blackjack helped Nevermore into the room. Like Trojan Fox, she'd taken the heavy sunglasses approach, while covering much of herself in a baggy sweatshirt.

"We gotta talk," Blackjack said, tossing Nevermore roughly to the couch next to me.

"What about our archnemeses? Why aren't they here?" Odigjod asked.

"They didn't want to deal with this, so they called me," Blackjack explained.

"What about Circus?" I asked. "Shouldn't he be here too?"

"He's what we're here to talk about," Blackjack said, idly playing with the clasp of one of her revolvers. "You guys don't remember?"

"Odigjod does," the imp said, holding his head with a moaning wail. Nobody else answered.

"Circus was so fucking stoned out of his mind that he OD'd and had a seizure in the middle of your job. He wasn't s'posed to be captured, but with him on the ground like that, they didn't have no choice but to take him in. If any of you were in better mind, you coulda stopped this. You coulda rescued him. But you were all so shitfaced you could barely stand, let alone mount some half-assed rescue mission. Seriously, JUST WHAT THE FUCK WERE Y'ALL THINKING?"

We'd heard Blackjack yell plenty of times, but she never roared with this kind of anger. It was scary.

"WE'VE SPENT SO MUCH TIME, SO MUCH MONEY ON YOU, AND YOU PISS IT ALL AWAY ON SEX, DRUGS, AND ROCK 'N ROLL?"

"Very little rock 'n roll was involved, I think," Trojan Fox said wryly. With that same lightning speed, Blackjack whipped out her revolvers and fired a shot from each into Trojan Fox's mechanical feet. As quickly, she reholstered them.

"FUCKING BITCH!" Trojan Fox yelled, trying to stand but unable to.

"I shouldn't have done that," Blackjack said, taking her hat off and setting it on the table. "We got a field trip ahead of us, and I need you mobile. Shooting your feet was stupid. Any of you gentlemen feel strong enough to carry her?"

"I can," Geode said.

"Good."

Trojan Fox protested, "I don't need to be—"

"Yeah, you do," Blackjack said, pulling a Tri-Hole generator from her pocket and opening it in front of us. "You kids need to see some harsh truths, and whether you believe it or not, I'm doin' this for your own good. The other heroes thought we just oughta kill one of ya as an example for the others. My way might be more painful, but at least you'll all survive it. Now get in the damn hole."

We cursed and grumbled, but God help us we did what she said, walking single-file through the Tri-Hole with Geode carrying Trojan Fox.

We came through in a large white room with a high ceiling. The wall we'd stepped through was lined with at least a dozen triangular frames, perfectly sized and shaped for Tri-Holes. The rest of the room was sparsely furnished, save for a row of massive doorways built into the opposite wall, some ancient couches, some low wood paneling along the walls, and a few potted plastic ferns to give the place color in a cheesy, 70s sort of way. Some low, poorly digitized Muzak filtered in from unseen speakers, the Carpenters, I think, probably hoping to set us at ease.

If it weren't for the pair of fifteen-foot-tall robots that stood in front of us, this might have even succeeded.

They were vaguely human shaped, though lacked heads and walked on four spindly, steel legs. The thickness of their pale white armor, aged and dented in places though it was, made it clear that fighting them was not an option.

"White Knights . . ." Trojan Fox said, her voice full of wonder. "I thought they stopped making them when they formed the Protectors."

Instead of attacking us, they stretched a banner between the two of them.

WELCOME TO THE TOWER

There were screams. Curses. All of us turned and ran for the Tri-Hole, but Blackjack blocked our path. Nevermore, Geode, and I raised hands to fight her. She just raised a small controller in her hand and pressed the button.

Agony, blinding and fiery, burst from my Creeper, dropping me to the floor, screaming and thrashing alongside Geode, Nevermore, and Trojan Fox.

"Stop it! Stop it! Hurting them!" Odigjod pleaded in some faraway place.

After what felt like hours of agony, Blackjack let off on our Creepers. I didn't want to get up. I just wanted to lie down and die. I couldn't live here. I couldn't go in. I wouldn't. I'd just swallow my tongue, or focus on my head, cause an embolism or a stroke or an explosion, or . . .

. . . or I'd just slowly get to my feet with Odigjod's help, sulking and looking angrily at Blackjack as she went on in her angry drill sergeant voice.

"Now you ain't stayin' here. Like I said, this is a field trip, and a warning. You got off lucky this time. Fuck up again, and the capes up top will arrange an extended stay."

She opened one of the tall doors along the far wall and led us into the dark corridor beyond.

It didn't stretch on for miles, but it did seem to go on forever. Like the foyer, it must have looked classy and high-tech in the 70s, but now looked like some industrial alien abduction nightmare. On either side of the metal walkway were large, heavy glass tubes full of a thick, clear gel. Hundreds, thousands of them maybe (*remember the other doors, **tens of thousands***), only broken up by the occasional White Knight stationed between every few tubes.

A person floated in each tube. Some of them wore gaudy, super costumes, others street clothes. Most were human, but not all. Some had small black hoses piercing their skin, leading to machines at the tops of their tubes.

Each of them wore a face-concealing, bright-yellow smiley face mask.

Miles and miles of smiles . . .

Blackjack guided us further down the hall. "Back when the War began and we proposed setting up our own inescapable prison for villains, the brass at the DSA and the Ministry of Metahuman Concerns only gave us one guideline: no killin'. Even though these were villains, scum o' the earth, they knew the people would turn on us if they knew we were killin' 'em *all*. So, we had to get creative. Our best and brightest got together, combinin' the best technology we had with the best we could acquire elsewhere, to make this."

188

For emphasis, she rapped her knuckles against one of the tubes nearest to her. The glass and gel were so thick that it barely made a noise. The man on the inside, one of the ones with black hoses going into his skin, skull, and spine, didn't move. His smiley face mask leered down at us.

"We couldn't just leave the villains up and about, since on their own they'd eventually figure a way out. Thankfully, we found this gel in a crashed Gray scout ship down in Roswell, New Mexico, back in '47. It completely shuts down all bodily functions, from your shitter to your thinker to the aging process itself. You're basically immortal, but nothing but alive once you're forced into one of these. I've been told by folks who've tried it out that you don't even notice the passage of time from when you're put in and let out, but I gotta wonder, what's it like if you're never let out? Does life just end? That's one for the philosophy majors out there."

She chuckled, but the laugh sounded forced and bitter, as if she was imagining being in one herself. "The smiley masks, well, back when we used to have heroes workin' this place, it used to get depressin' seein' all those faces behind the glass. Minuteman, I forget which of him exactly said it, but he put out the idea to put masks on 'em to make this place cheerier."

"He was wrong," I said.

Blackjack shrugged. "To each their own. Just know that, once you're put in one of these tubes, you're in here until we say you can leave, and that's probably never gonna happen. Especially if you got a gift like our friend here that can be put to the betterment of po-lite society."

"What does that mean?" Nevermore asked.

Blackjack pointed at the black hoses attached to the man's spine. "It means that this villain's body produces an enzyme that can aid rich bitches in losing a few pounds, or a unique kind of magnetic field that'll allow our listeners out there to better hear the phone calls of dissidents. *Anything* they can use. Just be glad you didn't have anything they wanted. Otherwise you wouldn'tve been given this chance."

"What chance is that?" I spat out. "The chance to be lectured by a has-been superhero and—"

She hit the button on her Creeper controller, and again I was on the floor. The pain was more severe this time, burning and dancing beneath my chest.

Death. Death. Just get this fucking thing out of me!

Blackjack turned it off, her voice solemn when she continued. "No. I'm offering you a chance not to end up like these pitiful fucks."

The tubes rumbled, moving down the hall like clothes on a dry cleaner's rack. Even though I was on the ground, I could see the tubes that rotated into place beside us as clear as day.

Carnivore. Circus. Other drummers.

Showstopper. *Ghost Girl.*

I cried out, some impotent, sad, angry, animal sound. I wanted to focus on Blackjack. I wanted to rip her limb from limb. I wanted to destroy this whole place. But I couldn't do that. If I tried, if I even seriously *thought* about doing it, they'd put me in here (or use my Creeper to prevent me from ever doing anything else). All I could do was be angry.

"Look, I'm sorry I had to burst y'all's bubble, but I wanted you to know the stakes. You fuck up again, and you're all in here. So, for now, we're gonna make some changes. We're givin' you some time off to rehabilitate. You can still leave the island, but you can't have nothing in your body harder than smokes, pot, or a glass or two of alcohol. You feel your Creeper movin', and you'll know when you've had enough. There's gonna be no more parties. No more spendin' time with the heroes until you kids learn to take better care of yourselves. Do you understand?"

One by one, the others reluctantly agreed with Blackjack. Of course, I had to be last. I had to be the one left steaming in anger and fear. I had to choose between the lifestyle I'd fought so hard for and survival. I had to make a choice that really wasn't much of a choice at all.

"Yes," I finally said. "I understand."

#Supervillainy101: The Battle of Skull Landing

The history books paint World War II as a slam-dunk victory for America and her allies (but mostly America) due to the involvement of El Capitán and the Protectors, but in reality it was anything but. Though won in a few short years, Germany and her allies in Italy, Japan, Lemuria, and the Rebellious Imperial Possessions (Canada, India, and Egypt, among others) had amassed an impressive army of supers and mad scientists to their cause. The fights were fierce, literally changing the face of the earth, and it would have remained a bloody, years-long stalemate unless one side found some advantage to put them over the top.

Thankfully, America found that advantage first.

The Golem of Prague had been used by Jewish resistance fighters in Czechoslovakia. Twelve feet tall (and nearly as wide) and made of near-indestructible stone, it was incalculably strong and completely loyal to whoever had control over it. Taking it off the resistance fighters' hands, the Protectors put it to good use breaking battle lines and destroying anyone who would dare defy them.

The Golem's most dramatic use is generally regarded as the Battle of Skull Landing. A group of German scientists had set up a lab for experimental weapons, as well as unethical human genetic tampering and research into creating the *Übermensch* on a small island in the Mediterranean nicknamed "Skull Island," probably because it was such a cheery place. The island was heavily fortified and had some of the strongest supers the Germans could have collected, including two artificially created Titans. Not wanting to risk any of the Protectors on taking the island, they simply air-dropped the Golem in and told it to wipe the island clean of any traces of life.

Three days later, the job was done. The Golem, covered in blood but otherwise none the worse for wear, had killed every living thing on the island. Not even plants and nesting seabirds survived its wrath.

America put the science and research obtained from the station to good use in pumping up the economy postwar, and the Golem has been one of the Protectors' greatest heroes since.

#**LessonLearned:** Superheroes can be real assholes sometimes.

16

COLD VELOCIRAPTOR

I wish I knew who first came up with the term "cold turkey" so I could find them and shove some focus up their ass. I know, they've probably been dead for something like a hundred years, but if it takes years of research and finding a time machine to do so, I think I might.

Either way, they didn't know what they were talking about. Turkeys are fat, waddling birds that taste good on sourdough with mayonnaise and don't have much resembling a brain. I've heard some say they got a temper, and that they're not *that* stupid, but in my limited experience with them, they always struck me as oversized chickens.

Withdrawal isn't docile. It wouldn't taste good on sourdough with mayonnaise. It's ill-tempered and it claws at you, agonizing and constant like the worst sick and hunger you've ever felt.

Cold velociraptor always struck me as a more accurate name.

When Blackjack first dropped us back at the mansion, we made our way to the healing pods, seeing if they could clear our systems.

They couldn't.

That would have been too easy.

They could heal broken bones, torn flesh, and most diseases, but they couldn't rid our bodies of the drugs we flooded our systems with any better than they could have gotten rid of scars or tattoos. In a mad, desperate bid to find the easy way out, I spent close to a day calling Helios to see if maybe he could get me into some kind of rehab program that'd fix me up quick.

The only problem was, he didn't answer. I knew he saw my calls and texts, I knew he read them and heard my voicemails, but I got nothing back. The one time I did get through (maybe he picked up by accident), the call was disconnected almost immediately. I raged and cried and wiped out an entire hallway of the mansion when I lost control of my powers. I bounced so many times between wanting to kill him and wondering what I did to make him hate me that the two extremes began to merge and I started wondering if he would hate me if I killed him (*Ghost Girl could tell you*).

It was on the second day when the withdrawal symptoms really started to kick in. That's when things got real bad.

I hadn't slept. I was awake and in the black all at once, and I was scared. I could hear screams and moans coming from down the hall. I was sweating and cold and throwing up when I didn't have anything to throw up but bile with bits of blood in it. My powers were on the fritz, sometimes burying themselves deep, hiding when I needed them, other times exploding out unexpectedly and violently, taking most of my room with them. When I could think rationally, I thought of how I could make this better. I thought of asking Odigjod to take us off the island, of finding one of the dealers, of getting my hands on a little bit of Montage, just enough to take the edge off without setting off my Creeper.

This seemed like the greatest idea in the world. Agonizingly, I got to my feet and padded my way down the hall to Odigjod's room. I knocked on his door. Nothing. Harder. Still nothing. I started pounding on it, screaming his name.

"Aidan. We need to talk," Trojan Fox said.

"I'm busy."

"We all are," she said. "Everybody's downstairs."

"What time is it?"

"I don't know, but everyone's in the rec room and there's some serious shit we need to clear up here."

So that was where Odigjod was. Fine. I followed her. I'd even listen to her, some, but first chance I got, I was going to talk some sense into Odigjod.

The others were all stretched out on couches, all in pajamas, all looking as strung out and fried as I felt. Trojan Fox didn't look much better. Her eyes were bloodshot, her hair frizzed out, and her hands shaking heavily as she tried desperately to light a cigarette.

She waited for me to collapse on a couch before saying, "We're on our own. The heroes don't give two fucks about helping us. The only people who can, are us."

"But they're our friends!" I protested.

"No, they're our captors!" she proclaimed back, stretching out her arms. "You hear that, you fucks? We all know what you are, and we won't take it!"

"Are you done poking the sleeping dragon?" Geode asked.

"Oh they're not sleeping. They're just biding their time. It won't suit them to deal with us off camera like this. No, they're going to wait for something nice and public before they do anything to us. But until then, we have to get our acts together."

"But I liked my act where it was before!" I complained.

"Yeah, and look where it got you. Look where it got all of us! This isn't living! This is sedation!"

"So if we are sedated, what do you propose we do about it?" Nevermore asked, twirling a finger through her hair and coming away with a clump of it in her hand.

"We go cold turkey." *There's that phrase again.*

She continued, "We keep an eye on each other. We make sure we get better! If the five of us work together, I know we can survive this. So . . . are you all with me, or what?"

This wasn't what we wanted. This wasn't what we fought for. She had to know that. We wouldn't give in so easi—

Wait, why did Odigjod stand to join her? And Geode? No, that wasn't right, especially not Nevermore joining them, even if she did so very begrudgingly. She was the biggest party girl of us all, she would never join in on something this crazy!

She gave in to peer pressure.

Thunderhead was right, that is some really insidious shit.

No, this wasn't right at all. Trojan Fox didn't lead the team. *I* led the team. I was Apex Strike! I was the greatest supervillain in the world. I knew what I had to do. I was going to outspeech her. I was going to convince the others that we could fight for our right to have fun and party. I would tell them how we had to appeal to the heroes, or maybe find some way of resisting them that wouldn't tick them off.

I would be eloquent.

I would make them see the truth.

I stood up. I cleared my throat. I tried to say the words. When I couldn't, I leapt at Trojan Fox with fists balled, shrieking about how none of this was fair and trying not to let the others wrestle me to the floor too quickly.

The next days and weeks followed a very similar pattern. I'd spend most of the day in bed, crying and cursing and occasionally screaming, drinking water whenever it was given to me, eating whatever food was brought my way. Some days the others would begin to rage like I did, putting me in the position of helping hold them down no matter how much I might have agreed with the way they felt. Trojan Fox was easy enough to deal with once we hid her legs, but Odigjod and Nevermore were really tough when they started to lose their shit. Between the two of their powers running amok and my seriously altered perceptions, the mansion looked like a goth nightmare for a few days.

I was pretty sure I was getting better.

I had to be, since I was feeling worse.

After a while, things started feeling more normal. Pain became more sharp. I started remembering life outside of the mansion, even going so far as wanting my mom and Helios to come and make this all better. After the first week, I stopped throwing up as much and was even able to keep some food down. I made trips to the kitchen in the middle of the night, grabbing cereal or some fruit, whatever my body felt like it could handle. I didn't mess the bed anymore, and might have even started to get some real sleep, not in the black. Which was nice.

It was during one of these moments of blissful, real sleep that reality decided I'd had enough of a vacation from it and called me back.

With a cavalry charge.

An honest-to-God, trumpeting cavalry charge.

I woke up screaming, kicking my blankets aside.

"Betcha didn't know I could play the trumpet, didja? You should see what I can do with a tuba, then we'll *really* start rockin'."

I knew that voice. I never thought I'd hear it again.

"Showstopper?"

He crossed the room to me, spinning the trumpet on his finger and smiling. His shadow was so wide it nearly blocked out the sun streaming in my windows.

"How's that for a plot twist?" he mused, sitting at the edge of my bed. "One moment the tube closes around me and I think I've seen my last glimpse of the world, the next I'm out again and being told that I'm needed on the team because you guys fucked up so royal."

Seeing him again was such a surprise, I couldn't stop myself from diving across the bed and wrapping him in a huge bear hug.

"Okay, that was sweet for like the first three seconds, but now that I know you're naked and you're not letting go, it's getting a little weird."

"Sorry!" I said quickly, parting from him. "And we didn't fuck up," I clarified.

The look he gave me said that wasn't good enough, so I added, "Not royal, at least."

"You say to-may-to, the heroes say you fucked up royal, and with enough of 'em from the Empire to know royal, who am I to argue? Doesn't matter to what degree you did or didn't fuck this team you got up, because in your fucked-uppedness you got me paroled. So please, if you can find another way to fuck up that benefits me like that, fuck away."

"I will," I said, running a hand through my hair. *I need a haircut.*

"You smell like shit," he said.

"Showers and me haven't exactly been on speaking terms lately," I said. I looked to the tray of food, and felt my stomach growl. "That your doing?"

"Yeah. Ghost Girl and me have been here about three weeks while you five have been playing your zombie game, making sure you didn't die. You've all had it pretty rough, but you, mate, I thought you were going to die there for a while. Almost had me wishing they'd taken Spasm out instead of me. *Almost.*"

His words sunk in slowly. "You've been here three weeks?"

"Indeed we have. You guys needed a lot of time to recover. You *really* know how to party."

"And Ghost Girl's with you!" I said, leaping to my feet (well, trying to leap at least).

"Yeah. She and the others took a field trip up to the Chin to try and get some fresh air." I started for the door. "Well, let's go then!"

"Need I remind you about your still being naked?"

"Right," I said. I found some boxers, shoes, and a bathrobe, and gobbled down the sandwich he'd put at my nightstand as we left my room and headed to the Chin.

"By the way, you do know that dick pic you tweeted is one of the most retweeted in the world, right?"

"That happened?" I asked, feeling green.

"Oh yeah."

"Fuck."

"Well, it's not all bad . . ."

My muscles started to scream after the first few steps from the house. My lungs hadn't had a breath of fresh air in ages and started to complain, and the sun felt like it was searing my skin off. I wanted to go back to the mansion and just wait for them to return, but Showstopper prodded me, and I kept pressing on.

We made it to the Chin in good time. I could hear laughing. Talking. Happiness. *Real* happiness.

When we finally climbed to them, I could see that they had a bag of golf clubs and were using them to chip balls into the jungle. Geode used his superstrength to send one sailing far into the distance, causing a large ripple when it bounced off the force field. Odigjod and Trojan Fox laughed, exchanging high fives. Nevermore went up next, and through summoning her pendulum tattoo managed to match Geode's shield-hitter. I couldn't quite read her smile at first, before I realized that it was genuine. *Has anyone ever seen that?*

And there she was. Ghost Girl. She was dressed in civilian clothes (loose, but flattering), but still wore that creepy porcelain doll mask to cover her face.

She was a sight for sore eyes.

"Hey guys, who's winning?" Showstopper asked, pulling a club from the bag.

Everyone turned to us. The more I looked at them, the more I saw that they were every bit as haggard as I, but their happiness was infectious. Ghost Girl's eyes briefly flashed gold on me, but as ever she remained difficult to read.

I didn't care.

I hobbled to her, throwing my arms around her neck.

"I've missed you."

"I noticed," she said. Her voice was neutral. She made no move to hug me back. *What the hell?*

We separated, quietly. I knew we never got the chance to say good-bye to each other, but I thought she'd have looked on me a little more fondly than that.

"So the gang's all here now, is it?" Showstopper asked. "Feels like we oughta celebrate. Whaddya do for fun 'round here?"

"Party with celebrities and do a lot of drugs," I said, eyes never leaving Ghost Girl. She barely acknowledged my existence. *Maybe she wouldn't be so cold if she'd been here with us . . .*

Or maybe she just doesn't like being sent to the Tower while we fucked everything up out here.

"No, I meant what do you really do for fun around here?" Showstopper asked, laughing.

"He's serious," Ghost Girl said. Showstopper looked to the others for confirmation, and they nodded.

"I thought they were joking when they told us to keep you out of trouble," Showstopper said. "Well, fuck me, that changes things some."

"We could stay here. Video games. Board games. Odigjod has always wanted to learn Twister," Odigjod said.

"No, no, that won't do," Showstopper said, shaking his head. "You've been cooped up too long. We need to take you out. Do something fun."

"But with no alcohol or drugs," Trojan Fox grumbled.

"Right. Wholesome. Got it. Who's got a tablet?" Showstopper asked. Odigjod tossed his to Showstopper, and within minutes he was rattling off ideas and shooting them down before we could say anything for or against. As ever, he had the energy of a puppy and enough power to keep us all just the slightest bit afraid of him.

Like old times . . .

"Boom, got it!" Showstopper exclaimed, his smile broadening like a kid on Christmas morning. "There's a Mary Rising tonight. Any of you ever been to one?"

I'd always heard those were pretty cool, but had never actually been to one because my parents didn't want to make the trip.

It wasn't going out and partying with superheroes, but it could be fun. The others must have thought the same, because nobody opposed the idea.

So we were going to a Mary Rising. Cool.

Maybe there I'd get to find out just what Ghost Girl's problem was.

#Supervillainy101: Mary

Have you ever heard of the Grand Sorceror? No? I don't blame you. Although he was a fairly famous superhero back in the Golden Age, he was almost scrubbed completely from the history books because he kinda created one of the twentieth century's most dangerous supervillains.

You see, our friend the Sorceror had a problem keeping it in his pants, and this came back to bite him when he knocked up some school marm in rural Pennsylvania. She became obsessed with him and started following him everywhere, begging him to take care of her and their unborn child, but he wanted nothing to do with her. When she threatened to make this misfortune public, he arranged a magic spell to silence her permanently. Instead, he mispronounced one word in the spell and wound up killing her with an as yet unknown curse. He dumped her in an abandoned coal mine in Centralia, wiped his hands, and presumably walked away whistling whatever superheroes in the 20s whistled.

Unfortunately, the mine he dumped her in was severely haunted from a cave-in and cursed by said cave-in's victims. This, combined with the Sorceror's botched curse, transformed the unknown school marm into Mary, a hulking, thirteen-foot-tall, one-thousand-pound zombie with no real memory or intelligence but enough rage and superhuman strength (enough to give the Golem a run for its money) to more than make up for it. Time and again she has fought the Protectors, sometimes on her own, sometimes after having been roped in by some supervillain team or another, and time and again she's proven herself to be a force of nature. Every time she's killed, she appears ninety-six days later in that same mine, clawing her way to the surface and ready to rampage. Her clockwork resurrections and the superheroes killing her have created a booming tourist industry in the area.

As for the Grand Sorceror, well, there's few records of what happened to him after the Mary incident, but I'm a fan of the theory that he was fed to Mary by a bunch of pissed off, Golden Age heroes as payback.

#LessonLearned: Don't fuck with magic users.

17

THE WORST THINGS ALWAYS STICK AROUND

Maybe it came from hearing too many stories about how awe-some Mary Risings were when I was a kid, but I was a bit let down when we first teleported in and saw that it was really just an overcrowded, small-town carnival. There were rides and games, cheap food and screaming kids, poorly piped in music, and that ever-present smell of popcorn and vomit. The early evening air was cool and bracing, enough to wake you up and remind you that winter was right around the corner.

It reminded me a lot of home, actually.

My old home, at least.

The mine entrance itself was the centerpiece. It was sur-rounded by large light towers and cordons to keep people out of harm's way, and vendors selling hero pennants, Mary balloons, and "Genuine Mary Teeth." There were no heroes yet; they would come a few minutes before sunset (when Mary typically rose) to get ready and probably sign a few autographs. Until then, we had to make our own fun.

Showstopper acted as master of ceremonies, trying to cheer us all up at any cost. He talked us into games, terrible fried food, and one by one even got us all onto the mechanical bull. We couldn't use our powers—not if we didn't want to attract any attention—but it was actually pretty fun. Nevermore and Trojan Fox were naturals. Showstopper and I weren't. I tried to hold on, but wound up wrapping my legs around my head when I faceplanted off the front. Showstopper's fall was more spectacular (weighing three hundred–plus pounds will do that, I guess), but he took it in good humor, waving to the crowd and bowing as he hobbled back to us.

"That was awesome," he said. "I need food."

"Don't mention food now," Geode said, holding his stomach. I tried to look stronger, but I shared his queasiness. Maybe combining fair food and mechanical bulls wasn't the best idea after detoxing.

"More for me then," Showstopper laughed.

He may have been fat, but he was a breath of fresh air. He was energetic, he was positive, and he didn't judge us. He was just glad to be free.

I couldn't say the same for Ghost Girl.

I'd never seen her in public (it was weird seeing her with that scarf wrapped around her face instead of her usual mask), and maybe that gave her some of the awkwardness, but that could only account for some. The way she looked at us . . . it seemed like she was only hanging around out of a sense of obligation, talking when spoken to, following us where we went but never adding anything. She wasn't hostile, but she wasn't friendly.

She wasn't the Ghost Girl I'd remembered.

I was glad when we'd decided to split up. I knew she would make a break from us, and it was easy enough to follow her, for a while.

I'd forgotten how fast she was—and in what poor shape I was in. She might have actually gotten away if I hadn't put up a small wall of focus in front of her.

She stopped.

"Let me go, Aidan," she said without turning around.

"No. Not until you tell me what your problem with me, with all of us really, but especially *me* is!"

She turned around. Her eyes weren't angry, not really, but they were pretty close to it. "You want to know my problem?"

"Yeah, I think I've earned that much!" I said, doing a pretty good imitation of sounding strong and confident. "I mean, after what we shared—"

"You earned *nothing*! We had sex, Aidan. Desperate sex because I wasn't sure if I'd ever see the light of day again and because I briefly thought that you might still have some human decency hiding within you. Seeing you now, I'm beginning to regret that decision."

That hurt. A lot.

I didn't love Ghost Girl—at least I was pretty sure I didn't love her—but I did like her a lot. Probably more than any girl I'd ever known (even more than Kelly Shingle). Though she was creepy and quiet a lot of the time, she was also kind, smart, and hid a pretty good sense of humor.

She was my friend. One of the best friends I'd ever had (and a mostly hot one, too). I'd hoped beyond hope that I would see her again someday, even knowing that it would likely mean seeing her as a drummer, just so I could show her what a big man I'd become.

And now she was looking at me like I was the worst person she'd ever met.

"Back in training, I thought you all might be decent people. That beneath the pretext of villainy we were all just scared, misunderstood kids who got roped into this because the capes backed us into a corner. That we did this because we had to, not because we wanted to."

"But we *did* want to do this. At least, I know I did."

She shook her head. "I know that, now. I knew it then, but I thought you stood a chance at being something different. You had this naïveté and sweetness to you, beneath all the selfishness and stupid fucking posturing, that I thought might have made you into a better man once you saw what supervillain life was *really* like."

"You were wrong about that," I laughed.

She started to walk away, further into the carnival, but did nothing to stop me from following.

"You let this life poison you. You let *them* poison you," she said harshly when I caught up.

"The heroes?" I asked. She nodded. "Nah, they're cool, mostly, when they're not being dicks I mean, but we're all friends when they're not."

"And where were these friends when you were screaming in withdrawal? They made a good showing of not cleaning you up while attending their premieres and galas and their courtship of the paparazzi, while Showstopper and I made sure you didn't die!"

I may have still been pissed with Adam some, but I shook the thought off. She didn't know them like we did. "They're busy people. You'll see that once things get back to normal, once you know them like we do."

She laughed. "I don't want to know them. Not after what they have made of you."

"And what did they make us?" I said, defiantly.

"Puppets."

"Yeah, but we knew that going in. We get to be *their* puppets; they let us live like celebrities, it's pretty sweet," I said, proud to have outmaneuvered her.

"Okay, how about we find another word for it: whores."

That word wasn't nearly as cool-sounding as puppets. Not that puppets inherently sounds cool, but whores was much worse.

"We're not whores."

"You're paid to do something illegal."

"Hello, it's called a job!" I shot back.

"So none of those heroes you fucked ever paid you for sex?"

"No!" I exclaimed, indignant.

"Did they ever give you gifts?"

"Sometimes!"

"Did they ever give you drugs in exchange for sex?"

"No! Wait, yeah, maybe a couple of times. Maybe more, but definitely less than half!" I said. There were some fuzzy memories of some of the older superheroes propositioning me, me considering if I wanted to do anything with them, then them offering me some Montage or pills to get things going.

"Then you're a whore. So, is being a celebrity whore everything you'd hoped it would be?"

I was trying to raise defiance again, but with her eyes (*human eyes, this time*) boring right through me, I couldn't do that.

"People liked—*like* me. I mean, they say they like me. I think they mean it, but maybe they don't. But even if they don't, it's a lot more than I got before. I never had people even pretend to like me before. And the sex . . . so what if it's meaningless? I never got any before, and now I'm fucking some of the hottest women on the planet."

"You do know how pitiful that sounds, right?"

"Some, yeah."

"And that they were only ever fucking Apex Strike, not you, right?"

I shrugged. It sounded right. It didn't sound as bad as she was making it out to be, but it did sound worse than I'd had it in my head.

"Would you like to hear a story?" she asked.

"Do I have a choice?"

"No."

"Then go right ahead."

"I wasn't always like this . . ." she said, motioning to her face. A sick sense of anticipation filled my stomach.

Is she finally . . . ?

"I was pretty. I was happy. And I had a family. A mum, a dad, two younger sisters, and the coolest older brother in the

208

world. Justin was into surfing, biking, extreme sports . . . everybody loved him; it was hard not to, he always had a kind word or a present for me . . ."

I could see where this was going. I put a sympathetic hand on her shoulder. "He raped you, didn't he?"

She looked at me, confused. "Oh, God no! Ewww. What would make you—"

"I'm sorry, it just seemed like—"

More Afrikaans cursing. "—you watch too much telly—"

"—I SAID I WAS SORRY!"

". . . Do you want to hear the story or don't you?"

"YES! Yes, I mean yes, I'm sorry."

"Good," she shuddered. "My powers manifested when I was fifteen. They scared me at first, just like everyone's I'm sure. But once I realized what I could do, I thought it was the greatest thing in the world. I always wanted to help people, and looking into their auras I thought I could really help with that. The only real problem I saw with these new powers was the Black Strings."

She'd talked about these during training. The way she'd described it, auras appeared as a mass of swirling, multicolored strings in front of and behind a person. They couldn't tell you everything about their life, but some things stood out better than others. Events that were really bright and important showed up behind a person in white. Terrible, negative events showed up in darker shades.

The worst things people could do showed up in black.

"I hated seeing people's deepest, darkest secrets, because in all my sheltered life, I didn't want to believe they were possible. That was why I didn't test it on my family, at first, but finally, I was just so excited that I couldn't help myself and I looked, and I saw Justin's Black String.

"I didn't want to know what it was, at first, and for months I tried to ignore it. But when another appeared . . . I looked deeper, and I saw a vision of he and four of his friends beating a homeless man to death for kicks after a night of drinking. The second string was the same, but worse, because this time they weren't drinking. They were *hunting*. This was getting worse, and he had no remorse for it. I . . . I knew I was the only one who could do something, so when we were home alone one day, I confronted him in the kitchen while he was cooking lunch. I thought, coming from me, that he'd see the light, that he'd get just how wrong what he did was."

"I'm guessing he didn't?"

"No. He yelled at me like it was my fault for finding out, then he forced my face down in a pot of boiling oil."

My stomach churned at the thought. The fact that I was just admiring the smell of a fried-food booth a moment before didn't help.

"I should have died. I wanted to die. Instead, I grabbed a knife from the counter and opened his belly. After he let me go, I was able to scream. Then I opened his throat. The police came. They took me to the hospital. What I'd done was clearly self-defense, so I wasn't punished. Doctors told me I was lucky to keep my eyes, tongue, and most of my lips, and that they might be able to restore some of my face in time. I told them I didn't want them to. I wanted the reminder of what happened when I allowed myself to be willfully blind to the world. My parents thought I was mad, and maybe I was," she said, her voice trailing off.

"I knew his friends were still out there. I knew they still needed to be stopped. So once my face had healed enough, I found my first mask and cloak in a Johannesburg antique store. I became Ghost Girl, and I did things to them that were very much *not* in self-defense. They are Black Strings on my back that I can never lose and they bother me always when I use my powers, but they are also peace of mind."

"I'm sorry," I said. The words felt inadequate, but what the hell else are you supposed to say to a story like that?

"Be sorry all you want, but don't ignore what I'm saying. I didn't let myself see evil until it was too late because I didn't want to. I care about all of you too much to see you make the same mistake."

I could see where she was going. I wanted to tell her how many ways she was wrong, how great the heroes really were once you got to know them, how good and decent and fun they were to be around. I mean, sure, some of what she said felt true, and maybe the heroes were using us more than we thought, which was something we'd need to talk about with them, but it wasn't as bad as she thought.

It *wasn't*.

It couldn't be.

We weren't *that* stupid.

We were *supervillains*.

I sighed. "Maybe you're right."

"I am right."

"*Maybe* you're right, but can I say something?"

"Of course."

The words didn't come easily. Being honest has never been one of my strongest suits, but with Ghost Girl it was easy, and not just because she could use her power to see through you.

"I'm a supervillain. I'm a son of a bitch—not literally, I mean, since my mom was pretty nice, but I've done bad things, and I've made a lot of bad decisions. And you know what? If I could go back and fix all my mistakes, I wouldn't. And it's not just because of the sweet island lair or the sex and the drugs and the partying and the fame, though those have all been pretty awesome. It's because of you guys. You . . . Helen, Felix, Nick, Odigjod . . . Nevermore?"

"Angelique. Her name is Angelique."

Now I knew.

". . . Anyway, I *think* I love you guys. You're assholes a lot of the time, but you're also the best friends I've ever had, and I wouldn't give that up for anything."

She looked me up and down. "I don't even need my powers to know that you mean that."

Now for the really hard part. I quickly closed the distance between us, pulled the scarf down the lower half of her face, and kissed her twisted, mutilated lips. It felt weird, kissing her, and my stomach didn't entirely appreciate it, but I kept everything down. She resisted some at first, no doubt it'd been a while since she'd been kissed, but she didn't push me away.

I parted from her.

"You know, you make it really hard to hate you sometimes," she said, contorting her terrible lips into something resembling a smile.

"What can I say, I'm maybe, almost, kinda cute."

"Sometimes," she said, pulling the scarf back up.

It was almost dark. Loudspeakers kicked in, announcing that the Mary Rising was beginning. As if on cue, a glowing green Tri-Hole opened in the distance, spitting out a half-dozen of heroes too dark to see from where we were. Silently, we started toward them. No way were we going to miss the main event.

"Anything interesting happen while I was coming down from all the drugs?" I asked, trying to fill the silence.

"Well, Spongeman died," Ghost Girl said, offhand.

"Really? What happened?"

"He drowned."

"Seriously?"

"Yes. He fell in a pool while chasing some criminal. He was absorbent. His lungs weren't."

"Huh. Did they do one of those National Days of Mourning for him?"

"Not really. The Deputy Mayor was supposed to give a speech at some park, but they couldn't figure out how to turn off the sprinklers and had to cancel."

"That sucks. I guess."

"Not for Sponge Lad."

"There's a Sponge Lad?"

"Not anymore. He got promoted to Spongeman."

"Huh."

The others had saved us a spot pretty close to the front of the cordon around the mine entrance, so we got a good view of all the heroes who had come out for this Mary Rising as they signed autographs and took pictures with those audience members who had paid for tickets to meet them in advance. Some of them I knew, like Helios, Shooting Star, Photon, and Armada. The other two (*the more famous two*), Arcana and the Golem, were not a part of Project Kayfabe. There's no way they could have known who we were, but their presence was the only thing that kept me from waving to Helios.

"So much death here," Ghost Girl muttered. Her eyes were glowing, and her body shuddered.

"Are you all right?" Geode asked her.

"I think so," she said. "But I can't stay for this."

She pushed her way back through the crowd. I wondered if I should follow her, especially now that we seemed almost back on good terms, but then the ground began to rumble beneath me, and all thoughts of Ghost Girl disappeared.

Mary was rising.

The lights all blacked out at that moment, and a voice over the loudspeakers told us to quiet down and be aware of potential side effects. Sometimes, due to the imperfect nature of her curse, the laws of physics didn't entirely behave when she was rising. Some Risings have reported mass hysteria, gravity fluctuations, and the sudden appearance of a field of sunflowers in front of the mine. I was kind of hoping we'd see something, for the full experience, but that wasn't to be.

At once after the announcement, a few hundred hands rose into the air, aiming their phones' cameras at the pitch-black mine entrance. Slowly, faintly, a glowing green mist began to pour from it. Green light soon began to come from the thick cracks in the earth, brighter every second as the ground began to rumble even heavier. A primal roar came from the mine.

A massive shadow stood silhouetted in the green, pulling itself out by the edges of the mine.

Then they turned the lights on her.

We'd all seen pictures of Mary, but it was another thing seeing her in person. With flat, gray skin, patchy, almost non-existent white hair, and a muscular physique that almost made her look to be a giant gorilla, she barely looked female, let alone a former human. Only her tattered black funerary dress gave her any clear identity. Her flat, ugly face contorted on seeing the light, her massive lips and broken teeth curling into a grimace. She raised one giant hand to block the light as she looked around at the audience, confused.

"Have you seen my lamb?" she asked, her voice high and pitiful.

In a flash, the heroes were on her. Photon ran around her at superspeed, creating a disorienting whirlwind that unsteadied Mary on her feet. Helios and Shooting Star flew around her, unleashing energy blasts from their hands, while Armada unleashed everything from his impressive arsenal of experimental artillery on Mary's head and neck. Mary roared in pain and confusion, falling to her hands and knees as she waved impotently at the attackers.

The crowd was eating it up, cheering the heroes and cursing Mary as they took pictures and high-fived each other.

The four heroes let up on their attack, allowing the Golem to jump in and wrap its arms around Mary's chest. Slowly, Arcana floated in to meet them, her robe fluttering around her. The air took on a weird charge just by her presence. Dark-skinned, beautiful, and quite possibly immortal, she was supposed to be the strongest magic user on the planet. Her face held a look of utter serenity and ferocity as she pulled the deck of enchanted tarot cards from her belt. They flew around her like a swarm of insects, glowing and showing us brief glimpses of the ornate artwork on each card. The only question was, which would she use to finish Mary?

With a flick of her wrist, she flung one card at the ground near where Mary knelt. From it sprung a ghostly, tall figure in a medieval robe and wielding a massive sword. The crowd went wild when they recognized the card.

Justice.

Mary looked up at the spectral judge and asked, "Have you seen my lamb?"

One thrust of the sword between Mary's eyes was all it took to end the party.

Slowly, the crowd dispersed, though some hung around in the vain hope that the heroes would sign more autographs. Some of the heroes carted off Mary's remains to be disposed of at the Tower and . . . well, I wasn't sure how I felt about the whole thing. It was cool to watch, no doubt, but something in the crowd's reaction to this unsettled me.

Probably just your imagination.

Just before he entered their Tri-Hole, Helios turned back to wave to the crowd. Briefly, his eyes met mine, and he smiled. He flashed me a thumbs-up, and I shot one back.

Maybe things really were getting back to normal.

#Supervillainy101: Love & Superheroes

If you're a superhero, odds are that you're good-looking, a celebrity, and rich (unless you're Spongeman, rest his soul). Because of these things, odds on you're going to have your share of groupies, lovers, and spouses, and odds are they're going to have a high mortality rate.

I've already told the stories of the unfortunate girls who were with El Capitán and the Grand Sorceror, but they're hardly the only ones who've lost loves to misfortune (or being a jackass, in the Grand Sorceror's case). Minuteman's first girlfriend was caught in the crossfire of a supervillain battle and killed. ATHENA lost two husbands in household accidents (one falling down a flight of stairs and one to a mysterious fire that claimed him and his mistress). Crystal Skull's wives and girlfriends have been so frequently attacked, beaten, and crippled by thugs from various villainous syndicates that few stay with him for more than a year or two.

And the less said about the tragedies of the many girlfriends of Locust Lad/Man, the better, though he still holds the distinction of being the only superhero known to have sold a girlfriend to alien slavers in exchange for saving his city from a rogue comet.

Many superheroes get around this by sticking to casual sex or only sleeping with other superheroes. The Gamemaster has gone on record saying that he prefers dating former or current supervillainesses. When asked about this controversial philosophy, he's gone on the record saying that he does it because, "They know how to take care of themselves."

#LessonLearned: If you mean to date a superhero, have a will filled out.

18

THE BALLAD OF ADAM &
ADRIANA

Our chairs were in a circle and there was plenty of coffee and cigarettes to go around. Aside from having comfortable chairs and this not taking place in the backroom of a YMCA, it was pretty much exactly what I'd always imagined group therapy to look like.

It was Showstopper's idea that we do this, saying it would make us work better as a team if we understood everyone. It's not like he really knew what he was doing—none of us did really—but it passed the time in a depressing and getting-a-weight-off-your-shoulders sort of way. This time we were supposed to talk about what got us into supervillainy.

It was as depressing as you'd expect.

"I've never liked myself. Who I am, what I've done, how I look . . . The doctors thought it was clinical depression, triggered by the onset of a particularly abnormal superhuman ability. That's what *they* thought, at least. I thought after a while that maybe I was doing the world a favor by just punishing myself," Nevermore said, taking a drag on her cigarette to hold the tears back.

"That's not true," Showstopper said, getting nods from the rest of the group.

Nevermore laughed, mockingly. "No? I have stolen many things. I have hurt people. I have broken many hearts for fun. I have hurt myself more times than I can count. I have committed many crimes, just because I wanted to feel alive, and I should not be punished?"

She dropped her head. "I am a bad person. I have always been a bad person. I have always thought that perhaps . . . perhaps I should just find some dark, lonely abyss, a quiet place to die where the world cannot miss me. Then I will no longer be a burden, then I will only have myself to hurt."

Suddenly her infatuation with Poe made a lot of sense.

That was the most honest any of us had ever seen from her. She wasn't looking for validation or praise. She was just getting all of this off of her chest. I didn't know what to feel. Out of everyone here, I'd probably spent the most time with her. We were never really into talking—at least not about our lives before this—so this was all news to me. Part of me felt bad for not asking her more about this earlier, since it was something that she'd clearly been holding on to for some time and wanted to get out there.

Then I remembered what she looked like naked, and excused myself for not thinking of talking to her.

She was sobbing. Showstopper and Trojan Fox comforted her, telling her that we were all here for each other, but I had never seen her look more relieved. *I guess drugs and a painful detox will do that to you.*

What they didn't do was make it easier to listen to everybody else's stories. To Odigjod and Geode's family issues. To Trojan Fox talking about being unable to follow her dreams due to crippling debt and Showstopper making every sacrifice imaginable to try to make it as an artist who never knew if he'd be able to eat the next day. To Ghost Girl going into graphic, horrible detail about the fight with her brother.

I didn't have absent or dead or hateful parents (or parents *literally* from hell). I was never attacked or discriminated against. I just came from a mediocre, upper-middle-class suburban American upbringing and took the easy way to being something more. I mean, I didn't have many complaints about where my life was now (except for the occasional broken bones, and the whole drug withdrawal thing, and that uneasy feeling I'd get whenever my Creeper started to twitch beneath my sternum), but I was starting to realize just how much of a selfish prick I'd been.

When group therapy broke up, everybody started trying to figure out what to do with our night. Showstopper wanted to take in a musical in London, Trojan Fox a robot deathmatch in Tokyo. I was more interested in moping and wasn't of much use to any of them when the one thing that could have truly brightened my spirits (with the possible exception of a threesome with Nevermore and Ghost Girl, but that was never gonna happen) happened.

My phone was ringing.

The name that showed on the screen was one I hadn't seen in a long while.

Adam.

I smiled. *It's about damn time.*

I slid my finger across the screen and pulled it to my ear.

"What's up!"

There was a long, empty pause on the other side of the phone before I heard him slur, "Aidan. God, I've done . . . I need . . . Oh God! What have I . . . I need you. Please, please come here now! I've done . . . Oh God, oh God . . . fucked, so fucked . . . come here now! Something's . . ."

Was he sobbing, or just drunk, or—

"Please, please, Apex, Aidan, I need you man, OH GOD, I'M SO FUCKED!"

"Are you all—"

"NO I'M NOT FUCKING ALL RIGHT! I'M FUCKED! I'M . . . I'm, I'm sorry. I'm sorry. God, please . . . can you come here now, Aidan?"

"Where are you?"

"My place. Come alone . . . and wear your costume!"

I'd been to Adam's Beverly Hills estate a few times before. Like most rich people's homes, it was pretty much just white, steel, and glass, with lots of plants and pools outside and a spiked wall surrounding the perimeter. The solid gold statue of himself in full Helios regalia that stood in the planter in the middle of his driveway and read passages from his autobiography on the hour might have been a little gaudy, but bigger heroes had even more ostentatious monuments to themselves, so why couldn't he have his?

I didn't get to see that this time. Odigjod teleported me behind Adam's pool. It was dark out. The heads-up display of my helmet said that it was just after midnight, local time. *Fuck, time moves weird on Death Island.*

All the lights on the ground floor were on, and one of the rear sliding glass doors that led to the pool was shattered. Odigjod shuddered.

"Chaos happened here. Not the good kind for you, methink," he said.

"You can say that again," I said. "Can you tell what happened?"

"No. But bad, Odigjod knows that surely."

"Thanks for the warning."

"Being careful, Apex Strike. There's an bad smell tonight. This is not what it's looking like," he said, putting one of his clawed hands on my knee.

"I'm always careful," I said, patting him on the head.

"Not really. But better getting," he said, waggling his hand back and forth.

I smiled at him, just before closing my helmet's visor. After agreeing to come back for me when I was done, he teleported away in his usual puff of black smoke.

It felt weird, being in the suit again, but it gave me the strength to keep moving despite the cold feeling of fear that was creeping up the back of my spine.

I stepped through the shattered glass door.

"Knock, knock!" I said, trying to sound playful because I knew it covered up my fear.

Adam darted around the corner, his hand glowing bright gold. He was a mess. He hadn't shaved, his eyes were wild and bloodshot, tears ran down his cheeks, and his skin was sallow and slick with sweat. If I wasn't mistaken, those were also bloodstains on his tank top.

"Aidan, thank God! Thank God!" he said, putting out the energy burst in his hand and hugging me fiercely. "I was so scared, thought you wouldn't, oh God, oh God!"

He bent over, coughing.

"Are you all right?" I asked, patting him on the back. I had a sneaking suspicion, so I followed up, "Are you on coke again?"

"No, and yes, and I can handle my coke," he said, standing up and wiping his nose clean with a burst of golden energy. "But this . . . I can't . . . I mean . . ."

He sobbed, pointing to the kitchen.

I looked up to see Adriana Alton lying dead in a puddle of blood on the kitchen floor, her neck twisted at a terrible angle and her beautiful eyes bulging almost all the way out of her skull. Her dress was torn and her limbs were twisted and shattered, almost making it look like he'd tried to fold her into an oversized wallet.

I turned away, opening the helmet's visor so I could retch.

"DON'T PUKE, DON'T YOU DARE PUKE!" Helios roared at me through his sobs. "THAT'S EVIDENCE! YOU CAN'T BE PUKING HERE!"

"Then what do you want me to do? What the fuck happened?"

Hands shaking, he pulled a pack of cigarettes from his pocket and tried to light one up. "We . . . we got into a fight . . . it . . . I was screaming, she saw . . . we both had some drinks, some drugs, and then . . . and then she was just . . . and . . . IT WAS AN ACCIDENT AND . . . OH GOD, WHAT HAVE I DONE! I CAN'T GO TO THE TOWER! GOD FORGIVE ME!"

He fell to the floor, sobbing uncontrollably. I didn't know what to do, so I just patted him on the back.

I didn't really have an opinion of Adriana; she was nice, if ditzy, and damn hot. I don't think she cheated on Adam as much as he cheated on her (though I had this vague image of her giving me a blowjob once, but whether that was real or a Montage binge vision, I couldn't tell you), but they'd seemed happy together.

"Help me, Aidan. Help me. We're pals, right?" he said, looking up at me with teary eyes.

"Of course."

"And you know how important I am, right? And that I can't go to the Tower for this, right?"

"Of course," I repeated. "But I mean, you've got lawyers, and the Protectors—"

"No! None of them will understand!" he said, finally lighting his cigarette. "They can get me off for this, but I'm not fucking famous enough to get off in the court of public opinion! I'll be a legally innocent man, but I'll be an innocent man who everyone knows got away with murder! We control enough of the courts and the media, but, people won't forget! I'm gonna lose my sponsors, and they're . . . and they're gonna make me another Dart Lad!"

"I don't want you to be another Dart Lad," I said. It felt weird being around another man crying. I didn't like it. "What do you need me to do?"

He perked up some at the question. "I need you to hit me as hard as you can."

"What? The last time I did that I got Icicle Man all over my shoes."

"It's not that crazy!" he said. "My telekinesis can offset it. I need you to beat me and destroy my house. I need you to make it look like you broke in, we fought, and then when Adriana got in the way you killed her before fleeing. Then I need you to run out front, put on a show for the paparazzi, and let them all put together what happened. You get blamed for her murder, I get to be a hero, and we live to fight another day."

The more he talked, the calmer he became. It was only slightly unsettling, but I had seen him bust out that voice before, and only good things came out of it. But, Adriana . . . ?

"You want me to take the fall?" I asked. That also didn't sit right. I was fine taking credit for Icicle Man's death, but taking credit for something I *hadn't* done? That just felt wrong.

"No, I don't want you to. I *need* you to. For me. For *us*. You have no idea how much of Kayfabe I hold together, do you? How many of our plans for you require me? And that without me, it'll start to fall apart, and maybe you and your friends will be left alone, and then be caught by bigger and more powerful superheroes without us to protect you?" he said, gravely.

"Adam?"

"Yeah?"

"I'm on your side, you don't have to threaten me," I said, patting him on the back. He jolted away, as if my hand were electrified, before smiling unevenly.

"I'm sorry, man, this is just . . . this is just fucked. You can understand why I'm a little paranoid, right?" I'd never accidentally murdered my girlfriend in a coked-up rage and then asked someone to help me cover it up, but I had an idea of where he was coming from.

So I surrounded my fist with focus, and punched him in the jaw.

He flew through the air, smashing into the wall, shattering his framed gold record from the time the Protectors recorded that anti-domestic violence benefit song.

"I WASN'T READY YET!" he yelled, spitting out blood.

"I'm sorry!"

"But I like your enthusiasm," he continued, laughing. "Come on, do it again. We really have to trash this place."

So we trashed his place. I threw him around, smashing him into walls, floors, the ceiling. At his suggestion I broke his nose, a few of his ribs, and his right wrist. He blasted holes in his walls with energy bursts (and used them to eliminate all his drugs) while I ripped up the floor and the ceiling and flung pieces of furniture. Adam didn't want her body messed up too much, so he folded her into the fridge. Then he got the idea for me to hurl it out on the front lawn with her still inside.

"I can see it now," he said. "Grainy, black-and-white picture of the fridge on its side, right next to my statue, the door cracked open slightly, her bloodstained hand poking out. Top trending, cover of every newspaper and magazine . . . somebody's going to win some awards for that one."

You can never say that Adam lacked vision.

We'd just tossed the fridge through his front wall and stood staring out at the road a good distance away. It was late, so there were few signs of life, but you could see a couple of lights on at the parked paparazzi cars.

"They're probably wondering what the hell is going on. They don't know that they're gonna get the story of their careers tonight," Adam said, cradling his shattered wrist.

"So, are you going to call this in?"

"No, I'm emotionally traumatized by what I just went through." He started snorting heavily, forcing more tears to come. "This is how they're going to find me. Kneeling by the refrigerator. Crying. Calling her name."

"Showing that you're just like everyone else. I like it."

"Still better than them, but, yeah, that's the idea."

There was blood and dust on my hands. I rubbed them on my cape, not that that helped terribly much. I stared at the refrigerator, at the statue. Something nagging just pulled at me, something I had to get out.

"Hey Adam? What were you guys fighting about?"

"We're pals, Aidan, right?"

"Of course."

"Then don't ask me that question again."

"Sure," I said, not sure if I should be worried or calmed by his smile.

"Cool. Thanks. It's just . . . it's rough. It's love. It's life. It's all so complicated."

Even with that nagging uncertainty, I knew that was all I'd get.

"Come on, let's get into character," he said.

I nodded, closing the visor of my helmet and running down his driveway.

I wondered what this would look like in the morning. Though I knew I was sad about what had happened to Adriana, I couldn't help but feel that my career was back on track.

#Supervillainy101: The Stereotypes

In the early 70s, when the War on Villainy really started to kick into gear, the Protectors began receiving criticism for their lack of diversity, in that most of it—and its subteams—membership were made up of heroes from the United States, the British Empire, and the Soviet Union. Seeking to improve public relations on this front, a new subteam, "The Worldwide Protectors," was created. Consisting of Zulu Warrior, Comanche Princess, Dark Djinn, Miss Mekong, Lady Jaguar, and Maui, these teenaged heroes dressed in costumes based on their traditional heritages were supposed to usher in a new, "globally conscious era of heroism," according to their press releases.

Not long after they were introduced, the public gave them a new nickname: the Stereotypes.

Their costumes were bad jokes, their stage personalities were poorly written, and with all the money and time put into promoting the team, the Protectors kept them far away from the front lines, making them the punchline of pretty much every tabloid and late night host. After two years of this, and rumors that the team might be disbanded, the Worldwide Protectors went vigilante and started fighting crime on their own time.

Of course, with vigilantism outlawed, they were quickly branded as villains and were all promptly taken down by the Protectors.

Ever since, the Protectors have tried to pretend that this team never existed.

#LessonLearned: Sometimes, even superheroes make mistakes.

PUBLIC RELATIONS

I'd forgotten how bright the War Room could get. Dozens of small holographic projectors lined the walls, allowing heroes on the other side of the world to walk among us and explain our missions while transporting us to an almost video game quality recreation of where these missions would take place. As usual, Fifty-Fifty gave the main portion of our briefing, while today he was backed up by Helios and Shooting Star.

We had a unique opportunity coming up, Fifty-Fifty told us. Word through the grapevine was that one of our old teammates had some high-powered liberal lawyer who wanted to give them their day in court. While there wasn't word on just which teammate it was, with the hearing set in the Old Amber City Courthouse (a nine-story, 50s-style office building that would make an easy target), the chance to free them would make for great publicity. Security there was poor, and aside from the SWAT team escorting the prisoner, resistance would be minimal. It would probably be the easiest Black Cape Job we would ever have; a perfect way to get back in the game before working us up to some of the big plans they had ahead.

Easy. I liked the sound of that.

Now that we'd mostly succeeded in detoxing, the itch to do something big was coming back.

I wanted to be Apex Strike and play supervillain with my friends again. But, as usual, leave it to Trojan Fox to throw a wrench in things.

Right as Fifty-Fifty was finishing up, she raised her hand. This wasn't unusual; Trojan Fox was a stickler for details and would always ask at least a dozen more questions than any of us would think of. They always turned out to be good questions, but it still got annoying.

"What are we going to do about Jimmy?" she asked.

This made the heroes chuckle, slightly. Fifty-Fifty said, "Jimmy's been dealt with."

"*Dealt with* like he's stuck in the Tower *dealt with*, or *dealt with* like buried in a shallow grave *dealt with*?" she asked.

"The Tower, 'course," Shooting Star said.

"We're not animals," Helios added.

"That's up for debate," Trojan Fox muttered, glaring at him. She wasn't the only Offender who hated Helios for making me take the fall for Adriana's death, but she was the one who hid her contempt the worst.

"Excuse me?" Fifty-Fifty asked.

"Nothing," she said, toying around with her tablet until one of the walls exploded with pictures of a burning school, charred skeletons, and an idiot with a grin on his face screaming how awesome he was.

I was really getting sick of seeing him.

Adam, Adriana, and I were the top trending news story for four days after her death. There was another wave of stories about how terrible Apex Strike was, more mourning for a super-hero's lost girlfriend, her funeral, and lots of footage of a teary Adam, mourning her and vowing to bring me to justice.

And then Jimmy had to knock us out of the top spot.

Jimmy Janks was a high school freshman from Pensacola, Florida. Everybody said he was a quiet kid who mostly kept to himself and played a lot of video games. Nobody expected him to come to school with his newfound pyrokinetic abilities and burn it to the ground. Almost three hundred people (299 to be exact) died in the inferno. He waited on the school's front lawn, occasionally tossing fireballs at emergency personnel and giving interviews to the media until the Protectors opened a Tri-Hole and took him down. At the end, he was screaming and laughing and smiling so wide, you'd have thought he was crazy if his words weren't so clear.

"THE NEW OFFENDERS KICK ASS! WOOO! IF YOU GUYS ARE RECRUITIN', I AM *SO* IN! LOOK ME UP!"

After that, Adam, Adriana, and I were replaced by memorials to the lost kids and commentaries wondering if we, as supervillains, had gone too far in inspiring such a catastrophe. Talking heads argued that it was our duty to turn ourselves in to prevent further incidents, while others argued for more media responsibility, saying that the sensationalizing and glorification of our actions was the true danger (these voices were quickly shot down, since who wants to hear something *that* depressing?).

Trojan Fox followed up with another question. "I was wondering if there was anything we could do. Maybe put out a video denouncing Jimmy Janks' actions, try and discourage other dipshits from attempting something similar again?"

The heroes got a good laugh at this.

"Now why would we want to do that?" asked Fifty-Fifty.

"Well, first off, because it makes us look bad. By saying nothing, we implicitly approve of what happened. And second, we do want to discourage uncontrolled villainy, don't we? I mean, every act of supervillainy that is not perpetrated under your intelligent leadership runs a greater risk for tragedy than is acceptable, doesn't it?"

"Yes and no," Helios said.

Fifty-Fifty elaborated, speaking like he was reading off a script, "We do mourn for the unfortunate loss of life in this case, but we cannot have you trying to prevent it, because acts like this show the world how truly insidious your influence is. We need them to see that you are contagious, that you affect even the most innocent of children and transform them into monsters. So yes, their loss is tragic. We will shed our tears and we will throw benefit concerts. And we will be grateful, for they further remind people how desperately their heroes are needed to prevent things like this from happening again."

"Even though you won't," Trojan Fox said.

Fifty-Fifty sighed. "Are we done here?"

"I suppose," Trojan Fox said. The heroes looked like they would rather be rid of her. Then again, they always looked that way. If it wasn't for her way with that mech suit, I'm sure they'd have gone drummer on her ages ago.

One by one the holographic projectors flickered out as the others left the room, studying their tablets. I was hoping Ghost Girl would wait up for me, but she was gone. She was still upset with me for what had happened at Helios's mansion, but thankfully seemed even more pissed with him, so I was pretty sure she'd get over it if given enough time.

Them leaving early did give me one opportunity, though.

I ran up to Adam's projection before it disappeared.

"Helios!" I called out to him.

"Hey Aidan, what's up?" It was just the two of us now in the room.

We'd only talked a few times since that night at his estate. He'd always sounded calm, relieved, and occasionally even a bit giddy, in stark contrast to how he appeared on the news. He was a good actor. I doubted he was having trouble sleeping. He didn't see Adriana joining the ever-growing list of dead people he'd known in his nightmares.

"I just . . . I just wanted to see how you were."

"I'm great," he said without hesitation. "Kind of glad for the media circus to move on. And I've already begun looking for a new place, so the timing on this worked out well."

"How was the funeral?"

He shrugged. "It was a funeral. A lot of tears. A lot of black. You remember Venera, from Archnemesis Day? Yeah, we hooked up afterward."

I had to be honest with him. "Adam?"

"Yeah?"

"Something about this . . . just doesn't feel right to me. It's like, eating me up inside even though I didn't do anything, really, this time. You got any advice?"

He put a digital arm around my shoulder. "Aidan, Adriana was a great girl, really, and I had a lot of fun with her, but what's done is done. She died. We gotta move on. And besides, she had her problems which you never saw. She was nosy as hell and damn near destroyed everything we'd worked for."

"She did?" I asked. That was certainly news to me.

"Yeah, but she didn't, so don't go worrying your pretty little head off about it. Is there anything else?"

"I guess not."

He smiled. "Good, 'cause I got a date with an Atlantean."

His hologram blinked out, and suddenly I was in an empty, dark room. What he said should have comforted me; he was usually good at doing so. But why wasn't it working this time? Why did I still have that nagging feeling of emptiness? Why didn't his answers seem like enough?

Most importantly, when the hell did I become so curious?

Curiosity is a lot like syphilis. You only need to introduce the smallest dose into your body before it spreads everywhere, eventually taking over your mind and your life before driving you insane. Of course, curiosity doesn't end up with your body rotting to pieces (usually) and can't be cured with a few rounds of antibiotics, but that's the real insidious thing about it.

The only cure for curiosity is to look into it.

Getting Showstopper to agree to the plan I had in mind was easy. Getting Ghost Girl to agree wasn't.

I started trying to mend fences with the ever-classic chocolate and flowers. When that didn't work, I tried the even more classic getting down on my knees and begging. When that didn't work, I offered to eat her pussy. This got her to laugh, and to say that she might've taken me up on the offer if she was convinced that I'd be any good at it. Still, this must have been enough, because it got her to read my aura and agree to my field trip.

So, dressed in black and bearing bouquets of flowers, we got Odigjod to teleport us to the Forest Lawn Cemetery in Hollywood.

We had to teleport in at the far edge so no one would see us, but aside from some huffing and puffing on Showstopper's part, we were clear.

"Angelique's gonna be jealous; she loves cemeteries," Showstopper said.

"It's better if we keep this small. If all seven of us showed up, they might get suspicious," I said.

"Should Odigjod go?" Odigjod asked. As usual on field trips, it felt strange to see him in human form.

"Nah, stick around, Odigjod," I said. "Take in the sights if you want; I don't think we'll need you till we leave."

Smiling, he pulled a camera from his pocket and took off running down the road, looking for celebrity graves.

"Well, he's gonna sleep well tonight," Showstopper laughed.

"You know, if he actually slept," I said.

"Figure of speech."

"I hate to be the voice of reason here, but do either of you know where we're going?" Ghost Girl asked. I looked to Showstopper. He shrugged.

"Dunno, but I can find out," he said, bounding off towards a greenskeeper not too far away. He turned on the waterworks, throwing his arms into the air and ultimately getting a hug from the confused-looking workman. He bounded on back to us with a folded napkin in his hand.

"Got a map!" he said enthusiastically. "Now if my services are no longer needed . . ."

"They are," I said.

"Well, shit, are you sure?"

"Positive," Ghost Girl said. "We need you on crowd control."

"But if you're really good, we'll take you grave hunting afterward," I added.

"And perhaps buy you some ice cream," Ghost Girl said, without missing a beat.

"You know, you guys can really be cocks sometimes," Showstopper said.

"Supervillains," Ghost Girl added.

"Can you guys at least tell me *why* we're here?"

Ghost Girl and I exchanged looks, but didn't say anything. According to what Trojan Fox and Odigjod said, the abilities of our Creepers were greatly overstated by Blackjack. They weren't really listening devices, but they could get a good read on our emotions and intentions, apparently, so long as we didn't feel too outwardly traitorous, we probably wouldn't get in any trouble. That being said . . .

"It's better you don't know," I said.

"Awww, come on!" he pleaded. "I can keep a secret!"

"No you can't," Ghost Girl said.

Showstopper grumbled, "You know, if I had a secret plan, I'd tell you guys."

"Next time," I said, though I sincerely hoped there wouldn't be a next time like this. I wasn't really into running around in secret, it felt too much like I'd get caught. I much preferred the straight-up, costume battle side of supervillainy where I was guaranteed an easy getaway.

Still, despite his bitching and grumbling, he led us to the gravesite. There were dozens of bouquets and wreaths around her tombstone, pictures, teddy bears, everything you'd expect from a hurried memorial. There were a few tourists taking pictures there, and a few mourners for other gravesites within eyeshot.

"Can you take care of them?" I asked.

"Please," Showstopper said. "Watch and learn."

My heart skipped a beat as he clapped his hands. I almost expected him to stage one of his elaborate musical numbers, which wouldn't have made for a very subtle visit. He behaved himself, though. Raising his hands only slightly, he got each and every single person within eyesight of us to walk away.

He explained, "The trick is not making them go away, because if that's all you're doin', then they're gonna come back and probably find themselves wonderin, *Hey, why'd I go over here again?* No, you need to make them go away with a purpose. Make them think there's something they ought be doin' somewhere else more important than what they were doin' here. Like in this case, remindin' those tourists that there's some far more interesting superhero graves over yonder hill, or those mourners rememberin' that they left the lights on in their car, or that groundskeeper over there remember he's got a break comin' up and a pretty good porno on his phone he'd rather watch."

"You are an artist," I said.

"Damn right I'm an artist."

"Think you can stay one while we take care of this?" Ghost Girl asked.

"Are you kidding? This is the most fun I've had since I got out of my tube," he said, putting in his earbuds as he ambled a short distance away.

She looked at me. "Are you sure you want to do this? I can go in on my own."

No, I wasn't sure. She'd told me that people had seriously freaked out when she tried sharing her power with them, and I didn't want to lose my mind any more than I already had.

More than that, I was afraid of what I'd see.

"No," I said. "I'm not sure."

She sighed. "Aidan . . . do I have to force you to make the choice you already know you want to make?"

"Would you?"

"With pleasure," she said, grabbing me by the wrist, shortly before the world around me exploded.

Well, not really, but all the colors went crazy. The grass took a shade of bright blue, swirling as if it were underwater. The sky became a pale, empty pink. Ghost Girl herself was glowing a bright gold, with thousands of strands of auras of every color of the rainbow hanging off her back, some of them lazy, some of them darting about as if trying to escape or grab my attention. So many came straight out of her front that it appeared she had a double, a double that moved in ways she hadn't yet moved.

Then there were the five thick, black strands that floated just above her shoulders, each bearing the faintest hint of a face locked in an angry scream.

"Don't look over your shoulder," she said. Naturally, I did. Icicle Man's screaming, half-skinned face stared back at me, all black and darting at me like a snake.

I screamed. I looked away. That was even worse. The ground was covered in dead bodies, or at least what looked like dead bodies. Brown outlines of what were once people, writhing with still living strands of auras, some vibrant and active, others faded and sluggish from time underground. Adriana's dead, brown aura lay down in front of us, her hands crossed under her breasts as her body writhed violently with aura strings.

"Dear God . . ." I said, trying to hold back my breakfast.

"Yeah, you thought they looked bad when they were just bodies," she said, waving a hand over the aura and making the strings dance, pushing some to the side while others grew and lengthened. "Ah, here we are . . ."

A small handful of glowing brown strings arced up from Adriana's head, chest, hands, and knees, swirling together to form an image that looked almost like her, sitting on a couch. She was looking at a tablet—shopping maybe, or perhaps looking at tabloid stories about herself by the way she was laughing. She looked up. Then she was at the front door, accepting a thick envelope from a messenger. Back on the couch, she tore open the envelope, spilling out papers. She looked confused.

The aura jumped.

It was some time later. She was hugging, kissing Helios, welcoming him home. They shared some drinks, some food, some drugs, had sex. They were getting ready for a night out when she mentioned the messenger and the paperwork. In a rage, he turned on her, yelled at her for going through his personal things. She was confused. She was crying. He hit her once.

That was all he needed.

She was folded in half.

She died.

She never knew why.

I wrenched free from Ghost Girl, doubling over and spilling my breakfast on the still-blue grass. My powers flickered, flattening the grass around me, then making me feel as weak as a kitten.

She patted me on the back. "It's a lot to take in the first time. When I first manifested this power, I screamed for nearly a day."

"Did you throw up too?"

"No," she said. "Did you get what you wanted?"

"Not really. He just turned on her like *that*. I mean . . . I don't think he meant to kill her, he was crying way too much, but . . . what the hell was in that envelope?"

"One moment," Ghost Girl said, her eyes again flashing gold. "She didn't get a good look at what was inside, but she did get a good look at the outer label: SITUS CONSTRUCTION. Does that name mean anything to you?"

Strangely enough, it did. "My dad did some consulting work with them. They're one of the biggest urban renewal companies in the country."

"Why the hell would that set Helios off?"

"I don't know," I said. "But we know someone who could find out."

#Supervillainy101: Otis Shylock

Though the official War on Villainy was declared in the United States, other world powers had been fighting their own versions for some time. In the early Silver Age, higher-ups in the British Empire created the Ministry of Loyalty & Security for the sole purpose of rooting out subversive superhuman elements within the government.

They may have even succeeded, too, if they hadn't hired Otis Shylock to head the Ministry.

On paper he sounded like the ideal candidate. A decorated veteran of World War II (having fought across France, India, and the Pacific) and an experienced MI5 operative, he was charming, handsome, intelligent, and unquestionably loyal to the crown.

Unbeknownst to his superiors, he was also a superhuman sociopath with mind control powers and the ambition to make himself into a modern day Moriarty. While he did his job well, he used his influence and powers to create a network of human and superhuman operatives with a near cult-like devotion throughout the Empire. While they spent these earliest years setting up a number of criminal enterprises to build capital and influence, his ultimate goal was nothing shy of global domination.

And he would have gotten away with it too, if it hadn't been for a joint intelligence operation between the Soviets and Atlantis. Their spies within the Empire exposed Shylock's dealings, forcing him to go underground (though not before making nearly one thousand of his followers commit suicide). The Empire was embarrassed and paranoid, the Ministry of Loyalty & Security was disbanded, and despite his failure, Shylock had the infrastructure in place to make him one of the world's greatest supervillains for decades to come.

#LessonLearned: Nothing sets people on edge like a good conspiracy.

20

THE AMBER CITY CAPER

We usually stayed out of Professor Death's old laboratory, partly because Trojan Fox had claimed it, partly because it was one of the island's creepier corners. Aside from the heroes taking some of Professor Death's more creative toys, it was mostly left like they found it: full of half-built robots, torture devices, and shattered genetic experiment tubes. The giant death ray that held a place of pride in the center of the expansive chamber was supposed to have been deactivated, but I'd seen Trojan Fox tinkering with it in her spare time.

She'd installed more lights since I'd last been in, put in some carpeting and removed all the cobwebs, so it seemed about as homey as an old cave could get.

Ghost Girl, now wearing her doll mask, and I went to see her right after we got back from the cemetery. As usual, she was working in the small, enclosed workshop off to the lab's far end. She said she liked it in there because it was quiet.

She was dressed up nicer than usual and, if I wasn't mistaken, was wearing makeup.

"What do you want?" she asked, irritated.

I smirked. "Were you expecting someone else?"

Ghost Girl chuckled, lightly. "We're in the way of a hot date."

"Really?" I asked.

"No!" Trojan Fox said defensively, then looking at Ghost Girl, "Yes, fine. What's going on? Make it fast."

I looked up around the workshop's walls. "So . . . you say you like it because it's quiet in here?"

She got my meaning quickly enough, crossing the room and closing the door.

"These walls don't hide everything, but I've made them so they put our Creeper signals on a feedback loop. Talk."

And so I did. I told her about what I'd seen the night Adam killed Adriana and the things he'd said that made me curious.

Ghost Girl then told her about what we'd seen at the cemetery.

"So you came to me because you want to use my technological aptitude and utter hatred for the superhero fucks who put us here to find out why Helios killed his girlfriend based on the paperwork from this construction company, and why he believes that this information, if leaked, could ruin us all?"

"Pretty much, yeah," I said.

She smiled. "Of course I'll help! You do want me to dig up info to blackmail or disgrace him, don't you, because if so I could really work something up with Adriana's mur—"

I cut her off, "NO! I don't want to hurt him, I just . . . I just have to know why he asked me to do what I did."

Reaching for an earring on the table, she looked like a kid who'd been told she couldn't go to Disneyworld. "So, all I get for this is your peace of mind?"

"You'll get my peace of mind too, if that helps," Ghost Girl said.

"That's better," Trojan Fox said as she put her earring on.

"And if you ask really nice, he'll probably eat your pussy," Ghost Girl joked.

"Hey!" I exclaimed.

"Ew," Trojan Fox said, shuddering.

"HEY!" I exclaimed, even louder.

"I'm sorry, but that's just gross," Trojan Fox said.

"Oh come on, he's not *that* bad," Ghost Girl added.

"You do know I'm still here, right?" I said, ready for them to change the subject.

"Peace of mind, got it," Trojan Fox said. "Now get the hell out of here, all right?"

I started to feel better the moment we walked out of the workshop. Despite her personality and volatility and, well, pretty much everything else about her, I really respected Trojan Fox. She was easily the smartest person on this island, was more invested in keeping the team alive and together than just about anyone, and was a strong contender for the second best showman on our team after myself. She gave me a lot of shit, but she smiled enough after doing it that I knew she liked me.

I could hear Odigjod teleport into the workshop behind us.

"Sounds like her ride's here," I said.

Ghost Girl looked over her shoulder, her eyes gold. "In more ways than one."

It took a second for this to sink in. "Odigjod?"

"Oh yeah."

"And her?"

"Yes."

"Ew."

If Trojan Fox found anything in those next few days, she didn't tell us. It was business as usual around the mansion as we hung out, attended therapy (which was a mixed bag, since therapy had Nevermore on something of an abstinence bend while she tried to rediscover herself), and spent every available moment planning for our Amber City job. It may have been an easy Black Cape Job, but in our state we didn't want to fuck it up.

There was a lot of talk about which one of our old teammates we'd be rescuing. Circus seemed the most likely, given his age, but odds were that it was probably some drummer we wouldn't even remember from our Montage binge.

Finally, the day came.

It felt good to see everyone back in costume as we entered the Green Room. Even better to see Showstopper and Ghost Girl in their new, professional uniforms. True to form, Showstopper's was gaudy and colorful, with a domino mask that looked like it shouldn't even fit on his wide, smiling face, and a wild, heavy wig that would have put him at home in an 80s hair metal band. Ghost Girl's was similar to her old one, with a black hooded cloak and a tight white bodysuit with some armor and tech built in. They wanted to give her a newer, higher-tech mask, but she flat-out refused.

She looked good. We all did. We were happier, we were healthier, we were ready to be supervillains again.

"All right people, it's showtime," Fifty-Fifty said over our radios. "This is gonna be easy. They've got only one SWAT team guarding the prisoner, they've only got a skeleton crew on duty at the courthouse itself, and it seems they've evacuated a few surrounding blocks in case there were any surprises in store. You're gonna give them that surprise."

"Got it," I said, looking to my team as our radios cut out. *My* team.

I knew, as their leader, I should make a speech, and though I didn't really have one planned out, I did my best. "You all know what you're supposed to do, and where you're supposed to be. Just follow the script and have fun. You're the best team a supervillain could hope for."

"Thanks, boss," Trojan Fox said, sarcastically.

"Hey, come on, he's just trying to be nice," Geode said.

"Yeah, do we all get a hug and a kiss to send us off too?" Showstopper joked.

"Odigjod would enjoy a hug," Odigjod said, transforming into his bigger, furrier, villainous form.

"And he is not that bad a kisser," Nevermore added.

"Thank you, Nevermore. But like Fifty-Fifty said, it's showtime. Hellspawn, see us off."

Tapping a clawed finger to his forehead, Odigjod grabbed Nevermore tight and disappeared. He popped back and forth every thirty seconds, taking Geode, Ghost Girl, Showstopper, and Trojan Fox, leaving me for last. The brief gaps gave me a moment to think and be hopeful. Hopeful that the whole Helios thing . . . that'd turn out to be nothing. We would work fine as a team. So fine that they'd see that maybe the whole drummer idea was a bad one, or that maybe the eighth member of our team (if we were adding one on after this caper) would be a more suitable drummer than any of our seven. We would have to talk to the heroes, but I was sure that we could make them see—

There was static in my earpiece, and a voice I hadn't heard in a long time.

"New Offenders, Apex Strike, is anyone there?"

"Blackjack?" I asked.

"Thank Christ," she said over the radio. "Abort the mission! The others, they don't know!"

"Know what?"

"Abort! Repeat, abort! They don't know it's a tr—"

Odigjod was at my side, grabbing me, taking me with him to a dingy, empty hallway, before teleporting away to his position. I couldn't hear Blackjack anymore. In fact, I couldn't hear much of anything but the other confused voices in my ear.

"My sensors are on the fritz, I can't read anything," Trojan Fox said.

"This place is a ruin, there is no way this is an active courthouse," Geode said.

"I'm getting no auras here. Something's very wrong," Ghost Girl said.

Everything they said set off alarms that Blackjack had just started ringing. But . . .

"We've got a job to do," I said, my voice shaky. There was no way we could back out. Blackjack didn't have the authority to abort missions, only Fifty-Fifty, Helios, and Everywhere Man could, and they weren't saying a thing. This felt wrong, as wrong as anything had ever felt, but I didn't want to disappoint the heroes, not when we were just getting back on our feet.

"Let's just do what we came here to do and get out. No showboating, just get our man and get the hell out of here," I said, regaining some strength in my voice. We could hear them coming down the hallway in front of us.

Showtime.

I peeked out into the hallway. There were at least twenty of them, flanking a large steel coffin on a dolly that had to hold our prisoner. They all wore heavy body armor, face-concealing helmets, and carried automatic weapons.

We could handle them.

"Shock and awe," I said into the radio.

Nevermore and I stepped into the wide, long hallway from our hiding places. I aimed high, blasting out the lights and ceiling panels while she filled the air with ravens, disorienting the SWAT team. This allowed Odigjod to teleport in and take all their guns before Showstopper took over the crowd, put them into a quick dance number, and dropped them to the floor. Geode and Ghost Girl knocked down the few left standing while Trojan Fox rushed in to secure the steel coffin.

It took us only sixteen seconds.

"Now that's what I'm talking about!" I exclaimed. This even seemed to set the others at ease, enough that I was beginning to relax. Maybe there was something wrong, but maybe, just maybe . . .

Surprisingly, one of the SWAT guys near me stood back up. He was a big guy, taller than all of us and built like a linebacker. He stepped toward me, slowly, with one hand raised calmingly.

"Step down, young man. You don't want this to get any worse," he said. *That voice . . .*

"Step down?" I laughed. "Don't you know who we are?"

"I do. Do you know who we are?"

"That's . . . that's a weird fucking thing to say."

I raised a hand, let loose with a blast of focus to his chest, just enough to knock him off his feet.

But it didn't. He stood his ground. Didn't even stumble. I gave him a stronger blast. It just made a tear in his SWAT outfit. There was no blood, no flesh. Just . . . *gold and green spandex?*

"Oh shit . . . oh no no no no no FUCK!"

He tore off his SWAT outfit to reveal a tight, muscle-hugging suit of green and gold, a bright red cape unfurling behind him. As if the logo on his chest weren't enough, him pulling off his helmet to reveal that green and red luchador mask confirmed his identity.

El Capitán.

"Surrender now, and no one will be hurt," he said firmly, calmly. I was staring down the greatest superhero in the world, the guy I'd idolized before I could even talk, the guy whose posters decorated my bedroom wall until the day I became a supervillain. The guy who could—

There was a high-pitched, warbling scream somewhere down the hall. It took me a second to realize it was Odigjod. A glowing tree had sprouted in the hallway, nooses dangling from one of its limbs, tying around Odigjod and lifting him off the ground. His powers could do nothing against this as he tried to fight his way loose. Seeing the swirl of glowing tarot cards nearby, I knew what was happening.

At once, the SWAT team members all got to their feet and ripped off their costumes like novelty strippers, though instead of naked bodies beneath, there were at least twenty of the world's greatest superheroes.

El Capitán

Arcana

The Gamemaster III

Minuteman IV

Locust Man

Shield Maiden

ATHENA

Horus

None of them were Kayfabe.

None of them would show us any mercy.

"Your escape route is gone. Surrender," El Capitán said, levitating off the ground, his eyes glowing red with energy that would surely cut through me.

"What do we do?" Nevermore asked.

"I don't know."

Showstopper started, "How are we going to—"

"I don't know!"

"COVER YOUR EARS!" Trojan Fox yelled over the radio. Before I could ask why, a piercing shriek filled the air, forcing heroes and villains alike to their knees. One of her suit modifications, no doubt. My helmet kept the worst of it out, but that didn't help things make any more sense.

"Free Odigjod and get us the hell out of here!" she yelled at me, making a beeline for Odigjod in his magical tree. I followed. He squealed and fought, looking at us pitifully.

Before we could get him, Horus and Arcana stood in our way. Arcana slammed a card into Trojan Fox's chest, cutting the shrieking sound her suit made. Trojan Fox blasted Arcana through the air with energy from her gauntlets while

I surrounded my fist with focus and smashed it into Horus's falcon head. He slammed hard into the wall.

I'd never hit an actual god before. It'd have felt better if we weren't so royally fucked in every other way.

The heroes were on us as soon as they could stand, attacking in groups of three and four simultaneously and never letting up.

This isn't how it works in the cartoons!

It was madness. I was punched, kicked, and blasted with multiple powers all at once. Someone hit my suit's sound system hard enough to start a song. *No, Lou, this isn't a "Perfect Day."*

While I had to fight off Minuteman, Locust Man, Vulcan, and the Champion of Venus, I could only get glimpses of the others faring little better.

Geode tripled in size, grabbing El Capitán and launching both of them through the ceiling.

Several heroes piled on top of Nevermore, only to be pulled off by Shield Maiden, who Showstopper had gained control of. With some effort, he managed to seize Caveman's powerful mind and had him fighting the heroes as well.

ATHENA and several of her similarly mech-suited teammates surrounded and blasted Trojan Fox, and though her armor was as high-tech as any of theirs, she was taking a lot of damage.

Ghost Girl engaged Arcana and Horus with her quarterstaff and did well despite their great advantages. One hit to the throat sent Arcana doubling over, while one to the groin got Horus to fall on top of her.

And there I was, in the middle, blasting and trying to fight off heroes who weren't just pretending to try to capture me. Locust Man got me in a headlock and used his superstrength to twist me to face Vulcan as he approached me with a halo. *No no no, this isn't how this is supposed to go!*

The ceiling exploded above us as Geode and El Capitán, still grappling, smashed through and to the floor in front of us. Vulcan was nowhere to be seen. I got the impression he took the express elevator to the basement with El Capitán. *So that just leaves these three* . . .

Minuteman shouldered his enchanted musket as he pulled a halo from his tri-corner hat and approached me. I blasted the ground at his feet, intending to make a hole that would send him to the basement with the others. I must have aimed too high, however, as his legs exploded outward in awkward, horrible directions.

He screamed a lot louder than I would have expected.

"Holy shit!" Locust Man shrieked, loosening his grip on me just enough. I placed a hand next to his head and focused. He flew through the air, bouncing from wall to wall. He hit the ground moaning and writhing, his famous Locust helm shattered around what was probably a less pretty face than it was this morning.

There was no time for victory, but there was plenty of time for the feeling of fingers wrapping around my brain. I screamed, falling to my knees and clawing at my helmet trying to get them out.

I apologize for having to resort to such invasive methods of incapacitation, but you have given me little choice, a powerful, ethereal voice echoed in my head.

The Champion of Venus. He had one of the greatest grab bags of powers in the world: strength, flight, shapeshifting, the ability to smell colors, and telepathy, and was often called the second most powerful Protector after El Capitán.

Give in to my voice. Close your eyes, and all pain of this world will end, he intoned.

A battle cry made the Champion of Venus look up from me just long enough to see Shield Maiden run at him and smash him into a gooey, yellow stain on the wall. She continued to stomp on him as he tried to reform, keeping him in as many pieces as possible.

Showstopper ran to me, huffing and puffing, with blood running down his face from a gash in his forehead.

"Thanks."

"Any time, mate. You guys sure know how to party!"

"This isn't supposed—"

"I know, I was just kid—"

The crackle of a Tri-Hole opening filled the air. Turning to find it, I saw Arcana and another wounded superhero dragging the magical tree containing Odigjod through. He reached out a hand to us, his many eyes pleading as he called out for help.

Then the Tri-Hole was gone.

"Oh no," I said. "We're fucked! WE'RE FUCKED!"

"Apex Strike, clear the line! Everyone, Odigjod is down!" Trojan Fox said over the radio, her voice shaking but still in control. "Grab a Tri-Hole generator from a downed hero and make it home. We need to get the fuck out—"

A wall exploded down the hallway. I half-expected to see Geode and El Capitán pour through, grappling and exchanging blasts of crystal and laser vision.

What really came through the hole was much worse.

The Golem.

"WE'RE FUCKED!" I screamed again. This time Trojan Fox wouldn't shut me up.

El Capitán and Geode burst through the floor in front of the Golem. It just punched them both through a nearby wall and started running toward us.

"I got this," Showstopper said determinedly, cracking his knuckles. I didn't know what he planned to do. I didn't know what he *could* do. We had to run, we had to get out of here, didn't he see that?

He had complete control over Shield Maiden, two of ATHE-NA's lesser mech-suit teammates, and a Soviet heroine whose name I could never remember. He threw each in front of the Golem. The mech suits went by the wayside pretty quick, and Shield Maiden only slowed it for a moment. The Soviet must have had superstrength, because she was able to slow the Golem almost to a stop by digging in her feet. Irritated, the Golem grabbed her by the shoulders and flung her down the hall, smashing through wall after wall.

Showstopper's determination faltered. He turned to run, facing me. Faster than you would think for a monster so large, the Golem caught up and grabbed him in both of its massive hands. Lifting him over its head, the Golem ripped Showstopper in half, squeezing him to a bloody pulp for good measure.

He didn't even scream.

I thought he would scream.

The room went silent. I know there was a battle going on. I know nobody but me stopped fighting after seeing Showstopper killed, but as far as I was concerned, there was no world outside of that blood-soaked Golem and what remained of one of my best friends. There would be no more cheesy stories, no more late nights trying to decipher his Aussie slang, no more fat jokes.

Showstopper was gone.

Something popped inside me. I really, honestly think I heard a pop. My ears rang. There was a growing ball of rage that expanded beyond me. The world distorted. Debris swirled around me. My feet lifted off the ground. The walls in the hallway rippled and cracked.

I screamed, primal and inhuman.

FOCUS.

I don't remember the explosion, exactly. The news footage (from the two helicopters I didn't knock out of the sky) showed the courthouse exploding into the sky, the decades old structure reduced to shards of wood, steel, and stone, and never coming back down to earth. Buildings nearby fell over in a wave, knocking each other down like dominoes. In spite of the mass evacuations, thousands of people in the city were injured (mostly from being hit by pieces of the courthouse, some of which were found up to twenty miles away) and at least a dozen were killed.

It's been called the single greatest act of villainy on American soil since the Radiation Queens annihilated Detroit.

At the time, none of this mattered.

My feet touched the ground. I barely felt them. My nose gushed blood and I was blind in one eye, but I didn't care. I just wanted to sleep for a very long time.

I fell to my knees, aware that sound was coming back slowly, aware that there wasn't much of a courthouse anymore, aware that the top half of the Golem (minus its left arm) lay on the ground in front of me, looking confused and reaching out weakly for help. Tri-Holes opened all around in the building's smoking ruin. Voices were yelling over the radio, calling my name, seeing if anyone else was alive.

Two figures walked through the dust cloud in front of me, pausing to look at the remains of the Golem and curse.

Walking closer, I could see who they were. It almost brought out a smile.

Shooting Star and Photon. Kayfabe heroes.

My friends.

"Help," I said weakly. Her face sympathetic, Shooting Star reached a hand out to me. I reached back.

Then she blasted me in the chest with a beam of sparkling, red and blue energy. I could feel my leg breaking, vaguely, as I was roughly flung onto my back.

They both looked sad and scared as they approached me. Shooting Star said, "Sorry, cutie, but we can't have them interrogatin' you."

This wasn't exactly how I saw myself dying.

This sucks.

I saw the gunshot before I heard it. Photon's face from the nose down exploded outward. He quickly put his hands to where his mouth should have been, whether in confusion or pain I didn't know. He tried to run off at superspeed, but only managed a few steps before the rest of his head fell apart and he collapsed in a twitching heap on the ground.

Shooting Star turned to face the shooter and got a bullet through her bare midriff for her trouble. She doubled over screaming as another took her in the neck and a third blew off her lips, cheek, and most of her teeth. *Guess she's not going to be headlining concerts anytime soon.*

She fell to the ground, bleeding, twitching, and slowly dying. Another figure, small and shadowy walked out of the dust cloud, twin six-shooters in her hands smoking.

"Blackjack . . . help . . ."

"What are you doin' lyin down?" Blackjack said, looking around nervously as she ran to me. "Get up and run, you asshole!"

"Can't . . ."

"I got him," another voice said, lifting me off the ground and tossing me over her shoulders.

Ghost Girl.

Blackjack used a Tri-Hole generator to open an exit, and Ghost Girl carried me through.

Never had I been so glad to fly through the tunnel of green and screams in my life.

We landed in Death Manor's rec room. Ghost Girl set me down gingerly on a couch.

We weren't alone.

Nevermore and Geode were already there. They both looked pretty bad. One of Nevermore's arms was badly burned. Geode was broken and bleeding heavily from one of his legs while Nevermore tried to tie it off with a strip of leather from one of her boots.

"Help me, he's dying!" Nevermore cried out. Despite her limp and the gash on her belly, Ghost Girl walked across the room and began to help Nevermore tie off his leg.

Another Tri-Hole opened. Through it, the steel coffin was flung, clattering heavily to the floor. Trojan Fox followed.

Nearly half of her armor had been ripped off, and the other half was heavily damaged. She was covered in sticky, green blood.

"What happened?" Nevermore asked.

"Fifty-Fifty. He tried to kill me. I got him first."

In a rage, she ripped off her helmet and stormed to me.

"You motherfucker! This is all your fault!" she shouted and started repeatedly punching me with her one armored hand so hard she shattered my helmet.

"Helen!" Geode called out.

"We could have gotten out! We could have escaped! But *you* made us stay! *You* told us it was our job, you son of a bitch! They fucking killed Showstopper! They captured Odigjod! All because you didn't call it off when we told you that something was wrong! Are you fucking happy? ARE YOU FUCKING HAPPY?!?!?"

Ghost Girl thrust the broken, jagged end of her quarterstaff at the edge of Trojan Fox's throat.

"Helen, don't," Ghost Girl said.

"Don't *what?*" Trojan Fox asked.

"Don't think I won't do it. Don't blame Aidan for something he was forced into. Don't forget who the real enemy is. Take your pick. Either way, if you can walk, we'll need your help moving the rest into the healing pods," Ghost Girl said. She looked down at me, not unkindly, but not particularly happy with me either.

Trojan Fox stalked off, yelling in frustration and kicking a couch halfway across the room.

She knelt down beside the steel coffin.

"This better have been fucking worth it, so help me . . ." she said, prying it open.

I didn't see him sit up, but the last thing I heard before passing out was his voice.

"Took you guys long enough," Carnivore said.

#Supervillainy101: Eye Guy

When a bizarre experimental chemical accident transformed Indian scientist Vijay Thopi into a living entity composed entirely of disembodied eyeballs, he couldn't have been more thrilled. While being a living pile of eyes wasn't exactly the greatest superpower in the world, it made him unique, and he thought this was his ticket to a spot on a British superhero team.

It wasn't.

Undeterred, he started dousing himself in more experimental chemicals. In addition to putting himself in a state of constant agony, smelling absolutely terrible, and contracting three different types of ocular cancer, he also gained the ability to shift his form into any shape (so long as it was made of eyeballs), making his eyeballs harder than steel, and allowing him to see in every possible visible and non-visible spectrum. Hopped up on painkillers and chemo, he traveled to America, completely rebranded himself, and tried out for the Protectors.

They laughed him out of the room.

Embarrassed and furious, he rebranded himself again into the supervillain Eye Guy. While most hero teams wouldn't give him the time of day, there were plenty of villain teams who were interested in a guy who could fling rock hard eyeballs that could see through walls with deadly speed, and so he found himself bounced from team to team during the War on Villainy. Though it wasn't quite what he'd wanted, he was still glad someone was willing to pay him to use his powers.

Of course, medical treatments weren't cheap, and as his disease began to make him less reliable, work dried up. In the end, he attempted to commit suicide by superhero to go out in one final blaze of glory, hoping to seal his legacy. Instead, he collapsed in agony five seconds into his final fight and had to be carried off to the Tower in a sack by Black Blur.

#LessonLearned: Sometimes, no matter what you do, life just sucks.

254

21

THE MORE THINGS
CHANGE . . .

I fell into a sort of waking coma after Amber City, lying naked in bed with the TV on and its 'round the clock coverage of the aftermath. I was never quite dreaming, never quite awake, never quite sure of what was real and what wasn't.

I kept seeing the bodies. Showstopper. The Golem. The other heroes. Even the civilians the news said I killed. They got added to my usual nightly run of Icicle Man, Iron Bear, and Adriana.

My subconscious was starting to get crowded.

The civilians were mourned for, but not nearly as much as the heroes. The news had daylong retrospectives of the careers of Shooting Star, Photon, Fifty-Fifty, and Vulcan. Even though Vulcan was probably the only one the news should have been glorifying, since he was ugly as fuck compared to the other three, he got the least amount of screen time.

The greatest minds in the magical world gave interviews on how much work it would take to put the poor, damaged Golem back together, while hours were dedicated to talking heads

255

trying to figure out just why Blackjack had defected. There was some discussion about what Carnivore's escape meant, but even more gratuitous gloating about how the heroes had killed Showstopper and captured Hellspawn and how crippling a blow this was to the New Offenders, even though the captured villain refused to talk.

Time and again they played the clip of me utterly vaporizing the courthouse, knocking down building after building from my one, Golem-destroying burst.

I tried, for a while, to tell myself that this wasn't my fault; that this was just the life we led and that sometimes surprises like this happened, but the lies felt bitter.

It was my fault. I could still smell Showstopper's blood on my hands.

For a day or so, people tried visiting me, but I acknowledged none of them (unless they brought food).

Nevermore and Geode brought food and were clearly concerned.

Ghost Girl didn't bring food, but I could see her standing in the doorway, scanning me, leaving.

Carnivore crawled on my bed and straddled me, his face inches from mine, saying that as soon as I was well enough to stand, he'd give me exactly what I deserved.

His presence here was the ultimate cosmic joke, our punishment for doing this, probably.

Trojan Fox didn't come around and beat me again, even though I kind of wished she would. I certainly deserved it.

I'm sorry. I'm so sorry. Showstopper, wherever you are, if you're a ghost or a spirit or whatever, or if you're in hell with Odigjod's folks, please know I'm sorry. Please. I . . . I wouldn't trade places with you. I don't want to die, but you gotta know, I didn't want you to die either. You were my friend . . . I'm so, so sorry . . .

That damned clip again. The buildings dropping like dominoes. Helicopters falling out of the sky. The whole world exploding.

"You know, you got really lucky there."

Someone new, but not quite, stood in my doorway. He set a bag on my nightstand and sat at the foot of the bed.

"With that much power released, you're lucky you aimed it all at the Golem. Then it all went up. Otherwise you'd have killed everyone in the building, but like this . . . well, you live to villain another day."

Adam.

Of course he'd say I was lucky.

He wasn't there.

I rolled away from him. He sighed.

"We didn't know. You . . . you do believe me, don't you?"

I didn't say anything or roll back over.

"They didn't trust us, if you can believe that. They thought that because we never took you down, that a different approach was required. That's why we weren't there; they didn't tell us. They just wanted to capture you, in private, and be done with you like they were done with all the other villains. They don't have vision. They don't see your necessity."

"What about Shooting Star and Photon and the others?" I said, my first words in days.

"They were scared. Once we all found out what the other heroes were doing, they thought it might be safer to eliminate you before anyone could be interrogated and reveal Kayfabe. Thankfully, you got away before that could be an issue."

"Odigjod didn't. Showstopper didn't."

He brushed this off, almost casually: "Casualties of war. They can be replaced, though. Anyone can."

He must have heard how loud the silence in the room got because he playfully pushed my thigh. "Except you, of course! You're Apex Strike! What would we do without you?"

Good question. What *would* they do without me? All my doubt, all my fear fell into that one question.

All of it twisted together into an even crazier one.

"Do I belong here?" I asked.

257

Adam laughed. "What?"

"There were so many people in testing who were better with their powers or smart enough not to get their friends killed, and they got cut. Did I really earn my place here?"

"Aidan—"

"DID I?" I didn't mean to focus, but everything in the room lifted off the ground a few inches. At once, I could feel everything. I knew the texture of the wallpaper, the patches of carpet that were wearing thinnest, the pitiful death throes of dust mites as I crushed them in midair. Helios's breathing quickened—in fear, I was sure—though whether it was for what I had done or what he was going to say next, I didn't know. The field he made around himself moments later only kept that mysterious.

Realizing what happened, I dropped everything.

"You . . . you . . ." he said, his voice sounding remarkably like it did that night I helped him deal with Adriana's body. "You were guaranteed a spot on the team. You were so famous, how couldn't we? You and the imp, because Crystal Skull had a deal with the devil he had to make good on, and the mech, because the kids love 'em; you all had a free pass. We had to put you through the motions, but there was no way you wouldn't make the team."

Anger boiled inside of me as I faced him. "And because I made it, because I was so famous, you had me lead this team? You had me lead us into a deathtrap? You had me lose two of my best friends just so we could bust fucking *Carnivore* out of prison?"

Some of his composure regained, Adam shrugged. "These things happen."

"Get out."

"Aidan . . ."

"GET OUT!" I roared. Pain exploded in my chest. Every muscle and nerve in my body screamed as I thrashed.

Pulling the Creeper control from his pocket, Adam calmly said, "I really think you're forgetting who holds the power in this relationship, Aidan."

He let the Creeper do its thing as he stood up and brushed himself off.

"I know you're upset, and that's completely understandable. We'll be providing grief counselors to better help you cope. I've also made you a care package," he said, pointing to the bag on my nightstand. "It has some Montage, some E, some coke, some other party favors, a bottle of rather fine whiskey, and the numbers for a few very fine, very famous ladies who would be more than happy to make your acquaintance. We're sorry for overreacting over the whole Circus incident. Our big plans for you guys are coming real soon, and we want you to be happy again. We want to be *friends* again. As soon as something shiny comes along, people will forget about the attack on Amber City and we'll go out and party like there's no tomorrow."

Finally, right as he walked to the door, he turned the Creeper off. I curled up into a pained, fetal position.

"I'm sorry for all of this, but in the end, I think you'll understand," Adam said, closing the door behind him.

The tears came easily. I don't know if they were in fear, or pain, or that . . . what was that . . . betrayal? Yeah, I guess I felt like I'd been betrayed by Adam. He wasn't my friend. Friends wouldn't do that. Maybe, no, probably I knew that all along. I'm sure of that now, at least. Always that one little voice in the back of my mind reminding me that he was a superhero and I was a supervillain. I found that voice easy to ignore, usually, but now, with what happened to Showstopper and Adriana . . .

It can be like it was before. It can be so you don't have to hear that voice again.

I looked at the paper bag on my nightstand.

It called to me.

Even remembering the drugged out feeling of sick, even remembering the awful detoxing, I could feel the pull of that bag. I wanted to disappear in it.

I forced myself to sit up, gripping the edge of my bed.

I looked at the bag.

The door.
Fuck.

I padded down the hallway, now wearing boxers and a bathrobe. I tried reassuring myself that what I'd done was for the best, but enough of me felt that it was a shame to have flushed so much quality merchandise down the toilet. I just had to remind myself that I needed a clear head for what was to come next.

I made it about halfway down the hallway before Carnivore attacked me.

He leapt out of his room, his mouth curled in a wicked smile and his claws out.

"Finally," he growled. I flicked my wrist and he flew back into his room. I heard something shatter.

"I don't have time for this," I said, continuing down the hall.

That should've been the end of it. But then he charged again, quietly enough that I couldn't turn to face him. He knocked me facedown onto the rug, claws dug into my back through the robe.

"You don't have time for this?" he snarled.

"No, I don't," I said, trying to push off the ground. He pinched two of his claws at the base of my neck.

"*I* should have been *you*. You don't deserve everything they've given you."

"Way ahead of you there," I responded.

I wanted to laugh. I remembered, way back when I had feared and hated him more than anything else in the world. With everything that had happened since then, he didn't seem so bad.

Even with this, though, he was still pretty bad, especially with his claws wrapped around my spine.

"Any last words?" he hissed.

"He doesn't need any."

His yip was high and full of surprise when he was ripped from my back by the spectral sailing ship (*Grampus*?) projected from Nevermore's chest. Geode stood beside her, his arms, chest, and shoulders encased in crystals as he charged Carnivore, grabbing him by the throat and pinning him to the wall.

"Now you haven't been around lately, so we're going to cut you some slack this time," Geode said.

"But we are tired of taking your shit, you American piece of trash," Nevermore added, then looking to me. "No offense."

"None taken," I said.

"Fuck . . . all . . . of . . . you . . ." Carnivore choked out.

Nevermore laughed. "That won't be easy when we've cut off your cock and fed it to some dinosaurs, will it? Geode, pull off his pants."

Geode transformed his face into a terrifying, crystalline smile, placing his free hand on Carnivore's leg. Nevermore recalled the spectral ship only to send out that black, stylized orangutan with the straight razor in its hand.

"You can't do this!" he howled, looking down at me. "Apex Strike, tell them . . ."

Nevermore helped me to my feet. I brushed myself off and shrugged. "What can I say? We're supervillains."

If it was even possible, his eyes went wider.

"You don't get to fuck with us anymore," Geode said, his voice more gravelly as even more of him transformed into crystal. "We've seen so much, done so much together, that now, we are one. You fuck with one of us, you fuck with *all* of us."

Carnivore yowled, "You can't do this! I'll kill you! I'll kill you all!"

Nevermore rolled her eyes. "Some never learn. Make him a cage?"

"With pleasure," Geode said, tossing Carnivore roughly back into his room. He shot crystal spikes from his hands that rapidly grew into a wall, blocking off the door.

"Thanks," I said to Nevermore.

She smiled. "It's not a problem. We were going to do that soon anyway. You just gave us an excuse to make it sooner."

"Well, I'm just glad I could be your excuse then," I said. "Have you seen Ghost Girl and Trojan Fox?"

"Yes, they are both in the laboratory."

"Excellent," I said, storming off down the hall.

She quickly caught up to me. I didn't really want her to come, but I also didn't want to risk any of the consequences of telling her no, especially when she was in a cock-cutting mood.

She got right to the point. "I know we haven't talked in a long time. And I know, maybe, we never really talked at all. And I just wanted to apologize to you for everything."

"You mean for getting railed by all those superheroes?"

She frowned. "I meant more for using you. For using everyone. When we fucked, I fucked your mask, not you. I thought if I fucked someone with status, that it'd raised me up too, but it really just cheapened us both. It's not easy to see something like that, but I have, and I wanted to apologize. Will you forgive me?"

"Sure," I said again. I thought this might have gotten her off my back. Instead this only made her angry.

"You know, you are really terrible at this! You were supposed to say, '*I would forgive you if there was something that needed forgiving, but there was not because I was using you like a whore to make myself feel better, too!*' Then we would laugh, smile, maybe hug, and start learning what each other is like as a human being, no?"

In her rage, her tattoos almost seemed to all burst from her skin as one.

"Look . . . you're probably right about that, and this is something that I really think deserves serious conversation. But right now, just this second, I'm dealing with some shit that's bigger than you, and me, and all of us, and I really don't think I'll be able to talk to you like you deserve to be talked to until I get this

whole thing sorted out. I don't think I'm going to be as construc-
tive a talker as you need until I can figure out just what's going
on, and how I gotta deal with it."

It wasn't a great speech, nor was it enough to make Nevermore truly happy, but it was enough to get her to say, "We will
talk about this later?"

"Yes."

"Good. Because I need to make my amends to move on, and
you are the only one here I can do that with."

"Well that's—wait . . . you're doing Twelve Steps?"

"Fuck no. That would mean believing in a merciful God. I'm
thinking more like five or six steps. If I can get most of them
done with you, though, then I'm fine."

She laughed. I laughed. Neither laugh was all that bright
and cheerful, but it was progress.

She didn't have to see me all the way to the lab after that.

I didn't know how I felt about Nevermore anymore, not
really, not beyond thinking she was hot, and broken, now that
some shit experiences had helped clear my eyes, but I was pretty
sure I liked her in a non-sexual way too (though that was still
there, and nice).

It's funny the sorts of things grief will make you realize.

Trojan Fox had been busy. The lab was cleaner than I had ever
seen it, and she had clearly been working on her projects.

Ghost Girl walked out of the workshop. "She wants to see
you, and wants to kill you," she said.

"She does?"

"For different reasons. The part of her that wants to see you
is stronger than the part of her that wants to kill you, so you'll
probably live," Ghost Girl said, leaving the lab.

"Thanks for the warning."

Great. Now for the hard part. I steeled myself to enter her workshop, putting a small wall of focus in front of me that would deflect anything thrown or shot my way . . . unless it was a laser, which her suit had several of.

Then I'd be pretty well fucked.

She wasn't in her suit (or her legs, for that matter, and her balance on that stool looked damned precarious), but was working on it. The full ashtray next to her told me she'd been at this for a while. Pieces of the Trojan Fox suit were spread across the table, her hands working deftly as she soldered elements in place.

She didn't even look up to me to say, "He's a spy, you know."

"What?"

"Carnivore," she said, blowing a small bit of smoke away. "I'm not certain, but look at it logically. Why would they bait a trap with real bait unless said bait was intended as a backup plan in case we did find a way to escape the trap? Make him a trap within a trap? I'm not saying they found a way to turn him—he's far too much of a raging dumbfuck for that—but the real heroes probably have injected him with some nanites, or perhaps interdimensional implants intended to find us or ferret out information. The island's shield is strong enough to block out any of those transmissions, but we can't let them recapture him, at least not without letting me do a thorough exam to remove anything dangerous . . . or of course we could always kill him."

"Well, that's great," I said, "but—"

She pressed a button on one of her suits gauntlets, activating a holographic projector like we had in the War Room. News feeds, financial documents, pictures of us and the heroes flew across one of the walls.

"I looked up Helios and Situs Construction. I thought that rabbit hole might be deep, but I didn't know just how—"

"Trojan Fox, *Helen*, I want to—"

"—they're one of the biggest construction firms in the world specializing in cleaning up after superhero-supervillain battles, did you know that? Times have been tough for them the last couple decades, with the recession and the War on Villainy's end. But, what do you know, business is booming for them these days, and their stockholders couldn't be happier. Stockholders who operate a slush fund for payoffs to people with codenames like Crystal Skull, Fifty-Fifty . . . Helios . . . I could go on, but you know all the names already."

"Fuck."

"Fuck doesn't even begin to explain what's happened," she said, swirling the images to show some of our Black Cape Jobs. "I did some, well, a *lot* of digging. Nearly every job either indirectly or directly benefited the sponsors of Kayfabe heroes. Tearing down buildings and tenements they meant to develop the land on. Suppressing dissidence, preventing developing countries under imperial control from gaining traction toward independence. Hell, remember that Sasquatch village we destroyed up near the Alaskan border?"

"No."

"Really? Some Sasquatch youth swore a blood oath against you, which is pretty impressive since that tribe was entirely pacifistic."

"I was probably really high at the time."

"Weren't we all," she said, picking a lit cigarette from the ashtray and pulling it between her lips. "Well, that village's destruction made way for a new oil pipeline, and for a public relations coup when the heroes graciously moved the Sasquatches onto a new, modern reservation to better keep them safe from us."

This was a lot more than I expected. I mean, I didn't know what I'd expected, but it sure as hell wasn't this, and I sure as hell didn't think it was this big.

"So you're saying that, Helios killed Adriana because she accidentally intercepted a payoff from Situs, and he wanted to cover it up?"

"In a roundabout way, yes. He didn't have to kill her—there's no way she was smart enough to figure out what it was—but fill him with enough paranoia and cocaine and you get one dead supermodel."

"This is huge."

"Yes, but it's hardly surprising."

"It is?"

"Of course! The heroes have grown lazy. Once they saw that their lifestyles were threatened, they did what they thought they had to do to protect themselves. Once they think they're secure enough, they will get rid of us. It's the natural order of things."

I gripped a nearby workbench, dizzy, feeling like I was going to be sick.

"Don't you dare pass out on me," she said.

"Why not?"

Finally, she faced me. I'd gotten too used to her with those fake legs—it was kind of unsettling to see her without them—but it gave her a level of honesty that I had to respect.

"Because, insane as it may be, you *are* our leader. I despise much of what you have and have not done, but, somehow, you're still the center of this group, and if we want to do anything about all of this, anything to strike back at the heroes, to *save our friends in the Tower*, it needs to start with you, and we need you on your feet."

This was the first time I'd heard her seriously speak of rebellion. Sure, some of the villains back in training joked about it, but nobody ever meant it seriously.

Hearing it now . . . it scared the shit outta me. I half-expected our Creepers to explode, ripping our ribcages out and melting us down into a steaming puddle of flesh. When they didn't (and when my heart and bowels settled), I looked at her.

"This is crazy."

"I know, but what are we going to do about it?"

I wanted to say "I don't know," but that wouldn't fly with her.

Instead, I thought long and hard. I hadn't done anything against the superheroes without having my back put against the wall since I'd killed Icicle Man. Now she'd told me a horror story that had me feeling used. Combined with what Adam had said when we were alone and I wasn't a big superhero fan at the moment.

But, given time, maybe I could be again. Maybe if I thought on this, caught Adam on a good day, we could make things like old times again. Maybe he really was my friend, and I just caught him at a bad time.

The Amber City thing was rough on all of us.

I remembered the paper bag on my nightstand. I remembered how good it felt to flush its contents down the toilet.

That got me my answer.

"Escape."

#Supervillainy101: Rando

In the years following World War II, there was no rougher place to live than the Canadian Remnant. Following their traitorous alliance with Germany, Canada (no matter how much they protested that their alliance was simply to free them of British control) was split between the allies as punishment. Most of the western half was absorbed into the United States, the Northwest Territories were given to the Soviets, and what remained in the east was made into a British penal colony to set an example for the rest of the world. Quebec, having abstained from attacking the states, became its own independent nation of Free Quebec. With the world rebuilding and the Canadian Remnant not a top priority, near-anarchy raged for years within its borders.

It didn't take long for the supervillains to come in and start carving it up.

One of the most feared villains was the gene-job, Rando. Part man, part buffalo, part badger, all violent, he was used as an enforcer by many villains across Free Quebec. He wasn't known for his speaking ability (it was said he didn't know much more than his name, or at least the word everybody assumed to be his name), but he was known for his strength, ruthlessness, and unceasing devotion to his job. It's been said that he was once sent to break a man's legs and when the man fled to Mexico City, he followed him (on foot) until he had gotten the job done, before walking home.

Many said that the only thing soft about Rando was his fur, and that may have been true, at least until he was sent to kill a school administrator in Gatineau for ripping off a black market dealer on some textbooks. Seeing the bombed-out school in shambles and the teachers trying to teach their students with pitiful resources must have changed something in Rando, for instead of killing the administrator, he suddenly donated his entire life savings to getting the school back in working order and spent his days repairing the school himself and protecting it from brigands.

Though he remained one of Free Quebec's most feared villains until the day he died, the school was so grateful for his help that they commissioned a statue in his honor.

#LessonLearned: Sometimes even supervillains have a soft spot.

22

BIG PLANS

The heroes were true to their word; they gave us a couple weeks off before briefing us on our next mission. We killed time. We talked with grief counselors who tried, and failed, to help us through what had happened in Amber City. We kept an eye on Carnivore after he broke out of his room. He stalked around the house sullenly, but mostly left us alone.

The heroes didn't.

They were trying to make things up to us, teleporting in and playing games, bringing gifts, hanging out, helping put up Christmas decorations and even bringing a tree nearly the size of the foyer and piling presents beneath it.

Them trying to be nice was an improvement over them threatening to activate our Creepers. It did, however, mean that we didn't have much time to talk about more important issues, but we still managed.

In the beginning it was just me and Trojan Fox in her workshop. Since I knew there was no way we could hide any of this from Ghost Girl, I brought her in and the others soon after. We'd been through enough together that trust wasn't an issue.

Of course, we kept Carnivore out. Even if he weren't a spy, we couldn't trust him.

We never met up all at once, but in twos and threes we talked out plans for escape, though most of the exact details Trojan Fox and I kept between us. It was a shit thing to do, but it also meant they couldn't spill too much if something happened in the meantime (like getting kidnapped and tortured).

Trojan Fox said she'd been working on plans for getting the Creepers out for some time, and was confident that she could get them out if we all worked together.

I'd trust her on that (as if I had a choice).

She said that, if she could get access to it, she could rework the shield on Death Island so that only those we wanted on the island could teleport in or out. The island would transform from our prison into our safe haven.

Fine. I'd trust her on that too.

Then she started talking about breaking into the Tower.

This is where I dug in my feet. I missed Odigjod as much as anyone else, but even if we could teleport in (which we couldn't), and even if we could do it without the heroes catching us (which we couldn't), it was still too crazy to even consider.

We didn't have much time to argue, though, because after only a few days of our Tower arguments, we got our newest drummer.

Spasm.

I'd gotten along with him back in training. He may have been a terrorist, but he was good people, and a helluva lot more fun to have around than Carnivore. His body control and healing abilities could come in handy with our plans, but could we trust him on such short notice?

He reintegrated well enough with us for a few days. Ghost Girl agreed to feel him out and see if he would join us, but hadn't come to a conclusion.

We knew when they dropped him in on us that the heroes were getting ready for a new job. Maybe even the "big plans" they'd been talking about since training.

We just didn't know how big these plans would be.

With Fifty-Fifty dead, Helios led the mission briefing. You could tell he loved the power that came with the job. Dramatically, he announced, "Ladies and gentlemen, welcome to Washington, DC!"

The holographic projectors kicked in, filling the room with swirling images of the nation's (well, my nation's at least) capitol, mostly focusing on all the monuments and museums.

"Why do these things always have to happen in America?" Trojan Fox muttered.

"Sorry, what was that?" Helios asked.

She changed the subject. "So you're going to have us steal the Hope Diamond? Isn't that a little mundane?"

She kept the sarcasm thick, so Helios wouldn't see anything was off.

It worked. "Not quite, we've got something more ambitious in mind."

He swirled the images around until we reached our destination. "Welcome to the White House. One of the most heavily fortified facilities in America. Home of the executive branch of government, and our *democratically* elected president."

"You say that word like it's a bad thing," Ghost Girl noted.

"It wouldn't be if the people knew what they were doing," Helios said, bringing up an image of the president.

"In three days' time, President Patricia Perez will give a speech in the Rose Garden, thanking the heroes for their years of service, but ultimately arguing for a scaling back of private heroism in favor of government-sponsored superheroics."

"Well we can't have that. Lower pay, more oversight, more accountability, what is the world coming to?" Trojan Fox mused.

"Exactly!" Helios exclaimed. "And that is why you will all be crashing the speech."

"So you want us to wreck the place up. Then you will swoop in, save the day, and demonstrate just why independent superheroes are superior?" Geode proposed.

"No, we want you to kill her. And anyone else who gets in your way, obviously."

If anyone had any pins in the room and felt like dropping them, the sound would have been deafening.

"Nice," Carnivore growled, smiling wickedly.

"*Why*?" Trojan Fox asked.

"Isn't it obvious? Aidan, you know your history, help me out here," Helios said with a jaunty smile.

I did know my history. I could see exactly where they were going with this.

"You want to start another War on Villainy."

"That's the plan. Though our marketing guys are thinking the Second War on Villainy pops better. We thought we might be able to spin the Amber City gig that way after you went nuclear, but President Perez had a cooler head and calmed down the masses. Can you believe she actually talked the Protectors out of initiating worldwide martial law? Once she's gone, all the other powers, the Soviets, the Brits, Lemuria, Atlantis . . . they'll all be afraid to lose what they've got, and they'll come to us. They will call upon us to restore peace and order, and it will all be because of you."

That was a part of it, yeah. It also meant even more hardcore cracking down on supers, rights would disappear, hell, they might even institute a draft for all supers.

Or they might just disappear any and all they think could be threats before they actually are threatening. Just like last time, people, not even villains, would fight back, and just like last time thousands, maybe even millions would die.

Worst of all, everyone would blame *us*.

This was the heroes' big plan, and we were their pawns.

I didn't like being used to kill people. I liked being a pawn even less.

Pawns were meant to be sacrificed.

"Now I can't stress enough how important it is to not fuck this mission up. I know not all of you have killed before, and that might seem scary, but it's necessary for ensuring humanity's future. So, what do you think, Apex Strike? Do you think your team is up for this?" Adam said, flashing his million-dollar smile.

He meant this to be a cheeky exchange before leaving, and I wasn't going to disappoint him. "Yeah, we got this one, Helios."

"Glad to hear it," he said, starting to turn off the projectors. "As usual, you'll find mission briefing details in your tablets. We've set up the Tri-Hole access you're gonna use for the mission in the Green Room, but if you feel like using it for a little joyriding beforehand, well, we might be able to turn a blind eye. It's cruder than what you're used to. Had to use some older tech to make it look like you guys found your own way with a teleporter, but it'll work. Until then, study, keep in shape, and have fun!"

Flashing us one last wink and smile, he turned off his projector.

"Well that was a waste of fucking time," Carnivore growled, standing up. "Coulda just sent us a text with all that . . ."

For a second it looked like he was going to hang around, but thankfully he left the room. The rest of us just sat there in silence.

Spasm and I locked eyes. He smiled, a little nervous.

"So, this sound as fucked to all of you as it does to me?" he asked. I looked at Trojan Fox. She pressed a few buttons on her tablet.

"Creeper signals are quiet, for a few minutes at least," she said.

"Worse," Ghost Girl said to Spasm.

He rubbed a hand through his short, black hair. "I mean, I was all right with playing—"

"You hate them too, right?" I said to him.

"Of course," he said.

"Do you want to help us do something about it?" Trojan Fox asked.

Spasm looked around at all of us, probably wondering if this was some kind of trap.

"Like what?" he asked, cautious.

"Can we trust him?" I asked Ghost Girl. Her eyes flashed. She nodded.

Trojan Fox began, "We're dropping out of Kayfabe. We're going to deactivate our Creepers, and I'm gonna readjust the island's shield to keep the heroes from getting through. The island's got enough resources to keep us healthy for years, and once I can figure out how to alter the Tri-Hole access they allowed us, we're going to free our friends in the Tower and ourselves once and for all."

"And what about the assassination?" Nevermore asked.

Trojan Fox shrugged. "We don't do it."

"That's not good enough," I said.

"What, you getting patriotic on us here?" Trojan Fox asked wryly.

"No, but . . ."

I steeled myself up to argue with her, which was never easy, but she didn't know Adam and the other heroes like I did. She'd always kept them at arm's length. I'd let them in.

"They've put too much work into this. There's no way they're going to back out, even if we do. They might do it themselves and find some way of blaming it on us, or they'll half-ass something from some of the other Kayfabe kids they've got in the Tower. One way or another, they *will* do this."

A year ago, I'd have never thought of doing anything this crazy, but looking at these people and thinking back on how they'd all changed my life, I made myself say it.

"Guys, *we* have to stop the heroes' evil plot."

"Why us?" Nevermore asked.

"Because we're the only ones that can."

"Like it's just that easy?" Spasm asked.

"It won't be, no, but we can do it, I think. You can get all your Kayfabe files together quick, right?" I asked Trojan Fox.

"Of course."

"Good, because I think I got an idea."

Everyone looked to me. So this was it, the moment when I'd have to step up and really become the leader.

"It's got two parts. And the first is me stepping down as leader."

I didn't get quite the uproar I'd hoped for, but they did seem surprised, at least.

"I've been a real shitty leader. I let Ad—*Helios* get in my head. He made me think that he was a real friend, and that you were just the people I hung out with when I didn't have anything else to do. I thought because they made me leader, and because I was so famous, that I was the best leader this team could have, but I was wrong. Real leaders speak *for* their team. Real leaders don't let their team get hurt. That's why I nominate Trojan Fox to be our new leader."

I wish I had a picture of her face then, because she was never this surprised. "Wait—"

"Seconded," Ghost Girl said, raising her hand. Nevermore, Geode, and even Spasm were quick to raise their hands after.

"I hate you," she said.

"Get in line," I shot back. I was relieved. A great weight was taken off my shoulders (and put on hers, sure, but she could handle weight a lot better than I could), and I was fairly certain that this was the smartest thing I had ever done in my life.

I continued, "But I think you're going to like the second part of my plan, because for once, I don't think it's that terrible . . ."

It actually was that terrible, at first at least, but once Trojan Fox and Spasm put their tactical knowledge together, it immediately started to improve.

We waited until the day the heroes wanted us to do the job. I felt like I was going to lose my mind most of that time, that the heroes would figure us out, that they would come in and kill us or just set off our Creepers, but they didn't. Combine Trojan Fox's attempts at dampening their signals with the fact that they couldn't hear everything anyway and we were clear come game day, which was one hell of a relief.

Helios said they would take the Protectors' Tri-Hole access down for ten minutes during the president's speech for routine maintenance, which would be enough time for us to do our duty.

We wouldn't, but that ten minutes would give us enough time to turn the world on its head for the better if we could pull it off.

When it was finally time, Trojan Fox called Nevermore, Ghost Girl, and me to her workshop.

Spasm and Geode joined us a few minutes later, carrying Carnivore over one of Geode's massive shoulders.

"He's out?" Trojan Fox said.

"Sleeping like a baby," Spasm said.

"But he's bleeding."

Spasm shrugged. "What can I say, he's an awkward carry, fell down the stairs a coupla times before I could knock him out proper."

If she had a problem with this, she didn't show it.

"What do we need *him* for, anyway?" Nevermore asked.

"Because I'd feel a lot more comfortable if we tried this on a guinea pig first, and I think he might have some in him somewhere."

At her direction, Geode and I tied Carnivore to a workshop table with chains.

"Geode, hold him down, in case the chains aren't enough," Trojan Fox directed. "Spasm, keep him asleep, and numb."

"Done."

"Ghost Girl, how's the Creeper?"

Ghost Girls eyes went gold. "Its living components are nervous. It's trying to send a signal out, but your workshop's walls are keeping it silent."

"Good. Tell me if anything changes," Trojan Fox said, waving her hands at Carnivore's chest. "I'm going to neutralize its mechanical components. Then . . . then the *fun* begins. Nevermore, I need your bladed pendulum, perhaps half a meter high, just above his chest. And a raven."

"No problem," Nevermore said, projecting her tattoos and manipulating them to Trojan Fox's specifications.

"Excellent. Now we're going to want a horizontal incision, about eighteen centimeters wide, about ten centimeters below his sternum. Not too deep. And Apex Strike?"

"Yes?"

"Don't pass out on me. Your job's the most important."

"I wasn't gonna," I said, mostly meaning it. I wanted this to work, but I was freaking out a little. If this was successful, it would soon be *me* on that table.

The pendulum swung lower and faster, cutting a wide, clean incision in Carnivore's belly, his blood spattering the wall. Nevermore made the pendulum disappear after this, her raven hopping onto Carnivore's stomach before diving its head into the incision. According to Trojan Fox, she couldn't go in with any tools because the Creepers might sense them, and because Nevermore's tattoos could be both real and not real simultaneously, they were our safest bet. They may have been the safest, but they weren't the easiest to watch.

Don't think about being on the table.

Don't think about being on the table.

Don't think about that raven in your guts—

The raven flapped and fought for purchase, digging and pulling at the bloody flesh. Finally it twitched, digging its feet into Carnivore's stomach. Carnivore jerked violently.

"Got it," Nevermore said, her body straining from the focus.

"His vitals are going through the roof and I can only do so much; you better get that little fucker out fast!" Spasm warned.

Nevermore focused even harder, giving the raven strength as it dug even deeper into Carnivore's belly and ripped its bloody head free.

The Creeper in its beak was no larger than a salt shaker. Bloody and made of a small, dull metal, its six shaking, insect-like legs clamored to get back into Carnivore.

Trojan Fox smiled. "Well, that wasn't so ba—"

The Creeper let out a piercing, shrieking call that nearly put us all on our knees, its body glowing a dull orange. Dozens of long, thin tendrils burst from it and thrashed back and forth, reaching for Carnivore. Popping arcs of electricity shot from it, shattering glass cases and burning the concrete walls.

"FUCK!" I cried out, ducking and covering my head.

Trojan Fox was at my side. "Dammit, Nevermore, toss the fucking Creeper!"

The raven flung the Creeper into an empty corner of the workshop.

Now it was my turn.

Focus.

The Creeper exploded into a million pieces on the floor. Something small, meaty, and wriggling fell out of its remains, but Geode crushed it under his foot.

The room was a mess, we'd all nearly died, but Carnivore was still alive, his body nearly perfectly fixed up by Spasm.

"All right," Trojan Fox said. "One down, six to go. Who's next?"

#Supervillainy101: The Shot Heard 'Round the World

It didn't surprise anyone that Otis Shylock was the last of the major supervillains standing in 1993, though it did surprise many to see just how far he'd fallen. Once one of the leaders of the Villain's Union, commanding an army of nearly two thousand supervillains bent on controlling all criminal activity on Earth, by 1993 the heavy losses faced during the War on Villainy left him with less than thirty villains and a small mountain stronghold in Chile to his name.

Seeking to end the War once and for all, the heroes all banded together for one last assault on Shylock's forces on May 29, 1993. He vowed not to go down without a fight.

Though in his late seventies and not at the peak of his mind control powers, he and his diminishing army of loyalists fought off wave after wave of hero assault, killing and maiming dozens of the best heroes of the day. Still, with thousands of heroes against a handful of villains, the losses on Shylock's side grew heavy. The heroes soon realized that they just needed to wait him out, surrounding the mountain and blaring out psych warfare mixed with messages encouraging the villains to quit over loudspeakers 24/7.

The details of what happened inside are sketchy, at best. What is known is that Shylock demanded that everyone fight to the last man, to make the heroes' victory as hollow as possible. Not all the villains agreed, and a faction emerged intent on overthrowing Shylock and surrendering in exchange for leniency. A fight broke out, several villains were killed, and Otis Shylock took a single gunshot to the head.

The rebel villains left the mountain, surrendering themselves to the heroes in the hopes of getting a decent deal.

They were all rounded up and immediately sent to the Tower.

Moments later, the Protectors spoke to the media and declared that the War on Villainy had finally been won.

#LessonLearned: Everything ends.

23

TRYING SOMETHING NEW

Before we did anything else, we voted on what the hell we were going to do with Carnivore.

Trojan Fox and I wanted him dead.

Ghost Girl and Geode thought that, though he was an asshole and a murderer and probably a spy, here he was as much a victim as the rest of us and should live.

Spasm and Nevermore were pretty ambivalent to the whole thing, but Geode laid on the charm pretty thick and got them into the "letting him live" camp.

Fine. So he'd live. But at least we'd get some use out of him first.

The Tri-Hole generator the heroes provided was crude. The hole was smaller, sparked more, and looked pretty unsafe.

Geode dragged Carnivore, hands and feet tied behind his back, a burlap sack over his head and a GPS unit duct-taped to his chest, into the room. Though tied tight, he still thrashed and hollered.

"YOU CAN'T DO THIS! YOU CAN'T! I'LL KILL YOU! I WILL FIND YOU AND I WILL KILL YOU ALL!" he yelled, trying to fight free. "YOU CAN'T—"

"We just did," Trojan Fox said, nodding at Geode.

He threw Carnivore through the Tri-Hole, while Trojan Fox checked a holographic display on one of her gauntlets.

"Did he make it?" I asked.

"Ten kilometers outside of Omsk, Siberia. Vitals are stable. He may be a bit singed, but he's alive," she said, her lips curling into a smile just before she lowered her helmet's mask. "Let's see what he thinks of commie cheese now."

Anyone who cared about Carnivore would have probably had some sensible questions.

Even if he makes it to civilization and lives, won't he probably wind up in some gulag?

This is the middle of winter and I think he's coldblooded— won't he freeze to death?

Thankfully, none of us gave enough of a damn about him to have sensible questions.

We had a war to prevent.

We finished pulling on our costumes while watching the Green Room's TV. The president's speech had already begun. There weren't any heroes present, but there were plenty of Secret Service and DSA agents on hand. It wouldn't be easy, but we could manage them.

"Recalibrating the Tri-Hole for DC," Trojan Fox said. "We're going to have to go through fast; they'll be on us the second we step through. We won't have long before some group of heroes is on us, but we should have long enough to do what we have to."

She closed the mask on her Trojan Fox suit and held out a hand. "Should anything happen to me, I just want to say that it's been my greatest pleasure working with all of you."

Geode put his crystalline hand on top of hers. "The pleasure has been ours."

Nevermore shrugged, putting her hand on his. "It's been a lot of fun. I can say that much."

Ghost Girl joined silently, while Spasm just shrugged and put his hand on the pile and said, "Well, I haven't done the shit you've done, but what the hell."

"Well, are you gonna join us or are you just gonna stand there?" Trojan Fox said, looking to me.

"I'm just gonna stand here," I said. Their eyes glared at me with sharp edges. "What? This is one of those rituals you do when you think you're going to die, and I don't want to die."

"If not for you, then do it for the fucking team, all right?" Trojan Fox demanded, training a laser sight on my chest.

"Fine," I grumbled, putting my hand in the pile. "Long live the New Offenders?"

"I've heard worse toasts," Trojan Fox said. "Now, come on guys, let's kick some superhero ass!"

Normally you're supposed to only go through Tri-Holes alone or in pairs. I don't know if six people ever went through all at once, let alone through the cheap version they got us here, but we did it. The trip was faster and rockier than the regular Tri-Holes we'd taken, and I could've sworn my suit was beginning to smoke.

We made it through in a heap, but we made it through, and even managed to get ourselves in action poses before anyone started to scream.

It was a nice day out, cold and brisk with blue skies and a light dusting of snow on the grass. There were simple and elegant Christmas decorations around the edge of the garden, boring, but colorful enough. Dozens of reporters and camera crews occupied the rows of seats that had been set up for the speech, while the president herself stood at the podium, staring at us in shock.

Truthfully, I was kind of in awe to be standing this close to the White House.

It was hard to stay in awe, however, when a bunch of Secret Service and DSA agents opened fire on you.

Some reporters started screaming. Most of them tried to get pictures or good video.

"Take 'em down!" Trojan Fox yelled, taking off and blasting their guns with her lasers and energy pulses, and taking more of them down with her tranquilizer darts. Nevermore unleashed her tattoos and Geode jumped in, taking them on by force.

That left Spasm, Ghost Girl, and me to get to the president. *Piece of cake.*

A voice in my radio. Adam. He was confused, yelling.

"—not time yet, and we can't read—"

I cut him off, "Sorry we jumped the gun, we got a little over-enthusiastic. Just keep the Tri-Holes down and your eyes on the screen; we think you're gonna like this!"

"Cool, just wanted to make sure!" he said. "See you soon!"

Probably sooner than you'd like.

Nearly twenty agents surrounded the president, trying to cart her off. A dozen more stood between us, opening fire with conventional and Atlantean screamer weapons they shouldn't have had.

Cheaters.

I threw up a wall of focus between us and them, taking most of the abuse. His eyes intent and bloodshot, Spasm waved at the crowd of agents between us and the president. Most of them fell to the ground unconscious, while some, the stronger ones I guess, were taken to their knees grabbing their heads and screaming. Ghost Girl easily took them out with her staff. We approached the president at the podium. She stood still, defiant. There may have been a tremble, but she stared us down.

"Kill me if you want, but the Protectors will be here in five minutes and the military in seven. Whatever you do today, you cannot expect to get away with this."

I took a step forward, and a slight look of fear crossed her face.

"Madame President . . . we're not here to kill you. Hell, my parents voted for you, and though you're a little too blue state for my taste, you seem like a pretty cool chick."

Of all the things I could've said, I don't think she expected that (let alone to be called a "chick").

"Believe it or not, right now, we're the good guys," Ghost Girl chimed in.

"Kinda," I amended. "This microphone still working?"

The president nodded, warily. I strode to the podium and looked out at the field of reporters. Geode, Trojan Fox, and Nevermore had taken out the rest of the Secret Service and came onstage to join us. The reporters stared with a look of fear and awe, but none of them made a run, all holding their microphones and cameras and phones at the ready.

Perfect.

I tapped the mike. "This is on? Yes? Good."

I looked to Trojan Fox. By rights, this should have been her speech, being that she was the leader and all, but the public didn't know that yet. This would have to be my show for just a little longer.

"Madame President, ladies and gentlemen of the press, and everyone watching around the world, my name is Apex Strike. I am of the New Offenders, and I am a supervillain," I said proudly.

Adam's voice in my ear, "Aidan, what the fu—"

"Trojan Fox, cut our radios."

"Done."

I spoke to the crowd again. "I've made a lot of mistakes in my life, and maybe being a supervillain was one of them. But today, I, no, *we* are here to fix some of those mistakes. I can't save Icicle Man, or the lives lost in Amber City, or anyone else that we've hurt. But I can save the president."

They looked at us, dumbfounded, raising hands and calling out questions.

"Make this fast," Trojan Fox said. "My sensors on the Tri-Hole network are picking up faint signals."

I continued, "I can save her, because I was sent to kill her."

This got a pretty good reaction from the audience.

"I was sent to kill her by members of the Protectors looking to jumpstart a Second War on Villainy and increase their stranglehold on mankind. Trojan Fox, show 'em what you got."

She pressed a button on one of her gauntlets, and simultaneously all of the phones and tablets of the reporters began making noises.

"What you're receiving now are detailed files we have collected linking a number of superheroes to a conspiracy to create the New Offenders, orchestrating crimes to increase their own fortunes and protect their images including, but not limited to: extortion, robbery, terrorism, and murder. In addition to you, we have sent them directly to all of your papers and networks. We know that some of them favor the heroes, but not all, and even if they do you'll probably want to report on this because, well, today's going to be a pretty big news day."

"We've got incoming," Ghost Girl said, her eyes flashing.

"How soon?"

"Put a bubble around us now, soon."

Even though I didn't have that much experience with shield bubbles, I did what she said. I'd found it best not to ignore Ghost Girl.

There was a sound of something heavy and wet smashing violently into the side of the shield as blood sprayed across it, streaking over the bubble and slamming into one of the White House's pillars with a bright-red, wet explosion of gore. Even through all the mess I could see the tattered black fabric and the glimmering rings of half a dozen shattered halos mixed in with the mess.

Black Blur . . . or what's left of him.

Ghost Girl nodded at me, and I dropped the bubble. Spasm and Trojan Fox set about reviving a number of the Secret Service agents.

"Madame President," I said. "I'm sure you've got a bunker down there somewhere. You might wanna get yourself and your family and as many guys with guns down there as you can . . . this next part's not gonna be fun."

"Even if anything you said is true," she said. "Nothing changes."

"We know. Doesn't mean we can't do the right thing sometimes."

Though the Secret Service guys looked more interested in taking us down, the president ordered them to take her and her people to the bunker. *So that's one problem down, that just leaves—*

"Fine, you want to do this the hard way, we'll do this the hard way!" a commanding voice roared from above us.

Yeah, that just leaves that problem.

Surrounded by gold and white energy, Helios flew in and landed in front of us so hard that he cratered the lawn. Comet Girl landed beside him, as did Armada, shutting off his jetpack. From Tri-Holes around us emerged Everywhere Man, Silver Shrike, Morningstar, the Voice of the People, and Extreme Man.

Eight against six. Real fair, guys.

"Don't bother looking for rescue or trying to run," Helios continued. "*We* control the Tri-Hole network now. Sure, they'll get it back sooner or later, but not before you're all a bunch of greasy smears on our fi—"

Fuck monologues.

I blasted him through the air. It looked like I got at least a mile or two on him.

That'd buy us a few minutes.

The others weren't interested in monologues. They just wanted us dead.

They attacked all at once, Armada and Extreme Man with their guns, Silver Shrike with his arrows, Morningstar with her enchanted mace, the Voice of the People with his superpowered scream (which shattered windows for blocks around), and Comet Girl and Everywhere Man with themselves (or in Everywhere Man's case, many, many copies of himself).

With my focus, Nevermore's brick wall, and Geode and Trojan Fox's bodies, we were able to keep the others safe. The reporters weren't so lucky, a few being taken down by stray bullets and energy blasts, but aside from the few who ran, most kept their ground with cameras on us.

Trojan Fox broke formation first, taking off and unleashing all of her lasers, chain guns, darts, and rockets on the heroes, getting them to scatter even though she didn't seriously hit anyone aside from a few Everywhere Men.

After that, we made a beautiful mess of the fight.

I took Armada down first. He aimed an anti-tank rocket launcher at Spasm, so I focused on the barrel, bending it just enough to explode the rocket in the tube. In defense of his armorer, his costume saved his life, but all his bandoliers and ammunition started to cook off, exploding and igniting the fuel in his jetpack. He ran off screaming and exploding, setting off small fires as he went.

"Dodge to the right about a foot?" Spasm said.

I obliged him, just in time to see him force Extreme Man to double over, vomiting explosively.

"Thanks."

"Don't mention it," he said.

There were enough Everywhere Men on Geode to overwhelm even his superstrength, pulling him down so the Voice of the People could scream at him. His crystals began to crack under the sonic attack. Spasm and I tried to get to the Voice, but too many Everywhere Men got in the way.

"Duck!" someone yelled.

We did, quick enough to see the giant bladed pendulum swoop over our heads, cutting most of the Everywhere Men down. Nevermore ran through, using Geode like a ramp to leap up and over the Voice's scream. She landed behind him, generated an ax from one of her tattoos, and buried it into his shoulder.

His eyes went wide and his scream went high, blowing a hole in the White House. Another ax swing, this time to the back of his head, silenced him forever.

The screaming didn't end there.

Trojan Fox had Comet Girl impaled on the retractable blades of her gauntlets. Though she screamed bloodily, Comet Girl was blasting pieces of Trojan Fox's armor away with her freezing vision. Silver Shrike had found some arrows capable of piercing Trojan Fox's armor and had shot two straight into her back.

He approached her from behind, tauntingly nocking another arrow.

"You want this one, dear?" he joked.

"Oh, can I?" Morningstar said as she started to swing her glowing, magic mace in arcs of green and blue light. One hit from that would end Trojan Fox *and* Comet Girl.

Ghost Girl saw that, too, diving at Trojan Fox and Comet Girl and knocking them down.

Morningstar had built up so much momentum she couldn't stop herself from slamming the mace down onto Silver Shrike's head, turning it (and pretty much everything down to his pelvis) into a chunky, red paste.

"STEVEN!" she cried out. "OH GOD, STEVEN!"

She collapsed, bawling, next to the mess she'd made of her husband.

If I hadn't suddenly been surrounded by a couple dozen Everywhere Men, that might have made me a little sad.

But I *was* surrounded, so I had no time to grieve for her fallen husband.

I didn't know how many copies of himself he could make, but I think this might have been a personal record. There had to be at least a hundred of him, with more joining the fray every second. We hit them with everything we had: lasers, debris, crystals, ravens, axes, and even our bare hands. Ghost Girl was surrounded by fifteen of them, and kept them in a circle around her, beating them back with her quarterstaff and kicks. Geode was back on his feet, smashing them with his giant, crystalline hands.

Yet for every one we destroyed, two more joined the fight. They were unarmed, sure, but enough of them working as one . . .

Show them what you showed the Golem . . .

No. That was only a last resort.

Ghost Girl slid next to me. "We need to find the root!"

"Can you see him?" I yelled.

"Of course! But that's the easy part!" she cried out, whirling her staff around and beating three of them back. I could see her point.

"Where is he?" I yelled back, pulling together a plan.

Remember Spongeman.

Her eyes flashed, briefly. "Northwest of you, about eight meters."

I wasn't sure exactly how much that was supposed to be, but I gave it my best guess, ripping up a large chunk of earth covered in Everywhere Men and lifting it into the air.

"You got him," she said, whirling her staff around and preparing to throw it again.

It felt like if she could land the hit that this fight would be over and we'd be able to get out of here with just a few cuts and bruises to our name.

Not so bad.

Then Helios swooped in.

I'd never really felt him hit; he was usually good at pulling his punches. This time, though, he hit me with the full force of his flight and superstrength.

My suit and my powers softened the blow some, but not enough.

I could hear, and feel, my ribs crack, and I could taste blood, and all of that was in the split second before he ripped my feet from the ground

I knew we were flying away at a great speed, and I knew he was punching me, blasts of his brilliant golden sun energy shooting off in every direction with every impact.

I reached out and focused blindly at him, blasting myself away.

I was falling and, like the previous time, was glad I didn't know how high up I was. I just knew which way was down, and that was enough.

Focus.

I blasted downward with my hands, slowing the descent and trying to touch down gently.

Trying to, at least.

Where I was expecting ground, there was water, so I stumbled and fell in face first.

Everything hurt. It felt like I was bleeding out of every orifice. My suit was torn, my helmet so badly shattered that water started to fill it. It wasn't even that deep, knee-high at most. Dying like this, drowning in a big puddle, wouldn't have been particularly dignified, but it would have been easy. A few breaths in, a little struggling, fading into darkness, that's all it'd take. I didn't want to die, but I could have if I wanted to.

And if you do, Helios wins.

Fuck that, I thought, forcing myself painfully to my feet.

The helmet was a lost cause; I couldn't even think it open. I just ripped it off and tossed it in the water, quickly taking in my surroundings.

No way. Cool.

I was standing in the middle of the reflecting pool on the National Mall, the Lincoln Memorial to my left, the World Wars Memorial and the twin obelisks of the Washington and El Capitán Monuments to my right.

I'd always planned on visiting someday, I just never expected it'd be like this.

Tourists stared at me in awe, taking pictures with their phones. I waved to them.

A golden blur to my left. Helios was coming at me.

He was fast. He could fly. I couldn't.

Remember your training.

I couldn't fly, but I *could* half-ass it.

I aimed my hands down and focused off the ground as hard as I could, launching myself backward through the air like a cannonball while creating a massive jet of water that blocked out Helios. I could keep ahead of him, barely, by holding the focus out, narrowly aiming myself between the obelisks and landing on the grass of the mall, harder than I'd have liked, but alive.

Unfortunately all this did was buy me an additional three seconds before Helios was back on me.

I focused a shield around myself, able to deflect most of his energy blasts and even his heavy punches. It couldn't hold it, not forever, and he took advantage of a flicker in my focus, breaking through and blasting me through the wall of the second floor of the Smithsonian Museum of American History.

I must have been a mess. I could barely stand. I tried crawling through the shattered debris and artifacts, attempting to escape down one of the halls. The tourists who weren't running and screaming and were taking the time to take my picture must've gotten one helluva show.

I wheezed, "Run you stupid fuc—"

Helios smashed a hole through the wall and was on me before I could finish. He kicked me in my broken ribs, forcing me to cry out in pain.

"It wasn't supposed to be like this! *I'm* the hero! *You're* the villain!" he yelled, tears streaming through his mask as he kicked me harder. "The hero always wins!"

I focused on a broken slab of marble and hurled it at him. He blew it apart in midair.

"Cute."

He grabbed nearly a dozen jagged pieces of debris and a few display cases and hurled them at me. I was able to dodge most of them, but the glass display case hit like a dump truck, knocking me down before shattering against a wall. Dazed and bloodied though I was, I couldn't help but feel some grim amusement at what fluttered from it.

Well, Aidan, now you can say you've seen the Gettysburg Address.

"You fucked up, Aidan. We could've had something special. We could've been archnemeses for the ages, but you had to grow a conscience! You, the fucking *murderer*, had to grow some morals! What the fuck is wrong with you?"

"I'm not evil," I spat out. "Not like you."

"LIAR!" he roared, forming a massive ball of swirling gold and white energy between his hands.

Before he could launch it, he was hit by a giant black cat with claws the size of butcher knives. They tore through his suit and into his flesh, making him scream as he fought it away. Random bursts of energy from his hands blew holes in the wall, the ceilings, the display cases, even setting fire to the Star-Spangled Banner.

"That was very foolish what you did, Apex Strike!" my savior said mockingly.

"Thanks, Nevermore," I said.

"You're welcome," she said, standing in one of the holes in the outer wall Helios had made. "Also, you look like shit."

"Feeling worse than it," I said, looking down at my torn, battered body. "Didn't I used to have a pinky?"

"You still do. It's just bent all the way back."

"Oh. That's where that went," I said, thankful for the pain-dulling nature of shock.

"Come on, let's get you out of here," she said, putting an arm underneath my shoulders. A pair of massive, black raven's wings burst from her back, and though she was wobbly in flight and clearly unsteady with them, she was able to glide us back onto the mall.

I started, "The others—"

"Are fine, and they are en route. Trojan Fox's flight units were damaged, so I was the only one who could follow fast. But they are coming soon. Until then, you just have me."

"Lucky me."

"You could do worse," she said, flashing her rare, human smile.

If I weren't all covered in blood and dying, I might have kissed her.

Before I could, I heard people screaming and the terrible sound of a mountain being ripped apart.

Helios had used his energy blasts and telekinesis to destroy the base of the Washington Monument and was tipping it right on us.

"Helios, what the fuck is *wrong* with you?" I yelled.

I focused a powerful bubble around Nevermore and myself. For good measure, she threw up a few brick walls from her tattoos in a box around us as well.

Thousands of tons of stone slammed down around us. It took every bit of energy and focus we had to hold the barrier. So much weight, so much focus, we were pushed into the ground like a peg.

But we held.

A little more focus, and I blasted us a path to the surface.

We crawled out, looking at the chaos and devastation around us. Helios was nowhere in sight, but there were plenty of cop cars and news vehicles on their way. We were already being circled by helicopters and drones, but they kept their distance.

"Maybe they scared him off," I said.

"Maybe *we* scared him off," she said.

She laughed. I joined her. It felt like we were losing our minds, but somehow we were still alive.

Then a blast of golden light made her body go rigid, and she gave a brief cry of pain. She was lit up like an angel, so bright I had to close my eyes.

When I could open them again, all I could see was the charred skeleton that used to belong to Nevermore.

I couldn't process. I couldn't feel. I couldn't do anything but roar blindly into the sky.

Helios hovered in front of me, looking at her blackened bones. "Bitch."

My body began to heat up as though I was on fire. With that energy, I focused a heavy blast right at his chest, knocking him back down onto the mall. He countered with his own energy. We were blasting each other back and forth so much, screaming and yelling impotent, animalistic sounds as we tried to finish the other but couldn't quite.

He threw another chunk of the monument at me. I blocked. That was enough distraction for him to blast me in the right foot with one of his energy bursts. My suit took most of the heat away, but the force still shattered my ankle sideways, flooring me to the ground.

"We've got an audience. Any last words, supervillain?" he said, floating twenty feet off the ground, his hands glowing.

I looked behind him and managed a broken, awful smile.

"Yeah. *Long live the New Offenders!*" I roared out, laughing.

He turned to follow my gaze and got half a dozen mini-rockets from Trojan Fox for his trouble. He was able to project a protective aura around his body which saved him from serious damage from these. Her lasers, on the other hand, they hurt him.

Before he could retaliate, he screamed in fear.

"I'm blind! Give me back my eyes you supervillain fucks!" he cried out, spinning around and firing blindly, shots smashing into museums, police cars, the sky, the ground.

Thank you Spasm.

"Now, Geode!" Ghost Girl called out. Geode lifted her into one of his massive hands and tossed her through the air. Her gloves were off, and when she hit Helios, she tightly wrapped them around his neck. His screams stopped, and a look of pure terror took over his face as the two of them slowly fell to the ground. The glowing aura around his body began to flicker, then fall apart when they hit the ground. Ghost Girl seemed to be the only one able to walk away.

"What did you do to me? What was that?" Helios roared.

Spasm was at my side, fixing my ankle and my ribs and some of the worse cuts.

"You'll need some time in a pod to fix the worst of it, but I'll get you on your feet," he said, pulling me to my feet to prove he was true to his word. I was wobbly, but I managed.

"WHAT DID YOU SHOW ME? WHAT DID YOU SHOW ME?" Helios repeated, looking around with blank eyes.

"I showed you who you are, and all the ugliest skeletons in your closet," Ghost Girl said, punching him in his beautiful jaw hard enough to send blood and teeth flying.

"OOOOOOOOOOOOOOOOOOOOW!" he slurred.

I walked up to him, flexing my hands, trying to direct my focus. Small bits of debris began to float around me as I walked past, and I could feel everything and everyone on the mall. The others didn't try to stop me.

"Spasm, give him his eyes," I said.

He did, and Helios looked up at me fearfully. He tried to focus his powers back, but the hangover from what Ghost Girl had shown him had hit too hard.

I focused, lifting him off the ground by his outspread arms. He moaned pitifully, then started thrashing and yelling.

"You can't do this to me! You *can't*! I'm a superhero!"

"You're not a superhero," I said. "You're just an asshole."

(Witty quips are hard to come up with when you've lost a lot of blood.)

Focus.

His body jerked and shuddered in a very familiar way, and that same slurping, crunching sound that Icicle Man made was practically music to my ears as I turned Helios inside out and dropped the steaming mess onto the ground.

"We need to get the hell out of here," Trojan Fox said. "They got the Tri-Hole network back up, and the Protectors will be here any—"

Helios's remains jerked, starting to rise.

"No fucking way—"

An ethereal, ghostly form of gold and white light rose from his body. Briefly, it turned its alien and serene face to me, and smiled.

"I am the Charioteer, one of the fourteen Keys of the Cosmos. Thank you, Aidan Salt, for freeing me. One day, *soon*, when your planet's reckoning is at hand, I will return and repay your kindness," it said in an ethereal voice, rocketing into the sky with a blinding flash of light.

A brief moment of awkward silence took over our chunk of the mall.

"What, *the fuck*, was that?" Spasm asked.

Trojan Fox shrugged. "Shit like that's always happening around superheroes."

She pulled a stolen Tri-Hole generator from her belt and pulled up an exit for us.

"Wait!" I exclaimed, motioning for Geode to help me. Taking Helios's bloody cape, we gathered up Nevermore's bones.

She deserved to be buried with friends.

One at a time, the five of us stepped through the Tri-Hole, each of us landing around the Christmas tree in the middle of the foyer back home.

I was tired.

I was hurt.

I was sad.

But I was also relieved. It felt, for now, that for the first time in close to a year, we might have been free.

Someone started clapping slowly from the shadows.

"Not bad. Not bad at all, kids," she said slowly.

We all drew our weapons and powers on her, but Blackjack made no move to fight back as she walked out of the shadows.

"You did good, but want to do even better?"

#Supervillainy101: Flight of The New Offenders

It's a rare occurrence when everything goes to hell in your favor, but when it does happen, it's a beautiful thing.

After the Battle of Washington, DC, most of the surviving heroes (Everywhere Man, Comet Girl, Armada, and Morningstar) were taken into custody and placed in a hardened DSA facility for questioning. Extreme Man escaped in the chaos, though since it's hard for a guy with a graying mohawk covered in pouches and guns to hide, he shouldn't stay hidden long.

Most governments and the superhero hype machine tried to gloss over the conspiracy, but the Protectors made enough political enemies to make sure they would be held accountable to the accusations. President Perez has called for hearings, the Supreme Soviet isn't far behind, and though they're dragging their feet, British Parliament should join soon enough.

Sponsors of the Kayfabe heroes caught in the Battle of Washington, DC, have already dropped them, and those whose names Trojan Fox released have slowly started shedding them.

The Protectors and many of their satellite teams have temporarily been shut down for "internal review and restructuring." Though superheroics still take place, they're more apt to be vigilantes or privately held.

Or El Capitán, since nothing could stop him from saving people.

The New Offenders are still recognized as a terrorist organization by most respectable world powers, but there is a growing swell of support for our actions after we made our story public, and not just among the enemies of the empires (though the aid we've received from Lemuria, Atlantis, and New R'lyeh has been nice). Some have started to call us folk heroes, which does have a pretty good ring to it.

We may even manage to earn that title some day.

When we're not being villains, of course.

#LessonLearned: Everything changes.

24

THERE'S SOMETHING ABOUT MARY

In retrospect, I shouldn't have taken my helmet off in DC.

With my face all over the news, it was impossible to be myself in public. A baseball cap, shaggy wig, and sunglasses were all that protected me when Ghost Girl and I attended the next Mary Rising.

"They won't notice you," Ghost Girl said. "You'll be fine."

Nervously, I spun a pen between my fingers.

"It just feels like—"

"They're here to see Mary rise, not you. So look like you want to see some death, and you'll blend right in," she said, comfortingly as we walked through the crowd. I laughed.

"What's so funny?"

"I got into this . . . lifestyle because I didn't want to blend in anymore. I was tired of being just another face in the crowd. I wanted people to notice me. I wonder if I went a little too far."

"I think, in this case, going too far was a good thing. The whole world is changing because of you."

"Because of *us*," I clarified.

If her face weren't wrapped in a scarf, I imagine that would have gotten a raised eyebrow. "I was wondering if you would give us all credit."

"What can I say, I'm growing up," I said, catching my gaze wandering down to her chest. "Mostly."

"Good to see you haven't changed completely."

"That's not a matter of changing, that's me just trying to get something nice to hold onto while I'm in—"

Spasm pushed his way through the crowd towards us, tossing a lit cigarette on the ground and crushing it out. "I hate to break up your flirtation, but it's time."

"Hey, keep your pants on, we've got time," I said as we made our way through the crowd.

"*You've* got time, I'm just here until this job's done. Then it's back to Belfast and giving the redcapes all the hell I can."

"Whatever floats your boat. Just be glad you don't have to go where I'm going."

"And we *are* glad you're helping us with this," Ghost Girl added.

True to what Spasm said, it was beginning. A few heroes had come in through a Tri-Hole, but no heavy hitters. Too many people had been implicated in the Kayfabe files, and many others had been taken off duty as potential accessories. It would take a while for them to figure everything out, but until then, most active heroes we'd seen were second- and third-stringers. That would make this next part easy.

The loudspeakers told us to quiet down, again.

Green mist and green light came from the mine entrance.

Mary roared.

Right on schedule. No other side effects, yet . . .

"You can do this," I said.

"I know," Spasm said, gripping the fence hard. "I've never attempted anything this big, but don't think Liam Long's not one to try."

His eyes rolled back into his head as every vein and muscle stood out rigid on his body.

At first, nothing happened. Then everything did.

In a wave around him, people fell to the ground, unconscious. First the people in the audience, then the people working crowd control to keep us back, and finally the heroes. It happened so quickly that nobody would have a clear idea of just what happened and would write this off as just one of the many side effects of a Mary Rising.

Spasm fell to his knees by the fence, his eyes bloodshot.

"I'm fine, I'm fine . . . just give me a second . . ."

"Rest all you want, you did awesome," I said, surveying the hundreds of unconscious people that littered the fairground.

"Ready for Part Two?" Ghost Girl asked.

"No," I said.

"By which you mean yes?"

"Obviously."

We both pulled off our backpacks, pulling out my spare Apex Strike helmet and an oxygen tank made to hook into it. I stripped off my disguise and the street clothes covering my costume and put the helmet and tank on, just as Mary began to heavily stomp out from the mine.

Ghost Girl and I hopped over the fence, running to the mine entrance before Mary could climb all the way out.

Giant and stupid-looking, she cocked her massive head and looked down at us confusedly. Her one eyelid blinked heavily as drool and black slime snaked between her cracked, blocky teeth. Nobody knew if she remembered anything from execution to execution, but looking into her eyes, I got the impression that she did. I think she remembered most of the heroes who had killed her, and knew we weren't them.

"Have you seen my lamb?" she asked.

"No, Mary, we haven't. I'm so sorry," Ghost Girl said.

Mary took a step back as if struck, her eyes confused and frightened. I imagined that nobody had talked nicely to her in a very, very long time.

Slowly, Ghost Girl removed her scarf to show Mary her true face. This put Mary more at ease, as she took a slow step forward, her shoulders lowering.

". . . seen my lamb?" Mary asked again.

"Your lamb has been dead for a long time," Ghost Girl said, approaching Mary slowly. She held out her hand.

"I know you have felt more pain than almost any other being on this planet, and I can never apologize enough. If I could promise you relief from this life, I would, but I don't know how. What I can do, though, is promise you freedom from this cycle of death and rebirth in your pit. Would you like that?" Ghost Girl said, taking another step closer.

Mary looked at her, some of the fear returning, her shoulders raised defensively.

"Touch my hand, Mary. Know I'm telling the truth," Ghost Girl said.

Mary looked torn. ". . . you seen my lamb?"

She reached out, touching Ghost Girl's hand. Mary was the first person I'd seen who hadn't completely lost it when Ghost Girl shared her power with them. Her body went rigid and her eyes became completely black, but when Ghost Girl parted, Mary smiled crookedly.

"Have you seen my lamb?" she said.

Ghost Girl smiled. "So you will help us?"

Mary nodded. ". . . my lamb."

"Good," Ghost Girl said. "Now this next part won't be pleasant, but once it is over, I swear to you, everything will get better."

Mary barely moved when Ghost Girl pulled the hunting knife from her backpack and approached her.

"Oh God, it's so awful!" I yelled into the radio.

"Oh quit bein' such a little bitch, it's dark and your suit's sealed, you don't have to see or smell nothin'," Blackjack said over the radio.

"But it's so gooey!" I yelled again.

"It may be, but it's the best way in. Trust me kiddo, this'll work."

"Has anyone ever told you that you were one sick bitch, Blackjack?"

"Daily, if I'm lucky."

"Must be why we get along so well," Trojan Fox said.

"You're going to be fine, Aidan. Just relax, breathe," Geode said.

"You try fucking relaxing and breathing!" I yelled back.

"He is, actually. He's on a tropical island with a mai tai," Trojan Fox said.

"I fucking hate all of you!"

"Love you too, asshole," Trojan Fox said mockingly.

"Just . . . try remembering why you're here. What you're doing. That will make this easier," Geode said, trying to be calming.

That worked. Some.

But it didn't change the fact that I was currently curled up in a ball, trapped inside Mary's stomach, waiting to burst out of her like a goddamn alien the moment we got to the Tower.

It was all Blackjack's fault.

She was waiting for us back on Death Island after the Battle of Washington, DC. At first I thought she was there to try to take over the team, but she wanted the exact opposite. She offered us her assistance and centuries of experience in supervillainy to help us with our plans, and in exchange she wanted to build a small home on the island to retire.

Trojan Fox agreed to her terms, and said that, once we were all healed up, she wanted to free all our friends from the Tower.

Hiding me inside of Mary like some satanic Jack-in-the-Box was Blackjack's solution to the problem. According to her, the Tri-Hole hookup to the Tower is more secure than the rest of the network and would have had all its codes changed after DC, making the generators we took off the heroes useless.

With no permanent staff of the Tower, we couldn't sneak in with a supply shipment or any work crews.

That just left Mary.

After she was killed, her body was carted off to the Tower for cremation. If we could talk Mary onto our side, and if we had a really small group member . . .

And that's how I wound up stuffed inside Mary's stomach cavity, covered in slimy zombie guts and hating my life.

I was glad that Ghost Girl carved a big hole in Mary's stomach, which made getting in easy. I wasn't as glad that Spasm had to seal the hole behind me, but we had to sell the illusion.

Mary, thankfully, had no problem playing dead.

"All right," Spasm said over the radio. "Everyone's getting back on their feet. They're all wonderin' what exactly went down. The heroes're looking at Mary. It's good, real good. They're thinking everyone passing out was a Rising side effect, and that something in it must've hit Mary, too. They're raising their arms, posing for the crowds . . . and there goes the Tri-Hole. Looks like they're—"

"You've disappeared from GPS," Trojan Fox said. "You're there."

"Great," I said. "Can I get out now?"

"Not yet. Wait for it . . ."

There was a devastating blast of distorted energy over the radio. A few seconds later, Mary stopped moving. Then they dropped her.

Trojan Fox was back. "Want to hear what they're hearing?"

"Why not?" I said.

She connected me to the heroes' earpieces.

"... IT'S GOING DOWN, DEAR GOD ..."

"... EVACUATE! ..."

"... CAME OUT OF NOWHERE ... LASER ..."

"... HIT THE OCEAN, WHAT DO WE—"

"... *THE PEARL* IS DOWN. REPEAT, *THE PEARL* IS DOWN! ..."

"... WHAT THE FUCK DO WE—"

"Now, Apex Strike!"

Thank God!

I focused upward, blowing a hole in Mary's stomach and climbing out. *So gooey.*

The three heroes carrying her were distracted. Hearing their base had been shot out of the sky by a supervillain's death ray has a way of doing that to you. I never thought that Trojan Fox would get that old, giant gun working, but boy was I glad to be wrong.

Three blasts of focus got me two unconscious superheroes. The third was hardier, but Mary, guts hanging out and dragging on the floor, jumped to her feet and smashed her out against the wall.

"Thanks, Mary."

She smiled at me, wiping away drool with the back of her hand. "... my lamb?"

I wiped her black goo off my visor, finally letting me see clearly.

The White Knights began to stir. I ripped the garbage bag that Ghost Girl duct-taped to my chest open, pulling out Trojan Fox's small, centipede-like gizmo and chucking it at the nearest White Knight. It quickly crawled across its chest and latched to the back of its neck.

The White Knight stopped, shuddered, and cocked its head. Then it spoke in Trojan Fox's voice, "I'm in."

It turned, reached to a wall panel, and plugged in. The other White Knights shut down.

"I found him. Maximum Security, VIP Wing, he'll be so proud," Trojan Fox said. One of the doors in the wall opened. "I'm opening a path."

"Do you think *The Pearl*'s gonna be enough of a distraction?" I asked. "I'd hate to get a bunch of heroes on my ass with just a White Knight and a giant zombie for backup."

"It should be, but just in case . . ." Trojan Fox said. I heard a klaxon blaring further down one hall, and another door opened. "I just freed all of the minimum security offenders. That should give you a good head start. There's some friends, and other interesting ones too, in higher security, but I can't free them from here. Mary?"

Mary climbed to her feet. "Have you seen . . ."

"I'm going to light their tubes bright red. Could you break them out?"

". . . my lamb!" Mary exclaimed.

"Cool," Trojan Fox said. "You guys know what to do."

"Yes, sir!" I said jokingly. I may give her shit, but I didn't doubt my choice to make her leader.

I ran down the hall of tubes that Trojan Fox opened for me, following her every direction so I wouldn't get lost in the twisting corridors that made up the Tower's Maximum Security wing. I could see a lot of scary people in here, and was as impressed as I was scared.

Down a dark, twisting, metal stairway, Trojan Fox opened one final door to the deepest depths of the Tower.

The room was poorly lit by flickering fluorescents, and there were, at most, a dozen tubes. All of them were thicker, stronger, and had a faint ripple of energy to them that I had never seen before. They were all occupied, most of them by people, some of them by large, twisted, monstrous shapes, and one by a tiny little imp wearing a white shirt and a tie.

Odigjod.

I walked over to his tube, put my hands a couple feet away from its surface, and focused.

A blast of crackling purple energy, about as strong as the focus I put out, blasted me back, nearly crushing me against the wall.

Magic. For him, of course.

I tried an even stronger blast of focus, and got blown back even harder. It almost had an effect on the tube, its energy barrier flickering slightly, but it quickly steadied itself.

Now may be a good time to remember the Golem . . .

I clapped my hands together and tried to remember every bit of anger and fear and surprise I had the day Showstopper died. I could feel the focus grow in front of me. Everything in the room began to rattle. My body shuddered, my feet left the floor. I could feel everything, *everyone* in the room, even through their tubes.

Focus.

It felt like the whole world exploded. It *sounded* like the whole world exploded.

I fell on my hands and knees, but this time, knowing what to expect, I could almost get to my feet without a lot of trouble.

My ears ringing, my vision blurring, I tried to get my bearings. I was looking at the shattered tube. Whose it was, I didn't know, but it was big. Bigger than Odigjod's.

A large, clawed hand grabbed me by the shoulder and steadied me. "Careful, kid."

I looked up and stared into the face of Bad Bug.

"You break us out?" he asked.

Us?

I looked around. Multiple tubes were smashed open, their occupants stumbling around, trying to get their bearings.

Dr. Tongue.

The Radiation Queen (the real one).

Otis Shylock. He actually tipped an imaginary hat to me before running from the room.

"Thanks, kid!" Bad Bug said before darting out.

Shit. Trojan Fox isn't gonna like this.

I hadn't broken all the tubes, thank God. But I did get the one I'd come for.

"Apex Strike?" Odigjod said, his eyes fluttering wearily as the effects of the paralyzing agent, tech, and magic began to wear off. "Really you, yes?"

"Yeah, it's me," I said, opening my visor so I could smile at him.

"Going home is sounding good to Odigjod."

"You and me both."

He couldn't walk, not yet, but he wasn't too heavy to fling onto my back.

Of course, walking out of the Tower's Maximum Security wing was a lot harder than walking in. Whatever power I had unleashed had twisted the metal floor like a piece of taffy. Nearly every one of the hundreds of tubes was shattered open (the ground was littered with broken glass and smiley-face masks), some with occupants still unconscious, others which had already been vacated. Some serious, heavy-hitting villains wandered around, dazed and confused, while others had started to fight each other as they took out old grudges and petty jealousies.

I did my best to go around them.

*Unleashing a biblical plague of high-level supervillains on the world? Trojan Fox is **really** not going to like this.*

Back in the lobby, more than a hundred villains were crowded around the various Tri-Hole emitters in the wall, getting the hell out of dodge before the heroes arrived.

"Apex Strike!"

Now *there* was a voice I hadn't heard in a long time.

"Circus?"

He ran to me, all clown, and actually threw his arms around me for a huge hug.

"This is the Tower?"

"Yeah."

"What a shithole. You're breaking us out?"

Us? No, I just came here for Odigjod and . . .

. . . and there was Circus, standing with Artok and most of the other cut Kayfabe villains and a bunch of others in our age range, some wearing clothes and costumes that dated back to the 70s. Most of them didn't look like supervillains. They just looked like scared, confused kids who didn't have a place in the world.

You're a supervillain. You don't have to sympathize. Just let them go on their way, and . . . and . . .

"Trojan Fox? We're gonna have some houseguests tonight," I said, waving Circus and the rest of the group over to one of the free Tri-Holes.

Setting in the coordinates to home, I sent each of them through. Odigjod and I followed Mary, the last of our group headed for freedom.

I was worried about what I'd find on the other side. Trojan Fox would yell at me, sure, for fucking up and accidentally freeing the Maximum Security villains, and God only knew what the rest of the villains thought of me (most of the ones from training weren't exactly my biggest fans), but I guessed . . . well, I guessed I'd have to deal with that once I got home.

The world exploded in cheers when I landed back in the foyer. Somebody violently pulled my slimy helmet off just to kiss me on the lips (guy or girl, I didn't know). I was pounded on the back, hugged, and had my hand shaken more times than I could count. Even Trojan Fox didn't give me shit, hugging and kissing me on the cheek before taking Odigjod from my arms.

Spasm and Geode lifted me onto their shoulders, letting me look down at the cheering crowd as they all chanted my name (well, all of them except Mary, who couldn't). Looking down at the crowd, I felt bad for the faces I couldn't see.

Iron Bear.
Showstopper.
Nevermore.

Good people this life had destroyed. People I would never see again.

Even with those losses, I looked down and was glad to see those I still had.

Geode.

Trojan Fox.

Odigjod.

Ghost Girl . . .

Ghost Girl leaned up against the display case that held her costume, staying out of the party atmosphere all our new arrivals brought. Tipping up her mask for only a moment, she smiled at me and nodded, and I found myself thinking: *I can get used to this.*

#LessonLearned: Sometimes, friendship and teamwork really are all you need in life.

Yeah, I didn't see that one coming either.

ACKNOWLEDGMENTS

As always, I'd like to start off by thanking my wonderful agents at Literary Counsel, Fran Black and Jennifer Mishler, for everything they have done, will do, and are always doing for me. Thank you for taking a chance on both me and *Almost Infamous*.

Thank you to everyone at Talos Press and Skyhorse Publishing who helped sculpt my fairly raw words into something that could actually be called a book, especially my editor Jason Katzman. Your infinite patience and editing expertise made this book as awesome as it is today.

Dad, thank you for always being there for me; for teaching me the value of character development and making sure I never grew into a half-assed supervillain. Thank you for reading everything I've written, no matter how much it didn't suit your personal tastes, even if the main thing you took away from this book was it being the first time you ever saw your son write the word "cocksucker." Though you didn't live to see this book published, I hope wherever you are, whatever you are, you know that I finally pulled this off.

A special thanks to everyone who's ever put pen and ink to page to bring superheroes, good, bad, and otherwise to life, and for making us believe that people can fly.

And final thanks, of course, to my wife Fiona. You are forever my inspiration and the greatest partner in both writing and life I could ever hope for. Thank you for always believing in me, and *Almost Infamous*, even when I doubted myself. And thank you for helping correct my grammar and teaching me how to use a comma. I swear, one of these days I'll get it right!